After t

Peter Tonkin

First published 2018 by Sharpe Books.

For
Cham, Guy and Mark
as always.
*

And in memory of a dear friend:
Jill Andrews
1929 – 2017

Table of Contents

PROLOGUE

i

The dead man's name was Gaius Amiatus and he was standing in front of a makeshift altar shouting at a sizeable crowd. He didn't yet know he was dead. Or even that he was condemned to die. He was dressed in a loose-fitting black tunic because he was in mourning. In mourning for the god to whom the altar behind him was dedicated. A god called Gaius Julius Caesar. Who had recently been so violently translated from the earthly sphere to the ethereal.

Gaius Amiatus, his altar and his audience were in the *Forum Romanum*, where Caesar's corpse had been cremated by vast crowds running dangerously out of control after his funeral. The gold that had been thrown into the flames as sacrifice by the grieving multitude and had run molten from his funeral pyre's blazing foundations still gleamed on the stones of the Forum's *pavimentum* pavement. Still gathered brightly in the cracks between them. Having survived more than a week of inclement March weather. And the soles of thousands upon thousands of sandals and boots.

'I am the grandson of the great General Gaius Marius, Caesar's relative and mentor,' Gaius Amiatus was bellowing. 'If anyone should be leading you in acts of vengeance against his murderers, it is I! Think what Caesar has done for you! The money he left you. The gardens he has opened to you. The lands, farms and townships he has promised you. He loved Rome! He loved you as though you were his sons! He was truly *Pater Patriae*, the father of his country. And he was divine! We should call him *Divus Julius*! Julius the God!' Gaius Amiatus gestured to the altar behind him. 'This altar should be at the heart of a shrine! A temple!'

The crowd stirred and muttered.

'Yet those ruthless butchers slaughtered him without a second thought.' The rabble-rouser continued. 'They stole from you the pledges he made, the promises he embodied! The legendary wealth of Parthia. The lands beyond, perhaps. Like Alexander, he would have brought the fabulous wealth of the *Orientem* to you! Laid it before you in triumphs and in games! Shared it with you in golden gifts and *sestertii*. Hundreds of *sestertii* for every man here! But Brutus, Cassius, Decimus Albinus, Trebonius and the rest robbed you of all that when they robbed him of his life. They robbed us of a living god! Kill them all, I say. Burn their houses. Slaughter them as they slaughtered him. Without hesitation. Without compunction. Without mercy!'

9

Like the rioters who immolated Caesar's body here, this crowd was largely composed of old soldiers, many of them from beneath the banner of the bull. Caesar's own. Who had come to discover what would happen now that the man they worshipped – as a leader if not quite yet as a god – was dead. They raised a raucous cheer at the rhetoric. Gaius Amiatus looked at them proudly, impressed by the power of his words.

In the front row stood two men who were clearly legionaries. Or had been, at least. Perhaps still in uniform. Though it was hard to tell beneath the cloaks they wore. Long and mud-coloured – nothing like bright red military *saga*. But they both wore soldiers' *caligae* boots. They looked like useful men who would make excellent lieutenants when the real rioting began. And the looting. One was tall, lean-faced, with a dark, square jaw, short red-brown hair and blue-grey eyes. All just visible within the shadow of his hood. Beside him almost his twin in build. But slightly shorter. Fair haired and brown eyed. With a deep cleft in his chin.

When Gaius Amiatus swung round and began to lead his ragged army across the Forum, past the *Domus Publicus* where Caesar had lived, and up towards the Palatine Hill where, he reckoned, the aristocratic murderers might still be richly housed, these two men fell in at his shoulders. Like legates beside a general. Like Antony and Lepidus beside Caesar in the wars. He raised his left hand again, gesturing his little legion onwards. In the manner, he imagined, that his grandfather, the great General Marius, might have done. Revealing, through the sag of his loose black clothing, a dark-haired armpit. Thick black fur matted over the curve of ribs. Reaching round to an equally hairy chest.

But as he did so, completely unexpectedly, it seemed to him that a hornet stung him beneath his raised left arm. The pain was sudden. Intense. Piercing. It winded him. His steps faltered as he fought for breath. The hooded soldiers at his shoulders did not slow. They marched on towards the *Via Sacra*, side by side.

Gaius Amiatus' raised arm fell abruptly. Too heavy for him to hold aloft any longer. The rabble behind him began to gather round, frowning in confusion. The two cloaked soldiers vanished. Gaius Amiatus staggered. Went to his knees, still fighting for breath. He put his right hand into his left armpit, where he thought he had been stung. Pulled it out and stared at the palm stupidly. Seeing only a tiny smear of blood. 'What in the name of the *Divus Julius* has happened?' he wondered.

It was his final thought. He pitched forward. As dead as the cold stones he crashed down onto.

The two soldiers lingered in the mouth of an alleyway, looking back. 'That was neat, Septem,' said the man with the cleft chin. Pulling back his hood. Watching his companion wipe his dagger clean. 'The way he raised his arm opened up the ribs to your *pugio* dagger. You may even have stabbed him to the heart. In and out so swiftly I don't think he even realised...'

'You sound like a physician, Tribune,' answered Septem, the taller of the two, sheathing the dagger on his left hip. Pushing his own hood back onto his broad shoulders. The movements revealing the uniform and badges of a centurion of the Seventh Legion. Which explained the name the tribune was using: *Septem* – Seven. 'General Mark Antony said to make it quick and quiet. But get it done in any case. He really wants to keep the streets safe now that Brutus, Cassius and their friends are on the run. I think he'd rather be going after them than stuck here keeping the peace.'

'He ought to be able to trust Gaius Lepidus to do that. Lepidus commands the Seventh Legion camped out on Tiber Island and can bring them onto the streets if he has to. That's why Antony's promised him the governorship of Narbonese Gaul and Nearer Spain. To keep him loyal.'

'But this near-riot makes it clear yet again that Antony has to find a way to avenge Caesar – to placate the Caesarian factions in the Senate and on the streets. Not to mention the legions,' Septem the centurion answered. 'Until he does that or moves the old soldiers out, this sort of thing will just keep happening. Only he can't go after the murderers too publicly or he'll lose the majority of the Senate who still support them. He needs the Senate and the power they confer on him. Will do so for a good while yet. And meanwhile his problems are starting to multiply. Were doing so, even before we began questioning witnesses to the murder itself and assessing their evidence against the Twelve Tables of the law. What they actually saw in Pompey's *Curia* as Caesar was being slaughtered. Saw and heard.'

'Well at least he has plenty to occupy his mind and time while he's trapped here – trying to enact Caesar's plans and wishes as he's been commissioned to do,' said the tribune.

'While fighting to keep Rome as quiet as possible as quickly as he can,' agreed the centurion, Amiatus' *carnifex* executioner. 'But only so he can leave the city and start to settle all these soldiers on the farms Caesar promised them. And that's just the first task on the list that Caesar left. It's as well he claims to be descended from Hercules. He has almost as many labours to fulfil.' He paused, looking back at the swirling crowd in the Forum, which was beginning to disperse now, leaving the black-clad corpse for someone else to deal with. 'And that's the Gordian knot, of course. Because it's the retired soldiers who are making most of the trouble on the streets. That mob Gaius Amiatus was just about to lead in a riot was mostly old soldiers.'

'But settling a couple of legions on new farms and townships will take a fortune. One way or another…'

'From a man who is famous for the massive debts he owes rather than the limitless riches he can call on. I almost pity General Antony. He's been offered the chance of a lifetime. At the moment when all the Fates seem to be in league against him…'

'Still, back to the matter in hand,' shrugged the tribune. 'Do we come back and tear down the altar later? Has the general told you?'

'It stays. And there's talk of erecting a column in Caesar's memory too. That's to go ahead as well. We have more important work than hanging around here keeping the peace like *vigiles* policemen. So, in fact, have Lepidus and the Seventh Legion. Not to mention Antony himself, as I say. But our hands are tied until the city's under some kind of control and the streets are safe. We'd better report back to him and see what the next set of orders are.' He glanced back at the last few men hovering uncertainly around the corpse beside the altar. Looking up at the gently weeping spring sky as they shrugged and walked away. He could understand their confusion. They'd be lucky even to see the dagger-wound beneath all that hair. They probably thought Gaius Amiatus had been struck down by jealous Jove. For singing so loudly the praises of another, lesser, god. 'The general thinks that if they start worshipping Caesar, they'll be less worried about avenging him,' he concluded.

The tribune nodded. 'We can pray that *that* at least is true. What is it our Jewish friends say when they address their one and only god?'

'*Amen*,' answered Septem the centurion and *carnifex* executioner. 'Amen to that.'

I

The three men ran through the darkening streets. Two were hunters. The third was their quarry. Around them, the city snarled and howled like a wild beast. Dusk was gathering swiftly. The dangerous air of lawlessness intensified as the light thickened. Mobs of men and women charged madly from place to place around them. Armed with kitchen knives and cleavers. Sharp-pointed spits torn from the cooking-fires. Clubs. The sprinkling of ex-legionaries amongst them with *gladius* swords and *pugio* daggers. Even a few ex-gladiators with the bizarre weapons from the arena. Appearing and disappearing like wolves in a forest. As the shadows deepened, they lit flaming torches, which only served to add to the feral threat they gave off. The atmosphere was one of utter lawlessness.

The man hurrying home alone glanced increasingly nervously from side to side. All too well aware that he had made several serious miscalculations. Any one of which might prove fatal. Which, taken all together, he would be lucky to survive. To start with, he should never have agreed to visit the villa he had just left. Certainly not in secret and unattended by the guards and servants which were his right. Next, he should have been much more acutely aware of the passage of time. For the gathering darkness had come as a complete surprise. But the conference he and the villa's owner had just concluded – in itself another dangerous mistake – had seemed to both men to be vital and secret enough to warrant a little danger. So he had not asked for an escort from his host's personal squad of gladiators to see him safely home. Which now appeared as another grave miscalculation. For the danger was not so 'little' after all.

The route home he had chosen to follow, carefully avoiding the Forum, had seemed a safe one. But now, he deduced, he had overlooked a simple probability. That the soldiers whose duty was to keep the peace during the night would assemble there at sunset. Making the Forum itself safe. While driving the murderous mobs out into the suburban streets and minor forums east and north of it. Through which he was now fleeing so desperately. The local *aediles* magistrates should have *vigiles* watch patrols out, too. But probably not yet – for night had not quite fallen. And in this dangerously darkening half-light, it seemed that the law was asleep. While its exact opposite ran riot.

The white of the fleeing man's *toga* glimmered for an instant in the distance. As he ran from one shadow to another at the far end of an *angustum* alleyway.

13

Too narrow to admit a cart. But not too narrow to admit ruffians, thieves and murderers. 'Do you see him, Septem?' one of the hunters asked.

Septem nodded. 'I see him, Tribune,' he answered.

Both hunters were in full military uniform once again but without the hooded cloaks. Septem was now wearing a helmet bearing a centurion's brightly coloured lateral crest. His companion wore the armour and trappings of a tribune on the general's staff. His helmet was crested with a black plume that fell almost to his shoulders at the back. Both men were seconded from military duties to serve as spy and spymaster. The man code-named Septem, Centurion Iacomus Artemidorus, was the leader of a group of secret agents, undercover operatives, *agents provocateurs*, *carnifex* torturers or executioners and *interfectores* assassins. He himself being a master of all the skills involved in his work. As the unfortunate Gaius Amiatus had recently discovered. The Tribune Domitus Enobarbus his direct link to the Co-consul and General Mark Antony who had assumed command of them on Caesar's death. Had in fact employed them to keep his friend and mentor safe on the *Ides* of *Mars*.

Artemidorus and Enobarbus stood at the centre of a new concept in military organisation. A covert cadre dedicated to the gathering of military intelligence. Or, as in more recent times, political intelligence. A secret service. Something that had grown in strength and importance during the latest decades. First conceived, perhaps, by Scipio Africanus in the Punic wars against Hannibal and Carthage. Organised by Caesar more recently. Working, now, for Antony.

'He's beginning to slow, Tribune,' grated Septem. 'We'll catch up to him soon.' But even as he spoke, the pale gleam of the *toga* vanished into the dangerous darkness once more. He redoubled his speed. The iron nails on the soles of his *caligae* boots struck sparks off the cobbles in the stygian alley. The walls of which seemed to brush both of his shoulders at once. Their bricks striking against the tip of the *gladius* sword on his right hip and the lethal *pugio* dagger on his left, which they were only able to wear legally within the *pomerium* city limit because they were soldiers in uniform and on duty.

The lone man could hear the hobnailed footsteps echoing out of the black throat of the alley. He too redoubled his speed, his nervousness blooming suddenly into full-blown fear. He had no idea why he was being followed. Or by whom. But he was certain that his pursuers had no good intentions. He was, in fact, increasingly convinced that anyone he was liable to meet tonight was likely to cut his throat first and ask questions later. Despite his fame, wealth, social standing and political importance. All evidenced by the senatorial stripes on his formal clothing.

14

A minor forum opened before him. A lake of grey shadows into whose depths he plunged. The beat of his own sandaled footsteps echoed in his ears almost as fast as the drumming of his heart. Those of his pursuers joined in, making a strange, confusing rhythm. Which was somehow more threatening still. Almost as threatening as the smell of burning that hung in the grey air all around him. He glanced right. A *vicus* street leading south towards the *Forum Romanum* seemed full of flickering light. He wondered whether he should run towards it. Hoping for *vigiles* watch patrols. Or legionary peacekeepers. But then, over that unsettling rhythm of footsteps and heartbeat, he heard a baying. More animal than human. As though Cerberus the multi-headed hound of Hades had joined forces with Harpies hunting blood.

But straight ahead opened a friendlier thoroughfare. A proper *via*, wide and familiar. And, with a stab of relief that was almost agonising, he realised he was nearly home. He tried to put on a final spurt, spurred by the promise of safety. But he was at the end of his strength. He was by no means a young man. And the *toga* he wore was designed for stately, dignified progress. Not wild dashes through benighted streets. Which was one of the reasons he normally travelled in a litter borne by slaves. Preceded by torchbearers and *lictors* guards.

A kind of helpless incredulity swept over him. As he realised that his legs were going to let him down. Even though he was in sight of salvation. He slowed, desperately willing his limbs to stay sturdy. But within a step or two they turned from reliable tree trunks. Strong – if gnarled and knotty nowadays. To unsteady candle flames. Burning – wavering – guttering helplessly as he stumbled. Unable to bear his weight for one more heartbeat. One more step.

ii

He felt himself toppling forward. As though he had been cut off at the knees. He put out his hands and was just able to break his fall. So that his face at least was saved from striking the cobble stones. Even so, he was winded. And lay, gasping helplessly, as he waited for his strength to return. Something that did not promise to happen at all quickly. In the meantime, he rolled over and levered himself into a sitting position. Only to observe that the flames filling the southern roadway belonged to torches carried by a mob of men and women. Who were rushing towards him in a manner he could only compare to wolves in the wild. Or ferocious animals in the arena.

Because he was shocked and disorientated, they appeared to approach and surround him with superhuman speed. His ears were ringing so he found it hard to understand what they were saying at first. They seemed simply to be howling and roaring. The yellow brightness shone in their wild eyes. Gleamed on their

15

spittle, their drool. And their teeth. Turned their horrific, inhuman expressions into an array of terrible masks. It was disturbingly like being trapped in the middle of one of Sophocles' most appalling dramatic tragedies. Orpheus surrounded by Thracian Bacchantes ready to tear him apart.

The largest rioter strode forward. A monster of a man carrying a bloodied club in one hand and a flaming torch in the other. He leaned down closer. Lowered his torch. And spoke more clearly. In a deep *plebeian* voice. 'Here,' he said. 'I know you. I know who you are.' He straightened. Looked back at his cohorts with something like triumph. 'He's with *them*.' He shouted. 'He's with the treacherous scum who murdered Caesar!'

But before any of the mob could react, two new characters arrived on the stage. One dressed in the armour of a centurion of the VIIth. The other in that of a tribune. Only two of them. But carrying enough authority to stop the mob in its tracks. The ex-legionaries amongst it came to attention automatically. The rest, sensing their respect, also fell silent.

'No!' said the centurion, his voice ringing with command. 'He's with *us*.'

'He is if you can take him,' sneered the leader. Straightening. Striding forward to confront the centurion, chin to chin. 'You might be soldiers, but there's only two of you. And there's twenty of us. You might have your pretty swords but we've got knives and clubs and...'

His threats stopped suddenly. For the centurion had drawn his dagger so swiftly that the gesture seemed too quick for human eyes to follow. His left hand simply flashed down to his hip and struck back upwards like a snake. The blade gleamed for an instant in the torchlight and then was gone. As he drove it straight into his opponent's throat. The sharp steel went through the pit of the man's gullet. It punctured the tubes of the throat, stabbed the root of his tongue and separated the bones of the neck immediately behind. Without even touching the massive blood vessels on either side. Slicing the spinal cord as it went. For the briefest instant as the hilt rested against the skin below his voice box, a finger's length of the point stood out above the collar of his tunic at the back of his neck.

The centurion slid the dagger free and sheathed it. All as part of that one swift, flowing movement. Stepped smartly back. Stood shoulder to shoulder with the tribune. Protecting their seated quarry. The corpse stood still for an instant longer. His death had come upon him so swiftly and absolutely that his body had no time to react. His lungs emptied as his rib-cage collapsed. A soft, flute-like note sounded briefly as the expelled air went out through the hole in his windpipe as well as through his gaping mouth. Then the torch tumbled from the numb fingers at the end of his falling arm. Skittered away across the ground, making those

16

nearest dance back. His club dropped. His knees gave. He toppled backwards, smacking his head on the cobbles. The sharp sound echoed in the quiet, above the restless roaring of the flambeaus. His eyes continued to move for a moment. Met those of the man in the *toga* seated beside him. Then they froze. Wide. Shocked. Dead. As with Gaius Amiatus, there was no blood. Hardly any wound. Just a black slit as wide as a thumb, as narrow as a thumbnail, on the front of his throat. And another, invisible now, on the back of his neck. But he might as well have been beheaded. And the execution had been completed in half a dozen heartbeats. To the man sitting on the ground, it was all still a part of the strange play going on around him.

'He's with us,' repeated Septem the centurion. His tone like iron. His eyes like steel. 'Does anyone else wish to discuss the matter?'

As the mob backed away then turned and ran, the soldiers stooped and lifted their quarry to his feet. The moment they did so, his ears began to clear. As did his eyes. Reality jumped back into place like the slamming of a door. 'I know you!' he said. It apparently did not occur to him that he should thank them for saving his life. 'I know you both. You work for Mark Antony.'

'We work for General Antony, yes,' said Septem. 'And he wants to see you.'

'There's a couple of legal points he wishes to discuss. So he sent us to invite you to visit him, Senator Cicero,' added the tribune.

iii

Marcus Tullius Cicero leaned forward. Flickering lamplight gleamed on his high, balding brow and the scalp beneath his thinning hair. Sparked in his deep-set eyes. As his hooded gaze flicked from face to face across the room. He was approaching his sixty-fourth year and had supposed he had only retirement and academic study to look forward to. But Caesar's death changed all that. It thrust him back into the deadly arena of Roman politics. To fight or die like a gladiator.

Secret Agent and Centurion Iacomus Artemidorus had never seen him look so nervous. Even sitting on the cobbles in the minor forum surrounded by the mob, he had simply looked confused. The spy glanced across to his superior, the Tribune Domitus Enobarbus. They exchanged cold gazes. Then returned their icy glares towards the nervous jurist.

Cicero had many reasons to be apprehensive.

First, there was the fact that the two soldiers, who had escorted him here after rescuing him from the mob, were still in full armour. In spite of his evident distress they had half-carried him home. Organised his litter so swiftly he had no time to change his battered clothing. Grudgingly allowed him to summon his secretary, Tiro. And escorted them both here, Cicero in the litter and Tiro running beside it.

Their swords still sat now on their right hips. Daggers on their left. Helmets on the floor beside their *caligae* boots. And his host, General and Co-consul Mark Antony and his brothers Gaius and Lucius were equally warlike in their attire. They looked as though they had just left a battle. Or were just about to start one.

Cicero's anxious gaze returned to the centurion's almost magical dagger. Which brought the vision of the dead rioter with that tiny, bloodless cut on his throat to linger distractingly in the famous jurist's memory. The flute-like note as he breathed his last. There were rumours that the murderous centurion himself had simply thrown his beautiful young lover to the mob. In spite of the vital information she had discovered while undercover in Cassius' household, working as one of the team tasked with preventing Caesar's murder. But the centurion discovered she had betrayed him to the conspirators Gaius Trebonius and Minucius Basilus. Blamed her, in the final analysis, for the failure of his mission to keep Caesar safe. It was said he had acted coldly and without a second thought. And for all Cicero knew, the mob had torn her limb from limb with their bare hands. As they had ripped apart the innocent *Tribune Plebis* and poet Helvius Cinna, mistaking him for the guilty Cornelius Cinna a hanger-on of the conspirators. As the wild Thracian women tore Orpheus to pieces.

Secondly, there was the panel of interrogators the two soldiers had brought him to face. Who they were as much as what they wore. Co-consul and General Mark Antony. His wife, the icy Lady Fulvia, at his side. Antony's fully armed brothers Gaius and Lucius scowling at their shoulders and the consuls-elect Aulus Hirtius and Gaius Vibius Pansa at theirs. The latter pair in *togas* so white that they emphasised the sorry state of Cicero's. In spite of the fact that Hirtius was a life-long friend, all of their expressions were set alike. As though they were modelling for a bust of Nemesis. Deity of implacable Justice. And inescapable Revenge.

Only Co-consul Publius Cornelius Dolabella and Master of the Horse Marcus Aemilius Lepidus were missing from this roll-call of the men currently ruling Rome. Dolabella was out, apparently making sure that every *aedile* magistrate in the city had mounted *vigile* watch patrols. Lepidus had no real legal authority or constitutional power, the battered legislator knew. For he was merely deputy to a dead dictator. His power and position terminated with Caesar's last heartbeat. But he was also on the streets. Or in the *Forum Romanum*, at least. With the Seventh Legion. Nominally searching for the ringleaders of the riots that erupted after Caesar's funeral and continued nightly since. Like Gaius Amiatus, General Marius' grandson. Like the leader of the mob who had nearly killed him earlier. Though Cicero himself was privately certain that the people truly responsible for at least sparking the murderous anarchy sweeping through the city were sitting in this room. Watching him sweat.

Thirdly, most importantly, there was the deadly dangerous subject of the legal discussion he had been brought here to join. For they were clearly trying to circumvent the express will of the Senate and People of Rome. To twist Cicero's legal knowledge to their own devices.

Most of the men whose crimes were under discussion had escaped from Rome and the wrath of the mob by the skin of their teeth in the early watches of the nights soon after the murder. Including Gaius Cassius and his brother-in-law Marcus Brutus. Who had been forced to barricade their villas and fight off outraged crowds attempting to burn them out. As they had burned the *Curia* in Pompey's Theatre where the *Libertores* had slaughtered Caesar. The majority of them were fleeing east, via their country villas and estates. Only one or two hardy, well-protected souls like Decimus Albinus lingered.

iv

It had been Decimus Albinus, in fact, who Cicero was visiting earlier. Decimus, still protected by the *centuria* of one hundred gladiators he had arranged to give a display in Pompey's Theatre on the *Ides* of *Mars* itself. Apparently to guarantee that his good friend and mentor Julius Caesar was protected as he attended the Senate meeting that promised to declare him king. Actually to ensure the safety of the murderers as they ran red-handed from the deed; most of them waving their bloody daggers in the air. Decimus, to whom Caesar had promised command of the northernmost parts of Italy for the next year. *Gallia Cisalpinus* Cisalpine Gaul: the land between the Alps and the River Po, the Apennine Mountains and the Rubicon. The most potent power base in Italy. Who had wanted so urgently to discuss with Cicero whether Antony had the legal powers to cancel, change or delay his appointment. Or, worse, to take command of Cisalpine Gaul himself.

'There is really nothing left to discuss,' said Cicero. He sensed rather than saw Tiro get ready to record his judgement in the shorthand the secretary had invented for the very purpose. Which was the shorthand now used by the slaves who kept the public records of Senate meetings. But Cicero knew that what he was about to say would never be promulgated. Or even repeated. Not in the records of his speeches, of his letters or of his philosophical treatises. Should he survive to see them published.

'The Senate has ruled. And that is that. Even if you have now discovered witnesses willing to describe the terrible act in detail. It should make no difference under the law. Brutus, Cassius and the men who executed Caesar did so in the belief that he was seeking absolute power. *Tyranny*. Kingship. Killing a tyrant is

19

not a criminal act. It is a highly patriotic one. Like executing anyone the Senate has declared *hostis* outlaw. And as leader of the group, Marcus Junius Brutus has attested to being motivated by the actions of his ancestor who drove the last tyrant and king, Tarquin the Proud, out of the city four hundred years ago.'

'But the Senate has also ruled that Caesar was not a tyrant,' Antony reminded Cicero, eyes narrow. Probing. Testing. Twisting...

'They did that simply because if he was declared a tyrant then all of his actions, plans and appointments would have been cancelled,' insisted Cicero. Meeting Antony's cold stare. 'There would have been utter chaos. Not only in Rome but across the empire. Hundreds of senators forced to seek re-election. City officials high and low seeking reappointment. Legions no longer disbanded. Some needing to be re-formed. Both looking for officers to reassemble them. Pay to be handed back to the legions' *quaestors* paymasters. Farms to be relinquished. Returned to their original owners. Entire towns to be vacated. Towns completely peopled by retired legionaries such as Valentia in Hispania. Governors returning for reassignment. Every local government officer in the empire reapplying for his post. Whole regions left without governance as they did so. Revolution. Invasion, even. The Gauls and the Germans always straining at the leash in the north. Sextus Pompey and his pirates at Sicily in the south. The Getae in the east. Anarchy in any case...'

The new calendar disbanded, thought Artemidorus. The eight-day week reinstated. All the work Caesar had done with Cleopatra's Egyptian mathematician Sosigenes of Alexandria would be undone. Time itself would be broken...

A brief silence settled. Rain pattered softly into the pool of the *impluvium* at the centre or the *atrium* behind them. The *Mars* breeze stirred icily, though it was nearing the end of the month. The lamp flames flickered. Almost all of the seven men facing Cicero across the old-fashioned Tuscan style *atrium* had legal training as well as military. Many of them had been *praetors* judges as well as soldiers and senators. And Fulvia was one of the best-educated women in the empire. They all knew as well as Cicero that legally and practically undoing Caesar's plans would simply tear Rome and the states she governed apart.

'*Mayhem*...' Agreed Antony, breaking the silence. Picking up on Cicero's short speech without a beat. 'And that is why I have taken possession of Caesar's notes and plans as well as his will and other papers. In due legal process.' He paused, locking gazes with Cicero. As though daring him to disagree with the legality of his actions. 'Because the Senate, wisely, ruled that Caesar was *never* a tyrant. Thus preserving his actions in the *past*. But also meaning that now his plans and

20

dispositions for the *future* need to be confirmed. Enacted. And only I, as named executor, with these powers and documents, will be able to hold everything together in the immediate future. And put his wishes into action as he would have wanted. Only me.'

Because you have Caesar's plans, General, thought Artemidorus, and are the one man telling the rest of us exactly what they were. And you have the keys to the city's financial resources in the Temple of Ops. But is even that treasure going to be enough? Neither he nor Tribune Enobarbus shared Antony's airy confidence in this matter.

Cicero grew paler. But the purple stripes of the tunic he wore beneath his *toga* grew darker. Damper. 'That is true, Lord Antony. But it does not alter the facts which you know as well as I do. The Senate may have declared that Caesar was not a tyrant. Not only making you his executor but also making Brutus and the rest all guilty of conspiracy, treason and murder – murder at the very least.' He closed his eyes. Took a shuddering breath. 'But only at first glance.' Cicero's eyes opened. Narrowed. Moved from Antony to Fulvia as he added to his explanations. 'For they *would be* guilty of all these things had the Senate not pardoned them. In a unanimous vote. Just as complete as the vote that exonerated Caesar. So they cannot be guilty of any of the crimes we have discussed. By order of the Senate and People of Rome.'

v

'Just so,' nodded Antony. He paused for a heartbeat. Seemingly happy that the legal position had been established. But then his gaze switched to his secret agent. And he introduced into the discussion the one further question that Septem had suggested he should ask. The real reason for bringing Cicero here. To examine the one point of law that might undo all the defence strategies he had just laid out. In the case of one conspirator at least: the leader. 'What were Caesar's last words, Septem?' snapped Antony. 'And to whom were they spoken? According to the witnesses you have found and questioned?' His gaze flashed over to Tiro, making sure the discussion was still being recorded.

'They were spoken to Marcus Junius Brutus,' said Artemidorus, who had heard Brutus himself telling Cassius as they fled from the scene of their crime, calling for Cicero and his advice. And the secret agent had been looking for witnesses who had also overheard the fatal words ever since. Witnesses willing to come forward. Who were part of neither faction. For none of Brutus' friends would stand up before the Senate and accuse him. And none of Antony's men – such as Artemidorus himself – would be believed if they did so. Even if a large section of

21

the Senate suspected they spoke the truth. But Artemidorus had found a witness at last. A beautiful boy called Adonis.

The witness of whom Cicero had heard only the vaguest whispers.

Speaking now on his cue, Artemidorus was springing a trap which, they hoped, would catch the leader of the conspirators. And open a road down which they might, with luck and cunning, hunt the others. 'Caesar said, in Greek, to Brutus, "*Kai su teknon*? Even you my son?"'

'But what did he mean?' mused Cicero. Masking the shock in his eyes behind lowered lids. Not surprised, but deeply disturbed by this. Thinking again of Nemesis and the impossibility of escaping the grinding wheels of her justice. Or the terrible Friendly Ones who helped her. The Furies who were so powerful no one dared name them outright. For fear of summoning them. 'Like so many important cases this would turn on the meaning of a single word,' he prevaricated. 'That slippery Greek word *teknon*. *Child*. Now how are we to interpret that?'

'He said it to Brutus at the very moment that he died.' Antony's voice rang with certainty. '"*You too my child*?" Now, *you*, Marcus Tullius, and the murderers involved, might insist that "*teknon*" was merely a term of affection. Which might translate into Latin as, "You too, *puer* my boy?", "You too, *juvencus* youngster?", "You too, *catulaster*, lad?" Expressing simple surprise that someone so young and close in friendship could be involved in so terrible a deed.' He gave a bark of derisive laughter and leaned forward belligerently. 'Not a public declaration, you would no doubt argue, made with his dying breath. A pronouncement carrying, therefore, great legal weight – as you above all should appreciate. A deathbed confession, so to speak, from someone staring into the face of Charon the Ferryman to the underworld. An announcement that the last of his murderers was in fact his own *son*. Not to be translated as "You too, *filius*, my son?" Not "You too, *prognatus* my offspring?" Not a statement of *paternity*! Not a declaration of *fatherhood*. That old question. Which has lain between Caesar, Brutus and Servilia Caepionis, Brutus' mother, all these years…'

Fulvia spoke suddenly. 'Those who would deny the possibility say there is little more than fifteen years between them. Caesar and Brutus. Father and son. Could Caesar have fathered a child at the age of fifteen? On a girl four years his elder? Unlikely, they say! But *impossible*? I think not! We all know Caesar's reputation with women. That he started his philandering almost as soon as he was in his *toga virilis*. Which he assumed unusually early as someone of extraordinary mental and physical maturity. Sleeping around *before* his fifteenth year in fact. When Servilia Caepionis was well into childbearing age. Married at the time to Brutus the Elder, who was already old when the marriage knot was tied. Even though he served as

22

Urban Tribune a couple of years after Servilia fell pregnant. And he fell dead soon after that. But who never managed to impregnate her except, apparently, on this one unique occasion. By coincidence, perhaps, in the very year that Caesar really began his career as the seducer of half of the noble women in Rome! And, as everyone knows, Brutus junior's mother Servilia was Caesar's longest serving mistress. Rumoured to be his first. She may deny that Caesar impregnated her – but why should we believe her rather than him? How would she even *know*? For certain? Sleeping with old husband and young lover? But *he* would! Know his firstborn – even if he had to keep the knowledge secret? Of course he would!'

Artemidorus also leaned forward then, capturing the sweating lawyer's unsteady gaze. Sweeping back an unruly lock of hair from above his left eye. Revealing as he did so a long thin scar. 'And, although I hesitate to disagree with you, Brutus, Cassius and the rest, the moment in which one of your closest associates is just about to plunge a dagger into your groin. Into your *groin*, mark you. Having watched his friends stab twenty-two other daggers into your head, face, arms, shoulders and chest, seems a strange one to call forth a... What did Lord Antony say you might call it?... A *term of affection.*'

Cicero closed his eyes, his mind racing. The implications of this were disturbing in the extreme. It did not matter that Caesar had adopted his sister's grandson Octavian as his heir in his will. Leaving the boy his name and his fortune. Or even that he had nominated Decimus Brutus Albinus his heir in the second degree as well as Pro-praetor and Governor of *Gallia Cisalpinus*. There was almost no chance the full formal pardon would stand if the Senate agreed that Caesar's dying words admitted Marcus Junius Brutus, although unacknowledged in the will, was nevertheless really Caesar's *son*.

vi

Because according to Roman Law, of which Cicero was the greatest living exponent, there was only one crime worse than killing another citizen. Worse even than treason against the state. And that was killing your father. For the family was the heart of Roman society. And the *Pater Familias* stood at the head of the family as the dictator, *Pater Patriae*, stood at the head of the Republic. If Caesar's dying words were actually a claim of fatherhood, then the Senate's decision that Brutus was not guilty of Caesar's murder must be set aside. Independently of the quibble about tyrannicide. For if he was guilty of patricide, he had gone beyond the bounds of forgiveness. He had slaughtered not only his *Dictator* but also his *Pater*. If he was guilty of patricide then he must be declared *hostis* enemy of the state. Hunted by every citizen of the empire until he was caught. Then he must be brought back to Rome. And summarily executed.

23

Cicero knew the details of the penalty for patricide better than anyone. Which, he suddenly realised, must be one of the major reasons why the spy and centurion had hunted him down and brought him here. As he should have seen at once. Only his dazed state following his terrified flight and near death at the hands of the mob in the minor forum could explain why he had failed to make the link earlier.

For his most famous early case, the one that established his reputation, was the defence of Sextus Roscius of Ameriain, accused of that very crime. Which was why Brutus himself, in deadly secret, during the hours after the murder, had brought his horrible misgivings to his friend and lawyer. For Brutus, too, believed that Caesar's dying words claimed him as his son. Which in itself would be the most terrible revenge the dying man could possibly take. Now the jurist looked up at the stony faces opposite. The countenance of the cruel spy and soldier who had thrown his woman to the mob claimed his attention. The advocate knew his true adversary then. There was no longer any doubt about the rumours. Centurion Artemidorus had discovered someone willing to act as witness to what had been said during the moments it had taken Caesar to die. Who knew exactly what Caesar's dying words had been and to whom they had been spoken. And he saw how those three words of Greek could become the leading conspirator's Achilles' heel. If Brutus was found guilty of patricide, that guilt would tarnish all the others by association. Opening them dangerously to the hostility not only of the People, but also the Senate. The deeply split and wavering Senate who had stood by Caesar's murderers so far. Largely at the prompting of Cicero himself. As well as laying Brutus open to the horrific sentence called *Poena Cullei*.

In many ways *Poena Cullei* seemed to be an almost laughable punishment. In no way comparable to ejection from the Tarpeian Rock. Or even crucifixion. Though no Roman citizen could be crucified. And ejection would result only in a few heartbeats of terrified downward flight before you were smashed to pieces on the roadway below. If you were wise enough to dive rather than to jump. The former ensured death. The latter risked an agonising end as, crippled but still living, you were impaled on a great brass hook and dragged to the Tiber to drown. Worse even than this, *Poena Cullei* involved the ritual of stripping the condemned man naked while a leather sack big enough to hold him was prepared. Then, into the sack should be put a dog, a cat, a monkey, a fighting cock and a viper. When they were in place, the naked man joined them. The sack was sewn shut. Then it was thrown into the Tiber. Each of the animals had a symbolic significance long lost in time.

But Cicero knew all too well the nightmares of the terrified Sextus Roscius. Which, now, Marcus Junius Brutus might well be sharing. Dogs and cats have

24

teeth and claws. Cockerels have beaks and spurs. The sort of monkeys selected could be anything from chimpanzees to baboons. Large, strong animals, also well supplied with teeth. All in all, given the situation likely to arise in a slowly sinking sack with a man, naked and defenceless, among these terrified animals tearing at each other, the viper offered the best alternative. If it could be made to strike some vital part. Before the other drowning occupants tore the dying man to pieces. With their teeth, claws, beaks and spurs.

'Sextus Roscius most feared having his face clawed off before he drowned,' mused Cicero. 'I myself wondered whether having one's genitals rent asunder or one's intestines ripped out might be worse. But my thoughts were apparently too earthly. Sextus was terrified that his *anima* spirit would wander, faceless, blind and anonymous through the afterlife. Helpless and unrecognised for all eternity.'

The silence returned. The rain eased so that individual drops fell into the *impluvium* as though the gods themselves were counting the passage of time, thought Artemidorus grimly. So that the mere mortals in the *atrium* could all appreciate the length of eternity. And a man like Brutus' whole existence seemed to have been dictated not only by his standing in society but also his importance as the latest representative of his famous family. A living representative of the standing of his forefathers in the history of the city through the centuries. For such a man, the thought of wandering blind, faceless and unknown through the rest of time must hold horrors simply unimaginable to lesser men of no family. Who did not expect their names to echo through the *atria* of history. 'So,' he demanded. Breaking into the silence. 'If a case could be made that Caesar did, in fact, accuse Brutus of patricide with his dying breath, what would be the next step?'

vii

'The case would need to be presented to the Senate,' Cicero answered slowly, his mind clearly racing. 'Who would need to be convinced by the testimony of witnesses. Who in turn would need to be unimpeachable in such a terrible matter. Then, if convinced there was a case to answer, they would recall him in the name of the People of Rome to face the charge in person. Declare him *hostis* outlaw if he refused. If such a charge could be proven, not even the Senate could set it aside.

'And *could* such a case be made?' probed Antony.

'That is not a question I could answer immediately,' answered Cicero guardedly. 'It would turn around the evidence of witnesses, for instance. A prosecution in the proper forms…' His voice tailed off. As he realised with a lift of his spirits that nearly all of the men who had actually heard Caesar's last words were among the murderers themselves. And they had fled the city, almost to a man. Putting themselves beyond even Antony's reach.

25

'But you *could* answer it?' probed Fulvia impatiently. 'Eventually. If we can supply a witness or two…'

'It would depend on the standing and probity of the witnesses, of course. If a senator would stand up, for instance, his evidence would carry much more weight than that of, say, a slave…' he said. 'But in any case, I would have to consult some other jurists, both in person and through their writings. That could take time and may even require travel. To Athens, for instance. Or even, I suppose, to Alexandria… The library… What of it is left after Caesar set fire to the Museum of Ptolemy four years ago.'

'But you could do it?' demanded Antony.

'Perhaps… Perhaps…'

'Very well,' said Antony. 'Get started as soon as you can, then. My men will see you home…'

'Ah,' said the elderly jurist, his eyes brightening. 'If I might avail myself of your latrine before I go. And, perhaps if Tiro…'

'Of course,' said Antony.

Fulvia clapped her hands and a slave hurried in. Cicero rose and hobbled after him on stiff legs with his secretary solicitously at his side.

As soon as they left the *atrium*, the atmosphere changed. Antony and his brothers stood, shoulder to shoulder. 'So,' said the general, including his wife, his brothers, the consuls-elect and his secret agents in his plotting. 'We have a well-laid trap. For Brutus at least. And when he goes down he'll likely pull Cassius down with him. We need to discuss this further. Enobarbus, Septem.' He focused his most powerful stare on his spymaster and his spy. 'Rebuild your team,' he commanded. 'Recruit anyone you need to support the testimony of the slave you've questioned so far. Plan to go after anyone who could be made to stand up beside him and swear to Caesar's dying words. The more powerful and influential the better. But even the fact that Cicero is looking into the matter will start rumours at the very least! Excellent!'

'Yes, General,' said Enobarbus. 'But Septem here is also working on establishing exactly what was *done* as well as what was said. Precisely what was done. By whom. In what order.'

'To give us a list of the men we want to go hunting for first,' added Artemidorus.

'First after those *spuria* bastards Trebonius and Decimus Albinus. The one fooled me and the other fooled Caesar. That makes it personal. For both of us!'

'But don't let your focus on those two distract you from any others chance might throw your way…' added Fulvia, icily.

26

Like Minucius Basilus, thought Artemidorus. Basilus, whose perverted games and enjoyment of humiliation and agony had gone much of the way to making his lover Cyanea break down and betray them all.

'Look for more witnesses and don't make any secret of it either,' said Antony. 'Find out the truth of the matter. In as much detail as you can.' He paused. Rubbed his hands. 'That was an excellent notion of yours, Septem. *Patricide*! It would never have occurred to me! Even if it comes to nothing in the Senate it will terrify Brutus. Shock all his friends and associates. And stir the pot in a way that murderous crew won't like at all.

'And, talking of stirring the pot,' he continued. 'Aulus Hirtius, I think it's time for you to go to Decimus Albinus and make one or two things very clear to him. One – Caesar may have put him down as Proconsul for Cisalpine Gaul for the legislative year that begins with your appointment as Co-consul in *Januarius*. But two – Caesar didn't know what a treacherous little *blatta* cockroach Albinus was when he did it. Therefore, three – if Albinus thinks I'm going to let him take over the entire north of Italy with three full legions under his command, he had better think again, no matter what Caesar proposed and the Senate has decided! *And*, come to that, he'd better get out of Rome as quickly as he can or I'll send people after him who will simply chop their way through his gladiators until they can take his traitorous head and spike it in the Forum for everyone to see!'

The group had split up by the time Cicero returned. Tiro a step or two behind him. The tablets full of his dangerous legal wisdom clutched safely to his breast.

'Tribune,' boomed Antony, in his cheerfully ebullient offspring-of-Hercules persona. 'Would you and the centurion kindly escort our revered guest home. I have slaves with torches ready and waiting to accompany his litter of course, but I would feel happier if you who brought him here took him back again. Make sure that no harm comes to him...'

The two soldiers stooped, retrieved their helmets and stood, armour creaking. Making enough noise to cover the final word of their general's order.

'...*yet*...'

II

Artemidorus sprang awake as the morning *tubae* trumpets sounded across the encampment of the Seventh Legion. For the first time in what seemed like weeks he found himself in the centurions' tent which was his usual home. When he was not on secret assignment. On the camp bed which was his accustomed resting place. As a soldier. As opposed to as a spy. For much of the previous month he had been working undercover, bivouacked in Antony's villa. Required to attend the general at any hour of the day or night. Ready to come and go on secret and increasingly dangerous assignments at a moment's notice. Before, during and after Caesar's murder. Which it had been his mission to prevent at any cost. For which he still felt almost personally responsible. As, just like Caesar, trusting the treacherous Decimus Albinus as his closest friend, the spy had trusted his lover Cyanea. Who had betrayed them all in the end.

Last night, however, he had returned to camp after escorting Cicero's litter home. Marching through the benighted city allowed him to satisfy himself that the VIIth's patrols at least were keeping things quiet. Even if the *aediles'* watchmen preferred to linger round their watchfires.

The centurions' substantial leather tent was pitched in the grounds of the Temple of Aesculapius right at the southern end of Tiber Island. A carefully negotiated financial arrangement with the keepers of the temple allowed not only living and cooking within the grounds but also access to the roomy temple itself when the weather was unusually inclement. An agreement that suited all involved. Negotiated in the final analysis by Antistius, the physician. A leading member of the order of Aesculapius. Who was also a member of Artemidorus' *contubernium* unit of spies. And the man who had performed an autopsy on Caesar. The first recorded in history as far as the secret agent knew.

One of the centurions' servants bustled in with a bowl of steaming water, a polished bronze mirror and a phial of scented oil. Bringing the light of a grey dawn behind him with the chill wind through the tent's wide flap. Although these were far better quarters than the simple legionaries', it was agreed among the centurions that they would remain in eight-man unit *contubernium* tents. Though there were six centurions assigned to a cohort. Seven in the First Cohort's case as Septem had a replacement to stand in for him when he was working undercover. And, just like a legionary's eight-man *contubernium*, they had two servants per tent.

Tribunes and legates, of course, had quarters in city villas. Often owned by themselves or their families. Fully staffed with the usual range of slaves, therefore. Such senior officers were important men politically as well as militarily. Men who were usually climbing the *Cursus Honorum* ladder to supreme power. Their absence from the camps, however, was the main reason why the centurions – and their council – wielded so much influence in the legions.

The dawn light was beginning to fill the tent which Artemidorus shared with the First Cohort's other centurions, including Oppius, his replacement. All of whom were still asleep, having spent the night patrolling Rome's restless streets. Artemidorus, however, felt full of decisive energy. He flung his cloak back with a flourish. The heavy mud-coloured woollen garment, which had acted as a blanket during the cold night, billowed up off the truckle bed. Allowing the spy to step out onto the carpet which was the tent's floor. He pulled his sleeping tunic up over his head and dropped it on the cloak. Naked, he strode across the flooring, pausing at the foot of his bed to pull his dagger from its sheath on his uniform belt. Which, with his red *sagum* uniform cloak was folded neatly at the bed-foot.

The *pugio* was not a standard-issue dagger such as the majority of the legionaries wore. This was the dagger whose almost magical blade had dispatched Gaius Amiatus and the nameless leader of the mob pursuing Cicero. And he had not bought it. He had stolen it. In fact, this was the second time it had fallen into the spy's possession. The first time, he had purloined it from the household shrine of Marcus Junius Brutus on the night before Caesar was murdered. While he was also liberating Puella, a slave who had overheard several crucial meetings between Brutus and the men plotting to murder Caesar. In the hope that her evidence, combined with everything else his cadre of spies had learned, would convince Caesar to spend the *Ides* safely at home. On that occasion, he had left it wedged in the neck of Brutus' *ostiarius* doorkeeper who had tried to recapture the escaping slave girl.

Then it had found him again. Half a day later. Wedged in the groin of Caesar's corpse. Left there by Brutus as he fled in horror from the *Curia* of Pompey's Theatre. To hide with the other *Libertores* in the Temple of Jupiter Capitolinus. Protected by the treacherous Decimus Albinus' gladiators while news of their terrible deed began to speed round Rome. And, at the earliest opportunity the spy now knew, to discuss Caesar's dying words to him with Brutus' friend and lawyer Cicero.

ii

Artemidorus held out his left hand, cupped. The servant poured a little warm, fragrant oil into it. The spy smoothed this over his stubbled cheeks, chin and throat. Then he used the dagger to shave himself. Watching his reflection in the bronze mirror held by the servant. Measuring the face reflected back at him with calm, calculating eyes. The bronze gave them a golden cast he knew they did not possess. They were grey eyes. Cyanea once told him they were coloured somewhere between smoke and steel. Her eyes had been bright blue-green. And it hurt him to remember them. The blue-green eyes of a liar and traitor he had loved. His were Greek eyes in any case. To go with the Spartan brain behind the high, clear forehead. Though his eyebrows and unruly hair were as dark as any Roman's. As any Iberian's in fact. And the red cast given by the bronze mirror simply emphasised what was already there. The unruly fringe fell forward in scarce-controllable curls. One of which at least covered the white line of a scar running like a military road straight from his hairline to his left eyebrow. Lifting it slightly into a permanently quizzical tension with the right one. The lean face beneath was all cheekbone and nose. The nose was long and narrow, like a blade. Tending towards the Roman aquiline as much as to the straight Greek. The nostrils, too, were narrow. Like an eagle's. Apt enough for a man who followed the Eagle of the Seventh Legion, perhaps. There was no doubt about the straight slash of his mouth, though. Which, even at rest, looked brutal. Or the breadth of the jawline reaching into the square chin he was about to shave. A chin on which the stubble, like his hair, glinted with shades of red-gold.

But one glance was enough reflective introspection for today. He was in action almost immediately. Revelling in the way the cold steel seemed to glide across his oiled skin like a zephyr of breeze across a stream. Thinking that the edge was keener than any razor wielded by the legion's *tonsors*. By the *tonsors* on the street corners in the city itself. Even by Antony's own *tonsor*, who had been in charge of his shaving and barbering since he had removed the fox-red beard disguising him as a workman. Employed to fix some damage to the roof of Brutus' villa. And to discover what the traitor was planning – and whether anyone in his household was witness to it.

By the time the sun was a dull silver *denarius* behind the thinning cloud above the pines of the distant Quirinial Hill, Artemidorus was shaved. Washed. And dressed in full armour. *Casila* helmet on his head. Blood-red *sagum* swinging from his shoulders as though he was one of Leonidas' three hundred Spartan warriors. One of the Spartan king's *cryptaia* cadre of deadly special agents. Like Caesar, he took his *jentaculum* breakfast as he went about his business. Sipping a cup of *posca* vinegar and water flavoured with rosemary and thyme. Washing down a mouthful of coarse *lentaculum emmer* bread still warm from the legion's ovens. As he marched through the stirring camp, slave trotting at his side. Handing the cup back as they reached the riverbank and replacing it with a handful of dates. Then, alone, out onto the *Pons Fabricius* towards the *Campus Martius*. Pausing halfway across the bridge to eat the dates as he thought through his plans for the day. Spitting their stones into the green-black swirl of the Tiber.

On the *Campus Martius* Field of Mars, the cavalry *alae* division of the VIIth had their camp and the pen for their horses. Close by the massive funeral pyre that had been erected for Caesar near the tomb of his beloved daughter Julia. A pyre that had been dismantled because the dictator's body had been immolated in the Forum itself. Between the horse pens and the vacancy left by the pyre there was an exercise area where the cavalry practised their manoeuvres. Or, when they were not occupying it, the legionaries used as a parade ground. And, beside it there was a wooden-walled area set aside for weapons training. Usually, this was where legionaries sharpened up their skills with the swords, daggers and spears they all carried. The archers practised their archery. Though the truth of the matter was that most Roman cavalry and the majority of their archers left much to be desired. Which was why generals like Caesar took *auxilia* auxiliaries into battle, the centurion mused. *Alae* wings of Numidian and Gallic horsemen. Cohorts of Cretan and Thracian archers.

Although the training area was his final destination, Artemidorus marched past it, heading towards Pompey's massive theatre with its fire-damaged *Curia*. Burned by the mobs revenging the man who had been slaughtered there. Not far from the theatre another of the men who had fought so hard to keep Caesar alive was about his daily ritual. A man who, like Artemidorus, had warned the doomed dictator of specific threats against him. Too little, however. Too late. Spurinna, *augur* and *haruspex*, Equestrian and Etruscan both in his standing and bloodline, was assessing the auguries for the day. As revealed in the entrails of a ram. Particularly in its liver. The creature had already been blessed and sacrificed. Spurinna, red to the elbows, his *toga* tied back in the ritual Gabine knot, was sorting through the animal's steaming viscera. As presented on a great gold bowl. Which sat on a stand at one end of the altar. Where the dead ram's belly gaped emptily.

Around Spurinna stood his acolytes and priests. And, on the outskirts of the crowd, a strikingly beautiful young woman. Her figure, features, hair and colouring revealed Ethiopian ancestry. Her smile on seeing Artemidorus revealed a lot more besides. The young woman's name was Puella. Girl. That was all she had ever been called in the household of Marcus Junius Brutus where she had been a slave. Until Artemidorus stole her and took her to Antony as living proof of the conspiracy against Caesar. Too late, as things turned out. She was currently

31

in Spurinna's household. The safest place to keep her as a runaway. Though, to be fair, Brutus currently had a lot more to worry about than the whereabouts of a missing slave.

'Ah, Septem,' called Spurinna, looking up from the ram's liver. 'The day augurs well. Whatever undertakings you are considering are likely to prosper if you begin them before the sun sets.'

'You know what I have been ordered to undertake,' answered Artemidorus. 'And how I propose to go about it.'

'My villa would be a good place to start, then,' said Spurinna. 'Especially as your little *aulus* lark is sitting in a *cubicula* storeroom terrified out of his mind, explaining at length to anyone who'll listen what Caesar's last words were.'

Artemidorus nodded. Puella was not the only runaway hiding in Spurinna's ample villa. A record keeper to the Senate and slave to the Censor Gaius Trebonius was also there. A Greek boy of disturbing beauty called Adonis. Who had been unlucky enough to catch Artemidorus' eye as the spy ran into the *Curia* immediately after the assassination. The first to come into the murder scene as the boy was the last to leave it. Adonis had not been too hard for Septem's *contubernium* of agents to track and kidnap. Without even alerting the boy's owner, who was currently hurrying away from Rome, in any case. Like the rest of the conspirators. Soon to head eastwards planning to take up his promised post of Proconsul for Asia as soon as practically possible. And certainly in no mind to worry about a missing slave. The unfortunate youth was now languishing in Spurinna's house, until such time as his evidence could be checked further and recorded in legal form. In case this ever brought Brutus to trial – as Antony clearly planned that it would.

'If your duties allow you, come to me at about noon,' suggested the soothsayer. 'We will examine the boy Adonis further. Then we can eat and plan. I can send my slaves to summon anyone you wish to see. A couple of hours should be enough to set things in motion. And then we can bathe and dine at our leisure. Perhaps you might stay the night.'

'That does sound like a well augured day,' agreed Artemidorus, his gaze lingering on Puella's wide brown eyes and shy smile. 'And it does occur to me that our caged songbird may have a good deal more to tell us. If we apply a little further pressure. He heard Caesar's last words. And I'd bet he may well have seen exactly whose dagger went where as they slaughtered him. Though of the two areas of knowledge, the latter is likely to be by far the more dangerous. As the boy will have realised, of course. Naming names. Especially names of incredibly rich and powerful, deadly dangerous and deeply frightened men. That could be flirting with an untimely and probably unpleasant death. Remember poor Telos. Beaten to a pulp and crucified. Eyes and tongue ripped out. Before his throat was cut. All for getting too close to Brutus' and Cassius' plans for the *Ides*. In the meantime I have an appointment. And I do not dare be late.'

'Until noon, then,' said Spurinna, turning away. 'Go to the Senate House and the villas of both co-consuls,' he ordered his assistants. 'Inform everyone that today is well augured...'

Artemidorus also turned away. And retraced his steps to the practice area. There were two strapping legionaries guarding the door through the rough wooden wall. Who snapped to attention and saluted their centurion with thunderous punctiliousness. But there turned out to be only one other person present in the training area as Artemidorus entered it. Gaius Quintus Tarpeius, the last of the *triarii* stood in full armour. Like the old-fashioned *triarii* legionaries, Quintus was older than the average. A slight, whip-strong *gallus* rooster of a man; with something of the fighting cock about him. A comparison emphasised by the bright red crest to his shining steel helmet. Artemidorus was momentarily distracted by the thought of the fearsome bantam-cock Quintus sewn in a sack with Brutus as the *Poena Cullei* was inflicted. Tearing his face off would be the least of it, he thought, with wry amusement. For Quintus had a fearsome reputation as a soldier. He had at one time or another served round all the edges of the empire as well as at its heart with generals like Marius, Sulla, Pompey, Caesar and Crassus. Some said that it was Quintus who had killed Spartacus himself. Face to face in a duel at the climax of the final battle near the village of Quaglietta. A battle that remained nameless because it had been fought against slaves. Just before Crassus crucified six thousand of the rebel gladiators all along the Appian Way. Beheading the nightmare that always arose when slaves turned on their masters. And, some said, venting his spleen after Pompey, as usual, came in at the end of the campaign and took much of the credit for other men's work.

Quintus had joined the VIIth even before Caesar's uncle Marius had reorganised the entire army. He was an enormously rich citizen of ancient Patrician Tarpean lineage. With no family to survive him. The legion was his life. And he committed everything he owned – everything he was – to his beloved VIIth. Though he had only been seconded to it twenty-two years previously in 689AUC when Pompey raised it in Hispania. As a companion to the VIth *Ferrata* Ironclads. His armour was the best and most advanced that could be purchased. The best, but never the brightest or most ornate. Over the standard chain mail he habitually wore the overlapping steel plate shoulders, breast and backplates that

33

were only just coming into fashion. The steel of his *gladius* and *pugio* was only fractionally less advanced than that of the dagger on Septem's left hip. In battle, Quintus and his companions were traditionally placed in the third wave. Which was why they were called *triarii*. Thirds. This was because they were the most experienced. The best armoured. Best equipped. The shock troops who would break the weakening wave of opponents already flagging after fighting their way through the first two ranks. Or, if things were going badly, they would be the rock on which the rising wave of enemy warriors would founder.

It was Quintus' place in the undercover *contubernium* that Artemidorus ran and Enobarbus commanded, to act as weapons instructor and equipment officer. And the armaments in whose use he trained Septem and his agents were every bit as advanced and exceptional as the arms and armour that he wore. His wealth of both money and experience meant that whatever was most likely to serve Artemidorus and his associates would be brought to the VIIth's armoury. From the past and the present. From the ends of the empire and beyond. And then presented to the spies. Who would be trained in their use up to the highest possible level of expertise. Arms and equipment not only useful in whatever mission they were undertaking. But also in any assignment they might ever be required to undertake. This particular well-augured morning, Artemidorus observed, the practice was to be with sling-shots.

iv

Artemidorus liked the sling. It was a weapon that he thought was wrongly underestimated. Caesar himself found slings, their stones and bullets of every style and size extremely useful. From pebbles taken at random, through heavier, specially tooled lead bullets, to huge steel-tipped bolts, massive boulders and incendiary bundles hurled by huge *ballistae* and *fundibalae* catapults. Quintus was expert in all of these weapons too. Sharing ideas and experiences over the years with Lucius Cornelius Balbus, the *praefectus fabricum* chief engineer who became Caesar's secretary, and the military architect Vitruvius. Unlike bows, slings were easy to carry. Unlike arrows, the projectiles they fired rarely ran out. There was always a pebble or a rock somewhere underfoot – even on the busiest battlefield. Like Marius' *pilum* spears, but unlike arrows, the more advanced bullets could not be reused. They lost their form and edge on impact. They could easily be beaten back into shape but not in the midst of combat.

In the hands of special soldiers, trained in the skills of Thracian and Balearic slingers, slings were comparable to the bow and arrow in terms of range, impact and rate of fire. In some areas, indeed, superior to the bow and arrow. Arrows were slow and easily visible, for instance. He had seen *testudo* shield-covered tortoises formed by men waiting for arrows to fall. You didn't know a sling bullet was coming until it hit you. Then it was often too late. Therefore he worked as hard to keep his skills with the sling as well honed as those with the bow, the *pilum* spear, the *gladius* and the *pugio*. And Quintus would train up the rest of the undercover operatives. For the battlefield was by no means the only place where slings could be lethally effective.

What Quintus had prepared today was something unusual, however. On a long table that almost stretched from side to side of the range, there were several slings laid out. Short, medium and long. A trio of simple slings of traditional design, each longer than the other, and a staff sling with a short piece of wood attached. And piled by each sling was a range of bullets, from simple stones rounded by agitation on riverbeds to leaden bullets of various sizes, weights and forms. In front of the table, down the length of the range stood four posts. One at fifteen paces, then thirty, forty and fifty. On each post sat a watermelon. Impaled on a spike. Just as Antony planned to do with the *Libertores'* heads in the Forum when the time was ripe.

Each melon wore a legionary's helmet. In front of each post stood a *scutum* shield. The area between the top of the shield and the brow ridge of the helmet was narrow. In battle, just wide enough to allow a soldier to see ahead. There was about the width of a palm between the shield rim and the helmet edge. 'Target practice?' wondered Artemidorus as he came level with the table.

'A little more than that, boy,' answered Quintus. Sounding, as ever, short-tempered. As though the spy's simple observations were underestimating his plans and wasting his all too valuable time. 'Try the first. The short Thracian. Let's see if the last few weeks of undercover work have spoilt your aim. Notice the pouch is wider even on the short sling so that it holds the stone more firmly.'

'Making it more accurate,' suggested Artemidorus.

'Obviously!' snapped Quintus.

Smothering an affectionate smile, the spy placed a stone in the sling. The short sling was a shepherd's weapon. This one was of Thracian design, as Quintus said. There was little more to it than a long piece of woven fibre with a pouch in the middle and a knot at one end. It was exactly the same as the shepherd's sling that the Jews still saying mourning prayers for Caesar every night would recognise. From the duel between the shepherd boy David and the giant Philistine warrior Goliath of Gath. Which was recorded in the scrolls of the Nevim, second section of their Holy Tanakh.

With these thoughts running through his mind, he whirled it and fired almost casually at the nearest watermelon. The stone sped fifteen paces and over the top

35

of the *scutum* faster than the eye could see. It hit immediately below the helmet's ridge. If there had been a face there it would have shattered a septum or taken out an eye. On its way into the skull itself. Only the weight of the helmet stopped the melon from exploding.

'Good enough, boy,' allowed Quintus grudgingly. Who never called him by rank or code name when they were alone. Who stood on every ceremony in front of others. 'Try the next.'

The second was the longer sling, as used by the lethal Balearic sharpshooters. It was a more substantial weapon altogether. Instead of a knot there was a loop at the end. Artemidorus picked it up as ordered. It was the first – shorter – of two slings of the Balearic design. He slipped the loop over his finger and took a heavy lead weight shaped like a big almond with sharp edges. It sat firmly in the wide pouch. Artemidorus whirled it expertly and fired. This time, at the greater distance, the bullet clipped the top of the shield, making the curved wood rock back and forth. But it shot up off the rim and smashed into the watermelon with such force and at such an angle that the helmet lifted and everything beneath it shattered. Red flesh exploding into red mist.

'That's some poor bastard's face,' observed Quintus approvingly. 'And his brains, likely enough. But there's something else I want to try...'

Quintus sped down the thirty paces – never a man to walk when he could run. He stooped. Produced another melon from behind the *scutum* and replaced the red mess on the stake. This time he turned the helmet sideways on. The cheek guards hung down like broad metal daggers. Joined to the bowl of the helmet itself by a couple of hinges at the top. The opening for the ear gaped in front of the scoop of the neck protector at the back. Satisfied, he hurried back again. *If we'd been chasing Quintus instead of Cicero, we'd never have caught him*, thought Artemidorus indulgently.

'Don't aim for the ear,' commanded the bantamweight legionary. 'Try and hit the cheek flap. As near to the hinge as you can.'

Artemidorus accommodatingly removed his own helmet, placing it on the table. Ran his fingers through his hair as he assessed the target and the distance. Then he took a heavy lead bullet and placed it in the sling. Whirled. Fired. Faster than the eye could follow, the projectile flew down the range. And hit the melon precisely where Quintus had told him not to hit. In the unguarded ear section. The melon rocked. A black hole appeared in the near side. A lumpy red mist exploded from the far side. 'In one ear and out the other,' said Quintus. His tone conflicted. 'I told you not to do that, boy.'

'I apologise, *magister*...' said Artemidorus. His tone placatory rather than insubordinate.

'It's just a waste of my time and my melons,' grouched the armaments officer. 'Though it was an excellent shot. Let's see if you're more accurate with the long Balearic at forty paces...'

He doubled down the range and began to fiddle about with the third melon. Placed the helmet with a purposefulness verging on outrage. 'HERE!' he bellowed, slapping his hand against the cheek guard. Talking as though to a child. Or an idiot. 'Hit it here!'

Artemidorus took yet another heavy lead bullet and loaded it into the third sling. The strings to this one were slightly longer again. Of woven fibre. The pouch of soft leather that seemed to cling to the keen-edged, sharp-pointed metal. The loop gripped the base of his finger snugly. He swung it, feeling the motion begin to possess the whole of his body. While he narrowed his eyes and focused on the distant hinge. As soon as Quintus was out of range, he fired, with all his strength. There was a loud *CLANG!* The helmet seemed to jump. The melon rocked. When everything settled, Artemidorus could see that the hinge was broken and the cheek guard was hanging at a slight angle.

'Good lad!' called Quintus. 'Now come and look at this.'

Artemidorus ran forty paces down the range to where Quintus stood beside the damaged headgear. As the spy approached, he lifted the helmet gently off the melon. The green skin showed a decided dent where the hinge had been driven inwards by the force of the lead bullet.

'Where is that hinge?' demanded Quintus. 'On your own head and helmet where is that hinge?'

Artemidorus accommodatingly indicated the side of his skull just above his cheekbone. Between the top of his ear and the edge of his eye. There was even a little indentation there from the hinge of his recently removed headpiece.

'The bones there are not strong,' Quintus informed him with all the authority of their colleague the physician Antistius.

'I see...' said Artemidorus, his tone making it clear that he didn't.

'Go to the melon. Push the tip of your finger against that little mark your bullet made when it hit the hinge,' Quintus ordered.

Artemidorus obeyed. And as soon as he pressed his finger to the spot, the entire section beneath it collapsed. Red flesh dotted with black seeds burst out. 'Even beneath the helmet,' Quintus explained, 'the bones simply shatter. This one would be just as dead as all the others so far.'

'Interesting...' said Artemidorus, looking around for something to wipe his hands on.

'There's a cloth on the table,' Quintus informed him. 'Beside the staff sling. While you wipe your hands, I think I'll just...' He took hold of the third stake, which was held erect by a cross of wood designed to sit firmly on the ground. And he dragged it right to the far end of the range. Where he stood it just in front of the wooden wall. The better part of sixty paces from the table with its slings and bullets.

Artemidorus returned to the table and wiped his hands. When they were clean, he picked up the staff sling. It looked like slings he had seen in Egypt. He knew how to use it. And was as accurate with it as he was with the Thracian and Balearic slings. But it was different in more ways than in simply having a length of wood secured to it. The wooden handle made it more powerful, somehow. In the past he had seen these fired and heard the string snap with a crack like a whip. The idea of whips made him briefly think of Minucius Basilus and what he had planned to do to the treacherous Cyanea. A picture of her pale nakedness lashed to Basilus' whipping post flashed unbidden into his memory. But the spy drove such distractions from his mind with brutal efficiency. Focused on the sling in his hand. Whether it cracked like a whip or not, it certainly fired a heavier bullet. Faster. And across a greater range. Eyes fixed on the target fifty paces distant, he put the bullet into the pouch.

Aware of little besides its considerable weight, he began to swing the weapon. The technique was different. The balance too. He almost crouched as his thighs and knees joined his arm and shoulder to launch the weight while the sling snapped back on its staff with its distinctive whip crack. But the sling itself was not the only thing making a sound. For the bullet screamed a persistent, piercing, terrifying howl as it sped towards its target. It hit the shield which toppled backwards, allowing the missile to shriek onwards. It smashed into the stake in the centre of where the soldier's chest would be. And buried itself in the wood. The impact was so powerful that the melon rolled back and fell to the ground. 'Low,' called Artemidorus apologetically.

'True,' answered Quintus. 'But if that had been a legionary you would have smashed his ribs. Maybe done even more damage. If he'd just been wearing a leather breastplate you'd probably have killed him. Chain mail or fish-scale armour even. Only a solid steel one like mine would have survived that.' He beat his steel-shelled chest in illustration of his words.

'Always assuming the soldier didn't die of fright at the sound the bullet made...' added Artemidorus.

'Yes,' nodded Quintus approvingly. 'A couple of hundred bullets coming screaming in like that is likely to unsettle even a well-trained cohort, I should think. Superior to arrows. Especially as you can't see them. But just as deadly. I heard that in Gaul Caesar had some of the bullets made red hot and fired from special slings. Set whatever they hit alight. Or whoever, in some cases. And unlike arrows they came in invisibly. Particularly good for street fighting and besieging walled towns. Thatched roofs and wooden walls just burst into flames for no apparent reason. Most unsettling.'

As they talked, Artemidorus placed another bullet in his sling. Quintus stood the battered *scutum* up again, replaced the melon and stood clear. The spy swung the sling again, leaning into the movement, feeling the heft of the heavy lead weight in the straining pouch. When he fired, the bullet screamed away, its trajectory more accurate than last time. It was just possible to see the black dot as it whipped through the air. Just a heartbeat before his eyes told him it would hit, there was a *CLANG*. But before the sound arrived, the helmet had jerked back as though struck with a club. The melon fell off the post. 'Always assuming you didn't shatter his forehead, even through the helmet, you'd probably have broken his neck!' called Quintus grudgingly. 'Still, you don't seem to have lost your touch. Think you can hit the far one? Better part of sixty paces. Quite a distance...'

vi

Quintus watched Septem placing the bullet into the big Egyptian stick sling and beginning to move. The old soldier smiled with simple pride and affection. But he was careful to do so inwardly. It would never do for the centurion to know that he was the best slingman Quintus had ever seen. That he was, in fact, the best soldier Quintus had ever seen. Had the old *triarius* been lucky enough to have fathered children, Septem would have been the perfect son. The Vestal Virgins, in fact, held a will formally adopting the boy, although Artemidorus had not the faintest idea of its existence, let alone its contents. When Quintus died, the centurion would find himself the head of the Patrician Tarpean family and one of the richest men in Rome. Something that would cause almost as much surprise and consternation as the fact that Caesar had named his sickly nineteen-year-old great-nephew Octavian as heir to his name and fortune in the will published after his murder.

These thoughts took Quintus through the moments before Artemidorus fired. The stone screamed down the length of the range and slammed into the wall an arm's length to the right of the target. It stuck there, its sharp lead point buried deep in the wood. 'Again,' called Quintus.

Artemidorus overcompensated. The next bullet slammed into the wall on the left of the target.

'I thought today augured well,' called Quintus brusquely. 'Clearly not for your aim, boy.'

The third bullet smashed into the *scutum*. Wedged in the curve of hide-covered wood. Sending the shield skittering back to slam into the post. The melon rocked but did not fall.

'A bit better...' allowed Quintus. 'Might have broken his shield-arm. Numbed it at the least, I suppose... Try again.'

This time the melon exploded. The helmet spun away like a child's ball.

'At last,' said Quintus.

'Not much use if it takes four shots, though,' admitted Artemidorus. 'That would have been no use at all if I'd been slinging against some charging Ghost Warriors in the north of Gaul.'

'Ah, but you won't be, will you?' said Quintus. 'Come down here and use your wits as well as your eyes.'

Artemidorus joined the old soldier beside the wall. Quintus began to work the first bullet free. 'Look,' he said. 'The shots are all level. Same height – just above the *scutum*. It's just your lateral aim that's off.'

'I don't see what difference that would make. A miss is a miss.'

'Against Gaulish Ghost Warriors, yes. I agree. And against the bloody great Germans too unless they come at you in a Boar's Head wedge formation. But you won't be fighting any of them will you? Given what's happened and given the mission we've been handed, you know you're going to end up fighting legions. Brutus' legions or Cassius' legions. Or more likely both at once. And they'll come at you in a wall. A shield wall. But still a wall.'

'So if I miss the one in the middle, I'll hit the man on one side of him or the other...'

'Precisely! And even at sixty paces you'll do some serious damage. Before you get down to sharpshooting at forty paces and less...'

Artemidorus tried to pull the lead bullet out of the wall to the left of the mess that the exploded melon had made. Failed: it was buried far too securely. 'How much damage, do you think?'

'It's impossible to be sure,' Quintus answered. 'I tell you, though. I miss the old days when we could use slaves or criminals as targets. That way we'd know for certain!' He paused, then added. 'As it is, we'll just have to wait for the war.' His eyes almost vanished in his deep-lined face as he squinted up at Septem, dropping his voice to a conspiratorial whisper. 'Not, I think, that we'll be waiting all that long...'

Quintus called the guards in and the four men swiftly put the range to rights, vacating it as the next group arrived, all armed with short, reticulated Parthian bows. 'What,' called Quintus cheerfully to their leader, one of the *principales* junior officers in the cavalry division. 'Parthian bows – and no horses to shoot from? Or are you just going to practise running away and shooting as you go?'

'We're moving one step forward at a time, Quintus,' came the cheerful reply. 'First we learned to ride. Now we learn to shoot. I'm afraid I'll be as old and grey as you are before they can do both at once and graduate into proper *sagittariorae* bowmen! Right, you lot. Line up behind the table. Raise your bows and nock your arrows. The standard form with this weapon is the Persian method. Pull back the string with the bottom three fingers of your right hand, steadying the arrow with your index finger and thumb. Finger along the shaft. Bow in the left hand. Level with your chins. At an angle which what I remember of Pythagoras and Euclid suggests to be about forty-five degrees. And pull towards your chest. Your chest! Save your nose for sharpshooting with the Egyptian longbow...'

'I've seen them practising,' said one of Quintus' legionaries as the four of them trooped out through the door. 'If they tried both riding *and* shooting, they either shoot each other or fall off and break their necks.'

'Or both,' growled his companion. 'On the other hand they might do us all a favour and kill that *principale*. Too full of himself that one. Needs to learn some respect. *Old and grey...*'

They were Quintus' men, so Artemidorus did not discipline them. He watched as they doubled off. 'They're good lads,' said Quintus quietly. 'They take pride in what they do and try to pull the rest up to their level.'

The two soldiers turned and began to stride across the Field of Mars side by side. 'It's a while since I've done much practice with the bow,' said Artemidorus. 'Maybe we should catch up with that next.'

'As a matter of fact, I have a delivery of new bows coming. New types of bow. New types of arrow, bolt and dart. New techniques, therefore. To maximise range, accuracy and rate of fire.'

Talking about new and experimental types of armaments, the two soldiers walked towards the Gate of Fontus which stood astride the *Clivus Argentarius* main road leading in from the Field of Mars towards the Forum. Only because of the current state of emergency in the aftermath of Caesar's murder could they continue across the line of the inner *pomerium* city boundary fully armed as they were. Even so, as with last night, their armour and carelessly displayed weaponry gave them an air of danger. So the pair of them walked alone. As the good citizens of Rome, their servants and slaves, shopkeepers, stallholders, ex-soldiers, street gangs and even the occasional sorceress and fortune-teller all gave them a wide berth.

*

It was Artemidorus' plan to accept Spurinna's invitation and assemble the *contubernium* of spies and secret agents at the augur's villa. Where there was also the Senate scribe Adonis who he wished to question further. But between the Gate and the villa, there lay the *Forum Romanum*, showing clear signs of damage from the riots. Some of whose flagstones still showed gleams of the gold which had run, molten, from the ornaments and honours that had been thrown into Caesar's funeral pyre.

But, more relevantly, just off the Forum on the way towards the *Basilica Aemilia* market there lay several *tabernae* taverns and *lupanars* brothels where Artemidorus planned to contact one of the members of his *contubernium* directly.

He and Quintus walked side by side into the first tavern which the centurion knew to be a favourite of the man he was seeking. And there, immediately, was their objective. A big square Iberian ex-legionary from the Sixth Legion, the Ironclads. Who was known to Artemidorus, code-named Septem as a member of the VIIth, by his code name Ferrata – Iron Man. The secret agent had stayed clear of Ferrata recently. Because it had been to the tender mercies of Ferrata and the rioting men behind him that he had left his treacherous lover Cyanea. Naked and lashed to a whipping post in the villa of Minucius Basilus. One of Caesar's murderers. And a man noted for the perverse pleasure he took in the suffering of others.

There was a conversation there that Artemidorus was not yet willing to experience. But Ferrata was an excellent man. Cyanea had robbed him of too much to let her rob him of Ferrata too. '*Ave*, Septem,' said the legionary, catching his eye as he and Quintus came in. Not a difficult feat. Every head in the room turned towards them as they entered, armour gleaming, helmet crests bright, swords and daggers on their hips. Ferrata was seated at a small table piled with eggs, dates and *emmer* bread. In the middle of a ring of wine goblets. In the midst of a larger circle of rough-looking, half-sober ex-legionaries. Caesar's will had been read a good while ago now. Antony had the dead dictator's notes and knew his wishes. But nothing had actually been done as yet. So Rome was still full of the men who had come to collect their final pay and discover where they were going to be settled. Which made the streets more dangerous than usual. The taverns immensely profitable. And the girls in the brothels permanently exhausted.

'Finish your wine, Ferrata,' ordered Artemidorus, with the authority of a man paying better than standard legionary rates. 'We have a meeting we need to attend.' Then he and Quintus turned and exited.

Ferrata caught up with them moments later, juggling a cloth-wrapped bundle of olives and bread. One whiff of his breath confirmed that he had obeyed Septem's order and finished the wine. 'What's up?' he asked guardedly.

'New orders,' said Septem shortly. 'More details when we get where we're going.'

viii

The three men were admitted to Spurinna's villa by his slave Kyros. Kyros was a quick-witted and decisive young man. So much so that Artemidorus was considering adding him to the *contubernium* – though the secret organisation was rapidly expanding past the standard eight-man command. As Kyros led the three soldiers across the *atrium*, he brought them up to date with what he had been doing. For it was directly relevant to their immediate mission. 'Gaius Trebonius' slave, the Senate record keeper, is called Adonis,' he said. Artemidorus and Quintus exchanged glances. They knew the record keeper's name. But there was an unspoken agreement between them to indulge the excited boy. 'We have him locked in a storeroom and we have been getting him ready to answer your questions, Septem.'

'We?' asked the spy.

'Puella and me. Augur Spurinna has given us permission. I know it is unusual for a woman to be involved in such work. But she is very good at it. *Very* good.'

'In what way?' The spy and centurion was intrigued. He knew the young woman to be intrepid and resourceful. But this was a new side to her.

'It was Puella who suggested Adonis would be more amenable if we took his clothes. And tied him naked to the chair. All alone in a cold, dark storeroom. And it was she who thought of refusing to let him use the latrine. Then she suggested that she and I should stand outside the door and speak loudly enough for him to hear us…'

'Discussing what?' asked Artemidorus.

'Your techniques as *carnifex*. I said that you and Antistius the physician had been considering the most effective ways of getting answers quickly and accurately. And that you were surprised to learn that techniques such as gouging, chopping, flaying, burning and boiling were probably not as effective as you might suppose. Then Puella said *No*, it was apparently better to start with smaller

43

things. Like nails. Fingers. Toes. Teeth. Then *I* said the most popular technique was still crucifixion. And *she* said, *Wrong*: if you're going to hammer nails through bits of people, don't think in terms of wrists, ankles and crosses… Think *tables* and *testicles*…'

Ferrata gave a guffaw of laughter at this. And even Quintus suppressed a grin. But Artemidorus wasn't so sure. It seemed to him that Spurinna had behaved like an over-indulgent parent. Letting the youngsters play their cruel games. But what was done was done. He would talk to Adonis while Kyros and any other servant Spurinna could spare went about business that was much more commonplace. Puella, however, would stay with him. To watch. To learn.

Spurinna welcomed them and set about supplying a light *prandium* lunch. Ferrata shoved his empty cloth into his belt and assumed the look of a man who hasn't eaten in days. Kyros was given a list and sent out to summon those named on it. Artemidorus left Quintus and Ferrata considering a meal of cold meat, eggs, olives, bread and fruit. With Spurinna's permission, he took Puella with him. Though, to be fair, she was as much his property as the soothsayer's. He was the one who had stolen her from Brutus' household in the first place. During the dark and stormy hours before the *Ides* dawned. Spurinna was simply giving her a place to hide. In the unlikely event that Brutus' servants had time – or inclination – to look for her. After they closed up Brutus' Roman villa and headed south after him. As Artemidorus gestured for her to follow him, the spy kept his face stern, and met her wide, melting gaze with his steeliest stare. Until she looked down, silently abashed. Aware that she had somehow displeased him. All without a word having been spoken. Then, still silently, the pair of them went to talk to Adonis.

As Kyros had said, the terrified and desperate young man was tied naked to a chair in a cold, dark storeroom. As Artemidorus opened the door, letting light flood in, the Senate secretary jumped and just suppressed a cry of alarm. Artemidorus breathed in and his nostrils told him that in spite of Puella's refusal to let him use the latrine, he had managed to contain himself. What Kyros had not remarked upon was something Artemidorus had noted on first meeting the young man. His physical beauty. He was from the north. Of Germanian or Gaulish colouring. Like one of the forty thousand slaves taken after Caesar's famous defeat of Vercingetorix and the tribes at Alesia.

Artemidorus remembered that Trebonius had spent some time as Caesar's legate at war with the Eburone tribe in the north of Gaul nine years or so ago. Where this beautiful boy had been captured no doubt. As a ten or eleven-year-old. His hair was a helmet of tight blond curls. His eyes the blue of a summer's sky. In the evening, after sunset. His nose almost Greek in its perfection and his lips like the bow of Cupid himself. In the middle of his perfect, square chin, there was a *gelasinus* dimple. Not a cleft, a *fissura*, as there was in the Tribune Enobarbus' determined jaw. A dimple. No doubt his beauty was the reason his slave name was Adonis. 'Release him,' Artemidorus ordered. 'Give him back his tunic and guide him to the latrine.'

As Puella hurried to obey, he continued talking – to Adonis. 'You will use the facilities and return here. There are two other soldiers in the house and both are widely experienced veterans. If you make any attempt to escape they will kill you. If you come back here, there will be food and drink waiting for you. And you and I will talk. There will be no torture. I have served my time as *carnifex*, but I see no need to use my skills on you. If you tell me what I want to know. Is that clear?'

'Yes, Lord...' Adonis stood stiffly. Massaged his wrists where his bonds had been tightest. Pulled the tunic Puella handed him over his golden curls.

'You know I will keep my word, after our last conversation, when you told me about Caesar's dying words as you overheard them...'

'Yes, my Lord...' Like his features, his Latin was perfect.

'Good. Off you go. And hurry.'

ix

Adonis needed no further prompting and the chastened Puella hurried after him to guide him to the latrine. And return him as swiftly as possible. Artemidorus followed them out, his stern face softening towards a smile. Strode through to the kitchen and returned with bread, cheese and water. These were sitting on a table when Puella guided the boy back again. At a gesture from Artemidorus, the prisoner pulled the chair up to the table and fell-to hungrily. 'Wait by the door,' Artemidorus ordered and Puella obeyed. Standing half in the light, watching proceedings avidly. Hungry for knowledge. Not for food. Artemidorus perched apparently casually on the edge of the table. His position establishing both his superiority and the fact that he, too, was between the boy and the doorway. But not quite close enough to present a threat. The light was behind him, however. Shining over his shoulder into the boy's face. So the interrogator could see clearly every shift of expression. In the perfect features. In the wide, limpid eyes.

'You did well to remember Caesar's dying words,' Septem observed.

'I remember everything,' Adonis replied. The words coming less than clearly past a mouthful of bread and cheese. 'That is the reason Lord Trebonius had me trained in the shorthand and positioned as a recorder in the Senate. I have always been able to remember every detail of what I hear and see. And, since I learned to read and write, everything that I have seen written down. By my hand or another's.'

45

'I know you *heard* what was said at the murder of Caesar. Can you tell me what you *saw*?'

'I saw everything, Lord.'

'Tell me what you saw, then.'

The dazzling eyes widened. Adonis was pale with terror. Artemidorus was presenting no threat – quite the opposite. Therefore, reasoned the spy, the boy's fear came from the fact that he was preparing to disobey his order. Preparing to negotiate. To strike a bargain if he could. 'What I saw could mean death. To me and my…'

'Your… *What*? Family? Lover?'

'Sister,' he admitted reluctantly.

And Artemidorus understood something further about the boy's name. 'Your sister Venus…'

'We are twins,' the boy admitted. 'And apart from our sex, it has always been nearly impossible to tell us apart. Lord Trebonius was amused to name us as he did. For our beauty, he said…'

'And if I can guarantee that you and your sister will be safe, will you tell me what you saw when Caesar was murdered?'

'Yes, my Lord. If you can do that.' Something more stirred in those wide, blue eyes. Desperation? Cunning? Calculation certainly. Perhaps hope.

'What?'

'My Lord Trebonius has enjoyed us both in many ways, but lately Venus has failed to please him. He had allowed members of the household access to her. As punishment. But now that he has been named among the *Libertores* and fled the city, there will be no one to control matters. While the household prepares to follow him to Ephesus as he takes up his post of Proconsul of Asia Province.'

Artemidorus sat silently for a moment. 'And if I can rescue your sister and bring her here, everything in your astonishingly accurate memory will be mine?'

'Yes Lord. Everything. As will we. Venus and I. Body and spirit.'

'I seem to do little else these days but steal one slave after another. Very well. We have a bargain. I will take some men and bring your sister to you.' He stood. Looked down at the young man. 'And stop calling me *my Lord*. Call me Septem.'

As he went out through the door he said to Puella. 'Guard him but do not frighten him any further. You are a gifted interrogator and, like Kyros, you will make a fine addition to my *contubernium*. But you need to know. Sometimes you catch more flies with honey than with vinegar!'

Artemidorus entered Spurinna's *triclinium* dining room, to find that Kyros had returned already with some more members of the *contubernium*. Who were now taking advantage of the soothsayer's hospitality. As this was a quick meal taken on the wing, rather than a full, formal *cena* dinner, they were perched on the edges of the dining couches. Crowding round three sides of the central table. Antistius the physician was dipping a piece of bread into a bowl of olive oil, his face, as ever, folded into a thoughtful frown. Beside him sat Hercules, who as yet had only the sketchiest idea of why he was here. He was gnawing on a chicken leg. Hopefully not from one of the soothsayer's prophetic birds, thought the spy wryly. Hercules was tutor to the son of Marcus Aemilius Lepidus, the commander of the Seventh Legion.

Hercules, like Adonis and his sister, was given a slave name from antiquity, following the current fashion. And as Adonis was beautiful – and his sister, no doubt, all but a goddess – so Hercules was huge. And enormously powerful. Even more so than Antony himself, who claimed Hercules as a direct ancestor. And, as tutor to Lepidus junior, he was an expert not only in logic, rhetoric, philosophy, morals and mathematics. But also in wrestling, horsemanship and the use of weapons. He also had a cool head. Obeyed orders without question. And was nobody's fool. Furthermore, like Artemidorus himself, and Kyros, he was Greek. Albeit an Athenian rather than a Spartan. Best of all in Septem's mind, Quintus seemed to like him. There were potential areas of conflict as the two men's skills overlapped. But the older *triarius* seemed to take his huge associate cheerfully under his wing – and into his confidence.

x

'Right,' said Artemidorus, falling into full centurion mode as he crossed the dining room towards them. 'Finish up. Antistius, Puella is guarding a very nervous boy in one of the storerooms. Check him over, please. I want to be sure he is hale and hearty. We will have a long session of question and answer when I return. He apparently has an astonishingly accurate memory and I propose to test it to its limits. The rest of you. We have a mission…'

*

Artemidorus led his little band out of Spurinna's villa. As Kyros shut and locked the door behind them. His face a mask of disappointment at being left behind. Shoulder to shoulder, they followed the broad *vicus* north-east round the foot of the Viminal Hill. With the centurion in front, the legionary Quintus at his side. With Hercules and Ferrata close behind. Skirting the *subura* and marching towards the southern slopes of the Quirinial Hill. The *subura* particularly was heaving with activity. But the sight of two fully armed soldiers – accompanied by a muscular legionary and a giant – ensured everyone kept a respectful space around them. Though it attracted a good deal of attention. As nervous citizenry of

47

all types and statuses gave the four of them a wide berth. But kept a watchful eye on them as they marched away. In this circle of nervous silence, the spy explained the mission they were on. And his simple plan to make it succeed.

When they reached Trebonius' villa on the pine-fragrant slopes of the exclusive neighbourhood, Artemidorus knocked on the door. With the pommel of his *gladius* sword. He made sure his blows sounded businesslike. Slightly impatient. And loud. For there was a decided bustle of activity going on at the far side of the portal. Not too surprisingly. The wood of the solid entrance showed signs of damage by axes, spears, cleavers and fire. The mob out to avenge Caesar's death had clearly come knocking recently. The *ostiarius* doorkeeper opened almost immediately. Peering out nervously. Only a little relieved to see the murderous mob replaced by an officious-looking squad of soldiers. The centurion with his bodyguard strode past. Reaching out to tap the tile on the doorpost bearing the face of Janus, god of entrances and exits.

Artemidorus stopped in the middle of the *atrium*. The others crashed to attention behind him. 'I wish to see whoever is in charge,' he snapped, getting more deeply into his character as the impatient soldier. On an important mission.

'The mistress left this morning, following the master…' the *ostiarius* explained nervously. 'So there's just…'

'I am Colus the proconsul's *atriensis* steward,' announced a round-bodied, frog-faced, loose-lipped man with dark bags beneath greedy, gimlet eyes. And a suspiciously dark profusion of oily curls. Entering the *atrium* with all the pomp and dignity of the master here. 'How may the house of Trebonius be of service, Centurion?'

'I come from Co-consul and General Mark Antony. I speak with his authority.' Artemidorus' tone matched that of the pompous steward. With a telling edge of military impatience. 'As you are no doubt aware, the proconsul's slave Adonis is in the co-consul's custody as a witness to the murder of Dictator for Life, *Pontifex Maximus*, General, *Pater Patriae*, the Divine Gaius Julius Caesar.'

'Ah…' huffed Colus, clearly unaware of anything of the sort. 'I see…'

'The co-consul has sent us with express orders to find and bring his sister Venus, who, we understand, may have further information. And in any case will be of use to our *carnefaxes*.'

'Venus has not left the house since the *Kalends*. Fifteen days before the *Ides*! She can know nothing…' Colus wrung his hands, clearly unhappy at the thought of losing control of the young woman.

'You obviously do not understand the methods used by *carnifexes* in sessions of close questioning,' snapped Centurion Artemidorus, a thunderous frown

48

gathering. That the personal emissary of Rome's current ruler should have to explain things to a mere steward... 'There comes a time when even the acutest discomfort fades. And a subject will only answer further questions in order to protect a loved one. A sister, let us say. From suffering even greater agonies in his place...'

The pudgy face flushed unhealthily. Spittle gathered at the corner of those slack lips. The gimlet eyes lost focus for a moment. Turned inward rather than outward. The steward's mind was suddenly filled with pictures of what soldiers such as these might do to Venus. To loosen Adonis' tongue.

'Will you send for her? Or must we tear this place apart?' snapped the angry, impatient centurion. 'Make your mind up. Our time is short.' His fists rested on the hilt of his *gladius* and the pommel of his *pugio*.

'I will send! I will send!' Colus assured him. His voice reaching the upper ranges normally only attained by Queen Cleopatra's eunuchs. 'You there! *Ostiarius*! Make yourself useful. Go and get the girl.'

As the doorkeeper hurried to obey, the steward suddenly had a second thought. 'Oh! And make sure she is suitably dressed to accompany the centurion and his men!'

And, as a further afterthought: 'You may need to get one of the women to wash her...'

The doorkeeper vanished at last.

An icy silence descended. Under which stirred the bustle of a household preparing for departure. With only a skeleton staff likely to remain until the master and all his family and servants returned to Rome again. Sometime, thought Artemidorus, far in the future. If the treacherous Trebonius ever returned. A homecoming which it was now in his remit to stop. By *perimere* slaughtering the man in question whenever an opportunity arose.

Artemidorus' lips narrowed as time passed and his thoughts returned to the present. Adonis' fears for his sister were obviously well founded. Trebonius' punishment was still being lustily re-enacted. Venus was probably tied to a bed somewhere. Readily available. The spy began to wonder whether Trebonius shared his friend and co-conspirator Minucius Basilus' predilection for enjoying the pain and humiliation of others.

But then the doorkeeper returned. Followed by a young woman who had obviously just been washed. Her golden ringlets jewelled with drops of water. Her tall, slim body dressed in a tunic that was far too large for her. Which nevertheless contrived to cling to the outlines of her still-damp body. Her dark blue eyes wide. With speculation rather than fear. The three men behind Septem gave a concerted

49

sigh. Mixed of every emotion between spiritual wonder and naked lust. For in spite of the signs of trepidation and discomfort in her expression, her face was simply the loveliest Artemidorus had ever seen. 'Venus,' he said, fighting to keep his voice harsh. 'We have come to take you to your brother. Have you any personal possessions you might need to bring?'

'No, my Lord,' she answered, in a low, musical voice. Her tone bitter. Her perfectly dimpled chin square. Her spirit clearly unbroken by whatever had been happening to her recently. 'As you see, I cannot even call my clothes my own.'

'Very well,' he grated, his cold eyes sweeping over Colus and his cohorts. 'Let's go.'

As they stepped out of the doorway and into the street, the four men fell in around Venus as though they were her bodyguard. Trebonius' *ostiarius* lingered with the door half open, watching the woman departing with a wistful expression. Clearly, thought Artemidorus, glancing back, the doorkeeper had missed out on his chance to bed her like the rest.

xi

As the spy turned, something flew past his shoulder with a fierce buzzing sound. There was a strange sensation of air stirring against his ear and the section of his cheek not protected by the side-piece of his helmet. The solid *slap* of some kind of impact. The doorkeeper, so close behind him, staggered back. All of a sudden he had something sticking out of his shoulder. Something short, black, brutal. The man screamed, half-turned and slammed the door shut. Artemidorus blinked. Turned to Quintus. Another projectile buzzed viciously by. And a dart slightly shorter than his forearm slammed into the wood of the already damaged door. Where his head had been an instant before he turned. His mind was suddenly filled with pictures of exploding melons. But this was a bow of some kind, not a sling. Firing powerful metal-tipped darts, not leaden bullets.

'*RUN!*' he yelled.

The five of them took off in a tight unit, keeping low. Artemidorus had little idea of where they could run to. Trebonius' villa was clearly closed to them, and he knew no one living close by. But at least the Quirinial Hill was covered with pines as well as with ancient and excusive villas. And no matter how accurate they were, bows were of limited effectiveness in woods. Especially when they were being fired from some distance. As this one must be. For there was no sign of an archer as yet. Simply the telltale whirr of his incoming darts.

Artemidorus let Quintus take the lead. Then he gathered the others in front of himself, bringing up the rear. He was the largest of them protected by armour. Even if he was the target, he stood a better chance than any of the others should he be hit. His equipment wasn't up with Quintus' but it should be proof against arrows fired from any great distance. With Quintus in the lead, Ferrata and Hercules on either side of Venus and Artemidorus protecting their rear, they charged into the nearest stand of pines. No sooner had they done so than the next arrow whizzed over Artemidorus' head, sped past the three ahead of him and lodged in a tree just in front of Quintus. Without pausing, the legionary reached up to tear it free and then plunged on decisively. As though he knew where he was going, thought Artemidorus. With a feeling somewhere between surprise and shock. For he had never seen Quintus outside the camp lines of the Seventh Legion. So how in Jupiter's name did he know his way along the forest paths between the ancient villas of the Quirinial Hill?

'Get down!' ordered Artemidorus, dismissing all speculation from his mind. He did not pause to see his order obeyed. Instead he turned and slammed the full length of his body against the nearest tree trunk. Shielding himself with the solid wood as he looked back across the wide road. There, in the black alley between two lofty patrician villas opposite, a shape flickered and was gone. Half body. Half shadow. But there for just long enough.

Artemidorus saw a tall figure dressed in a long, hooded cloak. Just like the one he had worn when executing Gaius Amiatus. As the attacker moved, there was the gleam of weapons at belt level. But Artemidorus hardly noticed these. For he was focused on what the stranger was holding. In the heartbeat before he slid it under the cloak and vanished. It was a small, heavily reticulated, powerful-looking bow. Like a strange variation of the Parthian equipment he had seen earlier. Of a design the spy had never come across before. Halfway along its length, reaching back past the string and a little forward of the bow's grip itself, was a long lateral guide-piece. In the flash of movement it was impossible for Artemidorus to be certain of its composition or design. It might be wood or metal. It might be a tube or an open groove. There was no doubting its function, however. It was designed to give the short darts the weapon fired more range, more power and much more accuracy.

'Did you see that?' asked Quintus, appearing silently at his shoulder. 'That was a *sôlênarion*. Byzantine design, I'd say.' He held up the dart he had pulled from the tree. It was short but heavy. It looked dangerous. Powerful. The solid arrowhead was made of sharpened steel. 'Armour-piercing,' he added grimly. 'Nasty!'

Artemidorus nodded. Trying not to imagine what the first of these had done to the doorkeeper's shoulder.

Quintus continued, 'I have several coming in the supply I told you about. We'll see how effective they *really* are, eh? In the hands of a proper soldier rather than some fly-by-night *sicarius* dagger-man.'

'We picked him up in the *subura*,' added Ferrata, appearing at Artemidorus' other shoulder. 'Must have been following us since. Friend of yours?'

'Not that I recognised.'

'Well,' said Ferrata grimly. 'The list of your enemies is a long one. It'd take one of Caesar's new weeks to go through it all.'

'If word of our mission has slipped out, there are twenty-three names pretty high up,' said Artemidorus. 'Starting with Brutus, Cassius, the Casca brothers, Decimus Albinus, Trebonius...' His voice tailed off. 'Though this feels more like the work of someone particularly underhanded and treacherous. And rich. Able to hire professional killers at a whim. Someone like Minucius Basilus.'

'Basilus and twenty-two others there, then,' allowed Ferrata as the three of them turned and walked back to Venus. And Hercules. Who was lying protectively on top of her. 'And there's also the gang leader of the man you killed yesterday. Don't know the corpse's name but he was apparently right-hand man to a nasty piece of work they call The Gaul. Thinks of himself as king of the streets. Used to run with Titus Annius Milo. Took over the gang when Milo was banished for killing Clodius Pulcher on the Appian Way then died at Compsa, what, four years back?'

'I thought Milo and Cicero were friends. Why would his replacement want to kill Cicero?' Artemidorus thought of the raging mob from which he had rescued the senator.

Ferrata shrugged. 'Allegiances shift. Caesar was popular. With the gangs as well as the *plebs*. Cicero sided with his murderers. And Cicero promised to defend Milo in front of the Senate. Said he would get him forgiven and recalled. Pardoned. Reinstated, even. But he never did. And, talking of shifting allegiances, there's that treacherous green-eyed demon of yours. That Cyanea.'

'*Cyanea!*' the name hit Artemidorus with an impact like a bolt from the Sicarius' Byzantine bow. He actually staggered back a step. 'But Cyanea is dead.'

'Dead? No such luck. She was too much for me and my men. I'll tell you about it sometime. But no. She walked away. Left one or two bleeding in her wake. Killed both of the poor bastards who untied her, hoping to take first turn. Slit their throats from ear to ear. And set fire to Basilus' house as she went. Never seen anything like it. Hope I never see anything like it again, either. Nemesis – and then some. She could be one of the Friendly Ones reborn, that one. She's still out there somewhere. And she won't rest quiet 'til you are well and truly lying cold and stiff on your funeral pyre. And she's standing beside it with a flaming torch and a great big happy smile.'

III

'Shouldn't the general be here for this?' wondered Enobarbus.

The tribune was not really expecting an answer. He was simply thinking aloud. But Artemidorus spoke up anyway. 'He wasn't present for the original interview, when the boy told us what he had heard. Confirming what I overheard Brutus admit to Cassius as they ran out of the *Curia*. Before we realised what he must also have seen. Let's hear what the boy says now. He can note down what he tells us as he speaks. He knows the shorthand invented by Cicero's secretary Tiro. And he's a secretary to the Senate after all. He should be able to think, talk and write at the same time. Then we can take him or his notes to the general when we know exactly what went on.' He emphasised the point by holding up the bundle of wax tablets he was carrying. On which Adonis was going to write down all the details he promised to reveal to them. Now that they had rescued his sister and restored her to him. After a lengthy and extremely careful return journey from the life-saving pine grove on the Quirinial. The rest of the *contubernium* were in the *triclinium* dining room or in the simple bathhouse that Spurinna had added to the rear of his Equestrian villa.

'Will the details matter, though?' mused Enobarbus.

'I think they will. And I think we'll see that even more clearly when we discuss what we learn with the others. At the very least we can get some sort of a sequence established. Maybe start roughing out a plan of campaign. We know General Antony wants every one of the murderers killed in the fullness of time. But what the boy tells us could well give us some kind of list. In order.'

'Who dies quickest. Who lingers longest. That sort of thing?'

Artemidorus nodded. 'We certainly need some kind of strategy beyond the general's decision that he wants Gaius Trebonius and Decimus Albinus to die first. But despite what the Lady Fulvia says, we can't just go rushing all over the empire randomly slaughtering any murderers we happen to meet, trusting in *Tyche* or *Fortuna* to guide us. But, on the other hand, if we take the boy straight to Antony and he gives a full, detailed, report…'

'…as we're hoping he will. To *us*, at least…'

'…there's a good chance the general will simply explode. You know what his temper's like. Especially at the moment when he's being pulled every way at once. Everyone trying to second guess him. Even though he's the only man in Rome who can stop us going straight into another civil war, *Libertores* against Caesarians. Stabbing him in the back in the meantime. Dividing the Senate, not that *that* takes much effort. Cicero being... well, *Cicero*. And, as you observed when we had just dispatched that rabble-rouser Gaius Amiatus, he needs peace and quiet to be established as quickly and securely as possible. So he can go out and spread some harmony and goodwill. Not to mention farms, smallholdings and *sestertii*. Here in Italy first. And then further afield. Perhaps as far afield as Egypt. Which is also a major part of the problem.'

'Cleopatra?'

'Cleopatra.'

As they talked, the two soldiers walked through the *atrium* of the augur and *haruspex* Spurinna's villa and entered the little *cubicula* room where Adonis was happily reunited with his Venus. He was seated behind a solid little table. She was curled contentedly in his lap. Exchanging an embrace which was, perhaps, more intimate than was usual between siblings. Even ones as beautiful as these. The moment the two men entered, the young woman jumped out of her brother's arms. Stepped back. Stood. Dimpled chin raised. Expression set. Dark blue eyes speculative. Tiny red spots burning on the exquisite curves of her cheekbones. The loose tunic Trebonius' man had given her still did surprisingly little to conceal her other, equally exquisite, curves.

'Go to the slave quarters at the back of the house,' Enobarbus ordered. 'Ask for a young man there called Kyros. Tell him what you need in the way of clothing, food and drink and he will arrange for you to have it.'

Brother and sister exchanged a glance. 'It's all right,' said Adonis. 'They have looked after me well. They will do the same for you.'

'Until we stop being useful to them at any rate,' said Venus cynically. Her voice velvety and deep. Like the purr of a contented panther. 'Or until we cease to satisfy them,' she added.

'We're not all like Gaius Trebonius or Minucius Basilus,' said Artemidorus gently. 'No one will do anything to you here...'

'Though if you talked like that in most houses,' added Enobarbus, 'you'd lose some skin off your back for it. Whether your master was aroused by the sight or not.'

Venus shrugged and vanished. Artemidorus placed the tablets on the table in front of Adonis. 'Now,' he said. 'To business...'

ii

Artemidorus glanced across at Enobarbus as Adonis sorted out the pile and opened the first wax tablet. Both men had been intimately involved in the ill-fated

55

attempt to keep Caesar alive on the *Ides*. One as spymaster, the other as spy. Both, like Antony, had been on the steps of Pompey's *Curia*, when the murder was committed. Still fighting their losing battle against Brutus, Cassius, Decimus Albinus, Trebonius and the rest. Artemidorus had been the first man into the deserted chamber after the horrified senators and the jubilant, blood-smeared *Libertores* had run out. The man who had seen the terrified Senate Secretary Adonis slipping away from the scene of the crime.

It was Artemidorus who actually discovered the body, therefore. Lying like a garish pile of soiled washing at the foot of Pompey's statue. Gold and purple liberally splashed with darkening crimson. Who trod in the lake of Caesar's blood as he made sure the recently deified god was actually dead. Ensured that the folds of his torn *toga* covered his legs in a decent manner. And covered his head in the proper religious form. Particularly important as Caesar had been *Pontifex Maximus*, the chief priest of the city and its burgeoning empire.

Artemidorus was also with Antistius when the physician carried out his *post-mortem* examination of Caesar's body, cataloguing the number and severity of the wounds. Discovering, ironically, the list of suspected murderers that Artemidorus himself had given Caesar on the way to the *Curia*. Unopened and unread, still in the fold of his sleeve he used as a pocket.

But neither the spy–centurion nor the spymaster–tribune had been in the *Curia* to witness the deed. As far as they knew, no one had yet given exact details of who did what and when during that momentous incident. Even Brutus and Cassius themselves had been unable to recall the exact sequence, blinded and confused as they were by a heady mix of terror and elation. There were almost as many versions flying around the city as there had been men with bloody daggers.

It might have seemed incredible to Artemidorus and Enobarbus that so many should have seen the same thing and yet perceived it and remembered it differently. But then they had both spent many years sifting through the various reports of their secret operatives. No two ever quite the same. And both had served enough time with Caesar in Egypt, Gaul, and in those parts of the empire to which the civil war had taken him, to know that his published versions of these adventures often differed radically from their own memories. What Adonis was going to tell them, therefore, was the first actual blow-by-blow reconstruction of precisely how Caesar had met his end. And the promise of it seemed, to Artemidorus at least, simply breathtaking.

'We were outside,' he said brusquely. 'We saw for ourselves what passed between Gaius Trebonius and Co-consul, General Mark Antony.'

'And you need not bother to detail the comings and goings of Caesar's golden *curule* chair as he was rumoured to be coming and then not coming and then coming again,' added Enobarbus.

'Tell us what happened as clearly as you can from the moment Caesar entered...'

Adonis picked up the long bronze stylus he would use to make his notes in the firm-set wax of the first open tablet. 'Caesar entered hurriedly,' Adonis began, as he began to make his shorthand notes. 'Led by Decimus Albinus. By the hand. As though Caesar were a child. Albinus released Caesar and moved away as he came to the dais where his golden chair was standing. With a small work table just beside it. He was dressed in his gold-patterned tunic and his purple *toga*. He was wearing his royal-red *caligae* boots. And a golden coronet fashioned to look like a victor's laurel wreath. He was carrying papyrus scrolls, wax tablets. And a long bronze stylus just like this one.' Adonis held the stylus up. Its sharp point gleamed wickedly.

'Even before Caesar reached the dais on which his seat and table had been erected, the whole front row of the Senate, and many others beside, were on their feet hurrying towards him. They reached him as he stepped up onto it and prepared to sit. As Secretary to the Senate, I have to be able to name all the important Conscript Fathers, for sometimes in the heat of debate, the Father of the House forgets to name the next speaker he calls upon. I certainly knew most of the men coming forward, though towards the end there seemed to be almost a hundred of them milling around at the back.' His eyes opened wide and he frowned as he directed his intense gaze upon his two interrogators.

'My position as secretary was on Caesar's left, on the floor of the *Curia* and therefore below him,' he explained. 'Half a dozen paces distant, beside the keepers of the water clocks. My head perhaps level with his waist. While I was seated at any rate. And I was a pace or two behind him as well. But I could see quite clearly.' He lowered his gaze and his sharp-pointed stylus, making his notes on the wax in front of him as he spoke. 'The first senator to approach him was Lucius Tillius Cimber, who caught at the hem of his *toga* even as he was sitting down and arranging his scrolls and tablets. Piling most of them on the little table so he could attend to them during the debates, as he often did. But as soon as he had done this, Caesar half rose. A group of senators gathered round, supporting Cimber, though he had not yet begun to plead his case. The sheer weight of numbers seemed to make Caesar sit back again. Cimber rose to full height then and began loudly to plead for the return of his brother Publius Cimber, who had been exiled by Caesar. He kissed Caesar's hand, then his forehead, leaning down over him while the others crowded round. The Casca brothers, Publius Casca and Gaius Casca, were the closest. Then Marcus Brutus and Gaius Cassius, then Decimus Albinus, Pontius Aquila, Minucius Basilus…'

'Very well,' interrupted Enobarbus. 'You need not tell us who was in the queue. Tell us what order they struck in. That will be sufficient for our needs, I think. For the moment at least.'

Artemidorus nodded in silent agreement.

'So,' said Adonis. 'Caesar was sitting down again, as though overwhelmed by Tillius Cimber's kisses and demands. In the meantime, the group of senators I have just named closed around him. All at once, Caesar struggled to get up, spilling some of his scrolls and tablets onto the floor of the dais. As though suddenly alarmed by the crowd of senators and their demands.

'Then it began. Cimber abruptly grabbed a firm hold of Caesar's *toga* and pulled with great strength. This moved the heavy folds of material across Caesar's shoulder and laid bare the left side of his neck. Right across to the shoulder joint of his left arm. And his chest, down to the neckline of his tunic. Caesar made things worse for himself by pushing upwards, calling, "*Ista quidem vis est!* This is violent assault!"

'At the same time, Cimber called, "*Quid te amicorum exspectas*? What are you waiting for, friends?"'

The boy looked down, falling silent as he wrote rapidly on the wax of the tablet.

iii

After a moment, he continued to speak. 'Publius Casca produced a dagger then. His was the first of many that suddenly appeared. He had it hidden beneath his *toga*. Most of the others did too, but some of them had daggers hidden in writing cases. Publius Casca struck for Caesar's unprotected throat from behind his left shoulder. Aiming for the section of Caesar's neck uncovered when Tillius Cimber pulled his *toga* aside. I saw it clearly from where I was seated. Though I rose to my feet almost at once. As Caesar himself was still trying to do. Because of Caesar's sudden movement, Publius Casca missed. His arm went right across Caesar's shoulder. His elbow was almost in the crook of Caesar's neck, beneath his ear. The golden coronet Caesar had been wearing was knocked off by this. But Casca's dagger hardly scratched Caesar's breast. Seeing the dagger, Caesar must have understood the full danger then. He caught Casca's right wrist and stabbed his stylus completely through the forearm.' The boy held up his own stylus, its nib now caked with wax, but still looking almost as sharp as Artemidorus' *pugio* dagger.

'Publius Casca screamed out at that,' Adonis continued. 'Even as Caesar shouted, "*Contemptus* Casca! Contemptible Casca! What does this mean?"'

'By way of answer, Casca called something in Greek. I suppose it was a cry for help because the other Casca, Gaius, came to his brother's aid. For he too was very close beside Caesar. And still at his left shoulder. Caesar let go of the stabbed arm and half-turned, rising to his feet at last. The golden *curule* chair fell off the back of the dais. Gaius Casca pushed the little work table aside and came right up to him. And drove his dagger in under Caesar's ribs straight up into his chest.'

'That was the blow Antistius the physician said was the fatal one,' nodded Artemidorus grimly. 'None of the others were deadly in themselves...'

Enobarbus nodded too, his expression grim. 'Go on, boy. Who attacked next?'

'Cassius,' answered Adonis. 'Caesar tore free of Publius Casca, but kept hold of Gaius Casca's arm, almost as though he was using the murderer as a crutch to keep himself erect as they staggered together down onto the floor of the *Curia* itself. Even though Gaius Casca's dagger was still buried in Caesar's side.'

'Making sure there were no more up-and-under strokes...' suggested Artemidorus knowledgeably. 'Especially if he was facing Cassius. He's a real soldier. Knows his *pugio* dagger-work. Expert, in fact, with *pugio* and *gladius*. And Caesar would have known that. Besides, the moment Gaius' dagger came out, so would Caesar's blood. And he'd weaken pretty quickly after that.'

'Good point,' allowed Enobarbus grimly. 'And Gaius Casca would have been a useful shield for his vulnerable left side as well. That's possibly why most of the rest of the wounds were in the head, shoulder and arm on the right side. Go on, boy,' he repeated. 'What next?'

'Still holding onto Gaius Casca, Caesar stumbled forward. Cassius was there just beyond the edge of the dais. He stepped in and he stabbed Caesar in the face. Caesar saw the blade coming and turned away. Even so, Cassius opened him up from his hairline to his chin. Cut his eyebrow open to the bone. Nose and cheek. But missed his mouth. Caesar barged past him, staggering. Dragging Gaius Casca along as he moved. Then the rest closed round him and it's a little more difficult to be precise. Caesar was calling "*Adiuva me*! Help me!" and "*Proditio*! Treachery, treason!" In spite of the wound to his face, his voice and words were quite clear. There must have been six hundred senators there. And not one of them raised a finger. Quite the opposite. Most of them were heading for the door. In case they were next on the murderers' list after Caesar, I suppose.'

'It's a wonder you could still see what was happening with all that panic, hustle and bustle going on,' probed Enobarbus.

'Oh, they stayed well clear of the assassins,' explained Adonis. 'It was as though Brutus, Cassius and the rest had some kind of plague. There was a clear area all around them and I was standing up by then of course. And all alone, as a matter of fact. The other secretaries and the men keeping the water clocks had all taken off like frightened hares. So. The next thing I saw was Senator Bucolianus, Senator Caecilius' brother, coming round behind Caesar and stabbing him in the back. The rest closed in, stabbing him in the arm, head and shoulder. I think one or two of them wounded Gaius Casca into the bargain for Caesar was still using him as a shield. He stopped calling out for help. They were stabbing so wildly that they began to wound each other as well as Caesar and Gaius Casca. Marcus Brutus tried to join in but Cassius stabbed him right through the hand and he fell back. Minucius Basilus also missed Caesar and stabbed Rubrius Ruga in the thigh. There was blood everywhere.

'Caesar, blinded by the blood from the wound in the face that Cassius had given him, did not see Marcus Brutus, though they were almost nose to nose. Still leaning on Gaius Casca, he dashed his right hand down his face and cleared his vision for a few moments, swinging round again. It was then, as I told you earlier, he recognised Decimus Brutus Albinus. He said, "You too, Brutus?" Decimus Albinus was getting ready with an answer. A sneering one judging from his face. But someone slipped in the blood and rolled across the floor, distracting him. I couldn't see who it was too clearly, but I'm almost certain it was Minucius Basilus, still staggering back having stabbed Rubrius Ruga. I'd been watching Basilus because he looked as though he was really enjoying himself. In a sick sort of way. Even when he stabbed the wrong man.

'Senator Pontius Aquila helped Basilus up again and tried to stop him attacking Caesar once more. For it was clear by now that the poor man was dying. But Basilus tore free and went back onto the attack. Stabbing Caesar in the back once more before he went to join the others standing silently, looking on. So then, at the end, when they had all stabbed Caesar at least once and began to fall back, Marcus Brutus came forward a second time. That's when Caesar saw him and said, "*Kai su teknon*? You too, my son?" He said it loudly. Angrily. He was not saddened or defeated. He was outraged. He almost shouted the words as though he wanted everyone there to hear them clearly.

'And Brutus stabbed him in the groin. A low blow, curving upwards almost from his knees. There was no doubt in my mind that he was aiming for his genitals. That he was aiming to emasculate him. For Caesar had, as everyone knows, been sleeping with Brutus' mother throughout the whole of Brutus' life. But the word "*teknon*" son, seemed to hit him like a blow. And by then in any case, Gaius Casca

60

had finally pulled himself away and Caesar was beginning to collapse. There was a great cascade of blood as Gaius tore his dagger free. And that rush of blood was enough to make Caesar stagger and begin to crumble. So Brutus' dagger went into his hip as much as into his groin and wedged there. It tore out of Brutus' grip as Caesar turned away, beginning to collapse at last. I think he groaned, as I have told you. But he said nothing further. He staggered a step or two as his murderers stood back, apparently overawed by what they had done. Then Caesar finally fell at the foot of Pompey's statue. And they turned and ran like a flock of birds all taking flight at once. Caesar was writhing and twitching weakly as he finally succumbed. Trying to make sure his *toga* covered him properly and decently at the moment of his death.'

'That's Caesar all right,' nodded Enobarbus. 'Always careful of appearances.'

'Right to the very end,' Artemidorus nodded. 'Like Leonidas and his three hundred Spartans oiling their hair at Thermopylae... Go on boy. What next?'

'He stopped twitching and lay still and that was that. The *Curia* was empty and strangely silent. Everyone else had run away. And I thought I'd better get out of there myself. That's when we saw each other, Centurion. Me on the way out of that slaughterhouse. You on the way in.'

iv

'So,' said Antony sometime later. 'Of the so-called *Libertores*, who are twenty-two in number, not counting their hangers-on, we now have a shortlist of twelve.' The three men and Fulvia were in the *atrium* of Antony's house. Adonis and Venus were in the *culina* kitchen with Ferrata and Hercules keeping an eye on them. Waiting in case Antony wanted to question them in person. Quintus was on his way back to the VIIth. Spurinna was taking auguries at the altar on the Field of Mars with Kyros in attendance, having left Puella at home. And Antistius had gone back to his villa where several patients and a good number of clients were waiting. The three men and one woman were seated around the table Antony liked to use when holding meetings and formulating plans. A large *amphora* of wine in a holder and a big jug of water stood in the middle of the table. The one half empty and the other untouched. Of the four green glass goblets there, only one was wet.

'In the order of their involvement as detailed by our witness. Yes,' Artemidorus answered his general. 'There's a group of ten or so that the boy Adonis did not see clearly enough to name individually. But we know who they are from our own observations of who went up to the Temple of Jupiter Optimus Maximus Capitolinus on the *Ides*. Waving their daggers, showing off their bloodstained hands and boasting about their deed.'

61

'But the boy has given us twelve names in precise order,' Fulvia said. Her tone placing the words halfway between a statement and a question.

'Blow by blow,' nodded Enobarbus grimly.

Antony put down his goblet and held out his hand. Artemidorus passed him the papyrus scroll onto which Adonis had written the names of the men he had identified. In the order those names appeared in his account of the murder. As written on the wax tablets. And sealed in case it ever came to a law case. The three men discussed them as Antony read them aloud. Fulvia inserting her observations as the conference proceeded.

'Decimus Albinus and Gaius Trebonius were first on my list too,' said the general. 'So it's good to see them first and second here. When it eventually comes to spiking heads in the Forum, theirs will be well *ahead* of the others.' He chuckled at his play on words. No one else did.

'Yes, General,' nodded Enobarbus. 'You have made your wishes on that score clear.'

'Good,' said Antony. 'Then who's next?' There was a short pause, then he continued. 'Not that it much matters who *heads up* the list,' Antony tried for a laugh again. With no success.

'The heads belonging to the Casca brothers, perhaps,' suggested Enobarbus. 'Publius – who struck the first blow. And Gaius – who struck the fatal one.'

'I've heard a rumour that Publius Casca contacted Cicero a while ago – a bit like Decimus Albinus,' said Antony, giving up on witticism for the moment. 'He wants the old windbag to put a case together distancing him from the *Libertores* and the murder itself. Publius apparently says he's not guilty of anything. Because his dagger missed Caesar in the first instance. And after he was stabbed through the arm he took no further part in the attack. None of the twenty-three wounds was actually made by him. Though in my opinion, even Cicero will find it hard to make a decent defence out of that.'

'Won't stop him trying, though, if things get any worse for the so-called *Libertores*,' said Enobarbus cynically. 'Publius Casca will just be the first among many to desert when the going gets hard. And, talking of Cicero, there's still no legal ruling on Brutus and the patricide charge is there? It's been a while. And I hear Cicero's left the city…'

Everyone around the table shook their heads. Enobarbus paused for a moment, frowning, then asked, 'Who's next on the list?'

'Cassius,' Artemidorus answered. 'Really and truly, he should be first in the file, General. He's the main motivator of the whole thing. He was the one who really hated Caesar. Possibly for something as petty as being passed over for the post of *praetor urbanus* chief judge in the city, when Caesar gave it to Brutus. *Praetor peregrinus* chief judge outside the city and the promise of Proconsul of Syria were just not enough to satisfy him. And he's a good soldier. Outstandingly good, in fact. He led ten thousand out of the slaughterhouse at Carrhae when Marcus Licinius Crassus lost seven legions, his son and his head to the Parthians.'

'A defeat which Caesar should be marching to avenge even now,' said Antony quietly, picking up his goblet. 'We even discussed his battle plan and how he was going to do it.'

'But just as Cassius – and Cicero – wanted you to be slaughtered alongside Caesar, so we need to get rid of Cassius as quickly as possible,' said Fulvia, her voice trembling with outrage.

Artemidorus nodded his agreement. 'He's the only one of them who has the ability not only to build an army but to deploy it in the field against you, General. Brutus, Trebonius and Decimus Albinus are all good. But they're not in Cassius' league. If it was up to me, his head would be the first one spiked in the Forum. When the time comes, as the Lady Fulvia says.'

'That's where our hands are tied for the moment,' said Antony, with a frown of frustration. Finding his goblet empty, he reached for the *amphora*. He grunted with the effort of lifting it. Poured carefully. Replaced it in its stand. Glanced at the water. Looked away. Drank the thick, dark liquid neat. Then continued. 'Any action against Cassius or Brutus would do as much damage as taking the head of Cicero himself. Which the Lady Fulvia is also keen for me to do, incidentally. But I can't. Yet. The Senate would proscribe us all. Declare us *hostis* outlaws and enemies of the state. And that would mean the confiscation of all our moneys and assets. Villas. Everything. Put our families out onto the street or make them reliant on the generosity of those few friends willing to risk contamination by associating with us.' He looked at Fulvia for several heartbeats. Then added, 'Not to mention putting us personally at the top of everyone else's kill list.'

V

'Better get back to our own kill list then,' suggested Artemidorus. 'It was more brothers next, wasn't it? Bucolianus and Caecilius. Senators. Not really notable for anything else. Other than being friends of Cicero.'

'I'll put signs up saying who they were when I display their heads,' said Antony. 'But the first ones that go up must be easily recognisable. I want people to see them and say, "Look, that's Gaius Trebonius... He took Antony aside while Caesar was being slaughtered..." Knowing whose head it is and why it's there is the whole, entire point!'

63

'On the other hand, we could make Cicero stand beneath them and explain who they were to passers-by,' suggested Fulvia acrimoniously. 'He'd make an excellent *praeco* town crier announcing all the news as well.'

'And upcoming events,' added Antony, matching her tone. 'Such as his own imminent execution.'

Artemidorus and Enobarbus exchanged glances. Under his wife's bitter influence, the general's mood was darkening dangerously. This was what they feared and hoped to avoid by bringing the list themselves and keeping Adonis the witness out of the picture for the moment. For Antony in one of his rages could be fatally unpredictable. Only Fulvia could control him then. Or Cleopatra. But one of them was in Alexandria and the other seemed set on making things worse instead of better.

'Minucius Basilus is next,' said the spy grimly. 'He's top of my personal hit list. He tortured my friend Telos to death and turned Cyanea into a double agent by threatening to torture her as well. He enjoys making people scream and suffer. It's something I'd like to see if he enjoyed himself. Screaming and suffering...'

'I'd heard Trebonius likes the sound of suffering too,' said Antony, distracted. 'And the sight of it apparently arouses him.'

'If you want details of that, all you have to do is ask Venus and Adonis,' said Artemidorus. 'I'm sure they'd be happy to describe all his little predilections.'

Antony gave a grunt. 'Who's next?' he scanned the list. 'Pontius Aquila! Now he and Caesar did have some history. Do you remember when Pontius refused to stand as Caesar went by at... oh which of the triumphs was it?... And for weeks afterwards, every decision Caesar made was capped with the words, *if Pontius Aquila will allow me...*' His chuckles grew deeper. His mood was lightening. 'Made a laughing stock of the pompous little *nothus* bastard. Well, that only leaves one name on your secretary's list,' he said.

'Marcus Junius Brutus,' nodded Artemidorus.

'Brutus has the respect of the populous,' emphasised Fulvia shortly. 'He's dangerously popular. Men like that should be among the first to die! Him and Cassius.'

'And, as we keep saying, General, Cassius is one of the few men able to raise an army and bring it to the field against you. There is no end to how dangerous he is.'

'But as long as he stands with Brutus, he has the love of the *plebs* and the protection of the Senate. I cannot proscribe him. I cannot have him killed by my secret agents and assassins. Even if he was struck down by the gods themselves, his death would be laid at my door. No. We need to watch. Watch and wait. For Cicero's ruling if for nothing else...'

'Where are Brutus and Cassius now?' demanded Fulvia suddenly. 'I know their villas in the city are closed. But they must be somewhere...'

Enobarbus glanced at Artemidorus. 'Septem?'

'The most recent intelligence we have,' said the spy, 'is that they are both staying at Cassius' villa in Antium. It's a big place by all accounts. Plenty of room for the two of them, their families and slaves. Overlooking the sea. Thirty military *miles* or so due south of here. A day's march. Straight down the *Via Appia*.'

'Have you got eyes on all of them?' Fulvia demanded.

'Not all of them,' answered Artemidorus. 'Only the important ones. The ones with disaffected or bribeable slaves. The ones that are the subject of gossip in the Forum. Decimus Albinus is still in his city villa, surrounded by his gladiators – in spite of the message you sent him, General. Cicero is in Puetoli. I guess he plans to stay for a while. Maybe until *Ludi Megaleses* are over in mid *Aprilis*. He doesn't approve of the riotous games that are part of the festival. He'll likely head back here from Puetoli then. That's a three-day journey. Still straight along the *Via Appia*. Minucius Basilus is down there too. But on the far side of Neapolis and *Monte Vesuvio*. He has a big place in Pompeii.'

'Now that's a town I'd like to visit,' said Antony, apparently oblivious to the glare Fulvia shot at him. 'No end of a good time to be had in Pompeii I hear. Wall-to-wall women and all of them wild and willing...'

We've lost sight of Trebonius, however,' concluded Artemidorus. 'But I'm fairly certain Venus or Adonis will have a good idea where he's headed. I just haven't asked them yet.'

vi

'Pompeii,' purred Venus. Her tone was calm. Measured. Her gaze level and steady. If she was nervous being questioned by the most powerful man in the world she did not show it. Not even Fulvia's steely glances seemed to discomfit her. She was clearly used to being looked at. In a range of ways. Artemidorus was impressed. And a little disturbed. This was a woman who liked to live dangerously. She reminded him of Cyanea.

'Pompeii again,' said Antony thoughtfully, swirling the thick dark wine in his goblet. 'Does Gaius Trebonius own property there, girl?'

'No, Lord Antony. He is staying with Minucius Basilus. Basilus owns a large villa in Pompeii. I believe it looks out over the bay beside Neapolis. My master often visits there.'

'Have you been there yourself?' asked Artemidorus, intrigued.

65

'No, Centurion. I have been fortunate. Very few of the women my master takes down there ever return.'

'What does he do with them?' wondered Fulvia. 'Sell them on?'

'To the brothels?' added Antony. 'I hear the place is full of...'

'I think not, my Lord,' Venus' throaty purr interrupted Antony's question. 'The household slaves say that the body-slaves – especially the young women – do not survive the visits. What Basilus and my master do to them.'

There was a brief silence. Then Antony said, 'Maybe you should go down and see what Trebonius and Basilus are up to, Septem. At the very least we might be able to tarnish the reputations of two such upright senators. Who apparently enjoy torturing female slaves to death. Not really consonant with old Roman *dignitas*, is it? Even if slaves count as property rather than as people. How soon could you get to Pompeii and back?'

'On horseback,' said Artemidorus. Careful not to let Antony's unique approach to *dignitas* – which famously included chasing enemies through the Forum drunk out of his mind and armed with a sword – interfere with his own aplomb. 'Three days each way. Maybe less. I usually reckon that a fast messenger can get right down to Brundisium inside a week. One of Caesar's new seven-day weeks. And that's twice the distance.'

'It's worth considering,' decided Antony. 'I'd like to know what the pair of them get up to. And, beyond that, whether Trebonius still plans on taking up the proconsulship of Asia that Caesar had planned for him. And, if so, where his loyalties are likely to lie...'

'Well, in that case, Antony, send Septem to Pompeii,' Fulvia said. 'And do it at once! While we wait for Cicero's ruling on Caesar's last words. In the face of all this political prevarication it is something we can actually *do*. Without upsetting the Senate. Without offending Cicero. Without just waiting for the next disaster to come down on us...'

The conversation had reached this point when Antony's major-domo Promus entered. 'My Lord... my Lady... there is a messenger from *Magister Equitum* Lepidus. A legionary from the Seventh. He says he brings important news.'

Antony shook his head. Gave a dry, humourless chuckle. 'Too late my dear,' he said. 'The next disaster has clearly arrived. Show him in, Promus. Oh. And take this pretty little thing – Venus is it? – back to the kitchen. We'll have more to ask her later.'

*

Artemidorus did not recognise the legionary who strode into the *atrium* a few moments later and slammed self-importantly to attention. Took off his helmet and cradled it against his chain-mailed chest with his right arm. As though it was a baby he was intent on strangling. 'General Antony! I bring a message from my general, Gaius Lepidus.'

'Go on, boy. Spit it out. I wasn't expecting a message from Mercury or Mars…'

'General Lepidus has just received word from the legate commanding the legions in Dyrrachium…'

'Dyrrachium?' interrupted Fulvia. 'What…'

'The city at the western end of the *Via Egnatia*, as you will remember, my dear,' said Antony easily. 'On the coast of Illyria *ad orientalem* eastwards across the *Mare Hadriaticum* Adriatic Sea opposite Brundisium. Caesar fought a great battle against Pompey there, in which I myself played a not inconsiderable part. Though I didn't feature much in the version of events he published soon after. That was four years ago. It is currently the staging post for no fewer than six legions, waiting to head for Parthia as soon as someone can mount Caesar's proposed campaign. Yes, legionary. Please carry on with your message.'

'My Lord, I have to report that the legate of the Fifth Legion, the *Alaude*, Larks, sent an urgent message to Gaius Lepidus as commander of the Seventh. The message contains the following information…' The legionary drew in his breath, his face folded into a frown of intense concentration. 'The legate wished Lepidus to know the following. That Caesar's nephew and heir Gaius Octavius has been training with the legions at Dyrrachium and Apollonia just south of it. In preparation for assuming his post as *Magister Equitum* to Caesar himself when the Parthian campaign begins. The young man has made many friends among the officers of the legions in Dyrrachium and has established himself as a firm favourite with the men.'

'Well done him!' said Antony, amused. 'Not bad for a sickly whelp who should probably have been drowned at birth. Yes, legionary? Is there more?'

'Yes, General,' answered the legionary, his frown of concentration deepening. 'The legate wished Gaius Lepidus to know that on receipt of news that Caesar was dead and that he had named Gaius Octavius as his heir, Gaius Octavius and two of his closest associates, Marcus Vipsanius Agrippa and Quintus Salvidienus Rufus, who had been studying together with him, took ship. Their plan was to land somewhere near Brundisium. The legate's messengers have travelled as swiftly as possible and it is unlikely that Octavius and his friends have made much progress other than coming ashore here in Italy. So far.'

'So that has Lepidus all girlishly aquiver, does it? A sickly boy and two near-nonentities. Who may or may not be a week to ten days' journey away from Rome?' Antony shook his head in exasperation.

67

'My Lord,' said Fulvia quietly. Her use of Antony's title and the tone in which she spoke focused the mind of every man there. 'A boy perhaps, and a sickly one. But a boy who may call himself *Caesar* and stand as heir not only to his name but his fortune. A boy, moreover, who has already made himself popular with six entire legions. Legions, I should add, that you will need to recall and control should anything go wrong with our current plans. A boy who I believe you should be careful not to underestimate. And, if the gods are with him, he might well have come ashore three days ago. If he landed then and gets some decent horses, he could be here in little more than ten days' time.'

There was the briefest of silences. Then Antony spoke. 'Very well. You are right, as ever, my dear. Septem. Forget Trebonius and Basilus. You can catch up with them later. Put Cicero and the patricide question on one side for the moment. We'll come back to it in due course. Leave for Brundisium as soon as you can manage it. Find young Octavius either there or on the road coming here. He can only use the *Via Appia* so it shouldn't be too hard to hit upon him. You were briefly in Spain with Caesar, weren't you? And saw the boy there?'

'From a distance. But I would know him again.'

'Excellent. There you are then. Find him. Bring him to me. With or without Quintus Rufus and Marcus Agrippa.'

vii

Artemidorus' first port of call was the Seventh Legion's cavalry unit on the *Campus Martius*. Ferrata and Hercules followed him. On the way there, he left his two companions and stuck his head through the gate in the wooden-walled practice area and called to Quintus, who was testing a range of nasty-looking bows there, with an assistant. Who was left to clear everything up as the *triarius* answered the centurion's summons. Under Quintus' eagle eye, the legionary in charge of the cavalry *turmae* squadron, selected the best horses he had available and put four of the swiftest and a brawny packhorse at the disposal of the spy and his little cohort. Together with the four most comfortable saddles the unit owned.

The need for four fast horses had arisen out of a brief conversation in the *culina* kitchen of Antony's villa earlier.

'Straight down the *Via Appia*,' said Ferrata round a mouthful of boiled egg. 'You'd better pray that the news of young Octavius' arrival hasn't leaked out too far yet. And that no one could ever guess Antony might send someone to greet him. The first few *miles* of the Appian Way are lined with tombs. Perfect for ambushes and murder attempts. You'd better watch your back, Septem.'

'I've got a better idea, Ferrata. Why don't you watch it for me?'

'*Stercus*! Shit! Me and my big mouth. And who's going to watch *my* back?'

'Hercules here. If Lepidus will spare him for a while longer.'

The gigantic tutor looked up with a smile. 'Better than being stuck in a classroom all day,' he rumbled. 'But I have a very large back myself. And unlike you, I'm a tutor not a soldier. And therefore possess little in the way of armaments and armour.'

'Don't worry. I have just the man to guard your back, even though it is pretty broad.'

'But if you're coming with us, Hercules, you're going to need a bloody great horse,' said Ferrata. 'Several, in fact...'

The four men rode into the city through the Gate of Fontus. Their arms and armour were packed with their other necessaries on the packhorse or in saddlebags on their mounts. They were all in warm, unremarkable travelling clothes. Even so, Artemidorus paused at the gate, showing the guard there the pass Antony had supplied them with. A pass requiring anyone who saw it to render Centurion Iacomus Artemidorus of *Legio VII* and his companions any aid or succour they required. On pain of death. 'That should sort out the matter or fresh horses too,' said Ferrata, approvingly. 'Even though the "on pain of death" bit may be pushing it. Even for the general.'

'I wouldn't bet on that,' said Artemidorus. 'What he says, he tends to do. Like they say in Egypt: *So it has been written; so it shall be done.*' He did not point out that Antony had given him not only the written order but also a sizeable bag bulging with golden coins.

The four of them clattered through the Forum and along the *Via Sacra*, heading for the *Porta Capena*, where the centurion showed the pass once more. Then they pushed through the bustle of tourists, farmers, tradesmen and beggars. Walking their mounts out onto the roadway itself. The *Via Appia* and the *Via Latina* both originated here and the *Via Latina* was a more direct route to the centre of Italy, and might actually get them to a meeting point with Octavius more quickly. But not if he was coming to Rome via the Appian Way. And Antony's orders had been quite clear. Once onto the *Via Appia*, therefore, they let the horses have their heads and galloped side by side along the ancient military road, apparently oblivious to the traffic that pulled, jumped or dived to one side or the other, getting out of their way. Glancing back, Artemidorus was relieved to see that the packhorse, on a long lead rein tied to Quintus' saddle, was well able to keep up with them.

Their initial charge down the road was not arrogance or officiousness. Artemidorus had taken Ferrata's warning to heart. It would do nobody any good if he set out on his mission with one of the nameless assassin's brutal arrow bolts in his back. But either the news about Octavius had not leaked out yet or whoever sent the anonymous assassin had neither time nor inclination to unleash him once more. The four men rode south through the forest of tombs unmolested.

They had set out in the early afternoon, and so they made fewer than twenty military *miles* before the sun set. Making even a fine road such as the Appian Way too difficult and dangerous to follow at full gallop in the darkness. They found a hostelry in the town of Campoverde. It was no mere drinking place, or *taberna* tavern. It was sizeable. A proper *hospitium stabulum* with accommodation not only for the men but also for their horses. For it was one of the first or last on the busy road running north–south. One of the busiest roads in the empire, in fact. And therefore in all the world.

The four travellers handed their weary mounts to a pair of waiting slaves who stabled the horses and made sure they would be ready before dawn next day. And would bring the packhorse's load up to the room Artemidorus was assigned. Then they took their saddlebags and went into the tavern itself, guided by the big brass lamp that hung above the door. Fashioned in the shape of a *fascinus* or winged phallus designed to ward off bad luck and black magic. To do this, they crossed the stable yard and then a tiny formal garden that would have been a tempting place to linger in the warmer months. Even in early spring, the fountain played gently and the flickering lamps made the statues seem to dance. The main entrance was lit by a series of lanterns which cast an enticing glow. Almost as enticing as the odour of roasting meat which wafted out into the darkness.

The interior of the *hospitium* would have flattered many Roman villas. The wide *ostium* doorway and broad *vestibulum* entrance hall opened into an *atrium* which was unusual only in that there was no opening in the roof or *impluvium* pool beneath. The large, square area was filled with tables, many of which had been pushed together to make one large board that was surrounded by neatly dressed, serious-looking men. The rest were filled with an assortment of people who were being served by what appeared to be a small army of *pedisecae* waitresses. The atmosphere was warm, settled and welcoming. The erotic pictures on the walls almost decorous. Certainly when compared with the ones in Antony's bathhouse, Artemidorus thought. At one side of the room stood a bar piled with *amphorae*, jugs and barrels. At the other a low stage where a young woman was playing a lyre as three girls, diaphanously dressed as Graces, danced. Beyond the stage, a short passage led to a staircase. Which mounted, no doubt, to the rooms above. Behind the bar, a wide doorway opened into what could only be a *culina*, from which the mouth-watering odours were wafting, along with a good deal of smoke.

A tall man wearing a tunic and an apron, who was obviously the *caupo* innkeeper, came out from behind the bar and hurried forward. 'Welcome, gentlemen. How may the *hospitium* of Campoverde be of service? Food? Wine? We offer only the best. And at very reasonable prices.'

'Accommodation. A room for the night.'

'Ah. Now there I must disappoint you, sir. All our rooms are taken.'

The spy reached into his saddlebag. Pulled out Antony's pass and showed it to the man. Who read it slowly and laboriously. But read it nevertheless.

'Well, Centurion, I don't know…'

'We'll pay fair rates. But we need a room. One room will do for the four of us.'

'Well, I suppose. I will discuss matters with my wife…'

'Excellent. Do you have a bathhouse?' asked Artemidorus.

'We do. And the water is hot. We can also supply masseurs if you have been riding long and hard.'

Artemidorus didn't bother to ask how the innkeeper knew they had been riding. Not only were they not local – and unlikely to have walked here. But they also stank of horses. Which was why he had asked about the bath. 'Very well,' he said. 'My companions will each discuss their individual needs but for me it is a bath, a drink, a meal and a bed for the night.'

'You have arrived at a most opportune time,' said the innkeeper, signalling to a woman who was clearly the *cupona* the landlady, his wife. 'We are very busy but I'm sure we can accommodate you.' He turned to his good lady, including her in the conversation. 'My wife and I usually sleep in the front overlooking the stables, but we will move out and arrange for more beds to be put in there…' She nodded agreement and turned away while he continued. 'And we are so busy tonight because the *collegium carnifexes* guild of butchers is meeting here as it does at the end of every month.' He gestured at the serious-looking men gathered round the largest tables. 'And the meal, in consequence, is best beef. And particularly fine.'

viii

Artemidorus relaxed in the *tepidarium*, allowing the warm water to lap at his chin as he made his plans for the night and the morrow. Stopping at the *hospitium* was an indulgence. But the general was right. Gaius Octavius and his friends could only be coming along the Appian Way – unless he wanted to go adventuring across country. Or unless he decided to turn aside and make a visit or two on the way. The *via* after all came past Puetoli, outside Neapolis, where Cicero was staying. And, indeed, past Antium, should he wish to talk with Brutus and Cassius for any reason. If either of those possibilities proved true then there would be no chance of meeting the boy and his companions. But it seemed to the spy that Octavius would most likely hurry straight to Rome. He was by all accounts an

71

intrepid youngster. He had smuggled himself across war-torn Hispania a couple of years back to join Caesar on campaign. But he was sickly. No way round that. Therefore he would likely be coming swiftly but sensibly up the *Via Appia*. And in that case, whether they stopped here tonight – or further down the *via* tomorrow night, they would come across him eventually.

But what then?

It was all very well for General Antony to order that Octavius be brought to him, but what if the young man had other ideas? Would a squad of four soldiers be enough to change his mind? Artemidorus doubted it. There had to be a better way than simply turning up and shouting the general's orders. As he had said to Puella, you catch more flies with honey than with vinegar.

He had reached this far in his thoughts when Hercules' massive shadow fell over him and the huge tutor stepped down into the water. Artemidorus hurriedly sat up. He knew enough about Archimedes' theories to realise that if he didn't move, then his face would be submerged the instant his huge companion sat down.

'Ferrata found a whore yet?' he asked as the waves washed over his shoulders.

'Not yet,' rumbled Hercules. 'He's too busy trying to eat an entire cow. Says he's never tasted beef before. But he's got his eye on the Three Graces.'

'It's only a matter of time. He has a nose for a willing girl that would put a hunting dog to shame. One of the dancers is certainly most likely. Or the girl with the lyre. Where's Quintus?'

'On guard outside the bathhouse door. He says there's something about this place he doesn't like.'

'His senses are always battle-ready,' said Artemidorus, frowning. 'I'd better be a little more careful myself.'

'At least we're all in the same room,' observed Hercules. 'Though I'll never fit on that little bed.'

'The innkeeper's bedroom,' nodded Artemidorus. 'The noisy one overlooking the stables and the road. Where he can keep an eye on whatever's going on.'

He heaved himself out of the water. Hobbled across the room like a septuagenarian. 'I think I'll see if the masseur can untie some of these knots in my legs,' he said. 'Full day on horseback tomorrow. And I'm not saddle-broken yet.'

*

A little later, Hercules, Quintus and Artemidorus were seated together at one of the smaller tables. Each man had a goblet in front of him with a bowl beside it. There was a jug of surprisingly good local wine and a jug of water beside that. 'Drawn from our own well, sirs. Clean and pure…' The bowls were full of fragrant beef stew, which was such a rarity that the spy was hard put to remember when he had last eaten it. The meat had been roasted over the open fire in the kitchen and was served in a sauce made of pepper, lovage, celery seed, cumin, oregano, dried onion, raisins, honey, vinegar, wine, broth, and oil. It was served with crusty bread fresh from the oven.

The three graces and their *lyricist* had gone. They were replaced by a comedian in a battered comic mask who seemed to be very popular with the butchers. Though that was as much to do with what they had drunk as with what he was saying.

'*No. Listen... There's this man, just back from a trip abroad. He goes to a fortune-teller, see? But he doesn't realise the fortune-teller is completely incompetent. So he asks about his family, how they all are... and the fortune-teller replies: "Everyone is fine, especially your father." Well, the man gets all upset at that and says, "What are you talking about? My father has been dead for ten years!" Quick as a flash, the fortune-teller replies: "So you think you know who your father actually is, do you?"*'

'We have to think this through,' said Artemidorus, raising his voice above the howls of laughter, refusing to be distracted by the way the joke's punchline made him think of Brutus and his questionable paternity. 'Who is most likely to get the boy to agree to come and see Antony? Four soldiers? Four messengers? Four ambassadors bringing gifts and tokens of goodwill?'

'I'd go with the last one. The men bringing gifts and good wishes,' said Hercules and Quintus nodded his agreement.

'I think so too,' said the spy. 'So the next couple of questions are these – how do we disguise ourselves as friendly emissaries. And where do we get goodwill gifts rich enough to impress young Octavius and his friends?'

'Gifts that might reasonably have come from Antony,' added Quintus.

The three fell into silent thought as they cleared their bowls and mopped up the sauce with the bread.

'*There was this bloke who really hated his wife, see? Then one day she drops dead. And there he is at his wife's tomb paying his final respects when this stranger comes up to him and asks, "Who is it that's resting at peace, friend?" And this man replies. "Me! I'm finally at peace now that the bitch is dead."*'

Artemidorus jerked as though he had been slapped. Looked around, frowning. Met Quintus' eyes and looked guiltily away. 'What?' asked Hercules.

'Nothing,' answered the spy shortly.

But the comedian's words echoed in his mind and memory. '*Canicula mortus est.*' The bitch is dead. The words he had used to Quintus a few days after the *Ides*

73

of *Mars*. Telling him Cyanea, as he believed, was dead indeed. For he had thrown her, naked, to the mob.

ix

Artemidorus woke a heartbeat before Quintus sat up. They were side by side in the bed belonging to the innkeeper and his wife. Ferrata was snoring in the low truckle bed assigned to him and Hercules was less restfully on a mat on the floor. The cloud cover had vanished. The light of a low full moon streamed in bars through the latticed shutter of the little window opening. Which let in sound as well as light.

'What?' whispered the *triarius*.

'Hush!'

The noise that had disturbed them came again. The jingle of tack. The soft percussion of an unshod hoof beat. Someone was leading horses in or out of the stable across the yard beyond the pretty decorative garden. Artemidorus rolled out of bed and crossed to the window. Thanking the gods for the deft ministrations of the masseur. His legs worked almost as well as usual. By pressing his face against the laths he could see down into the road-side of the *hospitum stabulum*. Two black shapes – scarcely more than shadows bundled in travelling cloaks – were leading horses into the stables. A lamp burned welcomingly inside, so that parts of them seemed cast in silver and parts of them cast in gold. His interest piqued, the spy caught up his own travelling cloak and wrapped it around himself. Then, barefooted and silent, he ran out of the room and down the stairs.

Heat and smoke lingered in the air of the big *atrium* but the guests had long since returned home or gone to bed. The *caupo* and *caupona* were both likely asleep in whatever chamber they had taken for themselves. Only the slaves in the stable seemed still to be up and about – no doubt guarding the horses. And entertaining some midnight visitors.

Artemidorus tiptoed into the black throat of the *vestibulum*, feeling his way forward in the dark towards the broad, welcoming *ostium*. Explored the door with his fingers until he discovered the great bolt and eased it back. Well greased, it slid silently. And the door swung equally quietly towards him. Cold night air washed over his bare legs and feet. Night sounds of whispering breeze and tinkling water flowed in with the chill. The lamp in the flying phallus above him was still burning. That, the moonlight and the brightness in the stable were sufficient to show him that the garden and the yard beyond it were empty. He ran forward into the darkest shadow available, just beside the open stable door.

'...No, I'm sorry, masters. This is not a staging post. These horses are not for sale or hire. They belong to four guests...'

74

'Money is no object. We need to get on. We have important business.' A hard voice. A soldier's voice. One with authority. An *equitum* knight or patrician. A man used to getting his own way. Angered by the slave's refusal to co-operate. Keeping himself under control with quite an effort.

'I can't help that, sir. These horses are spoken for. And by men I would rather not cross.'

'And yet you would cross me. Gaius Valerius Flaccus. And my employer Lucius Cornelius Balbus. One of the richest and most powerful men in Rome… Secretary to Caesar himself…'

'And the men who own these horses are soldiers too, sir. Another centurion. From the Seventh. And according to my master they are on a mission for Co-consul Antony himself. With a warrant over his own seal and sign.'

'Antony!' Another voice, lighter in tone. Breathless with shock. 'Are you sure?'

'If you doubt me, sir, then go and ask the master.'

There was an abrupt hissing sound. The eavesdropping centurion recognised it at once. Someone had just pulled a *gladius* from its sheath.

He stepped forward into the light. 'Good evening, *nobili* gentlemen.'

Four pairs of eyes regarded him. Two slaves, trembling on the knife-edge between worry and outright fear. A square, hard-looking soldier in centurion's armour – except for the helmet. Bareheaded except for the hood on his cloak. Legion badges covered. *Gladius* in hand. And, beside him, not, apparently, in armour, a younger patrician-looking companion. Behind them, two exhausted-looking horses. Necks white with salt sweat. Legs shifting uncomfortably, dragging worn hooves in the straw. The soldier was first to move, his naked *gladius* catching the light as he raised it.

There was a silent stirring at Artemidorus' shoulder. The grip of his own *gladius* was pressed into his hand. Quintus stood beside him, fully armed.

The stranger's sword point wavered. Fell.

'There are no beds here,' said Artemidorus.

'And no spare horses either, as you can see.' Quintus added.

'And the beef's all gone as well,' Ferrata's rough voice struck in as he arrived at Quintus' side. 'Not one sweet mouthful left.'

'So, I think perhaps Lucius Cornelius Balbus would prefer that you went on your way. I know Co-consul and General Mark Antony would. As I move at his order and speak with his voice.'

There was a moment more of silent confrontation. Interrupted by the arrival of Hercules and the sounds of stirring in the *hospitium* behind him. Then the stranger sheathed his *gladius* and led his limping horse out into the yard, heading back onto the moonlit road. His aristocratic companion followed. His patrician gaze sweeping over them, making no distinction between the soldiers and the slaves.

x

'Time to move on,' said Artemidorus as the hoof beats faded away down the Appian Way. 'Now we have the moonlight we can follow the road. Saddle our horses and load up the pack animal please.'

'We don't want those two to get too far ahead of us,' said Ferrata as the slaves hurried to obey.

'No,' agreed Artemidorus, turning and beginning to retrace his steps towards the gathering bustle of the *hospitium*. 'If they work for Balbus then they're on the same mission we are. And I want to get to Octavius first if we can.'

'Our horses are rested and theirs are tired,' rumbled Hercules. 'Is there anywhere else that they can get mounts that are better or fresher?'

'There are staging posts every fifteen miles,' answered Quintus, his voice echoing a little as they crossed the *vestibulum* into the brightness of the *atrium*. 'But I don't know whether there'll be horseflesh at all of them – or what it will be like if there is. No farms this near Rome; only huge *latifundia* estates. No horses there, either, I'd say. Not anywhere near the *via* at any rate. So it'll be as *Fortuna* dictates in whatever towns and villages they pass.'

'Well, as long as they're ahead of us, they'll get first pick of whatever they find,' said Ferrata as he mounted the first stair.

'Right,' said Artemidorus. 'Especially as they'll have limitless funds if Balbus is backing them. So we'd better hurry.'

They were ready in a surprisingly short time. Tab settled, basic breakfast in a bag and a wineskin which Ferrata carried. Horses saddled and pack animal loaded. It was still well before moonset, let alone dawn, as they led their mounts out onto the road. Artemidorus relieved Quintus of the packhorse's lead rein. 'As far as I can remember there is no other *urbs* city or *oppidum* town between here and Caserta or maybe Aquinum,' he said. 'Just one or two *vici* villages. And Caserta's almost a part of the *urbs* of Neapolis. Two days or so from here.'

'That's what I remember too.' Quintus nodded.

'Right. Then what I want you to do is this. Take this money and go to the market in Campoverde. Hercules will guard your back. Get yourselves breakfast there and then buy whatever you think would make an acceptable gift for young Octavius. I trust your judgement. And the market is a good one by all accounts. Then catch us up again. Ferrata and I won't go at full speed until you rejoin us. But we should still be able to get closer to Balbus' messengers. Their horses are blown and they'll have to rest them soon unless they plan on riding them to death.'

76

Quintus nodded once and turned his horse into the side road leading to the town. Hercules followed him downhill, and the westering moon kept the path between the gathering trees clear enough to follow. And to be fair, thought Artemidorus, the main town was not too far away, crouching behind its battered walls.

Then he turned his horse's head towards the long, straight, moon-bright line of the Appian Way and eased it into a trot. Ferrata fell in at his side and the packhorse trotted happily behind.

They ate breakfast in the saddle at an easy canter as the gathering dawn lit the eastern sky away above the mountains on their left and the moon at last set in the sea away beyond Antium. Overlooked, Artemidorus judged, by the wide balcony of Cassius' villa where he and Brutus were staying. The two soldiers were soon joined by the early traffic that usually filled the main road between Rome and the south. But it was never heavy enough to slow them – or varied enough to hide the two men on exhausted horses they were following. Even as dawn turned to day and the sun itself rose majestically over the eastern peaks.

'Something's just occurred to me,' said Ferrata suddenly, after a long, thoughtful silence.

'What?'

'Well, if news of the boy's arrival has got as far as Balbus, then it might well have got as far as whoever sent that assassin after you.'

'Yes. The same thought had occurred to me,' nodded Artemidorus. 'But they'd need to have a really good soothsayer or maybe an *encantatrix* enchantress to know for certain Antony would send me to greet him.'

'Anyone who could send that assassin with that murderous bow would probably be able to get a *striga* witch.'

'Then they wouldn't need assassins would they? A *striga* could strike me down with a curse! In fact I'm surprised I'm still upright if what you told me is true and that *striga* Cyanea is still alive.'

'Now there's an ill-omened thought if ever I heard one!' Ferrata clutched at the *fascina* good-luck charms hanging from his belt. Most of which were phalluses of one type or another. Smaller than the lamp above the *hospitium's* doorway. All erect. With or without wings and testicles attached. Pulled his horse away from the spy's as though expecting a thunderbolt to hit him.

Artemidorus drew in his breath to follow up his observation with a question. For Ferrata had been among the murderous mob to whose tender mercies he had left his treacherous lover. And yet Ferrata said she had managed to walk away from them. Having killed the first two men who released her from the whipping post to which she had been tied. And injured two others who had tried to stop her.

And then had set fire to Minucius Basilus' villa on her way out. All this while stark naked and apparently unarmed. The spy knew well enough that she had been trained as well as he. Had served as a *gladiatrix* just as he had featured briefly in the arena as gladiator *Scorpius*. She had known all of Quintus' weapons and how to use them. But to have done what Ferrata described almost made him believe she did in fact have magical powers.

But before he could ask his question, Ferrata called, 'Look!'

xi

Because he had pulled his horse over to the side of the road, pretending to fear a thunderbolt, Ferrata had given himself an excellent view downhill into a valley that sloped into a broad green field. And here there lay a carriage on its side. At the bottom of a track of torn and muddied grass. It was a light carriage, not quite a chariot. A wooden box large enough to seat two or perhaps four with a driver at the front. All on four sturdy wheels with a central shaft and enough tack to secure two horses to it. But the cart's horses were gone. And in their place, two exhausted, sweat-white mounts listlessly champed the grass nearby. And someone, presumably the driver, was sprawled on the ground beside the wreck. Face down. Unmoving.

The two men reined to a halt. Artemidorus looked around but the *via* was empty at the moment. He slid off his horse and ran down the slope to the vehicle. Everything was still and deathly quiet. He slowed, regretting the fact that his *gladius* and *pugio* were in the packhorse's bags. Then pressed on, thinking he was more likely to need a surgeon than a sword. For the grass around the driver was stained with russet darkness. And his head lay at a strange angle.

The shaft was still attached to the front axle so, even though the carriage was on its side, he had a foothold that allowed him to climb up and look down through the door. A young couple lay on the lower side, which was resting on the grass. A young woman and a handsome youth with their arms wrapped around each other. And, like their driver, they weren't going to get any older. The young woman was lying half on top of the young man. And, again like the driver, various parts of their bodies lay at odd angles, suggesting that their carriage had rolled over and over on its way down here. As, in fact, the state of the grass on the slope behind him attested. But the wounds in their chests made the ex-gladiator certain they had been stabbed before their carriage was rolled off the road. Even though he knew it was hopeless, he heaved himself onto the side of the carriage that lay uppermost now and lowered himself through the door as though it was a trapdoor. Both bodies were cold. And a swift but thorough search revealed that they had been stripped of anything that might identify them. Except for their clothing,

78

which was of good quality and looked expensive. The same was true of the roughly dressed slave who had been driving, whose corpse he checked after scrambling back out of the carriage. Not that slaves carried much in the way of identification. Unless they had been collared.

It didn't need much intuition for him to see that the two desperate messengers working for Balbus had taken the carriage horses in exchange for their own. Leaving the exhausted animals as they would only slow them down. Even unladen and led on a long rein like the packhorse. And when the youngsters and their driver had objected, the ever-ready *gladius* had come out again. As swiftly as it had in the stable. And there had been no one there to restrain him this time.

'I don't need to come down there do I, Septem?' Ferrata interrupted Artemidorus' thoughts.

'No. Three dead. Stabbed. And the horses tell us whose *gladius* is responsible.'

'That *nothus* bastard,' swore the legionary.

'Looks like they wouldn't sell their horses,' said Artemidorus turning and running back up the slope.

'No idea who they were or where from?'

'Nothing to identify them. We really ought to find and warn the local *aedile* magistrate. But we can't afford the time to get involved.' Artemidorus stopped by the packhorse. Opened the big bag and pulled out his *gladius*. Then, after a moment, his *pugio* as well. Strapped them to his belt.

'Pass mine too,' asked Ferrata. The spy obliged. The legionary hooked them to the only sections of his belt not covered with lucky phalluses.

Artemidorus took a short run and vaulted into his saddle just as he had seen Caesar do. Kicked his horse's sides and trotted forward. The packhorse moved accommodatingly behind.

'I might get involved if we find those two,' growled Ferrata. 'For just as long as it takes me to cut their guts out.' He eased his *gladius* in its scabbard and folded his face into a murderous frown.

*

He was still frowning at midday when the sound of galloping hoof beats rose over the general bustle of the busy road behind them and warned that they were being followed. The combination of the threat from the assassin and the murder of the young couple in the carriage was enough to make both men stop and turn, hands on sword-hilts. But the men galloping towards them were Hercules and Quintus.

'You made good time,' said Artemidorus.

'Thought you'd be further on,' gasped Quintus.

'Got distracted,' explained Ferrata. 'We found...'

'Tell them later,' ordered Artemidorus. 'What have you got, Quintus?'

Quintus urged his horse forward as he reached into his saddlebag. He brought out a bag bulging with what looked and smelt like bread and cheese. And a wine skin. All of which he passed to Ferrata. Then he reached in a little deeper and produced, with a flourish, an expensive-looking, ornate *gladius* in a tooled black leather scabbard overlaid with bronze. 'Bargain,' he said holding the impressive weapon almost reverently. 'Stallholder didn't know what he was selling. Said he got it from a sailor down on his luck.' He slid the sword out of the scabbard. 'Look at the work on that blade. It's superb. The quality of the metal's excellent too. And, I know it doesn't match, but...' he reached into his saddlebag deeper still and produced a *pugio* dagger. 'Steel's almost as good as yours,' he said. 'I have no idea where the stallholder got the dagger, though. Maybe from another sailor. Who knows? But the work on both of them looks like it's from *Mauretanian Tingitana* to me. North African certainly. Punic, maybe. Though I don't think either of them's old enough to have come from Carthage. African for sure but not Egyptian.'

'Pity they don't match,' said Ferrata.

Quintus threw him a look that would have shattered marble. 'Best I could do!' he snapped.

'They're perfect,' said Artemidorus. 'The boy wants to be a soldier. And what soldier doesn't love exotic weapons? These will be better than anything he's got...'

'Unless he's got a *gladius* that Caesar gave him, of course,' interrupted Ferrata. 'When they were together in Spain.'

'Ferrata,' rumbled Hercules, in obvious amusement. 'Are you just looking to get a whipping? Even if Septem hasn't got a vinestock on him at the moment, he'll be happy to use his belt, I bet, if you don't shut your big mouth...'

Artemidorus shook his head. Hercules was right. Quintus was getting genuinely angry. Ferrata was in danger of going too far with his needling. And, as he did not have the whippy club made of thick oiled vine stems which was one of the marks of a centurion's authority – and which was also a useful aid to discipline – he nevertheless had his wits. 'Ferrata,' he said. 'Now's a good time to tell Quintus what we found. There may have been news of missing people in the market.'

With Ferrata's mouth gainfully employed and peace restored, the four of them rode onwards. While Ferrata's last crack about Caesar's sword niggled in the secret agent's mind.

They caught up with the dead couple's horses at a *mansio* staging post late in the afternoon. The beasts were obviously working horses, not fleet stallions. A matched pair of brown geldings, broad in shoulder and haunch. Short-legged and powerful. But by no means built for speed. Though they, like the horses in the field with the corpses, had been ridden into the ground. Were covered in salt sweat and would take days to recover.

'Do you know who these horses belong to?' Artemidorus asked the man who owned the stable. A matched pair like that would be expensive, he thought. And, taken with the quality of the dead couples' clothes, suggested a rich and influential family. From somewhere not too far away along the *Via Appia*.

'No. Certainly not to the men who left them here. A right couple they were. Riding horses into the ground like that. Why do you ask?'

'Just wondering. So, you gave them a pair of horses in exchange for these?'

'In exchange for these and a fair quantity of coin.'

'Do you have horses we can exchange for these five – and a fair quantity of coin?'

'I do. And better horses than I gave those supercilious snot-nosed *nothi* bastards. I hate to see horses treated like that so I gave them a couple of nags they couldn't run to death.'

'That's perfect,' said Artemidorus, deciding not to ask how Balbus' murderous messenger had put the man's nose out of joint. Other than by their treatment of horseflesh. Happy just to thank *Fortuna* and his personal demigod Achilleus, hero of Troy, for the good luck. 'Quintus, would you oversee things here. Then join us in the *mansio* itself. Just food and wine. No bath this time. And we won't be staying. It's going to be another clear night and the moon's full. We'll push on as soon as we're ready.'

As he sat at the *mansio's* largest table, with Ferrata and Hercules opposite, Artemidorus laid the *gladius* and *pugio* that Quintus had bought on the table. They made an impressive sight, even though they did not match. He eased the *pugio* out of its sheath and tested the point against his thumb. Then sucked the blood off his wounded skin when the blade sank in as though his flesh was cheese. 'Sharp,' observed Ferrata.

The secret agent nodded. And pulled his own dagger from its sheath. Laid it on the table beside the sword. Ferrata gave a low whistle of astonishment. 'Yours is a much better match,' he said. 'They could almost be a set.'

'That's what I was thinking,' said Artemidorus. But the conversation stopped there with the arrival of food and wine. To make room for which the weapons had to be cleared away.

They were in the saddle again before sunset. And discovered with some pleasure that the stableman had not lied. These were four fast horses, and a pack animal strong enough to keep up with them as they thundered southwards into the brief darkness between sunset and moonrise.

*

Two days later at sunset they pulled their mounts to a stop immediately outside the gate of Capua city, just as they would have in Rome, and put their swords into the saddlebags. This was a civilised Roman town. There would be rules of conduct, *aedile* magistrates to see them enforced. Patrols of *vigiles* constables to back them up. So, armed only with their daggers, they entered the city and found the forum. It was easy to do so because although Capua was an ancient Etruscan and Samnite settlement, the Romans had laid it out in the Roman way when they took over its governance. The central square of the thriving metropolis was full of people going about the last of their daily rituals. Men and women strolling from the baths to their villas, planning *cena* dinner and their evening's entertainment. Going to and from the temples of Diana *Tifitania* and Hercules, both popular local deities. The markets, shops and stalls were still open, though business was easing off. Above two or three welcomingly open doorways, lamps in the shape of winged penises burned, draped with garlands that emphasised the fact that they were at least taverns, and probably *hospitia*.

'See?' grumbled Ferrata, who was tired, saddle-sore and increasingly mutinous. 'We could have come straight down the *Via Latina*. And it wouldn't have made any difference. Saved some time, that's all. And a good few blisters on my backside...'

For much of the afternoon they had been riding through increasingly populous country past the point where the *Via Latina* rejoined the *Via Appia*. Through great fields that would be green with spelt later in the spring. Past copper mines in the distant hills; foundries and workshops nearer at hand. And, lingeringly, past the infamous schools that produced the greatest gladiators of all.

'Didn't you do some training here?' asked Quintus. 'During the Third Servile War? Before you became *Scorpius*, scourge of the arena?'

'Just before you slaughtered Spartacus, you mean?' asked Artemidorus.

'That's only a rumour,' snapped Quintus.

'Can we at least pause here for long enough to get some feeling back on my *culus* arse?' demanded Ferrata. 'It feels as though Spartacus and half his army have been…'

'Very well,' nodded Artemidorus. But then he said, 'Wait! Look.'

Crossing the square towards one of the garlanded doorways, oblivious to the common bustle of their surroundings, strode the murderous soldier and his patrician companion. The setting sun struck across the square of the forum, lighting their faces and blinding them. Seeming to cast the pair of them in bronze. There could be no mistake.

Praying, aptly enough, to Achilleus that his legs would work properly, Artemidorus slid off his horse. 'Hercules, look after the horses,' he ordered. 'Quintus. Ferrata. With me.'

xiii

The *atrium* of the *hospitium* was almost as busy as the forum outside. The three companions stood for a moment at the inner end of the *vestibulum* entrance hall looking around. Lingering here, they were three steps above the level of the *atrium* floor. And that was just about the only difference between this and the *hospitium* of Campoverde. Though this was, if anything, larger and more sumptuously appointed. Just the sort of place for the short-tempered soldier and his supercilious associate.

A swift glance round was enough for Artemidorus to make out the pair of them as they shouldered their way to a table at the far side of the room. Pushing past *clientis* clients and *servi* waiters alike. The spy was in action at once, running down the steps with Ferrata at one shoulder and Quintus at the other in a tight arrowhead formation. It took the three of them a little longer to cross the room than the two men they were following. Artemidorus and his men did not shoulder the other clients, and the men and women serving them, so rudely out of the way. They did not push past, swagger by or stare down the quieter patrons. But they turned heads. And by the time they arrived at the inner table, almost every eye in the place was watching them. Except for those belonging to one or two preoccupied groups. And those of their two suspects, who were talking quietly to each other, apparently oblivious. Even when Artemidorus stopped, towering above them.

'Gaius Valerius Flaccus, I believe,' said Artemidorus. His tone icy.

'What's that to you?' sneered Flaccus, looking up.

'To me? Nothing. But it would have meant a lot to the young couple and their driver who you murdered as you stole their horses because you could not steal ours.'

83

Flaccus erupted, sending the table skittering back across the floor, reaching for the vacancy on his belt where his *gladius* should have hung. Finding instead the hand of his young companion on his forearm, restraining him. 'I am Marcus Fulvius Nobilitor,' the young man said quietly, his cultured tones carrying over the hush. Clearly trained by a master of elocution. Planning on a swift ascent of the *cursus honorum* ladder to political power. 'Can you prove this ridiculous accusation?'

'We found the horses you abandoned beside the carriage you rolled off the *Via Appia*. In which were the bodies of the couple you stabbed. With the *gladius* you are reaching for even now. Forgetting, in your anger, that you are forbidden to carry it within the city walls.' Artemidorus continued to speak to Flaccus, ignoring Nobilitor for the moment.

'But can you prove it?' insisted the young patrician, sounding unsettlingly like Cicero.

'My companion here saw as much as I did,' said Artemidorus, stretching the truth.

'So. It's your word against ours. Two against two. A couple of common soldiers' words against an *eques* Roman knight and a *patricus* patrician with an ancient name.' Nobilitor laughed and shook his head, dismissing the three men.

'Two honest Roman soldiers against a murderous horse thief and his supercilious accomplice,' answered Artemidorus. His voice carrying as far as Nobilitor's. And trembling with passion. Ringing with truth.

Flaccus lost his temper then. Even more quickly than Artemidorus had calculated that he would. He threw aside the table and the stunned Nobilitor along with it, launching himself straight at the centurion. Who stepped aside and let the enraged man barge past him. The three companions closed ranks behind Flaccus, presenting a solid wall as he swung round, knocking over two more tables and spraying water, wine and food over everyone nearby.

'Shall we take this outside, Gaius Valerius?' suggested Artemidorus, calmly. His voice steady. His tone reasonable.

'So you and your companions can dispose of me together, three against one?' snarled Flaccus. 'I think not!' He launched himself at Artemidorus again, knocking over yet another table as he did so. Spilling an *amphora* of wine and a jug of water over the three men who were sitting at it. Locked in quiet conversation. Apparently unaware of the events unfolding around them. Until now. They leaped up as though they were one person. Stepped back, shoulder to shoulder. A tight defensive unit, like the spy and his two companions.

Artemidorus froze. Stunned. As though the huge blow that Flaccus aimed at him had actually landed instead of whipping past his nose. He stepped back and, when Flaccus sprang forward swinging his fist in once again, the secret agent caught it in both hands and held the raging man still for just a moment as he spoke, his voice lowered but still carrying over the stunned silence. As he looked the young man standing in the middle of the wine-soaked trio straight in the eye.

'Centurion *Eques* Gaius Valerius Flaccus, may I introduce you to the man you have come searching for? Gaius Octavius Julius Caesar. Or, more properly, I believe, Gaius Julius Caesar Octavianus. And his companions Marcus Vipsanius Agrippa and Quintus Salvidienus Rufus.'

'What?' Flaccus was as stunned as Artemidorus. 'Is this true?' He pulled his fist free, stepped back and turned. Glared accusingly at the three men.

Who were, suddenly, the centre of attention. Everyone in the *atrium* seemed frozen, staring at them while they tried to comprehend what on earth was going on.

'May we discuss this outside, as you suggested?' said the young man Artemidorus had called Gaius Julius Caesar Octavianus. He turned decisively and walked towards the steps leading up to the *vestibulum* and out into the forum. Flaccus stood, as though he had lost the power of movement. He did not object when Artemidorus pushed his shoulder gently, simply swung round and followed on almost mindlessly. Artemidorus looked back at Nobilitor, who had actually been knocked to the floor by his raging companion. The patrician picked himself up, dusted himself down, straightened his clothing and began to catch up with the little group as they moved towards the door. Artemidorus followed Flaccus up the steps across the short vestibule and out into the forum.

The three young men moved to one side, standing in a shadow. Flaccus crossed to stand in front of them and Artemidorus stayed close with Ferrata and Quintus at his shoulders. Nobilitor limped out after them, his face thunderous. Artemidorus couldn't even begin to calculate the number of things that had happened recently which might have upset the supercilious patrician. But he reckoned that a good deal of his wrath would be aimed at Flaccus.

Then thoughts about Balbus' emissaries were suddenly thrust to the back of his mind. For he was being addressed directly.

'How did you recognise me?' Octavius' voice was calm. Gentle. But there was something in his tone that marked him as a natural leader. A confidence that he was equal to any situation. That he would be heeded. And obeyed without question. He stepped towards Artemidorus, bringing his face into the light of the lamp above the door. He had Caesar's broad forehead with an unruly fringe of thick hair falling forward above it. The eyes beneath delicately curved, slightly overhanging, brows were large, deep, burning with intelligence. Under the wide cheekbones capped with neat ears, the jaw fell away to a pointed chin. Which avoided weakness because it thrust forward into a slight cleft. He had Caesar's nose. And Caesar's mouth. Artemidorus thought, *I would have known you anywhere, Gaius Julius Caesar Octavianus*. 'I saw you in Spain, Caesar,' he answered. 'When you were with your adoptive father.'

If Octavius was surprised at being addressed by his new title, he did not show it. 'You were at Munda?' he asked.

'I was in Spain,' repeated Artemidorus. 'I saw you there.' He did not add that he had been the boy's secret guardian, ensuring – albeit almost invisibly – that he crossed the war-torn country safely and reached Caesar's side alive.

Octavius looked at his companions. 'And you have been sent to greet me,' he observed. 'By whom?'

Artemidorus opened his mouth to answer. But several things happened in rapid succession before he could form the words.

Flaccus thrust himself forward, arrogantly taking Artemidorus' place, saying, 'I have been sent by Lucius Cornelius Balbus with my companion Marcus Fulvius Nobilitor…'

Somewhere in the distance, Hercules bellowed, 'Septem, look out! *Hey you…*'

And, with a sound like that of an angry hornet, a short, black, arrow-shaft whizzed through the space Artemidorus' head had occupied an instant before. Slammed into Flaccus' head, which had taken its place. Piercing it completely. Wedging itself from one temple to the other. And smashing him onto the ground at Caesar Octavianus' feet.

'Well,' observed Ferrata. 'Now we know exactly what he's got on his mind…'

'Don't just stand there spouting jokes,' snapped Artemidorus, the battle-hardened centurion of the VIIth. 'Inside. Everybody. NOW!'

IV

Aedile magistrate Lucius Claudius Siculus was not a happy man. Artemidorus could tell by the still-damp blotches down the considerable front of his robes that he had been summoned in the midst of a truly epic *cena*. The stains were of wine, *garum* and various other sauces, enlivened, if the sharp-eyed spy was right, with morsels of unctuous eel, dark duck and pallid mutton. Olives, egg yolks and pomegranate, all still brightly coloured. Artemidorus' attention had been gripped by these spots and speckles because they were very like the ones on Nobilitor's white tunic. Only those were a uniform pinkish red. And had come from Flaccus' head rather than from Lucius Siculus' table.

The unhappy law officer had no idea who the men he was questioning about the murder of Gaius Valerius Flaccus actually were. Because no one had told the *vigiles* constables anything other than that the dead man had been shot with an arrow fired by someone who had escaped into the night. Hercules had described the assassin to them. A tall shape clad in a colourless cloak, carrying a bow with a long central section. Down which a shorter, more powerful arrow or bolt could be fired. With astonishing range and unsettling accuracy. Making Artemidorus certain that it was the same *interfector* assassin who tried to kill him earlier. A fact he had not yet disclosed. Certainly, whoever it was had used the same weapon. He and Quintus agreed on that. Hercules had seen the figure outlined against the evening sky, taking aim from a roof overlooking the forum. And had seen it vanish into the shadows. Before the *vigiles* had been summoned.

As far as the law in Capua was concerned, this was a party of friends who had been drinking in a *hospitium* when a slight unpleasantness had arisen, calling them out into the street. Where a person or persons unknown had killed one of them. Perhaps aiming for him. Perhaps aiming for one of the others. An unknown person with impenetrable motives. Who seemed to have disappeared almost magically into the night. They carried the body, escorted by the friends and witnesses, to one of the rooms attached to the Temple of Diana and sent for their boss.

'Certainly,' said the *aedile* now, his jowls quivering with insight, 'this atrocity must have been committed from some distance. A rooftop did you say? I cannot conceive of someone standing beside the deceased and driving this monstrous thing through his head. And even if I could, I doubt anyone would have the strength to push it right through from one side to the other side like that.' He

87

shuddered, his whole body shaking like a quince jelly. 'And all of you were gathered around him when it happened. Even the large slave who saw so much – Hercules is it? – was close by when the murder occurred. By my reasoning, therefore, you must all be innocent of this act…'

'Unless one of us hired the assassin,' Artemidorus observed. 'But we will only discover the truth of that idea when we get to talk to him.'

'My men are scouring the area at the moment and if they find any trace of this murderous monster they will alert me,' nodded the *aedile*. 'And I will alert you. In the meantime, you may return to the *hospitium* while I look further into the business. I would be grateful if you could warn me before you leave Capua.'

'We had not yet decided where to stay for the night, sir,' said Octavius, in his most modestly youthful tones. 'Would you be kind enough to recommend somewhere to us?'

'Well, the best places are expensive…'

'Expense is no object,' snapped Nobilitor. 'This young man is…'

'…is with me,' interrupted Artemidorus, well aware that Octavius would probably prefer anonymity. For the time being at least. 'I am Centurion Iacomus Artemidorus, Seventh Legion, on assignment for Co-consul and General Mark Antony. I have his letter of commission if you wish to see it.'

'No, no. That will not be necessary. Well, then, the *hospitium* where your friend died is among the best, but my personal preference is for…'

*

'His brother probably owns it,' observed Ferrata, sometime later, studying the frontage of the *hospitium* that *aedile* Siculus had recommended. Not in the least intimidated by the company he was keeping.

But to be fair, thought Artemidorus, this place looked even nicer than the one they had just left. And, unless news travelled with supernatural speed in Capua, they would be anonymous here. For the time being. That certainly did seem to be what young Julius Caesar Octavianus wanted. For the moment.

The six of them trooped in as Hercules and Quintus went to see to the stabling of their horses; the recovery of their saddlebags. Even Nobilitor's as he was part of the group now. The *aedile's* men had taken all of Flaccus' belongings as part of their investigation. In the meantime, the six men received a warm welcome from the innkeeper's wife. Busy though the town was, she said, there were plenty of rooms, a bath, and a delicious *cena* on offer.

'We need to talk,' said Octavius as she bustled off to prepare their rooms. His cool gaze swept over Artemidorus and the still-shaken Nobilitor.

'Table or *tepidarium*?' asked Artemidorus. When Octavius hesitated, he enlarged. 'Where we are least likely to be overheard. The bar or the bath?'

'I certainly need a bath,' said Nobilitor. 'I stink of horse. And I believe I have a certain quantity of Gaius Valerius' brains on me. A bath is only the beginning. I will have to go through a full ritual cleansing as soon as I get home! Brains!' He shuddered.

'Must be a relief to know that he had any,' said Ferrata, bracingly.

Only the fact that Nobilitor was still so deeply shaken saved him.

'Caesar?' asked Artemidorus.

'Bath first,' decided the young man. 'We all need to relax.' He glanced at Agrippa and Rufus, both of whom nodded agreement. 'I think we have a great deal to discuss if what you have said is true. That you...' he looked at the pale, blood-spattered patrician, '...come from Lucius Cornelius Balbus. And *you*, Centurion, and your tactless friend come from Mark Antony.'

'Whether,' added Agrippa, 'either of you has any idea who killed Flaccus. Or which of us that nasty-looking bolt was actually aimed at.'

ii

Marcus Vipsanius Agrippa had a square, fleshy face which looked almost petulant at rest, thought Artemidorus. He had overhanging brows, a pugilist's nose, a square jaw and a cleft chin. His right ear stuck out more than his left. His body matched his face. It was square. But muscular rather than fleshy. He looked like brawn rather than brain – an easy man to underestimate therefore. A mistake that Nobilitor seemed set on making. For he talked to young Caesar and his companions as though they had yet to assume the *toga virilis* of manhood. Caesar was difficult to read, so the spy could not work out whether he was amused or angered by this. The incisively observant Septem was certain, however, that the young Octavius was holding back a great deal of information. As he sounded out the men sent from Rome to greet him. Their motives and the motives of their masters.

Quintus Rufus was easier. He was simply enraged by the patrician's condescending manner and tone. Like Caesar Octavius, his face was narrow beneath a broad forehead. The most youthful-looking of the three. But his body, like his two companions', was muscular and hard. His hands covered in telltale calluses, similar to Artemidorus', Ferrata's, and Quintus'. Soldiers' bodies – though as yet unscarred. Soldiers' hands. Which contrasted with Nobilitor's body which was beginning to run to fat. And his hands which were as soft as a vestal's.

The five of them relaxed in the quiet end of a large, steaming *tepidarium*. Hercules was sorting out the baggage. Ferrata was testing the wine. Quintus was

89

guarding the door. With even more vigilance than usual. The *tepidarium* was as well-maintained as the rest of the *hospitium*. The water seemed clean and fresh. No yellow currents or little brown logs afloat which made some of the country baths the spy had experienced less than pleasant. And the whole place smelt faintly of lemons.

'Lucius Cornelius Balbus sent the unfortunate Flaccus and I to guard and guide you to him.' Nobilitor looked down his nose at Octavius. An unfortunate habit, thought Septem; perhaps he had problems with his eyesight. 'He supposed you would not wish a great fuss to be made – or he would have sent more. And had it even occurred to him that there might be *sicarii* assassins abroad, he would have sent a cohort; perhaps a legion. Clearly he wishes us to assure you of his good offices. You may call upon him for any sum you wish within reason, for he holds a great deal of wealth that belonged to *Divus Julius* your late adoptive father. In his position as his secretary. In the meantime, he sends through me, sufficient funds to take you to him. All you have to do is ask. His only concern, of course, is that young men who find themselves in possession of seemingly limitless funds simply fritter them away in excess and indulgence. Take, for example, the young Mark Antony…'

'Talking of Antony,' said Caesar Octavius quietly, switching his attention to Artemidorus. 'What helpful advice and guidance does *he* send?'

'None, Caesar. He sent gifts that he believes you will like. A bag of coin that you may use as you want – he can be the soul of generosity, as you may know. A message that he hopes you will visit him when you are established in Rome. He, too, holds more money and numerous effects that belonged to your adoptive father. But, as Marcus Fulvius was doubtless about to observe, I doubt whether he would feel that he was in any position to offer guidance. A little advice, perhaps. A little wisdom learned through bitter experience.'

'Bitter experience indeed…' sneered Nobilitor.

'Of which he has apparently had a great deal,' nodded Octavius Caesar, amused.

'May I ask what your plans are, Caesar?' asked Artemidorus.

'Certainly. I and my two companions are travelling to Rome. I believe the people there will welcome me, as they did in Brundisium, though I must admit I landed further down the coast and approached the town with some caution.'

'And when you get to Rome, young man?' enquired Nobilitor, officiously. 'A little fun, I expect? Invest at least some of your wealth in tasting what the centre of the world has to offer. It is not for nothing that all roads lead there. The taverns. The fleshpots. The games. The races.' He was blissfully unaware of the icy looks all three of the young men aimed at him, for his eyes were closed in almost ecstatic contemplation of the things he was listing.

'When I get to Rome,' said Gaius Julius Caesar Octavianus, his tone so formal and icy that he almost chilled the bath, 'I will invest every denarius I can get my hands on in building an army to avenge my father *Divus Julius*!'

*

Sometime later, all of them were gathered round a large table in a private *cubiculim* room just off the *hospitium's* main *atrium*. Caesar Octavius' simply stated objective of avenging his adoptive father seemed to have robbed Nobilitor of much of his arrogant decisiveness. Though, thought Artemidorus, the sudden death of his companion must also have shaken him deeply. But in the final analysis, the soldier and spy simply saw his opponent's weakness as a potential advantage. Whatever Basilus had in mind for Caesar Octavius and his friends, Antony's needs seemed greater. Especially as the young man's stated objectives chimed so perfectly with the general's.

The only problems the spy could see were that Balbus had not yet contacted Antony – so their plans might turn out to be different. Especially as Antony had taken control of a great deal of Caesar's personal fortune. Something Balbus, as the dead consul's secretary, was likely to deplore. Also Antony's plan of revenge against Caesar's assassins was a long-term project dictated by more pressing political imperatives. Whereas Caesar Octavius' aims seemed pure, uncomplicated and immediate.

And, most importantly, perhaps, Antony in every conversation so far, seemed to view Octavius much as Nobilitor did. As an unschooled youth who could easily be twisted to his mentor's more important ends. An unschooled youth, as the insightful Fulvia had observed, who already had firm friends amongst the officers and men of the six legions in Dyrrhachium. He really began to wish that it had been Antony rather than Puella with whom he had enjoyed the conversation about catching more flies with honey than with vinegar.

iii

'So, Centurion Artemidorus,' said Caesar Octavius as the last of the *cena* was cleared away. 'You said that Antony had sent gifts of friendship.'

'I did, Caesar. If you will allow me, I will go and fetch them.'

'And I,' snapped Nobilitor, not to be outdone, 'Will go and fetch the money Lucius Balbus has sent for your use...'

'And *I*,' announced Ferrata, who had consumed as much wine as all the others put together, 'will go and fetch the bag of coin that General Antony sent to smooth your way home to Rome. And I bet it's bigger than Balbus'!'

91

'I will take the gifts and the coin, Ferrata,' said Artemidorus as they left the private room together. 'I want you to keep watch on Caesar's door. I'm pretty sure that the assassin who fired the bolt which killed Flaccus was the same one as tried to kill me. But there is no guarantee that the same killer means it was the same target.'

'But Quintus…'

'You know very well that Quintus will be guarding my door. Now you go and guard Caesar's.'

'Very well, Septem,' capitulated Ferrata with bad grace.

'And I'll send more food up. But no more wine. You'll guard nothing well if you're drunk or asleep.'

'As you command, Centurion. *Faciemus quod iubet…* We will do what is ordered and at every command we will be ready. Sober or not.'

Artemidorus returned a little later to find that Nobilitor was already seated, a sizeable bag in front of him, made fat by the coin it contained. 'You need only ask,' the patrician was saying, 'and I will disburse what you need. As Lucius Balbus has instructed.'

Artemidorus eased himself onto a seat and slid Antony's bag of gold *aureus* coins, stamped with Caesar's profile, onto the table. Saying nothing. Then he put the *gladius* beside them. And, beside the *gladius*, a *pugio* dagger. Which was almost a perfect match for the sword.

Caesar Octavius was too courteous to interrupt Nobilitor. But as soon as the self-important messenger had finished relaying Balbus' further advice and strictures, he turned to the silent centurion. 'So, Centurion Artemidorus,' he said. 'What have you brought from Antony?'

'This bag of gold. Which is yours to do with as you see fit.' The spy pushed the heavy bag across the table. Octavius glanced at Agrippa and Rufus. None of them moved or spoke. Nobilitor, misinterpreting their silence, allowed his lip to curl disdainfully. Antony's bag was smaller than Balbus.' But he had no way of knowing it was heavier – filled with generous Antony's golden *aureii* rather than the silver *denarii* Balbus had sent. Rufus reached for it and hefted it in his hand, eyebrows arched in surprise at the weight. Agrippa reached for the ornately sheathed *gladius*. Slid the steely iron blade out of the gilded black leather. 'A fine weapon,' he said. 'Numidian?'

'Possibly Punic,' said Artemidorus. 'Not Egyptian, apparently. You may wish to discuss the fine detail with Quintus.'

Agrippa smiled. Nodded. 'A worthy gift,' he decided. 'But the *pugio*? It almost matches. However…'

Artemidorus lifted the dagger, held it out to Octavian. 'It is the *pugio* that is Antony's gift,' he said. Slowly and formally. 'The *gladius* was sent because they almost make a matching pair. And because it is a fine weapon. But this *pugio* is something truly extraordinary.'

Octavius took it. Closed his fist round the sheath immediately below the cross guards. Slid the blade free. Sliced into the flesh between his index finger and thumb. Swore and started sucking the blood off his wounded skin.

'Sharp,' observed Agrippa, impressed.

'That,' said Artemidorus, looking Octavian straight in the eye, 'is one of a pair bought by the Lady Servilia Caepionis for her son Marcus Junius Brutus. A pair that reputedly came from the farthest fringes of Alexander's empire. The metal of the blades is unique, I am told. They hold an edge and a point better than any other I have ever seen. The blades are stronger and harder-wearing. Brutus had this one. Cassius had the other. This is one of the twenty two daggers that were used to kill Caesar. Its companion is another. Antony took it from your adoptive father's corpse after Brutus himself had used it. And he sends it to you as a token. An assurance that he, too, will not rest until every man who wielded a blade that day is dead.'

iv

Gaius Julius Caesar Octavianus rode into Rome one of *Divus Julius'* new weeks later, as the sun was beginning to wester above a city still excited by the recent *Ludi Megalenses* holiday games. Artemidorus and his squad had accompanied Octavius and his friends on their journey north from Capua. At first to protect him from the possibility that the mysterious assassin would try to strike again. But later to try and keep some distance between the young Caesar and the ecstatic crowds who came to greet and cheer him as he passed. It was clear enough how word of his arrival had become current in Brundisium and then in Capua. Just how information about his progress and his imminent arrival in one town after another spread, was little short of magical. But spread it did. And crowds came out to see him pass as though every day was the feast day of a major deity and a holiday in consequence.

Artemidorus rode up the *Via Appia* beside Octavius, his mind preoccupied with several problematic matters. The first concerned the late Gaius Valerius Flaccus. Who had murdered him and who had *he* murdered? The second concerned Antony. How would he react to the popularity and ability of a young man he dismissed as an easily manipulated boy and how would he react to the news that he had sent gifts – and gifts of such momentous weight and promise – to the young Caesar?

But the greatest problem occupying his mind was the enormity of the error both Antony and Balbus had made in underestimating Gaius Julius Caesar Octavianus and his friends. Even Fulvia's streetwise insight had fallen far short of the mark. For this was not a nervous boy coming to kiss the hands of his elders and betters, accept their grudging charity and follow their sage advice. This was a general leading an army. The reputation of one and the sheer size of the other seemed both to be growing exponentially. And had been doing so, apparently, long before they all met in Capua.

*

Probably fortunately, Ferrata had fallen asleep on guard at Octavian's door. For the young man and his two companions had no intention of sleeping in the *hospitium* on the night after Flaccus' murder. They crept past him in the darkness and left the city altogether. Though the gatekeepers swore no one had entered or left after dark. Whatever the truth of that, the fact was that the three young men had somewhere far better to rest than the *hospitium*. As Artemidorus and the others discovered early next morning. For, on the plain immediately south of Capua, there was a modest army encamped. The better part of a thousand strong, it was the heart of the legion Caesar Octavius was building to avenge his divine father.

The people of Brundisium, it seemed, had more than welcomed him, as he had modestly suggested. After sacrificing in the Temple of Venus *Genetrix* – as the progenitor of his father's family – Octavius had formally adopted his new name Gaius Julius Caesar Octavianus. The name, under the dictates of a smiling *Fortuna*, that Artemidorus had called him from the beginning. The loyal citizens of Brundisium – augmented by a great number of soldiers – had immediately turned over several million *sestertii* waiting in the town's depository to finance Caesar's planned invasion of Parthia. And then, again by the working of *Fortuna*, possibly at the prompting of Venus *Genetrix*, Caesar Octavius had met with a military detachment bringing the annual taxes to Rome from the Eastern Provinces. Which were immediately added to the wealth of Brundisium, as the soldiers added themselves to his burgeoning command. Making two treasure carts necessary. Not that the money was allowed to lie unused within them. As they passed through Campania south of Rome, every village along the way threw up more volunteers, mainly old soldiers. To whom the young Caesar promised a bounty of five hundred *denarii* each, with a down payment made at once.

There were several carts in the increasingly lengthy military train in fact. Those containing the treasure. Several others containing clothing, equipment and camp necessities. And one containing the mortal remains of Gaius Valerius Flaccus. On top of which lay his armour, his helmet and several other items from among his personal effects. All released along with the body by *Aedile* Lucius Claudius Siculus.

They made slow progress. Overnighting at Caesar Octavius' insistence – and to Nobilitor's disgust – in the tent beside his. Both of which stood at the heart of each evening's camp. As though they were an invading army on enemy soil. So there was no need to change horses. But when they came to the *mansio* where, on the way down the *Via Appia*, Artemidorus discovered the matched brown geldings that had pulled the dead couple's cart, he stopped and went to look for the stableman. The horses were still there. No one had come to claim them. He explained the situation to Octavius, and then he purchased them at once. And spread some of the load that had been carried by his little cohort's' three packhorses onto the backs of five.

So Caesar Octavius' growing army moved ever onwards. Finally coming past Campoverde where Quintus had bought the *gladius* and the *pugio* that Artemidorus had swapped for the one he took from Caesar's body. Giving the latter to Octavius. After Campoverde they arrived in the little town of Aprilia, some ten *miles* inland from Antium where Brutus and Cassius still lurked. And still two days' march from Rome itself.

The day was coming to a close and the procession, as usual, had been halted by the overwhelming numbers of locals. Most of them come to catch a glimpse of Caesar Octavius. Some just to pass the time with some welcome strangers. And some, old soldiers, to join the growing army. Veterans who, on campaign in distant provinces, had dreamed of owning a little farm in Italy and settling with a wife. To keep some livestock, grow a few vegetables, grow fat and raise a family. Who were now bored with domestic and agrarian life and panting to get back in the action. For five hundred *denarii* a man.

But in Aprilia, another sort of visitor arrived. A tall, elderly man in black mourning robes. White haired, erect, distinguished. Artemidorus first noticed him looking not at *Divus Julius Caesar's* adopted son and heir but the livestock. His interest piqued, Artemidorus crossed to the old man, his mind racing. There was something familiar about him. But the spy could not quite pin it down. 'Can I be of service, *dominus* sir?' he asked.

'Those brown horses,' said the stranger, his voice gentle but carrying. His tone patrician. His eyes chilly and his face bleak. 'The matched pair…'

95

Artemidorus knew then. Not that the logic was difficult to follow. The black clothes. The matched pair. The lost carriage. The dead youngsters. But, just to be certain he said, 'Would you follow me, sir?' and he led the old man to the closed cart with Flaccus' armour on top of it. With the bits and pieces found amongst his possessions piled beside it. Silently, the old man reached out and took a gold chain gently between his trembling fingers. Lifted it until the tiny gold figure of Juno, goddess of weddings, stood upright above the corpse of the man who had taken it from the murdered girl's dead neck. 'They were going to get married,' he said. 'He was taking her to Campoverde. To the market there. To buy gifts for the guests. As is traditional. They never came back.' He turned his fierce gaze on the secret agent. 'I have a son,' he said, his voice bitter. 'But he is away studying. And then he will join the army. She was the child of my heart. The promise of my old age.'

'The man responsible lies dead in this carriage, if that is any consolation, *dominus.*'

The old man straightened, his face setting like stone. 'It is none,' he said. 'But it is all I shall get, I suppose. Now, if you would be kind enough, take me to Octavius. I wish to talk to him and, perhaps to accompany him.' His mouth twisted bitterly. 'There is nothing to keep me here. Now.'

'Of course I will, sir. But may I know who you are so I may introduce you properly?' A man like this, he thought, should be surrounded by guards and clients. Probably preceded by *lictors*, calling his name and demanding safe passage.

'I am Quintus Pedius, the late Julius Caesar's cousin and closest living relative,' said the old man. 'A relative therefore of Octavius' himself. I wish to offer him everything left to me by Caesar in his will. And my help. And support in the Senate and on the streets of Rome.'

V

By the time they reached the city to which all roads in the empire led, the army behind them numbered nearly two thousand. And word had reached the city of Gaius Julius Caesar Octavianus' approach, so that thousands more flooded out of the Carmenta Gate. Along the *Via Appia*. The beggars, hucksters, farmers and stallholders were all pushed aside. Inundated by the tidal wave of citizens rushing out to see Caesar's heir. They flowed like naphtha amongst the tombs and the tall pine trees. Climbing on top of anything that would give a good view. They shouted their welcome and cheered with joy as he approached.

Artemidorus rode just behind him, his place at Octavius' side surrendered for the moment to Quintus Pedius. Who he knew now – though only by reputation.

They had never met before their conversations beside the horse pen. And Flaccus' bier. Pedius who wore, beneath his black *toga*, the armour in which he had led legions as general, *praetor*, and legate to Caesar. Which he had worn when Caesar awarded him a triumph for overcoming, at Compsa, Marcus Rufus and Titus Milo the rebels. For defeating Sextus, the last of Pompey's sons. Appointing him Proconsul. Before he retired from public life to mourn his wife, educate his son, see his daughter married and raise his grandchildren.

The old man's back was as straight as a *pilum* spear, thought the spy. A masterclass in how to handle heartbreak. He glanced around the cheering crowd suddenly, the hair on the back of his neck prickling. He associated heartbreak with Cyanea. And he associated her with the assassin who had missed him twice now. Who might well be taking advantage of the current situation to try for a third time. The third, being the first odd number. The first lucky number therefore, to superstitious Romans. But there was no sign of anyone in a long, dun-coloured, hooded cloak. No one with a lethal barrelled bow. Just Quintus close behind. And Ferrata behind Quintus with Hercules at his side.

But then, just as they approached the gate itself, as Caesar Octavius himself was entering the city, there came a communal gasp of wonder from every throat there. For a thin skim of cloud swept across the face of the afternoon sun, framing the silver-gilt disk with a halo coloured like a rainbow.

'It is a sign!' called someone. 'A sign! A sign! The gods themselves have blessed him! Long live Caesar! Long live Gaius Julius Caesar Octavianus!'

And the crowd went wild.

V

'See him *now*?' snarled Antony. 'No of course I won't see him now!'

'It would only add to his inflated opinion of himself if my Lord answered his demands the very instant that they were made,' added Fulvia tartly. 'I mean, who *is* he? Really?'

'He's a boy with no experience,' answered Antony before Artemidorus could speak. 'A sickly child, scarcely bearded. With ideas far above his station. Because he has inherited a name. A name and nothing more!'

'I could call myself Alexander,' emphasised Fulvia. 'But it wouldn't make me ruler of the world!' She gave a short, ugly laugh.

The three of them were in the *atrium* of Antony's villa. The atmosphere was unusually tense. Something of the excitement outside seemed to have seeped into the villa and then turned sour. The shouting and the cheering whispered on the restless breeze like the threat of distant thunder.

The general and his wife were pacing almost apprehensively. The soldier stood at ease, his helmet beneath his right arm. His jaw set. His eyes narrow. The scar above his left eye pulling the dark wing of his brow upwards. Giving his set face a quizzical look. Which actually matched his inner thoughts. Disturbed that he had fulfilled his orders and brought Caesar Octavius directly to Antony, only to find the general's door locked against him. Shocked to see these usually insightful people making such an error of judgement. But still unable to find a way of convincing them that Caesar Octavius was a force to be reckoned with. That even the name *Caesar* seemed more powerful than either Antony or Fulvia imagined. That a man called Caesar was at least deserving of courtesy. Understanding that he had, in fact, inherited a great deal more than just a name. And doing all this immediately. Before their time ran out.

'He's brought three thousand men with him, General. My Lady,' he tried one last time. 'They're making camp on the Field of Mars now. While he is standing waiting right outside your door. Eager to make contact. To start planning an alliance to oppose the so-called *Libertores*. And when his men call him Caesar they mean it,' he persisted. 'They don't see a sickly boy. They see *Divus Julius* reborn.'

Artemidorus' concern was growing into a dull certainty that he was losing this argument. Antony and his wife were relentlessly joining the numbers of people all too willing to underestimate Caesar Octavius without actually having got to know him. 'He has two large wagons loaded with gold – taxes and gifts,' he persisted. 'And you know that money is power. He's now promised his followers five thousand *sestercii* each if they stay loyal. They believe him. Many of them are *Divus Julius Caesar's* veterans. Tried and tested. Armed and ready to follow him anywhere. Against anyone he proscribes. He has contacts with Lucius Cornelius Balbus – who has yet more of Caesar's gold. And he has brought Caesar's relative, the General and *Triumphator* Quintus Pedius along with him. Who has promised not only his support but the money Caesar left him in his will. And Quintus Pedius says the other beneficiary Lucius Pinarius Scarpus is willing to do the same!'

He drew an unsteady breath. Persisted in the face of the ill-disguised hostility of his temperamental general and his wife. 'Caesar Octavius may still be young but he is by no means the callow youth who accompanied the Divine Julius in Spain and went to Apollonia to study. He has grown in power and standing, General. And you need to understand this fact whether you like it or not. Your aims are the same as his, though his plans involve more direct action. The moment he arrived in Rome he came to see you, expecting a welcome and some sort of agreement between you. And he has been waiting outside your door for too long already. You must invite him in. Talk to him. Better to be friends than enemies.'

'This is ridiculous!' snapped Antony. 'If I didn't know you better, Septem, I'd suspect that some of the gold the boy has stolen has found its way into your purse!'

'As you say, General. You know me better than to suspect that. And, you may recall, that I am bringing him to you and suggesting that you see him under direct orders that you issued to me yourself.' The soldier fought to keep the anger out of his voice. Not very successfully.

'I, however, do not know you *better than that*!' snapped Fulvia. 'No matter what you think your orders were you have exceeded your authority! You are dismissed Centurion!'

Artemidorus waited a heartbeat until Antony, frowning, nodded. He slammed to attention. '*Faciemus quod iubet...* We will do what is ordered and at every command we will be ready,' he grated. Then he turned on his heel, putting his headgear back in place, and marched out of the *atrium*.

On his way along the *vestibulum* entrance hall, he met Enobarbus who had just entered. 'I think Antony is making a bad mistake, Tribune,' he said in a half-whisper, pausing, apparently to lace his cheek flaps together under his chin. 'You must convince him to see Caesar Octavius. Treat him with some respect.'

99

'I'll do what I can,' said Enobarbus as he strode past. 'But I wouldn't wager on my success. Particularly as the boy seems to have run out of patience with all this hanging around.'

When the secret agent stepped into the street outside Antony's villa he was struck at once by how quiet it was. When he entered to report to Antony, the broad *via* roadway had been crowded with boisterous supporters all grouped round Caesar ~~Octavian~~ Octavius, Agrippa and Rufus. They were all gone now. Frowning, he ran down the empty roadway until he reached the Temple of Tellus which stood nearby. And there, in the middle distance, he saw Octavius and his two friends walking swiftly at the side of Marcus Fulvius Nobilitor. On their way, no doubt, to see what sort of welcome Lucius Balbus would offer them.

ii

Some hours later, Artemidorus was seated in the tent he shared with the other centurions of the Seventh Legion's First Cohort. Which he used as an office when they were out on duty. Bitterly nursing a sense of failure to which he was unaccustomed. Like a general who has lost a battle for the first time. He heard the approach of Tribune Enobarbus by the sound made by the legionaries he passed. As they crashed to attention, one after another, barking his name and rank. The noise growing louder and louder.

The spy knew the news his tribune was bringing was unlikely to be good. Only something out of the ordinary would have brought Enobarbus here in person. He was rising warily to his feet, therefore, when the tribune raised the tent flap and stooped to enter. The movement of his head and shoulders made a leather bag swing clear of his hip. 'So, Tribune,' he said grimly. 'I see one of us at least has joined the general's *speculator* courier service. I wonder which it is?'

'He wants you out of the city for a while Septem,' said Enobarbus, standing erect and shrugging the bag off his shoulder.

'*He* does?' Artemidorus raised one eyebrow quizzically. The left one, which was already pulled higher than the right by the scar on his forehead. The effect was enough to make Enobarbus shake his head ruefully.

'You're right. *She* does. But the general's happy to give you something worthwhile to do while you're away.'

'Carrying letters?'

'Carrying very much more than letters, Septem. Looking like a *speculator* military courier perhaps, but using that as a cover, for *speculators* can also be spies, can they not?. Do you still have the pass he gave you directing anyone who read it to do anything in their power to help you?'

'I have.'

'Good. You may need it. But use it sparingly.'

'That goes without saying if I'm working undercover. My name and rank are written in the first line. And my *contubernium*? My nest of spies?'

'I'm keeping them here,' said the tribune. 'I have work for them to do. But you can take one companion. To watch your back.'

'It will need watching, will it?'

'From what you've told me about the stranger with the *sôlênarion* bow, Septem, I'd say it certainly does. And so do you. Back, front and sides.'

'In that case, I'll take Quintus if you can spare him.'

'He's the one I can spare most easily,' admitted Enobarbus. 'He's the only one I can't use for undercover work. It's all too obvious what he is. He'll never change. And at the moment I have no mission for a tough, experienced, bloody-minded, occasionally insubordinate *triarius*.'

'But he might make the perfect companion for a courier,' mused Artemidorus. 'Ex-legionary. Bodyguard. Ten a *sestercius*. Unremarkable. As good as a gladiator. Better, in fact...'

'Just so! Right. That's settled then. Let's sit down and I'll brief you with the general's thoughts and plans...'

iii

The bireme was called *Aurora*. She was a handy trading vessel. The crew, including the forty-eight oarsmen seated in two twelve-line decks, the twelve replacement oarsmen, ten deckhands and the *militari* officers who crewed her, were all freedmen. Like Lucius their *praefectus* captain. Earning varying quantities of the profits garnered from voyaging mainly in the Tyrrhenian Sea up and down the coast between Massalia and Neapolis. Occasionally venturing across the Bay under Vesuvio to Pompeii, as captain Lucius planned to do on this occasion. But rarely heading further south than that.

Aurora's home port was Ostia at the mouth of the Tiber. And that was where Artemidorus and Quintus joined her as she began a trading voyage southward. Promising to come to port in Antium as well as Neapolis and Pompeii. Where many of the letters in Antony's pouch were due to be delivered. And many of the messages passed on by Enobarbus during the briefing, were due to be discussed. The vessel was laden with Celtic cloth and jewellery as well as stone and other building materials – mostly wood from the forests in the north. The cloth and jewellery were destined for the markets inland behind Antium. The building materials were destined further south – Neapolis, Herculaneum and Pompeii, like Rome itself, were burgeoning. And in Pompeii they planned to pick up more building materials – mostly marble from the regions further south – that would be

101

transported back to Rome. Together with anything else they could purchase and stow. Lucius was hopeful for some southern wines from the vines growing on the rich slopes of Vesuvio that he would take back on his way up to Massalia.

The journey was among the first of the season, for the weather was only just becoming reliable enough to make commercial voyages possible. Even so, Captain Lucius Silus and his pilot Otho kept their vessel within sight of the shore at all times. Otho the pilot standing at the massive helmsman's Herculean shoulder counting off the bays and estuaries where they could run for cover if the weather turned foul on them.

Like most Romans, Quintus hated the sea. And with good reason. For, even in a near calm, he was uncontrollably seasick. 'If he offers any more sacrifices to Neptune and Poseidon,' observed Lucius Silus as he watched Quintus heaving over the side, 'he'll assure us of the calmest and most successful voyage ever.'

Artemidorus grunted his agreement, unwilling to be amused by his friend's distress. Or the wry humour of such a new acquaintance. He himself loved ships and sailing. He had spent some of his youth and young manhood aboard vessels ranging from Cilician pirate *liburnian* raiding galleys to the massive *quinquiremes* with their five banks of oars that Pompey sent to stamp piracy out in the days when he and Caesar had been friends. Not to mention the naval actions in which he had been involved as part of the civil wars that started when the two of them fell out.

The breeze was gentle but persistent and from the north – as usual this time of year. So the labours of the oarsmen were soon replaced by the full belly of the big square-rigged sail. With its fanciful depiction of the rising sun as a beautiful goddess. And even though the oarsmen were able to take a welcome rest from their labours, *Aurora* was making as good time as a horse might, moving between a canter and a gallop. But her route was directly from port to port to port without the need to follow roads. Even ones as straight as the *Via Appia*. And, of course, courtesy of the system of *faros* lighthouses spreading southward along the coast, she would continue running at this speed through the night as well as the day. Allowing for rest periods for the oarsmen when they began to row again.

But the distance between Ostia and Antium was little more than thirty Roman military *miles*. And even staying in sight of the coast, *Aurora's* course was as straight as any Roman road. Having sailed with the morning tide soon after *jentaculum* breakfast, *Aurora* should be docked and unloading soon after *prandium* lunch. Which would put Artemidorus and Quintus – if he recovered in time – at their first destination by the early afternoon.

Artemidorus and Quintus ran ashore as soon as the ship came into harbour and the work of unloading her began. The legionary recovering with astonishing rapidity the moment he stood on solid ground. Their destination sat on a clifftop overlooking the bay. They could have walked with little trouble – but the spy wished to arrive with the pomp that might be expected of Antony's personal emissary. And so they hired a pair of showy horses and rode. They clattered up the paved approach to the villa, therefore, and slid to the ground at the foot of a wide flight of marble steps as an *ostiarius* doorkeeper came out of the porticoed entrance to greet them and discover their business. Followed by a couple of house slaves who ran forward to take their mounts.

'I have come directly from Consul and General Mark Antony,' said Artemidorus with all the impatient swagger to be expected of the character he played at Trebonius' villa. 'I bring letters and messages by word of mouth for the two senators and senior judges staying here. Your master *Praetor Peregrinus* Gaius Cassius Longinus and his guest *Praetor Urbanus* Marcus Junius Brutus.'

'They are both at home,' said the *ostiarius*, bowing. 'Please accompany me and wait in the *atrium* while I advise them of your arrival and find out if they will see you.'

'They'd better,' whispered Artemidorus under his breath to Quintus as they strode into the *vestibulum*. 'Unless they want to start a war at once.'

iv

Unlike Caesar Octavius dancing attendance on Antony, Artemidorus and Quintus were not kept waiting at all. Quite the reverse. No sooner had Cassius' *ostiarius* doorkeeper whispered to the *atriensis* major-domo and the latter vanished into an adjoining room, than Cassius and Brutus both appeared. Their wives Tertulla and Portia beside them. And, indeed, Brutus and Tertulla's mother, Caesar's still-lovely ex-mistress Servilia.

Servilia's presence set off a chain of association in the spy's mind. One that took him straight back to the conversation Antony had had with Marcus Tuillius Cicero about Caesar's dying words. Here were Brutus and his mother. What had become of the legal case turning upon the possibility that Caesar himself was Brutus' father?

But then his thoughts were interrupted by the arrival of another unexpected guest. Another soldier and senator. Pontius Aquila. The solid-bodied, square-faced, senator who had taken offence when Caesar had divided up his estate nearby, giving some of it to Servilia. And then mocked him for his refusal to stand during a triumph. He had never forgiven the theft or the humiliation. And was, therefore, one of the most fervent of the assassins. He glowered at Antony's messengers now from beneath one long, thick eyebrow, as though adding them to the list of men he wished to murder next.

Artemidorus frowned as he met Aquila's hostile gaze. But not through any emotion other than surprise. Aquila was supposed to be with Decimus Albinus up in Cisalpine Gaul. His visit here must be fleeting. And probably political in nature; bringing messages from one element of the divided *Libertores* to another.

Cassius, his relatives and guests had recently risen from a late lunch in the *triclinium* dining room, by the look of things. Cassius stopped now, and stared, narrow-eyed at Artemidorus. His expression a match for Pontius Aquila's. 'Do I know you?' he snapped.

'I am a member of Consul and General Mark Antony's staff,' answered Artemidorus easily. 'You may well have seen me.'

'Perhaps that's it.' Cassius didn't sound convinced. Nor should he, thought Artemidorus. For he and Cassius had stood face to face before. During the hours after Caesar's murder. But his closest dealings with the leaders of the so-called *Libertores* had been from behind another careful disguise. In that case, a thick, red, bushy beard. From beneath a freedman's leather cap. His face occasionally further covered by the metal mask of a Samnite's gladiatorial helmet. As he spied on the murderers in the Temple of Jupiter during the hours after their crime. And occasionally carried messages between them, Cicero and Antony. He had worked undercover in Brutus' Roman villa as well. Not to mention kidnapping Brutus' favourite body-slave the lovely Puella. But the family had been far too important – and preoccupied – to pay a mere workman much attention.

'Come,' snapped Cassius and turned. He led the family group, the messenger and his fully armed bodyguard through the *tablinum* office area and into the *peristyle*. Whose far wall had been removed so that the garden opened onto a veranda. Floored and balustraded with the sort of white marble the *Aurora* was due to bring north from Neapolis and Pompeii. While the family took their ease on cushion-covered benches, Artemidorus took Antony's letters out of his bag. Then he passed them into the imperiously raised hands of Cassius and Brutus, who broke the seals. Unrolled the papyrus sheets and more or less laboriously read the beautiful script written by Antony's secretary.

As they did this, the two soldiers stood at attention while the women and Pontius Aquila talked quietly. Their conversation informing the spy that they had enjoyed a light lunch. That they were planning on bathing later. And that they were all due to visit Aquila's villa, where Servilia was currently staying, later still, for a formal *cena* dinner. Servilia and Aquila clearly having come to some sort of accommodation over Caesar's gift of Aquila's estate to his long-time lover. While his ears were busy, Artemidorus let his gaze wander apparently innocently over the gathering frowns on the faces of Brutus and Cassius. Then out over the edge of the balustrade to the blue calm of the sea. Out of the corner of his eye he could just see the dock where *Aurora* was still being unloaded.

'You know what is in these letters?' demanded Cassius abruptly. His tone silencing the social chit-chat.

'The basis, *Praetor*. Not the details.'

'Antony says in my letter that you have further suggestions to add, which he does not wish to commit to paper at this time.'

'Says that in mine, too,' added Brutus.

The frowns on both men's faces spread to those of their wives. Portia, noted Artemidorus, still looked pale and sickly. Caesar's murder had been almost as hard on her as it had been on the victim.

'The general suggests that it is not yet time for you to consider returning to Rome...' Artemidorus began.

'*But...*' spat Brutus at once.

'Even though you both still hold the posts of *Praetor* Senior Justice,' he persisted. 'And therefore have many duties and responsibilities. Not least the *Ludi Cerialis* games which Tribune Critoinius is overseeing. And the *Ludi Apollonaris* Apollo's Games for which you are personally responsible Lord Brutus, as *Praetor Urbanus* Senior Law Officer in the city. But which Lord Antony is pleased to inform you his brother Gaius will organise if it is still too dangerous for you to return to the capital in person.'

Brutus and Cassius will be calculating on giving the most magnificent games they can, Enobarbus had briefed his secret agent on Antony's behalf. *And using them to gain the favour of the* plebs. *But the general thinks he can outwit them.*

'It is still some weeks to the Games of Apollo,' said Cassius, as Brutus sat, white-faced with shock and outrage; almost as pale as his sickly wife. 'We will have plenty of time to discuss the general's generous offer. But there are matters of more immediate importance here...'

'Crete!' snapped Brutus. 'He says they're offering me Crete next year. After all the money I have invested in the games – which I won't apparently be presenting in person – he says they're offering me Crete next year! I'll never come close to recouping my losses there. I need Syria! Macedonia!'

'I seem to have a choice,' added Cassius drily. 'Sicily or Cyrene. Pirates or desert. Cyrene! They might as well have offered me Carthage! There's nothing there but dust.'

'No legions with either governorship! That's the point,' said Brutus angrily. 'Precious little tax revenue and no legions.'

'My general wondered whether you might like a little freedom to begin exploring your new responsibilities,' said Artemidorus gently. 'Though you cannot undertake them officially until next *Januarius*, of course.

'General Antony has convinced the Senate that now might be the perfect opportunity to offer you the post of Corn Commissioners for Asia,' he continued smoothly. 'He suggests that these appointments might well suit you on several levels. Firstly, they are lucrative. Overseeing the shipment of grain from the East offers all sorts of profitable opportunities to experienced administrators such as yourselves.' His gaze lingered apparently innocently on Brutus who was infamous for the rapacity of his administrations and governorships. 'Also the appointment as commissioners, which you could take up at once if you so decide, would automatically make you free to travel out of Italy. With your families and households, should you choose to take them. Without further permission or interference. And at the Senate's expense...'

'Very generous, I'm sure,' sneered Cassius. 'Antony's back is to the wall. He's running out of money himself. In spite of the speed with which I hear he's forging documents in Caesar's name and selling posts or taking bribes. Going through the treasury as fast as he went through the wines in Pompey's cellar when he moved into Pompey's villa.' He gave a dry, angry laugh. 'The Senate is against him. At least Cicero's letters say so. And they won't turn a blind eye to his barefaced corruption for much longer. Moreover, they've formally appointed Decimus Albinus as Governor of Cisalpine Gaul – with three legions – and he's already taken up the post I understand. Not even Antony could stop that! So Antony dare not leave Rome for any length of time in case our friend and ally Albinus steals it out from under him in his absence. Therefore, of course he wants us out of the way as soon as possible.'

'And,' added Brutus, 'there's the question of young Octavius. I hear he's in Italy. What effect will he have on Antony and his plans I wonder?'

'At the moment, Lord *Praetor*, young Caesar Octavius is putting together an army as quickly as he can. So that he can come after the men who murdered his adoptive father,' said Artemidorus with some relish. 'He plans to proscribe and execute them all.'

'An army!' Cassius shook his head with a patronising laugh as though he had only heard the beginning of Artemidorus' speech. 'And he's a sickly boy, what, eighteen years old?' Everyone on the airy balcony laughed, the sound of their

106

merriment blending with the screaming of the gulls riding the air currents nearby. Only Artemidorus and Quintus remained straight-faced and silent.

'So,' said Artemidorus quietly as the patrician mirth died down. 'What shall I tell Lord Antony?'

'That we thank him for his letters and his generous offers,' said Cassius smoothly. 'And that we require a little more time to think them over and to discuss them. Amongst ourselves. And with our friends.'

V

Aurora came into the narrows between the barren island of Procida and the huge military port of Misenum on the mainland just before sunset. The north wind had strengthened as she left Antium and blew her southwards with impressive rapidity. She slid into the Bay of Neapolis as darkness fell. The rowers eased her towards the city dock while the deckhands furled the sail and got ready to heave the cargo out of the hold.

'You have a choice,' announced Lucius Silus. 'You can either eat with the crew and sleep aboard at no extra charge, or I can recommend a *hospitium* in Neapolis where the wine is good and the beds are soft.'

'And the women are clean,' added Otho knowledgably. 'For the most part.' The pilot clearly knew about more than the local seaways, thought Artemidorus with an inward smile. Then he met Quintus' agonised stare.

'We'll go ashore,' he decided.

'Well, be back bright and early,' advised Lucius. 'It's not far to Pompeii. Ten military *miles* at most but we'll be off down there as soon as wind and tide allow.'

'I tell you what,' said Artemidorus. 'Swing up our baggage as soon as we dock and recommend somewhere we can hire good horses. I think we'll leave you here after all.'

'You've paid for the full passage. But it's your money. What I'll do is this. We'll swing your baggage up then I'll send a couple of brawny crewmen with you to carry your stuff and guide you. Men who'll guarantee you a good deal with the locals...'

As it turned out, they got two solid oarsmen from the relief team. And Otho the pilot. The three crewmen guided them through the city streets as the moon began to rise, on the wane now, but still bright. 'I suppose you're going to try and make it to Pompeii tonight,' said Otho companionably.

'That's the plan.'

'Well, I can show you where to get the best horses to take you south from here. But I'd recommend that you eat here first. It can be a long trip by land. The coast's by no means an even sweep so the coast road gets unusually twisty. Then I can

107

recommend a good place to stay in Pompeii when you get there too. Cheap but clean – the *hospitium* and the girls. Well, it's a *lupanar* rather than a *hospitium*. But this place is useful to know about. You can stay the night if you need to. And as I say, it's reasonably priced. Which is unusual. Pompeii's an expensive town. Rich man's playground.'

'Yes?' said Quintus, more like his old self now he was back on dry land. 'Where is this cheap, clean brothel, then?'

'You'll find it at the crossroads two blocks east of the forum. Ask for Restituta. Tell her Big Otho sent you...'

*

Under the steady light of a low moon the two soldiers rode southward on mounts from the stable Otho recommended, Quintus leading a pack mule. They were full of a tasty *cena* of fish, olives and figs washed down with water from the city *hospitium's* own spring. It was drinkable, but contained a decided hint of sulphur. They pushed their mounts quite fast, for the road round the dormant volcano's foothills was well maintained and wide. Though, as Otho said, it twisted in and out in a most un-Roman fashion. Artemidorus calculated they must be adding almost a *mile* going side to side for every couple of *miles* they made southward. There were villages every now and then, the largest of them the little port of Herculaneum. Wayside establishments with welcoming torches ablaze. And a steady traffic, coming and going. As Otho observed, Pompeii was a rich man's playground and it was served as such. Still, it took the two men much of the night to cover on land a distance that seemed almost twice the distance *Aurora* would cover after the sacrifices in the dawn.

But as they finally rode through the outskirts of the town, the moon vanished behind a sinister wall of cloud that soon snuffed out the stars as well and hung low over mount *Vesuvio*. The wind swung round to the south and freshened, bringing a sprinkling of raindrops with a warm breeze whose gusts grew stronger and stronger. Pompeii had no walls. And, therefore, no gates. The road they were riding ran on south beyond the town. And another came in from the east that ran past this road and down to the docks. Where the two roads crossed, there was the forum. And the weary travellers turned east here and went two blocks, as Otho had advised. Artemidorus was glad to see a proper *hospitium* with stables attached just down the road from the *lupinaria* the pilot recommended. Which recommendation seemed, unexpectedly, to have caught the ascetic Stoic Quintus' imagination.

They went to the *hospitium* first. Stabled their horses and arranged a room. Otho's advice about eating had been good. The *culina* kitchen was long closed.

The bar was empty. The innkeeper who welcomed them had clearly been summoned from his bed. He was able to serve them wine, however, as their baggage was taken up to their room. Then Artemidorus dismissed the restless Quintus, and wearily followed the innkeeper upwards.

As he prepared for bed, the tired spy reassessed his plans. He had hoped to get out to Minucius Basilus' villa under cover of darkness and scout it out before delivering Antony's letter to Gaius Trebonius in the morning. But the length of the road and the unexpected turn in the weather had frustrated that plan. On the other hand, he thought, the change in the weather was likely to frustrate Lucius Silus' plans for *Aurora* too, for the vessel was unlikely to set sail straight into the teeth of a southerly storm. So, all in all, he had made the right decision in coming ashore – unless the intrepid captain made a really spectacular sacrifice to the gods and goddesses of sea and sky tomorrow. Something sufficiently powerful to make them change a gathering storm for more gentle northerly breezes. Artemidorus had reached this point in his thoughts when Quintus burst through the door. 'Come with me, Septem,' he said. 'I really think you will want to hear this…'

vi

The *lupinaria* brothel was a cut above the common run, thought Artemidorus. Though his experience of such places was limited. He had hardly ever found himself in a position where he needed to pay. But, as now, he occasionally accompanied friends and colleagues. To the reception area if rarely beyond. Satisfied with watching others make selection amongst the working she-wolves who sat or stood provocatively all around the walls. Offering an apparent infinity of colour, size, strength, specialisation and experience. Promising an eternity – albeit a short, expensive one – of unmatched ecstasy. Rarely, if ever, feeling the desire to indulge himself. But once or twice he had used the she-wolf inmates as a source of information rather than of satisfaction. As was the case tonight. Though he was the only man other than Quintus there – except for a couple of employees. A wiry male slave who fetched and carried for the girls. And a brawny giant of an ex-gladiator who looked vaguely familiar to Artemidorus. Who was clearly that most vital member of staff: the bouncer.

'This is Restituta,' said Quintus as he led her out. 'The woman Otho suggested I ask for.'

Restituta was a woman approaching middle years from a youth that had clearly been blessed with great beauty. Much of which remained. Unusually, given her profession. The wear and tear of her profession had not, apparently, touched her. Nor had the dread hand of disease. Her appearance now seemed enhanced rather than undermined by the silver in her raven black hair. The laugh lines around her

109

generous mouth and intelligent, quizzical eyes. And if her figure was tending towards the matronly, that only added to her consequence. It was clear she was in charge here – rather than being on offer. She was much as Artemidorus imagined Cleopatra might look like in twenty years or so. So, treating her much as he would have treated Cleopatra, Artemidorus bowed in formal greeting. The girls round the walls gasped and giggled. Restituta's ready smile widened. 'Let's go into my room,' she said. 'My girls can see me vanishing with two handsome soldiers. Which will do my reputation no end of good.' She leaned towards him, lowering her voice. 'Stagger a little on your way out as though you are utterly exhausted. Both of you!' She gave a throaty chuckle which reminded Artemidorus painfully of Cyanea.

But the room to which she led them was an office not a bedroom. And once inside, she grew more serious. 'Quintus says that you are looking for the villa belonging to Minucius Basilus,' she said. 'What is your business with him?'

'I am a messenger. My business is not with Minucius Basilus but with Gaius Trebonius, who is his guest, I understand. What is this to you?'

The last of the laughter drained from her face. 'It is an evil place,' she said simply. 'They do things there…'

'To your girls?' asked Artemidorus.

'Not to my girls. No. But sometimes to the young, inexperienced or desperate ones. And to the slaves he sometimes brings down here with him.'

'Is there no one local you can turn to? To stop him?' asked Quintus.

'Have you any idea how rich he is? He inherited millions. *Millions*. Together with the name and all the property. He owns the local *aedile* magistrate. Everyone of any power or authority south of Herculaneum. All in the power of his purse together. The watchkeepers never go near him. Or his villa. No one does. It's as though the place has been cursed by *strigae* witches. Or by the gods themselves. The villa is remote. At the top of a cliff; not high but steep and rocky. Near a gully that is deep, dark, and flooded at each full tide. Which empties into the bay as the tide falls. Sometimes bodies wash ashore and we all suspect they came from there. But even if they are linked to Basilus in some way, there is always an explanation. For the ones that count – the ones that aren't slaves. Slaves just get burned or buried and forgotten of course. As to the others, it's always the same. She fell down the cliff. Or into the gully. The fish got her. A vessel caught her in the harbour with its ram.' She paused for a moment. 'Though there have been no bodies recently. So maybe he's found another way of disposing of them.'

'Or,' hazarded Quintus, 'perhaps he's growing more controlled. More moderate…' Though he didn't really sound convinced.

'How is it that the household do not rise against him?' asked Artemidorus. 'Even slaves cannot be so cowed and beaten down that they would not wish to stop something so evil...'

'He keeps hardly any staff down here. And those are all carefully selected. Just enough to run the household and the kitchen. Keep him fed up to the standard he is used to. Cater for his parties and *amusements*.'

Artemidorus sat in silent thought for a moment. 'So, it is unlikely that either he or Gaius Trebonius has slaves or servants here who have come from their villas in Rome?'

'Highly unlikely. Why do you ask?'

'Trebonius' housekeeper, slaves and servants might well recognise me. I have delivered messages there in the past.'

'And that would matter? If someone recognised you?'

'It might.'

She took that in her stride with a shrug. 'As far as I know, all the people in the household now are locals. Carefully selected as I say. Who are happy at least to look the other way whatever is happening.'

'What do you want us to do about this?' he asked.

'Kill him,' she answered coolly. 'There is no other way to stop him.'

'Not without Antony's direct order.' He shook his head regretfully. 'I would do so happily for I have scores to settle with him myself. But I cannot kill him without an order.'

'*You* have scores...' her face was blank with astonishment now. Her gaze swung to Quintus' stony face and back. That he was known to Trebonius' household was one thing. Even that he might wish to conceal the fact from the man himself. But this was something else again.

'He took one of my friends who was working undercover in the Roman villa belonging to a friend and associate. Had him beaten half to death by a gladiator wearing *cestus* gloves covered with metal spikes,' said Artemidorus, leaning forward to fix her with his most intense gaze. 'Then, before he died, Basilus ordered that his eyes be gouged and his tongue cut out. Then he was crucified against scaffolding in the street as a message. Finally his throat was cut. And he was left hanging there. Until I found him and took him down.'

'And Basilus did this?' She was white with horror.

'Basilus ordered it. Watched it done. Made the dead man's partner, who was my lover, watch it. So that she would tell him our plans and betray us. Which she did.'

111

'Then I was wasting my time trying to warn you about him. You know what must be done to stop him.'

'Perhaps. But I still cannot kill him without the general's order.'

She gave one decisive nod. Her gaze as intense as Artemidorus'. 'At least I am sure that the pair of you know what danger you may be going into when you step across his threshold.'

VI

'We have to treat the place like enemy territory,' said Quintus next morning. 'We go in as though we were going into a forest in Germania north of Gaul. A forest full of *Harii* Ghost Warriors.'

'I agree,' said Artemidorus. 'But that's only the start. Sometime during our visit today I want to work out how to go back and break in tonight. To find out what it is that actually goes on there. If I know that, I might be able to think of some way to stop it. Short of killing him. Until Antony orders it done.'

'Wise enough, given the general's current attitude towards you. You really do not want to get any further into his bad books. Or you *will* find yourself in some dismal outpost in Germania, surrounded by Ghost Warriors. But remember, you haven't been too successful so far in settling the score for Telos' crucifixion. Or Cyanea's betrayal.'

'No I haven't. Not yet...' Artemidorus looked down at the lean, hard legionary. 'But then, I haven't stopped trying.'

'Never will, if I know you.'

'Not 'til it's settled.' He concluded grimly.

They spent a good deal of the morning searching through Pompeii for things that might assist them in their intentions for the evening. Making Restituta a willing part of their plans. Which allowed them access to her wide circle of acquaintance amongst the lower elements of the town. And so they were able to gather a surprisingly complete gallery of tools and techniques. But as the time for *prandium* passed, they had to return to the primary purpose of their mission. They stabled the mounts that had carried them here, hired a couple of fresh horses and followed the directions Restituta had given them. Riding out into the early part of a stormy afternoon.

The villa Minucius Basilus had inherited from his uncle – together with his immense fortune – was huge. It clearly allowed the ex-soldier to retire in almost majestic magnificence. Angry though he was that Caesar had given him money instead of a province to govern after his term as *praetor* ran out. The two messengers rode through vineyards, orchards and olive groves as they crossed the huge *latifundium* estate that surrounded the white marble villa itself. Which sat like a summer's cloud on top of a coastal hill to the south of Pompeii. Glowing with snowy brightness, even in the overcast day. Cresting a rocky promontory that looked north across the bay, past Herculaneum towards Neapolis. The horses cantered easily out of the cultivated groves and onto a marble roadway leading to the villa itself. The broad roadway was lined with tall poles topped with woven metal flambeaus. 'I hope they light those tonight,' said Quintus. 'That would be a great help if this weather doesn't clear up.'

'I take your point.' Artemidorus glanced around. Clouds still hung low above the magnificent view. The bay was grey and lined with welts of white foam as though the water had been scourged. The land, gathering up dull and damp on their right, crested in the flat tabletop of Vesuvio. The bay, Artemidorus noted, was empty. It looked like *Aurora* was staying safely moored in Neapolis for the time being. For some unfathomable reason, that made the secret agent feel more exposed. As though Lucius Silus, Otho and the crew were backup. Insurance. Support. Which had suddenly been removed.

As they pulled their mounts to a standstill at the foot of an extravagant set of steps, the doors above them opened. A shiftless-looking *ostiarius* hesitated half in the shadow of the *vestibulum*. There was a marble balustrade running up each side of the steps so, in the absence of slaves or a welcome, they hitched their horses to the lowest upright. Then they swaggered up the steps to confront the hesitant slave.

'My master doesn't want to be disturbed,' said the doorkeeper before Artemidorus had a chance to speak.

'Then don't disturb him!' snapped the officious messenger. 'My business is with Gaius Trebonius. Tell him I am here bearing messages from Consul and General Mark Antony.'

A hesitant hand was pushed out into the gloom of the overcast afternoon. It had three fingers and a stump. The thumb was short of its top knuckle. 'Give the messages to me and I will…'

'The messages I carry, *morologus* idiot are to be handed to General Trebonius in person. And there is more to be discussed with him than what is written in them.'

'Well, my master…'

'What is it, *nothus* bastard?' came a voice from the cavernous shadows behind the trembling doorkeeper. Not Basilus' hissing whisper, nor Trebonius' booming nasal. A rough, *plebeian*, bullying tone.

The doorkeeper turned, flinching. 'Men with messages from Rome, *atriensis* steward,' he said. 'For Lord Trebonius…'

'Well let them in, *spurius* bastard,' came the reply. 'I will go in search of Lord Trebonius.'

114

The doorkeeper cringed back into the shadows, pulling the door wide as he did so. Artemidorus strode in. Quintus followed close behind him, right hand on the pommel of his *gladius*. The pair of them marched into the *vestibulum* and stopped. The entrance hall was almost as big as Antony's *atrium*. And the *atrium* beyond it could almost have contained the Temple of Jupiter Optimus Maximus Capitolinus in Rome. Even on an overcast and threatening afternoon, it was seemingly full of light. What little brightness streamed down through the opening above the *impluvium* pool was magnified by the white marble of the walls and columns. By the brilliance of the mosaics on the floor. And, noticed Artemidorus as he moved forward, the *impluvium* pool itself was stocked with silver and golden carp, the largest and fattest he had ever seen, whose scales also seemed to catch the light. Its surface brightened further with lily flowers whose plump petals were as white as the skin of vestals. As he studied the succulent leaves, he suddenly felt a shiver run up his spine. He began to check surreptitiously around.

Certain that he was being watched.

*

But his attention was immediately distracted by the arrival of three men. Two of them attended by a crowd of six or so obsequious, cowed-looking slave women. The first of the three, ushering the two behind him forward, was clearly the *atriensis* steward. Though he looked like the leader of a street gang. A Clodius or a Milo – not the sort of servant a respectable senator would employ.

And his employer came immediately behind him. Looking more like one of the desiccated mummies from Cleopatra's Egypt than a living man. Pale, parchment-skinned. With blade-sharp cheekbones, hollow cheeks, an arrogant beak of a nose, cavernous eyes and an unsettlingly full, red-lipped mouth. Only the richness of his purple, gold-embroidered tunic proved him to be a man of substance rather than a recently reanimated corpse. How Basilus had managed to establish himself as a successful general and an effective *praetor*, the spy simply could not guess. The last time Artemidorus had seen him was in his Roman villa as Basilus handed the captured secret agent over to the men who had tortured Telos. Together with the apparently terrified Cyanea. Both of them expecting to share Telos' fate – at the very least. He hoped that, like Cassius, Basilus would not recognise him without the bushy red beard he wore during that undercover assignment.

Behind Basilus, strode Trebonius like a lesser Antony. His stature not quite so Herculean. His hair nowhere near so thick, dark or curling. His beard lacking the virile waves Antony's achieved when he grew it. But a lesser Antony was still a considerable man. And Trebonius, unlike his host, carried about him an impressive air of power and command. He wore his simple cream linen tunic like

115

a suit of armour. Carried himself as though he was always ready for battle. Stood out from his emaciated host and the thinly clad troupe of terrified girls around him like one of Caesar's statues in the Forum.

It was this that had made him such an able general, reckoned Artemidorus. Such an effective legate at Caesar's side in Gaul. Such a useful *praetor* pushing Caesar's hugely unpopular debt reforms through a mutinous Senate. The man who laid successful siege to Massalia – commanding the land troops that broke down the walls while Decimus Albinus commanded the ships which blockaded the harbour. The harbour that, in these more peaceful times, was the furthest port to which *Aurora* sailed.

ii

'Well?' boomed Trebonius. 'You have something for me, *nuntius* courier?'

'I have messages from General Antony,' said Artemidorus, refusing to be intimidated by the bullying tone. 'Spoken as well as written.'

'You!' ordered Trebonius, defining which of his acolytes he was addressing by smacking her on her thinly covered *nates* bottom. 'Get the letters. *Cito*! Quickly!'

Even as the whip crack of the blow was echoing in the cavernous space, she hurried forward, hand outstretched, eyes wide and brimming with tears. Artemidorus reached into the letter pouch and handed her the last of the parchment scrolls. She turned and scurried back. 'Not *velox* fast enough,' he said as he took the dispatch. 'We will discuss that later.' He looked down at the letter. At Antony's seal. 'Out!' he snapped. 'All of you.'

Everyone except Basilus vanished. Even the brutish steward.

'You!' Trebonius pointed at Artemidorus. 'Come!' He turned and marched through into the enormous *tablinum* study, which could almost have housed the Senate. Artemidorus was simply awed by the scale of the place. He felt for a moment that he was in one of the larger Ptolemaic palaces in Alexandria. The constant feeling that he was being watched fitted very well with his memories of Alexandria. The *tablinum* was walled with columns that supported a balcony. A match, he suddenly realised, to a similar structure that had lined the *atrium*. Which he had scarcely noticed at the edge of his vision while he was admiring the fish-filled *impluvium*. But that upper level might well conceal someone spying on what was going on below.

Looking beyond the *tablinum*, the spy saw that the rear of the villa opened into a *peristyle* garden, rather grown to seed – but also lined with columns and balconies. Where Cassius' *peristyle* opened onto a balcony overlooking the sea, Basilus' had a huge metal trelliswork grille in the middle. With what looked like a gate built into the structure. A trellis which also overlooked the restless *Sinus*

116

Neapolis Bay of Neapolis. And, no doubt, given the scale of the place, all the balconies around the *atrium*, *tablinum* and *peristyle* were backed by doors into upper rooms. This palatial villa could house a huge family and an army of slaves to look after them. But now it only seemed to contain two men, the young women who were their potential victims and the fewest possible servants needed to cater for them. Servants, as Restituta said, whose silence could be assured, no matter what went on.

Basilus hurried into the *tablinum* at Trebonius' side, bouncing up and down almost comically as he tried to see over his friend's shoulder the moment he opened Antony's scroll. In the middle of the *tablinum* there was the traditional *paterfamilias'* chair which faced back towards the *atrium*. Trebonius sat in this as though it and the villa belonged to him. Basilus hovered beside him. The spy and his bodyguard came to a halt in front of them and stood at ease. Artemidorus had no helmet. He was wearing a heavy tunic and a rainproof cloak, hood thrown back. But there was no mistaking his soldier's stance as he stood, feet as wide as his shoulders, hands clasped behind his back. Quintus was every inch a *triarius*. Under his travelling cloak he wore full armour; instead of a hood, his helmet, and *caligae* boots on his feet. Ready for battle rather than parade.

As Trebonius observed the moment he looked up from the scroll. 'So. Antony sends a pair of battle-hardened soldiers with his messages. Hardly unexpected, I suppose. But you said something about spoken messages as well as these...' he waved the papyrus in Basilus' skull-face, 'I assume you know what he's suggesting in here...'

'Yes, General,' answered Artemidorus. 'That you accept the post of Proconsul of Asia Province as Caesar proposed you should. And as the Senate has formally requested.'

'Tempting, certainly. Asia is a rich province. But a province policed by surprisingly few legions. By no legions at all, in fact...'

'Legionary detachments and auxiliary cohorts,' nodded Artemidorus. 'That is all.'

'Therefore suddenly less tempting...' said Trebonius. 'What do you think, Basilus?'

'Antony wants you powerless,' hissed Basilus. His cavernous eyes focusing on Artemidorus as though daring him to challenge the whispered assertion.

'Not quite,' said the spy. 'There is money to be had in Asia. And money is power. If you find no legions there, you can still buy some. When you have collected the taxes. Or borrowed against them. There will be many moneylenders and businessmen willing to advance considerable sums to the Proconsul of Asia.

117

Or you might even get funds from friends willing to trust and support you. Close friends.' The final observation was by no means innocent. For Trebonius was a proud man. Prouder, perhaps, than Antony. The suggestion – as thinly veiled as the slave girls – was bound to drive a wedge between the friend and host who was twice as rich as Croesus and the guest too proud to beg or borrow from him.

The secret agent let the proposition hang in the air for a moment, poisoning the atmosphere. Watching with quiet satisfaction as Basilus eased himself away from Trebonius. Like a man confronted with a tiger who knows it is death to run. Then he added, 'And Lord Antony suggests that, as the post is a newly created one, you might like to take up your proconsulship at once instead of waiting for *Januarius*. That would mean several extra months of taxes. Enough to buy a legion at least, I'd say…'

The bribe was so obvious it was distracting. As it was meant to be. Artemidorus wanted Trebonius focused on it. Caught between admiration of its dazzling prospects and suspicion that it was too good to be true. He did not want him thinking beyond it. Asking questions as Cassius had done. Making observations, like Brutus. About how desperate Antony was to leave Rome and settle the restless legionaries before they tore the city apart. But how mistrustful he was of Trebonius' friend Decimus Albinus, Senate appointed Governor of Cisalpine Gaul. With three full legions under his *imperium* command. Less than a week's march away from the defenceless city, once the Rubicon was crossed. Likely to be welcomed, in any case, by a Senate swayed by the *Libertores'* spokesman, Marcus Tullius Cicero. And how completely Antony – and all of them so far – had underestimated Caesar Octavius. And the legions he was buying, bribing and building. He did not want Trebonius swallowing his pride and asking Basilus how many legions he thought his millions might purchase after all.

'What may I say to Lord Antony is your answer, Proconsul?' he asked after a few moments.

'Tell him I'll think about it. That he will hear from me. Yes. Tell him I am considering his offer and that he will hear my answer in due course. That is all. You can go. And you do not need to return.'

He waved a hand in dismissal. The two soldiers turned and marched away. *Oh but we will return* thought Artemidorus. *And sooner than you think.*

iii

Artemidorus and Quintus sheltered amongst the twisted trunks and low-hanging, overspreading branches in the olive grove at the end of the torch-lined roadway. Well back from the main road through the *latifundium* estate, in a space big enough to tether their horses safely and secretly. By a grassy patch where they could feed. The rain eased, as the overcast began to thin. The wind blew restlessly from the south, gusting towards gale force less frequently. But still making the olive trees sway and whisper all around them. The afternoon darkened relentlessly towards evening, shadows gathering and dancing.

Amongst the other things purchased in Pompeii was a satisfactory *cena* of cold chicken, boiled eggs and figs. Augmented by the tart green olives they plucked from the branches around them. Made more substantial by a loaf of soft white Greek bread worthy of legendary baker Thearion himself. Except for the olives, the food had been by no means cheap – Pompeii was an expensive town – but it was bought with Antony's gold. Along with everything else they were carrying in preparation for tonight's mission. Which, to Artemidorus at least, seemed fair.

Sufficiently full, warm and dry, wrapped in their cloaks beneath the thick covering of the olive trees, the soldiers settled down to wait. As though they were on sentry duty in the dark forests of the north. But, while there was still light enough to see by, they went through those other purchases made by Antony's gold that were not edible. And began to make their plans.

'Though,' said Quintus, 'you know what's the first thing guaranteed to fail in battle, don't you?'

'Yes,' answered Artemidorus. 'The plan.'

Just before the sun set somewhere beyond the overcast, a wagon came down from Basilus' villa, pulled by a slow but sturdy carthorse. And its occupants climbed up to light the flambeaus lining the white marble roadway.

'That's convenient,' observed Quintus. 'Now we don't have to stumble around in the dark.'

'Or use up the oil in our own dark lantern before we actually get there,' agreed Artemidorus. 'But the main question has to be – is this just a daily ritual? Or is Basilus expecting guests?'

'We'll find out soon enough,' said Quintus. 'And in the meantime, I'm off to water and fertilise the olive groves – make sure there is nothing in my bowels or bladder to distract me later.'

'Good idea,' said Artemidorus. 'I'll follow on in a moment. If you haven't brought a *spongia*, better use grass to wipe up – if the horses have finished with it. Olive leaves are prickly. And watch out for nettles.'

After waiting until the evening had gathered to full dark, the secret agents decided that Basilus was not expecting guests. As quietly as possible, they led their horses to the olive trees nearest the bright-lit path and tethered them there. Then, under the flickering light of the first flambeau, they began to employ some of the non-edible purchases they had made earlier. Like the Ghost Warriors of the

119

north, they blacked their faces, arms and legs. Pulled black *penulae* poncho-cloaks over their heads, letting the cloth hang front and back, to make them almost invisible in shadow. Eased their *pugio* daggers in their *balteus* sword-belts. Quintus also eased his *gladius* in its sheath. Artemidorus clipped their dark lantern in the space where his sword should have hung. Making sure the reservoir was still full of oil and the wick was standing proud. Taking care to check in his pouch for the flint and steel that would light it. Making certain he would not confuse it with the other, smaller, pouch that contained the Balearic sling he habitually carried now as though it was another of his *fascina* good luck charms. Then, side by side, they flitted like dark moths up the shadows along the outer edges of the bright-lit approach road.

While Artemidorus had been focused on the fish in the *impluvium* pool, the slave girls and the two men he was talking to, Quintus' eyes had been busy in other areas. Although he had not felt the shiver of suspicion that he was being secretly spied on, he had worked out the basic design of the huge villa. Its layout like its architecture was massive rather than original. His keen nostrils had sensed the location of the *culina* kitchen. And the likely position of the *posticum* back door, therefore. The door through which supplies would be delivered, crisp and fresh to the *coqui* cooks. So it was no great challenge for him to work out where the back door was located from the outside.

The *posticum* was like much else about the villa. Larger than usual but no more modern. It towered nearly twice as high as Quintus and looked almost as imposing as the main entrance. But its lock was an elderly Greek variant of an ancient Egyptian design. Modernised only by the introduction of a Roman metal movement. The mechanism was devised to allow an iron key to be inserted from the outside of the door. Then turned in such a way that it lifted a latch on the inside. Praying that there were no bolts also involved in the villa's old-fashioned security system, the two spies began to try the keys they had purchased in Pompeii. The third one opened the lock.

As he heard the latch lift, Artemidorus pushed the door gently. And it swung silently inwards. He grabbed the edge of it instantly and held it ajar, listening for sounds and looking for lights. In the absence of both, he opened the door a little further and slid in. His nostrils instantly filled with the smell of cooking. But the air that carried the odours was cold. *Cena* had been served long since. And it seemed that the cooks had vanished about some other business. The two men eased themselves into the corridor.

Artemidorus slid the dark lamp from his belt and set it on the floor. Crouched. Took the top off. Reached into his pouch for his flint, steel and oiled wool kindling. Then he struck the flint, using the brightness of the sparks to focus on the wool and the wick like someone using lightning to see by. The wool caught and he held it to the wick. Nothing happened. He held the wool in place until his fingertips burned. Then dropped it. In the waning light as it died, he pulled the lamp wick higher. Then he took more wool from his purse and tried again.

On the third attempt the wick lit and he shook the wool until the flame there died. Then he put the cover on the lantern and eased the sliding door until a vertical beam of light as thin as a blade lit the way ahead. He moved it from side to side. Defining the width and the depth of the corridor they were following. The odour of *cena* was replaced by those of burning hair and oil. The stillness in the villa was emphasised by the dying bluster of the gale outside. Quintus eased the *posticum* door closed. They pulled themselves to their feet and crept forward, silently, side by side.

iv

On their right was the wall of the *culina* kitchen. On their left, a series of doors opening, no doubt, into storerooms. Ahead, another door that would probably open into the huge *tablinum* office area or the massive *peristyle* garden. Above them, a ceiling that was effectively the floor of the upper storey. 'Did you notice where the *scalae* stairs were?' breathed Artemidorus.

'Somewhere close by I think,' Quintus answered.

And so it proved. A set of stairs led away to their right, rising from a little vestibule inside the second door. He pressed his ear against the wood but could make out nothing that made any sense. So, rather than risk opening it, he turned and allowed the sliver of brightness from the lamp to guide Quintus and him up the stairs to the balustraded gallery which, it seemed, looked down on all the central areas of the lower storey. If Basilus and Trebonius were in the *triclinium* dining room, they would be out of sight. But if they were in the *atrium*, *tablinum* or the *peristyle*, they would be easy enough to spy on.

Artemidorus closed the lamp as they emerged onto the gallery. There was enough light up here to see, for several of the areas below were brightly illuminated. Almost invisible in the upcast shadows, the two spies snaked across the cool, white flooring until they could peer between the marble columns. Their position gave them an excellent view down into the *tablinum*. And the great mosaic decorating the floor, which Artemidorus recognised at once. It showed his personal demigod Achilleus dressed as a woman surrounded by the princesses of Skyros in a scene from *The Iliad*. The princesses were even more scantily attired than the slave girls attending the villa's owner and his friend. No wonder Odysseus was looking almost awestruck as he observed the scene, thought the spy

121

with a wry smile. The red-headed sailor spying on the hero. Just as Artemidorus and Quintus were spying on the less-than-heroic Basilus and Trebonius. But no sooner had Artemidorus recognised the picture on the floor, than the quiet that had dominated the cavernous villa so far was broken. 'There's no room in here!' boomed Trebonius' voice, seeming to echo up from Hades itself. 'Basilus, get your people to move these couches!'

'*MORS!*' Basilus' whispery voice was raised as close to a shout as it could come. The brutish steward hurried across the *atrium*, answering his master's call. Vanishing into the *triclinium* immediately below.

'Get these couches out into the *tablinum*, and be quick about it!' boomed Trebonius.

A moment later, with a juddering scream of wood on tile, the first couch was dragged out of the dining room and into the spacious office area. Pulled by Mors and two strong-looking slave boys. Some moments later, the second couch joined it, pulled by three more young thugs. Then Mors the steward moved the massive *paterfamilias'* chair, clearing a sizeable area between the couches, while the boys brought out small tables laden with jugs of wine and green glass goblets decorated with gold designs.

Basilus and Trebonius strolled out of the dining room. Both wearing light, loose robes which caught the light like silk. Each man was attended by two young women, familiar from earlier. Whose clothing was short, scanty and all but transparent. Whose faces wore knowing and accommodating smiles. But whose eyes, thought Artemidorus, seemed to be brimming with terror. Or perhaps it was his imagination. He hoped so, but he doubted it. First Trebonius and then Basilus took his ease on a couch. And the girls attending them lay down beside them, one in front and one behind. Hands busy at once.

'Not yet!' snapped Basilus. He pushed the girl behind him so viciously that she fell off the couch entirely, crashing onto the tiles of the massive mosaic with a cry of pain. The nearest slave boy just stopped the table from tipping and the wine from spilling. His face pale with shock. His nearest companion smirked at him; leered down at the girl on the floor. Whose kicking legs revealed that she was naked beneath the scanty *chiton* tunic. Basilus sat up and swung round to face the fallen girl. 'Get up, *cunnus*,' he spat. She pulled herself to her feet. 'Come here, *canicula!*' As she obeyed, he punched her in the lower belly, just above the pubis. And, as she folded forward, winded, he slapped her round the face so hard she fell down again. 'Get up and get back,' he snarled. 'One more mistake like that and I'll make you draw lots to see which bit of you gets chopped off first!'

'You two pay close attention to your master,' boomed Trebonius, easing himself back and forth between his body-slaves. 'You can't begin to imagine what intimate little bits and pieces of a girl are included on those lots. It isn't all fingers and toes, ears and nose I can tell you!' He gave a great booming laugh as though he had cracked the best joke ever told.

'*Mors!*' hissed Basilus again as the echoes of Trebonius' cruel amusement died. Raising his voice as close to a shout as it came. 'Let's get on with it! Where are they?'

'Coming Lord Basilus,' answered the steward. And he led a troupe of three women out of the *triclinium* and into the spacious brightness between the couches. The first one was tall, fair-haired, dressed in a robe like Basilus'. But the material was so fine as to be completely transparent. As with many fashionable Roman ladies, her body had been depilated from the neck down. Her upper lips, nipples and lower lips were rouged. She wore an *indumentum oris* mask across her eyes. And she carried a *flagrum* whip.

Artemidorus gave her only the most cursory of inspections, for his attention was immediately captured by her two companions. Both were naked. Their bodies full, rounded, and as pale as the plump lily petals in the *impluvium*. They had clearly been matched as a pair. Both had large, slightly pendant breasts with full, dark nipples. Both had broad hips, full buttocks and thighs that tended towards heaviness. Slightly bulging bellies, darkly forested. Unlike the girls on the couches, who came from a range of ethnic backgrounds, these had skin of almost alabaster whiteness.

But it was not just their nakedness that claimed his attention. It was what they were wearing on their heads. Each girl had a centurion's helmet laced tightly under her chin. Immediately beneath the eye-ridge, there was also a blindfold. And the effectiveness of these was made clear by the hesitancy of the girls' stumbling steps. Their eyeless clumsiness was compounded by two further factors. First, that each girl carried in her right fist a sizeable vinestock. The springy, whippy club that was a centurion's badge of authority. And secondly that the girls' left hands were tied together by a cord about two *cubits* long secured from one wrist to the other.

An air of sick excitement seemed to ooze out of the two men, strong enough to be palpable up here. Artemidorus' mouth went dry. His stomach twisted, suddenly full of acid. His nostrils flared. But, he thought grimly, this was what he had come here to witness. Worse than this, in fact. For the first glance at the two blindfolded girls had told him what was to come. The masked woman pushed them to the centre of the area between the couches. Prodding them with her whip, she

123

positioned them, left arms stretched, cord tight, one facing Basilus, the other facing Trebonius. Looking blindly towards each other. The scene froze for an instant. Then, 'Now!' hissed Basilus, 'Begin!'

The whip snapped against the nearest naked back. At once the two girls began to strike out at each other with the vinestock clubs. Missing at first as they whirled and beat the air helplessly. Keeping the cord taut. Staying at arms' length. But the masked woman drove them on with her whip. Aiming the cutting blows more carefully at backs, buttocks, breasts and bellies. Lashing her agonised victims closer and closer together as they whimpered, danced and beat the vacancy between them. Until first one and then the other landed a blow. The blunt, brutal end of a vinestock slapped into a breast. Almost immediately another smacked low onto a hip, whipping round onto the side of a dimpled buttock. Pale skin blushed red at once, bruises blossoming. Darkening. One after another. Explaining all too clearly why these women above all the others had been chosen for this particular perverse entertainment.

'*Euge*! Bravo!' bellowed Trebonius excitedly. '*Iterum*! *Iterum*! Again!'

The two blindfolded combatants found their aim. Time and time again the vinestocks whipped home. Landed with fearsome slaps. Artemidorus closed his eyes briefly. Slid back. Rolled over to look up at the red-painted ceiling. Tried vainly to clear the images from his head as blow after blow echoed through the cavernous *tablinum*. Blows soon augmented with the *crack!* of whip-strokes as the victims began to tire, needing further motivation to keep beating each other with the brutal clubs. And gasps of pain that soon became grunts, whimpers and cries – then screams of pain.

'Enough!' boomed Trebonius at last, his voice hoarse with lust. 'Bring my *cunnae* to my chamber. To quote the poet Catullus, girls, "*Pedicabo ego vos et irrumabo*" I'm going to bugger your backside then fuck your face! So let's get down to it!'

Artemidorus rolled over and looked down. Trebonius was gone. Basilus was striding excitedly towards the *peristyle*, where the twin staircase to this one led up to his bedchamber. His two female body-slaves were supporting the helmeted girl after him. Her body a mess of ridged red whip-welts and big blue-black bruises.

The woman in the transparent gown watched them as they went. She flung her whip onto Basilus' couch and turned, reaching for her mask, shouting, 'Mors!'

Seeing her now, alone, the centre of his attention, Artemidorus suddenly knew. Knew before the steward and his five burly slave boys appeared to clear the room in answer to her call.

Knew before she reached up and took the black mask off her face to reveal massive, green-blue eyes.

The woman with the whip was his treacherous lover Cyanea.

Artemidorus' body was in motion before his mind caught up. His arms, shoulders and thighs tensed, ready to make him spring erect. His chest expanded as he gasped a breath to shout. The tiny movement seemed to catch Cyanea's attention for she looked up at the balcony. It was as though their eyes met. For an agonising instant.

Then Quintus punched him on the corner of his jaw, immediately below his left ear. A short blow using as little telltale movement as possible. But a blow of immense power all the same. The spy hit the floor. Face down. Silent. Unconscious and still before his body actually did anything at all.

v

Artemidorus came awake like a flame touched to a cauldron of Greek Fire. Only the firm grip of a hand on his shoulder stopped him starting up. Only the rigid clasp of another across his mouth stopped him shouting out. His eyes sprang wide. And saw only impenetrable darkness.

'This lantern is *excrementum*,' came Quintus' quiet voice. 'The trouble I've had with it. I know what you're going to say. Let's take it back and complain. But did you see the size of the *baro* bloke who sold it to us?'

The secret agent relaxed, and Quintus' tone changed. 'All right now? No more jumping about and shouting? You know it will only get us killed.'

The hand lifted from Artemidorus' mouth. 'I didn't…' he wheezed. Vaguely surprised that his jaw was still working after the blow that knocked him out.

'No, you didn't do or say anything. But you were going to. And we'd have ended up facing that treacherous bitch Cyanea, that nasty-looking steward Mors and at least five well-built *rectae* thugs that work with him. Together with a couple of very strange but well-trained, fit-looking generals. Not to mention whoever runs the kitchen and takes care of the rest of the domestic arrangements in this madhouse.'

Artemidorus sat up. Eased his jaw. 'Fair enough. But I'm in control of myself now.'

'That's what you say! Tell me what you plan to do next, then.'

'Find Cyanea.'

'Exactly what I thought, boy. All *colei*, no *cerebrum*. All balls no brain. And what were you going to do when you found her? *Futuo* or *ferio*? Kiss her or kill her?'

'Get her out of here. Take her to Antony. Use her as a witness before the Senate to get Basilus and Trebonius impeached. Just like I tried to do with Puella the night before Caesar died.'

'Good plan!' Quintus sounded hugely impressed. 'And look how well *that* worked. Not to mention the fact that Antony's not talking to you. And the Senate won't give a toss about a couple of slaves getting beaten to death – not that they were actually beaten to death in any case. Especially not given the current political situation the Senate is facing. That we're trembling on the edge of yet another civil war. Unless Antony can hold everything together. In spite of Cicero and co. And that's before we even start to consider Basilus' millions – which will buy most of them twice over and then some.'

'I'm still going to find her.'

'Fine with me. I've lived long enough and made my will. Best go about it carefully and quietly, though.'

There was a moment of silence, then Artemidorus asked, 'Did you say you'd got the lantern to work?'

'Eventually.'

'Right. Let's go.'

Artemidorus sat up and thus discovered he had been lying on a marble floor. Quintus opened the shutter on the dark lantern a finger-width and so revealed that they were in one of the *cubiculae* bedrooms; presumably the nearest one behind the spot that they had chosen to spy on this evening's perverse proceedings. Artemidorus knew Quintus possessed enormous wiry strength. But the legionary was unlikely to have carried – or dragged – his unconscious body any great distance.

The lamplight was just bright enough for the two of them to find the door. Then Quintus closed the cover as Artemidorus eased it open. Nothing outside but darkness and silence. The wind had dropped. The storm was easing, he thought. 'Light,' he whispered. The pair of them stepped out onto the balcony with just a shard of golden light to guide them. Artemidorus paused. Waited for half a dozen heartbeats, trying to sense whether the mysterious watcher was still observing them.

Particularly as it could well have been Cyanea.

'Start with the slave quarters?' breathed Quintus. 'They'll be at the back of the house.'

'Safer to start there than go blundering in on Basilus or Trebonius,' whispered Artemidorus. But he eased his *pugio* dagger in its sheath. Just in case.

They went back to the flight of stairs that led down to the kitchen corridor. Then opened the door at the end. It led out into the rear section of the *tablinum* and almost immediately out into the *peristyle* garden. Although the far end looked out through the metal trellis over the bay, there were rooms off the colonnade on the right-hand, northern side. Necessarily smaller than those at the front of the house. Confined by the nearness of the cliff. By the size of the garden. By the fact that the entire southern side of the *peristyle* was given over to the bathhouse. As revealed by the pictures on the doors, dully but clearly illuminated by the lantern's beam. Brightened further, unexpectedly, by the moon as it broke through the rags of cloud at the edge of the departing storm. And, ultimately, by the fact that the rooms nearer the front were so majestic in size. These, therefore, were most likely to be the slave quarters. But which rooms would be occupied by the steward and his bullies? And which by the suffering women?

Artemidorus solved that conundrum in the simplest possible fashion. By creeping along the colonnade under the inconsistent brightness from the sky. Intensified as it was by the white marble all around him. Moving from dark door to dark door. Pressing his ear to each in turn. One after another seemed to reverberate to the sound of Stentorian snores. But then he came to others whose rough surfaces transmitted the sound of quiet, hopeless sobbing. 'Here,' he whispered. 'This is where the slave girls are!'

'Alone?'

'I don't hear any men in there with them if that's what you mean.'

'And Cyanea?' wondered Quintus.

'I don't suppose she's far away. And one of the girls will be able to direct us to where she sleeps.' Even in his own ears, Artemidorus' voice sounded icy.

'You think all of the girls will be in here? All six?'

'Probably...'

'They won't have kept any back to warm their beds?'

'Doubt it. If you had done what they have done to those girls, would you want them lying close beside you while you slept?'

'Probably not. Unless I had some kind of death wish. I'd boot them out when I'd finished with them and have at least one of those nasty-looking thugs guard my bedroom. In we go, then...' said Quintus. And leaned against the door.

As soon as the door moved, there was utter silence in the room. Into which the two men stepped, framed momentarily by reflected moonlight, Quintus swinging the door closed behind him once again. But when the legionary opened the cover of the lantern and released a blade of light, there were gasps and whimpers of terror. Under Artemidorus' narrow-eyed gaze, the edge of brightness played

127

across a small room with six basic beds in it. On which lay the young women. Four relatively unhurt. The other two covered with whip-marks and bruises. All of them naked. Dishevelled. Obviously recently abused. Probably in the ways Trebonius had threatened when he quoted the pornographic poet Catullus.

'*Confuta*! Be silent!' hissed Quintus. And the fact that his was a completely new voice silenced the girls more effectively than the imperative.

'We are here to help you,' breathed Artemidorus into the shocked silence. 'But first I must talk with Cyanea. Where is she?'

The women looked at each other, wide-eyed. It was impossible to tell whether they were too scared to reveal Cyanea's whereabouts. Through fear of her or fear of what might happen to her. Or whether they had never heard the name Cyanea before.

But then events overtook their hesitation and confusion.

The door behind Quintus swung wide. Mercifully, he had stepped forward so the wooden edge did not hit him. Instead the door slammed back against the wall, fully open. With a crash that drowned the sounds of distress made by the women. And the steward Mors stepped in. He was naked. Erect. Holding a terracotta lamp with a big wick. Whose flame lit the room much more efficiently than Quintus' dark lantern. Had he not been so drunk, he would have registered what was happening much more quickly than he did. But he was very drunk. So drunk he did not appear to notice the two black-clad, black-faced ghost warriors standing immobile in the shadows. Though to be fair, his focus – such as it was – was on the women. 'Right, *cunnae*,' he snarled. 'Get ready for round two!'

Quintus reached for his *pugio* dagger.

The movement attracted the steward's attention. His face seemed to lengthen as he realised what he was looking at. And his jaw dropped.

'What…' He staggered back, his broad torso blocking the door. Quintus' dagger was out, but it was clearly too late to be of much use. The steward sucked in a breath. Obviously planning to shout at the top of his lungs and summon the rest of the household.

But the bellow never came. Instead, the lungful of air whispered out of his gaping mouth as his face folded into a look of utter astonishment. The lamp fell. Shattered on the floor and died. His erection wilted. His legs gave and he slid to the ground. Revealing as he did so, the figure of a woman behind him. A woman standing out on the moon-bright, white marble colonnade of the *peristyle*. A woman holding a long, thin-bladed *pugio* that caught the brightness. And gleamed with a red-silver glitter. Who looked down at Mors as he rolled onto his front and

128

lay still. Revealing the black-blooded, fatal stab wound beneath his left shoulder blade.

Cyanea.

VII

The cart Basilus' servants had used when lighting the flambeaus last evening creaked into the southern outskirts of Pompeii's forum after moonset, in the darkness just before daybreak. There was no one up and out. Not even slaves going to the early markets. Which hadn't actually opened yet. Though the weather was calmer and warmer. The breeze moderated but still from the south. It promised to be a fine spring day, when it dawned.

But had there been anyone on the night-dark streets, they would have stopped and stared, wide-eyed and open-mouthed at the spectacle creaking past. Going from brightness to shadow and back again as it passed the lamp-lit doorways. With a black-skinned legionary in armour driving the single carthorse. An important-looking officer sitting beside him. Equally dark of colour. Two fine mounts tethered behind and trotting happily, unladen. Not so the cart, however. Carts full of farm produce the locals were used to. Carts full of fish up from the docks. Carts full of construction material destined for the latest building project.

But carts full of nearly naked women were a rarity, even in the fleshpots of Pompeii.

As they crossed the forum, Quintus pulled the right-hand rein and the patient carthorse swung his head eastwards. A few moments later, the vehicle creaked to a stop in the pool of brightness beneath the flambeau outside the *lupanar*. The two men climbed down off the driver's seat. Quintus banged on the brothel door while Artemidorus began helping the bruised and battered women down. After a while, the door was opened by the wiry male slave, dishevelled and sleepy looking. 'We need to see Restituta,' snapped the legionary.

The slave looked at the soldier uncomprehendingly at first. With slowly dawning recognition. Then he looked over Quintus' shoulder and out at the cart. His eyes widened. 'Looks like you certainly do,' he said. 'We don't often get them arriving by the cartload like *rapa* turnips.'

The slave vanished but he left the door ajar so Quintus and Artemidorus were able to help the girls inside. Wide-eyed and silent, but shaking with cold and fear. Especially when the big bouncer arrived and stood in the corner, silently eyeing them. All six were safely in the brothel's dimly lit reception room by the time Restituta appeared. Adjusting her clothing and straightening her hair. Obviously aroused from slumber. Or something more active.

One glance was enough to tell her everything about the women. And probably about the soldiers' dark disguises. 'You'll need to hide these poor women,' she said. 'Basilus will tear the town apart. Or rather his tame *aedile* and the *excubiae* watchmen will. I don't suppose you took any paperwork along with them did you? Bills of ownership and so forth?'

'There wasn't really either time or opportunity,' said Artemidorus. 'Though I am apparently destined to become quite experienced at slave-stealing. I'll bear it in mind next time.'

'Our priorities were a little different,' added Quintus. 'Like getting rid of the body, for instance.'

Restituta's eyes widened. 'The body! Not Basilus…'

'Sadly, no,' said Artemidorus. 'His steward, Mors. His will be the next carcass to wash out of the gully and into the bay. We dumped it down there on our way round to the stable.'

'Well, we'll have to act quickly even so. I can hide them for a while. Give them food and drink in the meantime. And some clothes. I have a tame *medicus* who can check them over, tend their hurts and then keep his mouth shut. But I'm not certain they can stay here with any degree of safety for any length of time. We'd be better getting them as far away as possible as quickly as we can.'

Otho the ships' pilot appeared, straightening his tunic, just in time to hear the end of what Restituta was saying. '*Quid novi*?' He asked sleepily. 'What's up?'

At the sight of the girls his eyes widened and he came instantly awake. And, as soon as the situation was explained, he said, 'We'll take them aboard *Aurora* and drop them anywhere they like between here and Massalia. No one will be able to track them that far.'

'That sounds perfect,' said Artemidorus. 'As long it's all right with the women and if Captain Lucius is agreeable. When do you sail?'

'When the loading's done,' answered the pilot. 'And Lucius will leap at the chance. He's a good man. The women can have *jentaculum* here, get checked over by this *medicus* and be aboard by time for *prandium*. Then we'll be off.'

The six women fell into a swift, whispered conference. Then a tall, Gaulish woman with blonde hair and bright blue eyes spoke for all of them. 'Massalia. We all want to go there.'

That was all. No thanks. No further information. Fair enough, thought Artemidorus. The decision was all that was needed. Anything else would be superfluous.

'Just need to get rid of the cart and the carthorse, then,' said Quintus after a brief silence. 'That'll be too easy to track and too much of a giveaway unless we're quick about it.'

'Take the cart and one of our horses,' ordered Artemidorus. 'Get as far inland as you can then leave the cart and carthorse somewhere grassy and ride back here on the other mount. We'll be off round about *prandium* time too.'

'If you go inland for a *mile* or so, there's a sidetrack running north,' suggested Restituta. 'That takes you up onto Vesuvio. You can leave the cart up there. Plenty of grazing for the carthorse. It'll be a while before anyone finds it. And when they do, it will lead them in exactly the wrong direction. But the pair of you will have to clean up before you do anything else. There are no African cohorts in town so you stick out a bit. You'll have to scrub off with cold water, though. None of the baths will be hot for hours yet.'

The *lupinaria* was wakened unusually early that morning, therefore, thought Artemidorus as he dried his face and hands on a rough woollen towel. Leaving black smears all over the pale cloth. By the time Quintus left with the cart, heading for Vesuvio's lower slopes, everyone under Restituta's roof was up and about. Fortunately no clients apart from Otho had elected to stay the night. So it was only Restituta's she-wolves who knew about the extra six women. And there arose a kind of sisterly agreement between them as soon as the working girls understood what had happened to their visitors. Basilus' tame *aedile* and his watchmen would hit a blank wall if they came here looking for information.

The wiry slave was sent to summon the physician. Restituta's ex-gladiator bouncer was set to guard the door. Otho and Artemidorus went down the road to the *hospitium* to pick up the soldier and spy's baggage – as well as the packhorse. To settle the bill. And to warn the *culina* that the girls from the *lupanar* would shortly be needing breakfast. And would pay in the usual manner.

ii

'I still don't really understand what happened,' said Quintus. 'I'd have thought she'd have raised Hades and handed you straight over to Basilus. Then happily watched you being beaten like they beat poor Telos. Given what there is between you.'

'I was half expecting to end up like those two poor women. Beaten with a centurion's vinestock. Only in my case beaten to death…'

'Like in a decimation, you mean?'

'Like in a decimation. Just for a moment there…'

They were following the coast road back to Neapolis. What had seemed like a lengthy ride along an unfamiliar route coming south in the dark, now seemed much quicker going back north in daylight.

The horses had settled into an easy trot which the pack animal could keep up with. The road was wide enough to let them ride shoulder to shoulder and hold a conversation. Even amid the early afternoon bustle of other travellers going back and forth around them. A couple of turns of a water clock had taken them to the picturesque port of Herculaneum through which they were riding as they talked. They proposed to stay overnight in the *hospitium* Otho had taken them to in Neapolis, before swinging north of Puetoli in the morning and joining the Appian Way back at Capua.

'She *had* just killed his steward,' said Artemidorus, who was himself still trying to work out what Cyanea was up to. Killing Basilus' steward, then helping them organise the girls' escape – even after she recognised him – then vanishing back into the night-silent villa remained such an unlikely series of things for her to do that he was still, frankly, bemused.

'I'm not sure she was absolutely certain who we were. Just for that moment,' he said. 'And after that, she was committed...'

'Well, she got very certain pretty fast. The moment I opened the dark lantern. She knew you even with your face blacked up. Why help you then?'

Artemidorus shrugged in continuing confusion. What was she up to? He wondered.

Quintus continued, worrying at the problem like a dog with a bone. 'She was right at the top of Ferrata's shortlist of people likely to have hired that killer and his *sôlênarion* bow. Given that she had the money. Or access to the money. And she obviously does now – Basilus' money. *And* you can see Ferrata's point. If you'd have left me tied naked to a whipping post and handed me over to a rioting mob with rape and murder on their mind, I'd have been giving Nemesis herself a close run coming after you.

'Furthermore,' Quintus continued, 'as she escaped from Basilus' house the night the riots began, she set it all on fire. So why go back to Basilus? The one man she surely wanted dead and burning more than you. Why help him play his *aegrotus* perverted games?'

'For the money?' wondered Artemidorus. 'Or access to it at least. Money is power, as young Caesar Octavius is keen to observe...'

'Then why switch sides *again* and kill his steward?' mused Quintus, thinking out loud. 'Then help you rescue his victims? And after she helped us get the girls organised – the wagon was a brilliant idea, though; well done for coming up with it – why didn't she come with us? Why stay? *What in the name of* Jupiter Optimus Maximus *is she up to*?'

It was a question that lay unanswered through the rest of the day. And indeed, through the rest of the night in the familiar *hospitium* at Neapolis. Where Artemidorus lay awake trying to fathom an answer. They discussed it next morning as they travelled past the junction with the road leading away down to the seaside hamlet of Puetoli.

Artemidorus paused at the crossroads, looking down towards the coast. Cyanea at last driven out of his immediate thoughts. He was torn with unaccustomed indecision. Cicero owned a villa down there. As far as he knew, the politician was in residence. And, although he had no orders to do so, he was tempted to pay a visit. To find out whether the lawyer had come to any decision about the possibility of charging Brutus with patricide. The accusation, which had seemed so promising all that time ago, had apparently come to nothing. So far. Perhaps a little nudge would set the ball rolling again, he thought. Put that particular Sisyphus on a downhill slope.

But after a moment or two he decided against it. Pulled his horse's right rein and headed inland, up towards Capua and the Appian Way. Like a performer in the *Circus Maximus* riding two horses at once, he found his thoughts occupied with those two subjects. What had Cicero discovered about the charge of patricide? Why had Cyanea behaved in such an enigmatic manner? Questions that remained unresolved when events overtook them once again.

It was mid morning. They had stopped at a wayside *mansio* for something to eat and drink, and to give the horses a rest. The day was as warm as the previous one, more early summer than late spring. They were seated at a table outside, therefore. Side by side on a bench overlooking the road. Discussing the problem of Cyanea's impenetrable motivation, mulling over whether Cicero needed a nudge to bring a suit against Brutus and making plans for their return to Rome. When a crowd came boiling up the busy thoroughfare.

'He's coming,' shouted someone. 'He's coming! *Caesar* is coming!'

For the briefest moment, the deeply preoccupied Artemidorus expected to see *Divus Julius* in his triumphator's costume, his red and gold embroidered tunic and his regal red *caligae* boots. Entranced by the vision, he rose to his full height then stepped up onto the bench, towering above the excited crowd.

So that when Caesar Octavius rode by with Agrippa and Rufus beside him, it was easy for the young man to spot the familiar soldier. He reined his horse to a stop, and called over the hubbub of the crowd. '*Ave* Centurion! This *is* a lucky meeting. Will you ride with me? I have matters I wish to discuss.'

134

'A very fortunate meeting,' said Caesar Octavius again as they trotted onwards, side by side, with Marcus Vipsanius Agrippa and Quintus Salvidienus Rufus close enough behind them to join in the conversation. And Quintus a little isolated just behind them. 'The gods are certainly smiling on me today. I must make a sacrifice to thank them when we get to Rome. At the Temple of Venus Genetrix, the founder of our family. But to business. I am still finding it very hard to communicate with Antony. Which has been something of a problem. A problem that is likely to get worse during the summer unless we can get it settled swiftly. But it is a problem I think you can help me solve. You can take my messages, thoughts and plans to him on my behalf.'

'I can, Caesar. But whether he will listen to me...' Artemidorus shrugged.

'You should be getting used to that. Was it not you who passed to *Divus Julius Caesar* himself on the *Ides* of *Mars* a list of the men waiting to murder him? At considerable risk to your own life and freedom? A list he never read?'

'Yes,' said Artemidorus, surprised that the young man knew of it. Too caught up in the moment to consider the implications of that knowledge – and how it might colour Caesar Octavius' view of him. 'It is true.'

'I too am familiar with the feeling of being disregarded,' laughed the young man. 'I am on my way back to Rome having spent some time with Marcus Tullius Cicero. He has been extremely courteous. And has *talked* to me about a wide range of topics. But as for *listening* to me...' He shook his head and laughed again.

'It is your age, Caesar...' suggested Agrippa.

'Oh I know that, Marcus Vipsanius,' Caesar Octavius answered his friend. 'My age. And their age. I won't be nineteen until September. They look at me – Antony, Cicero and the rest – and they see an upstart boy. With plans too big for him ever to fulfil. And their reaction is either to dismiss me – as Antony does. Or to patronise me – as Cicero does. But both of them underestimate me. And that's all there is to it.'

'They will learn better, Caesar,' said Rufus.

'They will Quintus Salvidienus. Eventually they will...'

'Do they not irritate you, perhaps even anger you, Caesar?' wondered Artemidorus. 'That they all present themselves as being so wise, so experienced, so powerful, so important. And yet they are all so short-sighted...'

'Why should it irritate me?' laughed Caesar. 'As long as they underestimate me, it is a weakness in them. And their weakness is my strength! Think about it. Antony finds me and my ambitions an easily dismissed distraction. As well he might. For his priorities are clear enough. Keep Rome quiet. Settle the legions in

135

their villages and farms. (Which I hear, is what he has managed to do at last. A little way north of here in fact.) Get some sort of reliable power base that does not rely on the goodwill of the Senate. Move the main opponents – Brutus, Cassius, Trebonius – into positions of diminished power and influence. Well out of Italy and in places where there is limited access to legions. Come after the so-called *Libertores* who killed my father *Divus Julius*. Starting of course with Decimus Albinus whom he has to prise loose from Cisalpine Gaul. In case he brings his legions south...'

'Your logic is impeccable, Caesar,' said Artemidorus, wondering whether the young man had somehow gained access to the contents of Antony's letter pouch before Enobarbus handed it over to him.

'But I don't think he need fear Albinus as much as he does. I understand that Albinus himself is nervous. Of the tribes at his back in the Alps. Supplemented as they are by the Gaulish tribes north of the mountains. Who are in turn under pressure from the warlike peoples in Germania. And Albinus' focus – and his legions, therefore – is to the north and in the Alps, rather than to the south across the Rubicon. But in the meantime, as I say, Antony is far too preoccupied with these concerns to give a second thought to an overambitious boy. So, for the moment at least, I am safe from him. And can go about my business unmolested.'

'And these are thoughts you wish me to take to General Antony?' asked Artemidorus, half amused, half astonished. Not, as yet, suspicious, though he knew he was being skilfully manipulated.

'You may take to Antony anything I say,' answered Caesar Octavius airily. 'And I assure you, anything I do not wish you to take to Antony will remain absolutely unsaid!'

'And, if I may ask, what is the *business* you mentioned, Caesar?'

'To get money, Centurion. To sell every brick of building, every stick of furniture, every piece of art I own. To beg and borrow every denarius that might come my way. For, as you know, I believe that money is power. Possessions are weakness. Sometimes I think Antony understands that and sometimes he does not. Cicero does not. Antony thinks that power comes from leadership. Which in turn comes from reputation and standing – great houses to impress his clients and great deeds to impress his legions. That he need not worry too much about paying his soldiers for they will follow him for love. On the other hand, Cicero believes that the legions, being patriotic Romans to a man, will do what the Senate orders them to do. And the heart of power, therefore, is politics. The man who controls the senators controls their soldiers. He is not concerned with legions at all. But only with the Senate and the men who make it up. All his great battles are fought with words.'

'And both of them are wrong?'

'Yes. Power is money because money buys legions. And in the end it is legions that count. *Divus Julius* understood this, and passed his insight down to me. Pay the legions more than your opponents and they will follow you, not them. No matter that they love your opponent. No matter that your opponent owns the Senate. Pay them and you have them. Keep paying them and you hold them. All other stratagems are doomed to failure in the long-run, no matter what little sparks of short-term success they promise. I think, of the men who stand against me – against whom I stand – really only Cassius sees the truth of this. Which is something else working to my advantage. For Cassius is not very likely to get either money or legions while he's here in Italy. And if Antony and the Senate send him out of Italy, it won't be to anywhere that he can get either money or legions in the short term. So, if it is a race between us, then I am off to the better start. Perhaps that good start might even be enough to make up for his experience, reputation and leadership skills.'

'But, Caesar,' observed Agrippa, 'Cassius and Brutus are brothers in more ways than one. Kindred spirits. And Brutus will be in charge of Apollo's Games during the second week of *Quintilis*, which you would like to rename July in honour of *Divus Julius*. And *Quintilis* is closer than you think! You know how effectively a good games can sway the crowd. Particularly if sufficient extra money is spent to bribe a large cohort of cheerleaders. Power in Rome is not all with the Senate. There is also the People's Tribunal and the *Comitia*, and those are ruled by the *plebs*. I would bet that at some point in Apollo's Games a good large section of the mob will start to cheer for Brutus. And, perhaps, for Cassius. To come home and take up the reins of power once again.'

'How right you are, Marcus Vipsanius! Therefore not all of my denarii will go on buying the allegiance of legions,' said Caesar. 'I will present the *Ludi Victoriae Caesaris* Victorious Caesar Games almost immediately after Brutus' Apollo Games and my games will simply eclipse his in the minds of the people. I will make them so magnificent, I won't even need to bribe cheerleaders! But your point about the *Comitia* is well made. They indeed wield just as much power as the Senate. And are much more accessible to men such as us. Especially as Cicero has no power over them. But Antony, in all sorts of ways and for all sorts of reasons, does. So, Centurion, as we ride back along this road that – like all the others – leads to Rome, let us get down to some serious discussion...'

iv

137

'He understood everything, General. Everything that you planned. Everything I said to Brutus, Cassius and Trebonius. He is either an extremely astute strategist or he has a spy buried deep in your camp. In either case, it would be an excellent idea to co-operate with him. In the short term at least.'

Without Fulvia present, Antony was more relaxed and amenable. He had just returned from more than a week in Casilium, only a couple of *miles* north of Capua. While Artemidorus had been away, his general had managed to calm the city to such an extent that he felt able to achieve the first of his goals. He had ploughed the *pomerium* city limit of a new town, and settled the vast majority of Caesar's restless legions there. It was not just the general who was calmer and quieter. It was the entire city of Rome. For the moment at least.

But the fact that Antony had permitted Enobarbus to bring Artemidorus to this meeting seemed strong proof of his feeling of strengthening control. Proof further supported by the fact that he was willing to listen to what his centurion was saying.

'You are of course probably correct, General,' Artemidorus continued. 'Octavius may well have overestimated his strength. His power. The influence of his name and his money. But he offers a test that will allow you to prove it one way or another. A test which I believe you can use to your own ends – and possibly even outmanoeuvre him into the bargain.'

The secret agent's words were carefully chosen. Enobarbus and he had discussed this meeting at length. Planned it in detail. Understood that it needed to fulfil several major objectives. First, to put Antony in a more amenable mood towards Caesar Octavius. Secondly, to offer the general a realistic plan to achieve his next objective. And thirdly, to re-establish Artemidorus in his good books.

'Indeed?' mused the general. 'Outmanoeuvre him? Interesting. Well, Septem? What is this proof?'

'He assumes, quite correctly I believe, that you have probably put in place a plan that will allow you to counter the Senate's support of Decimus Albinus. Who is already firmly established up in Cisalpine Gaul. A plan which will give you the legal authority to replace him yourself at any time which may prove convenient to you.'

'Certainly, in Cicero's absence, the Senate is almost ready to fall into my grasp. You know he is thinking of going to Athens? He says it's to study; perhaps to research the question of Brutus' patricide. Which has been unsettling Brutus and his friends for some time now, I'm told. I say it's to hide from me...'

'Indeed, General. But in the meantime...'

'In the meantime? Yes? In the meantime there is this test the boy Octavius proposes. What is that?'

'General, Octavius believes he can deliver the *Comitia* to you. Make The People offer you the governorship of Cisalpine Gaul over the Senate's head. Perhaps for a period as long as five years. Available to you whenever you care to move north and replace Decimus Albinus.'

'Very clever – if he can pull it off. But you forget. Or rather he forgets. I have no legions. I have my bodyguard, my Praetorian Cohorts. But six thousand men is not even one legion. And Albinus has three. Battle hardened. Sharp and strong.'

'But, General, that is not the end of the matter. And this is where you can begin to outmanoeuvre him, as I say. Perhaps even to use his plan against him. For, as you will remember, Octavius was to be Caesar's Master of the Horse during the invasion of Parthia that never happened because of his murder. He was studying with Agrippa and Rufus at Apollonia for nearly a year in preparation. But he used some of that time to prepare himself physically and tactically. In Dyrrachium. A fact whose importance he himself seems to have overlooked...'

'Dyrrachium! Where the six Macedonian legions are still stationed...' breathed Antony. 'Now this is interesting. What would make the Senate give me control of the Macedonian legions?'

'Co-consul Dolabella has been awarded the governorship of Macedonia and control of the legions stationed there,' said Enobarbus following Artemidorus' lead, as planned, 'The Senate is happy with this because they believe you and Dolabella are enemies. But Dolabella can be bought, and that is crucial. Because, on his way to Parthia, Caesar was proposing to subjugate the Getae. A warlike, restless tribe, not unlike the long-haired Gauls and the Germans. Now the Getae have been causing no end of trouble all along the *Danubius* river and as far down as the *Mare Euxine* Black Sea. He made no secret of his plans. Word of his murder might well have seeped eastwards. It might be – might it not? – that the Getae, already on a war-footing in expectation of Caesar and his legions, might feel the inactivity resulting from his death could give them an excellent chance to strike first. To come westward into Roman Macedonia itself. To confront Dolabella who is young and inexperienced. Before a new general of experience and standing comes to make war on them in Caesar's place.'

'So, General,' concluded Artemidorus, 'if you could find a way to make use of the threat from the Getae *and* Octavian's offer. Keeping each well independent of the other, so only you and your immediate circle could see the whole picture...'

'I could get the *Comitia* to give me Cisalpine Gaul and the Senate to give me the Macedonian legions while bribing Dolabella into agreeing – which I have time to do because he has not yet left to take up the governorship. Legions which I would instantly bring home and march north. Six against Albinus' three. A

139

brilliant stratagem, Septem. Tribune. I really like the sound of it.' He rubbed his hands together jubilantly. 'As we used to say in Egypt: "So let it be written. So let it be done..."'

V

The chariots came charging round the northern turn in the *Circus Maximus*, Green in the lead. Four black stallions ran shoulder to shoulder, kicking up clumps of wet sand as they hurled the light wicker-sided chariot round the end of the *spina*. The *Circus Maximus* was a cauldron of midsummer heat. The bludgeoning sun's rays augmented by the body heat of a capacity crowd and the absence of even a zephyr of wind. The closing *curriculum* race of the concluding day of *Ludi Victoriae Caesarius* Caesar's Games entered its seventh and final lap. The other colours' *quadrigiae* four-horse chariots crowded behind, dangerously close together, a wall of thundering flesh a dozen stallions wide. Crowding the inner *currus* against the barrier of the central divide round which they had raced six times so far.

Two hundred thousand throats bellowed as one. Two hundred thousand men and women, citizens and slaves, rose to their feet. Arms raised, feet stamping. The noise was overwhelming. Deafening in the *Forum Boarium* immediately outside the *Circus*. Loud in Caesar's villa at the top of the Janiculum Hill on the far side of the Tiber. Audible in the Temple of Jupiter Optimus Maximus Capitolinus on top of the Capitoline. Forceful enough to stop conversations in the Forum and interrupt announcements from the *Comitium*. Echoing amongst the pine groves on top of the Quirinial, most distant of the Seven Hills.

The wooden scaffolding surrounding the racetrack creaked and reverberated dangerously. Artemidorus glanced up at it, momentarily distracted by concern that it might all come down. Though *Divus Julius'* new sections looked pretty stable. Even so, he was very glad to be standing with Enobarbus and Caesar Octavius behind Senator Gaius Matius, who was nominally in charge of the entire games – though the money to stage them had all come from Caesar Octavius himself. While Caesar, Agrippa and Rufus had done much of the planning for them.

They were all gathered now in the dictator's seating area. At the heart of the original marble sections that would withstand an earthquake – let alone a victory for the Greens. The six of them were up on their feet, like the rest of the crowd, caught up in the drama of the moment. Standing behind *Divus Julius'* ivory and gold *curule* chair. Which had been placed in the position of honour, as though he might be here in spirit, directing the games being run in memory and honour of his victories. In honour of Venus *Genetrix*, the founder of his family and the

140

patron goddess of his *gens* family. And, on this occasion, in honour of his life and death.

But, as everyone now knew, *Divus Julius* could not actually be here in spirit. Because his spirit had been blazing across the sky, light and dark, since the *Ludi Victoriae Caesaris* began five days ago. Easily visible against the unbroken blue of the sky during the day. Seemingly even brighter than the moon during the long, breathless nights. Astrologers – mostly Egyptian and Greek – called the phenomenon a comet. But the entire Roman world knew that it was really the spirit of *Divus Julius* being welcomed to Olympus by Jupiter himself.

The summer's evening was closing in. The traditional four-horse chariot race was the last to be run. The last of fifty that day alone. And those amongst the crowd not rejoicing at the dominance of the Greens were hoping to see the spectacle topped off with a *naufragia* shipwreck, which might include all of the chariots. Leading to the death and destruction of the wicker-sided vehicles, their drivers and their horses. A slaughter fit to match those of countless gladiators, criminals, prisoners and wild beasts which had filled the celebrations so far.

But Artemidorus, who had been a go-between linking Antony and Octavius for the last few weeks, knew that the young man wanted a clean end to the games. So he could make his planned announcements in the certain knowledge that they would be listened to. Here and now. Before they were repeated by the *praeco* town criers in the city. And posted as news-sheets in the Forum outside the Senate.

Greens won. Again. There was no shipwreck and all the chariots came in safely. To the gratification of some and the disgust of others. Which was, thought Artemidorus in philosophical mood, all part of the human condition. No matter who you pleased, someone else was displeased. For instance, it seemed on the face of it, that Caesar Octavius' pronouncements would go a long way towards pleasing everybody who heard them. But, even as they were promulgated, the spy could begin a mental list of men who would be less than happy with what was being said.

Starting, in many respects, with Mark Antony.

It was Gaius Matius, as *Magister Ludi* Master of the Games, who made the pronouncements as dictated by the young man himself. Fortunately so. For Caesar Octavius' voice was by no means loud, unlike Agrippa's. And he had a narrow, sickly chest. Which did not support speeches delivered with a Stentorian bellow. Or even those offered with an actor's carrying projection. Gaius Matius, however, was a man used to addressing the better part of eight hundred senators. And, although the *Circus Maximus* was not designed like a Greek Theatre – to carry a whispered word to the farthest extremities – nevertheless his words reached

141

everyone they needed to. Those who were also seated on the marble seats reserved for the rich and powerful.

The *plebs* could catch up later.

As the winning chariot was led away and the others followed. As the hubbub died into anticipation of the award of the final prize. As the massive audience sat down and Gaius Matius, the last man standing, strode forward, a tense hush fell on the whole of the *Circus*.

'My friends,' he declaimed, his voice carrying like that of a *praeco* town crier. 'Let it be known...'

He paused, hands raised. It seemed that every eye was on him, though Artemidorus doubted he was visible to a good number of the crowd. 'Let the following things be known! *Primitus* that the Senate and People of Rome will be asked officially to recognise the deity of Gaius Julius Caesar. That he be titled in future *Divus Julius* in all official records and documents. As he has often been called by many of us since his murder. That he be worshipped as a deity – part of the state's religion, his cult being led by Augur, Consul and General Mark Antony himself. *Secundus*, that, upon official recognition of the deity of *Divus Julius*, his son and heir will assume the name and title, Gaius Julius Caesar Octavianus *Divus Filius*. And will be known by these names and titles from this time forward. And *tertio*, that this month, the month of *Divus Julius*' birth and of the celebration of the games that honour him, this month should no longer be known as *Quintilis*, but from this time forward as *Julius*. July.'

VIII

The *sicarius* knifeman employed to kill Artemidorus was known as Myrtillus, though this was not his real name. That was something which sounded almost Hebrew, but he did not look particularly Jewish. In fact he was tall, saturnine, dark-skinned – though tanned by desert suns rather than African ones. He had a lean, rangy body usually concealed by a padded tunic and a long, hooded cloak. When not about his murderous business, he walked with a military swagger though he disdained to wear soldiers' *braccae* trousers or *caligae* boots. His face was framed by a thin, black beard that followed the lean lines of his jaw down from his neat ears, past the sharp angles of his cheekbones to the resolute square of his chin. His eyes were dark, intelligent, and at the moment, burning with frustrated anger. His hands were huge and powerful; callused and bony. Held together by whip-strong tendons that stretched the skin like restless wires.

The name of his calling came from the *sicarius'* knife he wore concealed beneath his cloak. Which he often used. It had a curved blade with one fearsomely sharp edge. The inner side of the hook. In consequence it was lethally effective, especially in close work. Slicing open throats, necks, arms, wrists. Occasionally thighs or genitals. Opening blood vessels that bled out in mere moments. Unstoppably. The *sica* was looked down upon by his fastidious Roman employers as an ignoble instrument – especially compared with their straight-bladed, two-edged weapons the noble *gladius* and the upright *pugio*. They preferred to go armed for battle rather than street fights. Though they indulged in both.

The *sicarius* Myrtillus was more enraged than he could ever remember having been. Some of his anger was directed at himself. He had never missed with his lethal *sôlênarion* bow before. Now he had missed twice. It was the damage to his reputation that was the root of his rage. Not the fact that he had killed two innocent bystanders – and without being paid for the deaths. A slave doorkeeper hardly mattered. But he had killed a patrician in Capua and executions of that sort usually came with a premium charge. All this and the fact that he had been pulled from one target to another with the first matter still unresolved. Which made him seem to be hesitant. Indecisive. Inefficient.

Apparently oblivious to the murderer's ill-concealed annoyance, his employer's representative leaned closer across the table that separated them. 'Forget the centurion for the moment. Keep the original down payment and accept this additional sum...' A leather bag slid weightily across the tabletop. 'Priorities have changed. The young Caesar has risen to prominence and the promise of power with a rapidity and in a manner that could never have been foreseen. This alters everything as far as my employer is concerned. Alters your target especially, as we have discussed. Furthermore, your original *scopum* target, too, has been moved. Reassigned. He is no longer with the Seventh, which is being disbanded and settled. He is now with Antony's personal guard of Praetorians and we want to wait and see what effect this has, if any. For although he is with a new cohort, his responsibilities seem much the same.

'My employer suggests that your new objective will require you to consider employing new methods. The *sôlênarion* may be your preferred approach...' The voice drifted into silence for a heartbeat and the professional killer detected a moment of disappointment. Perhaps disapproval. He closed his fist over the leather bag. The mass of what it contained began to soothe his wounded pride. The gentle voice continued. 'But it has not been effective so far. And it is unlikely to be a successful approach with your new execution. Also, you may consider that employing an associate – at least one associate – might also help. There is plenty in that bag to allow freedom in this area should you choose to follow it. The entire security system you are faced with employs so many men that my employer is certain you will be able to bribe or blackmail at least one crucial member.'

'Are you telling me how to do my job?' snarled the frustrated assassin.

'Of course I am. So far in our association you have failed to live up to the reputation that first attracted my employer to you. But, consider this. If you use your own methods and continue to fail then the fault is clearly your own. The damage to your reputation irreparable. If you accede to my employer's suggestions and things still do not go well, then the blame is at least shared. Your standing tarnished, but redeemable. Besides, if *Fortuna* smiles on you, then you might yet earn everything we have paid so far all at once. For the centurion is often so close to your new quarry that you could conceivably kill them both at once. If, as I say, things go well for you.'

'Things *will* go well,' snarled Myrtillus. 'No matter how I approach the problem. No matter who is there. Tell...'

'No names!' The representative glanced uneasily around the *popina* tavern as best as was possible given the depth of the hood keeping the face in anonymous shadow. 'One slip along those lines and you either have to kill everyone nearby. Or I will have to kill you myself.'

'If you are so accomplished in these matters, then why do you not undertake the mission yourself?' sneered Myrtillus.

'Because I have other duties,' came the icy answer. 'But, if you doubt my ability to do so…' The quiet voice drifted into silence. And the *sicarius* felt the icy point of a blade slide up his inner thigh. A line of chill that seemed to strike to the depth of the femoral artery that pulsed there as powerfully as the carotid in his neck.

Myrtillus leaned forward suddenly, careful to move only his upper body. 'You rely on the fact that you are a boy – or little more than a boy to judge by your voice – to make opponents underestimate you,' he breathed. 'What would I not give to tear back that hood and see your face without the mask of shadow.'

'You might do so,' answered his opponent. 'But my face would be the last thing in this life you would see.' The point of the dagger stirred, as dangerous as a sleepy serpent.

Myrtillus sat back, with a soft, unsteady laugh. 'Very well,' he capitulated. 'You remain anonymous. Your newly assigned Praetorian centurion remains alive unless, as you say, he is close to my new objective when I strike. And the new target dies, in company or alone. As agreed. For the moment.' He leaned forward once again, suddenly, threateningly, recklessly. 'But take good care, whoever you are, that I do not add your name to the list of those I will assist in their passage to the underworld. For should that happen, I would come after you more relentlessly even than the Friendly Ones.' He glanced around as he used the euphemism, as though fearing that the Furies might come in any case, alerted by what he threatened rather than what he chose to say.

The hooded stranger gave a quiet chuckle. The blade left the sensitive skin of Myrtillus' inner thigh. But the cold kiss of the icy steel lingered. 'And you, Myrtillus of Lycian Olympos, had better pray to whatever gods you worship that I do not come after you. For I too am as relentless as the Friendly Ones. And I have at least two advantages over you. I know who you are. And I know where to find you.'

ii

'It's strange,' said Caesar Octavius, 'how you always know where to find me, Septem.'

'It's my job, Caesar. I may be assigned to the Praetorian Cohorts for the moment as the Seventh is disbanded and settled but the only things that have changed are the badges on my uniform. If I am to carry messages between you and Lord Antony, I need to know where you both are.'

'Well, you have found me.' Caesar's tone made the observation light, almost joking. But his cool grey eyes matched Artemidorus' in that they shifted from smoke to steel. The pair of them were seated on horseback, side by side, looking

145

down through unseasonably sheeting rain to the half-built settlement of Casilium, whose *pomerium*, city limit, Antony had ploughed some time ago.

It was all very well, thought Artemidorus, for himself, Caesar, Agrippa, Rufus and their men to be sitting here wrapped in thick, waterproof cloaks. But the men and their families down in the mud of Casilium, were likely to be less than happy with the progress of their promised city and adjacent farmland. Those of them who understood agriculture would have wished to see their smallholdings and gardens well sewn by now – with hope of some sort of harvest in the fast-approaching autumn and then in spring. But it was getting far too late in the year for that. Therefore, suspected Antony's envoy insightfully, the young man's icy demeanour had more to do with what he was looking at and with Antony, who should be taking better care of his ex-legionaries, than with the general's emissary.

'What does Antony wish to say to me?' asked Caesar Octavius at last.

'That the law passed under his brother Lucius, the *Lex Antonia Agrarian* is designed to settle the ex-legionaries in Italy once and for all. Including even the Seventh.' Artemidorus gestured down at the mud-pit of the half-built city. All too well aware of the inappropriateness of his message. 'Lepidus has relinquished control of them and is travelling north beyond the Alps to take up his new post as Governor of Gallia Narbonensis. With five new legions under his *imperium*. Settling the last of the ex-legionaries should remove the threat of restless soldiers upsetting the peace of the countryside and the city alike…' he paused again, poignantly aware of the irony of his words. Antony, in distant Rome, assumed that the ex-legionaries were established happily and his problems with them were over. Caesar Octavius – and Artemidorus now – knew different.

'And Antony asks that I should do nothing to undermine this peace. By offering them bounty to leave their idyllic newly settled towns and fertile farms and follow me instead.' Caesar picked up the message, his tone as ironic as the situation. 'Also, I have no doubt, he would be happier if I stopped my own representatives from sounding out some of the serving soldiers as to how much their allegiance might be worth. We have discussed this already, Septem, and I have told you what I intend. All the more so now that Antony has sent orders recalling the Macedonian legions. In case the Getae go to war. An interesting battle plan. Worthy, perhaps, of Marcus Licinius Crassus himself. To fear a confrontation in the east of Macedonia and answer it by bringing the army that was stationed there home!' He did not bother mentioning the useless but rapacious governor-to-be Publius Dolabella, who had not yet dragged himself out of the fleshpots of Rome to begin his march eastwards towards his new, if depleted, command.

146

Caesar wheeled his horse impatiently and headed back towards the leather-roofed tent that was his own current home. It stood at the heart of a simple encampment – the sort Marius' legionary Mules erected each night after a long day's march through enemy territory. They passed through a gate in the stockade, where guards slammed to attention, alert in spite of the unseasonal cold and wet. Rode along the straight *via* to the centre of the camp where the commander's quarters were pitched. A guard of legionaries crashed to attention, then sprang forward to help them dismount and take their horses. Caesar Octavius strode into his tent. Artemidorus followed, reminded with unsettling forcefulness of *Divus Julius'* battle-camp fortresses in war-torn Gaul. They entered the tent side by side, surrendering their sodden cloaks to the legionaries who were acting as servants. 'Can I offer you a drink?' asked Caesar hospitably. Artemidorus knew the young man well enough now to answer simply, 'Water, please, Caesar.'

'I will join you,' said Caesar, who hardly ever touched wine. A legionary hurried to an *amphora* and returned with two goblets of fresh spring water. And a look of almost worshipful awe. 'Thank you Marcus,' said Caesar. Again reminding the spy forcefully of *Divus Julius*. Who seemed to know the name of every man following his banners and eagles.

The furnishings in the tent were Spartan to say the least of it. Artemidorus approved: he was Spartan by birth himself. But there were two chairs and the men sat, facing each other over a table big enough to hold a battle plan. As though they were equals. Certainly, thought the spy, it was a mark of Caesar's absolute trust that the pair of them were utterly alone. For the word on the street was that there were assassins about, tasked with killing many more men than Artemidorus himself. Caesar chief amongst them. But here he was, casually unguarded. Even Agrippa and Rufus were out about some other business. Subverting Antony's legions, like as not...

'Cicero is on the run,' observed Caesar, coming directly to the point – as though, once more, he was privy to Antony's most secret thoughts and concerns.

'He plans to go to Athens,' nodded Artemidorus. 'He says he will simply study there.' He sipped the icy water. It was very good indeed.

'Not what Antony wants?'

'No, Caesar. Antony asked Cicero to rule on a matter of law some months ago. And he has not done so. The general would prefer Cicero did not leave Italy until he has done so...'

'A point of law?' Caesar's eyebrows arched interrogatively.

The secret agent leaned forward, measuring his words carefully. 'Are you aware of your father's dying words, Caesar? What they were and to whom they were spoken?'

iii

'That explains a lot,' nodded Caesar sometime later. 'Not least why Cicero has paused at Elea in his flight to Athens in order to talk with Brutus and Cassius. Who are also, I understand, on the point of leaving Italy. Clearly something needed to be settled between them before they parted – perhaps never to meet again in this life.'

'Brutus and Cassius are also en route for Athens,' nodded Artemidorus. 'And then to Asia. To take up their posts as corn commissioners. Until they become respectively governors of Crete and Sicily.'

'And Antony believes they will settle for this, does he? In spite of the fact that I understand Brutus has sent his freedman Herostratus into Macedonia to try and subvert the legions there. As though a couple of corn commissioners need six whole legions to back them up. Even if the Getae are growing restless. Which I doubt.'

'But, as you know, Caesar, Brutus and Cassius have no money to pay for troops. If Cicero rules as Antony hopes in the matter of *Divus Julius'* last words, Brutus will be *hostis* proscribed, outlawed, in any case. Cassius' reputation tarnished by association. Both of them far from Rome and helpless. And the Macedonian legions are on their way back in any case. Five of them, at any rate.'

'Leaving one legion as a fig leaf to confront the warlike Getae. Commanded, when he gets there, by the redoubtable Dolabella. If Gaius Trebonius, as Governor of Syria, allows him passage and a measure of support on his way eastwards…' Caesar smiled cynically and Artemidorus thought how bad the boy's teeth were. 'But Antony's plan to hamstring Brutus and Cassius may bear fruit – who knows? So, let us leave things as they stand for the moment with the murderous brothers-in-law. They are certainly relatively helpless until they get their hands on some money, as you observe. What does Antony propose to do about Cicero and this troublesome point of law in the meantime?'

'There has already been much unrest in Rome,' said the spy, choosing his words with even more care than usual. 'The citizens feel that Cicero is deserting them. Having established himself as such an important figure in the aftermath of the murder. And now, instead of standing up for the so-called *Libertores*, he is running like a rabbit. It is shameful. Cowardly. A desertion that will go down in history beside the perfidy of Paris stealing another man's wife to start the war

148

which destroyed Troy. And the stupidity of Crassus losing seven legions to the Parthians. Seven legions, his son and his head...'

Caesar gave a bark of laughter. 'So these are the rumours you have started spreading are they? If that gossip doesn't bring him back, then nothing will. Cicero is as anxious about his reputation as Brutus is! They are both bound by their concern for their place in history as tightly as a criminal is bound by his chains. I think I will return to Rome and see what happens next for myself.' He glanced around the tent and its Spartan furnishings. 'Though I mustn't linger there too long. In case I get a taste for the high life. Which I can no longer afford...'

*

The pair of them rode back side by side along the Appian Way with a modest escort led by Agrippa and Rufus. They rode fast and were approaching the *Porta Capena* in the Servian wall late the next day under a clearing sky with a kindly late-summer southerly to welcome them. Only to find the entrance to the city blocked by a huge crowd of wildly cheering citizens. Just before they joined the outskirts of this mob, Caesar pulled his right rein gently and guided his horse into the space between two tombs shaded by a tall pine tree. 'Marcus Vipsanius,' he said to Agrippa, 'go and find out what's going on.'

'I'll go too,' said Artemidorus. 'Probably best on foot...' Caesar nodded and the two men dismounted. It took hardly any time for them to join the cheering multitude. And no time at all after that to discover what was happening. 'Cicero!' the ecstatic mob started chanting. 'Marcus Tullius, welcome home! Cicero has returned to us...'

Rather than steal the returning lawyer's thunder, Caesar waited until he could enter the city quietly and anonymously. Artemidorus waited with him. But soon after they had ridden through the gate, their ways parted. Caesar, having sold all of the property belonging to himself and his immediate family, was proposing to stay at the house owned by Agrippa's brother. Whose friendship Octavius had won by pleading with *Divus Julius* to spare him – even though he had sided against Caesar and fought with Cato's defeated army in the civil war.

Artemidorus went straight to Antony.

As soon as he entered the *via* leading to Pompey's villa where Antony was currently living and the Temple of Tellus beyond it where the Praetorian Cohorts were encamped, he was struck by the contrast with Caesar's quarters. And the accuracy of his words. This huge villa might well represent a weakness in his notoriously self-indulgent general. The very frontage of the villa, with its costly representations of the prows of pirate ships destroyed in Pompey's naval campaigns, looked so lavish. He rode forward almost in a trance, his mind racing.

149

Hardly noticing the soldiers lining the street and guarding the massive door. He dismounted, still in a dream, and handed the reins of his horse over. Only when he reached the door itself did he pause.

'Password?' demanded a familiar voice. His eyes focused on the speaker. It was Ferrata. Who had been transferred with the *contubernium* of spies into the Praetorians at the same time as the centurion and the Tribune Enobarbus. Though the network was still working all together, undercover in various places, at Enobarbus' command – answering Antony's requirements. Facilitating – and informing – his plans. But was Ferrata working undercover here? And if so, why?

'Let me in, imbecile,' he said.

The big ex-legionary of the also disbanded VIth snapped to attention. 'That'll do, Septem,' he said with a gap-toothed grin. Then he lowered his voice, 'Though if anyone asks, it's *Hercules*. Again.'

Ferrata turned and thundered on the door. Which swung open just wide enough to admit the spy.

Artemidorus walked towards the *atrium*, frowning. The whole area was bustling. But not with soldiers as in Caesar Octavius' camp. With partygoers. Men and women in varying states of inebriation and undress stood and staggered all around the space. Slaves were dashing to and fro, filling plates with sweetmeats and savouries, filling goblets to overflowing. And not with icy spring water. At the entrance to the lively chamber, the soldier paused, looking round. Confused by the contrast with his recent experiences. He could see neither Antony or Fulvia – host and hostess.

As the secret agent hesitated, bewildered by the comparative waste of time, energy and money that the party represented, Antony's mistress Volumnia Cytheris whirled past. Dressed as Cleopatra. But Cleopatra in one of Antony's dreams: wearing only a gown of Egyptian cotton so sheer as to be transparent. Which was secured by a snake made of woven gold. That circled her ribs rather than her waist. Immediately beneath the pale fullness of her naked breasts. Their nipples gilded. Reminding him disorientatingly of Cyanea even so. Cyanea in a disturbingly similar costume.

Then, over to one side he saw Enobarbus. He pushed his way ruthlessly through the cheery throng until he reached his commander's side. 'What's going on?' he asked breathlessly.

'Cicero's back,' said Enobarbus shortly. 'The general is celebrating the success of his clever stratagem. He proposes to party tonight and confront the old man at the Senate meeting tomorrow. Get him to rule in public right there and then about the Divine Julius' dying words and the patricide matter.'

'Does he? Why now?'

'Because he's run out of patience. Because the old man tried to run for it and might actually manage to escape next time. Not be fooled by the rumours we started that the People of Rome thought him a coward and a runaway – like Price Paris of Troy. An abject failure like Crassus. He might even get beyond Antony's immediate grasp next time. Because now that the Italian legions are settled, Antony wants the legal matter settled as well so he can get out and about. He can't stay here forever, not if he wants to boot Decimus Albinus out of Cisalpine Gaul any time soon. And to cap it all, the Macedonian legions are due to start arriving in Brundisium any day now.'

iv

'Sick!' snarled Antony just after dawn next day. '*I'm* sick. And I'm still here!'

He had proved the truth of the latter statement by vomiting in the Senate House a few minutes earlier. In front of the entire Senate. The Senate – apart from those in exile or in hiding. And except for the one senator still in Rome whom he needed to be present for his plan to reach fruition.

Artemidorus, standing outside the still-gaping Senate House door, wondered whether Cicero's sickness was the real thing – or a clever ploy on the lawyer's part. And, if it was genuine, whether it really was comparable to Antony's self-inflicted nausea. About which there could be no question. The general had been far too drunk to hear his report yesterday afternoon – and had been either paralytic or deeply asleep ever since. He hadn't even bathed or shaved in the interim.

Now he was in the worst of all possible conditions. In the grip of a crippling hangover – and yet still so drunk that he was well beyond self-control or reason. He paced the rostrum like a wild beast in the *Circus Maximus*. 'It's a trick!' he continued, his voice a throaty, phlegm-thickened roar. 'The old *pēdĕre* fart is trying to outsmart me! I want him *here*! And I want him here *now*! If I have to, I'll get a builder and go myself to rip off his front door. The whole front of his *fornicates* villa!' But then he suddenly seemed to have a better idea. He swung round to address Enobarbus who, as tribune, was permitted inside the Senate. 'Tribune!' he growled. 'Get as many of my Praetorians as it takes. Bring Marcus Tullius Cicero here. And if he continues to refuse my invitations, then burn the old *nothus* bastard out!'

There was a hiss of horror throughout the entire Senate. Co-consul Publius Dolabella, preparing to take up the governorship of Macedonia and by no means worried even about the fate of his ex-father-in-law, simply shrugged. Made a

151

pantomime of washing his hands – the legal gesture demonstrating that he gave up any responsibility in the matter.

Enobarbus turned on his heel and marched out of the Senate House door. 'Come with me,' he ordered Artemidorus. 'Bring Ferrata and some men we can trust.'

'Trust to burn Cicero out?' asked Artemidorus, his voice betraying his shock.

'Men we can trust *not* to burn the old fool out!' snapped Enobarbus. 'But men who will put on a good show of trying to do so, if it comes to it.'

As the squad Artemidorus assembled for Enobarbus marched across the Forum in the direction of Cicero's house on the lower slopes of the Palatine, Ferrata fell in at the spy's shoulder. 'Have you seen Quintus recently, Septem?'

'Not since we got back from our mission to Antium and Pompeii, while the legions were being disbanded and the Praetorian Cohorts set up, why?'

'He wants to see you. He has a surprise. After this is over – whatever it is that this *is* – I'll take you to him.'

'What's this about?' The spy abruptly realised that Quintus might well be in trouble. He had lived for the VIIth and they had never discussed what he might do if the legion was disbanded. Artemidorus suddenly realised that the old man might be down there in the mud of Castilium, trying to get some sort of shelter erected. Some sort of subsistence crop planted. But then he thought, *No*... Ferrata wouldn't be proposing a three-day journey in the midst of all this. Wherever the old *Triarius* actually was, he must be somewhere in the city. Perhaps with Spurinna, like Puella, Hercules, Venus and Adonis... But then he realised with a start that he really had no idea where any of his little *contubernium* of spies actually were at all.

He quick-marched up to Enobarbus' shoulder. 'Tribune...' he began.

'Right,' snapped the tribune. 'Here we are. Let's see what's going on shall we?' And he hammered on Cicero's door with the pommel of his *gladius*.

After a few moments, Cicero's secretary Tiro answered. One glance was enough. His face flooded with recognition and suspicion. 'The master is unwell,' he snapped. 'You cannot drag him to Antony, whether he wants to go or not, this time. He is in his bed and too feverish to leave it.'

'Right,' said Ferrata unhelpfully. 'Then we have the general's permission to burn him out. The general's direct order to do so in fact. After he decided against getting a builder and smashing his way in personally. And he was speaking as consul into the bargain...'

'That will do, Legionary!' snapped Enobarbus. 'Tiro. Would your master be well enough to see Septem and myself? For a moment or two only. So we may assess the situation...'

'Well, Tribune, I'm not sure...'

'The general and consul did issue the order as reported by the legionary, Tiro,' warned Artemidorus. 'But, remember, we are the men who rescued Marcus Tullius from a murderous mob. He is only still alive because of us. We don't want him dead any more than you do. We only wish to make sure we can honestly tell General Antony that the senator is so unwell that setting fire to the house would simply roast him to death – not frighten him into obedience.'

'Very well,' said Tiro. 'But only you two. And only for a moment. The master is exhausted. And he is asleep at the moment, so tread softly.'

Artemidorus was shocked by the change he saw in Cicero. Even though the senator had not been at his best during their last meeting, nothing could have prepared the spy for the deterioration in the old man's appearance since. What little flesh there had been on his face seemed to have melted away. There was nothing more than skull beneath the ivory skin. The high forehead, framed with white, woolly hair, was beaded with sweat. The eyeballs behind the closed lids jerked feverishly from side to side above big black bags. The body on the bed, outlined beneath the covers, seemed bloated. While the arms and legs had grown more spindly still.

'Do you know where Antistius the physician lives?' asked Artemidorus.

'Yes,' answered Tiro.

'Send someone to fetch him,' commanded the centurion.

'We'll explain matters to Antony,' added Enobarbus. 'There'll be no more summonses to the Senate today...'

'... or talk of builders and burning.' Artemidorus added.

V

Side by side, Artemidorus and Enobarbus led their little command back across the Forum to the Senate House. 'Antony's not going to like this,' said Artemidorus uneasily, all too well aware that he was still in the general's bad books – even though he had yet to present him with even more unpalatable news. News about Caesar Octavius and his plans; the sluggish progress of mud-bound Castilium and the recurrent restlessness of the legions Antony supposed were happily settled. Not to mention the fact that Caesar Octavius appeared to have surrounded himself with more than one legion. Perhaps two or three thousand men, all old soldiers. Who seemed to be almost on a war-footing in the heart of Italy just three *miles* north of Capua. And of course there was the fact that the young man was in Rome now, watching this farce with his two bosom companions and a great deal of cynical amusement.

153

But then the goddess *Fortuna*, perhaps at the prompting of his own personal deity the demigod Achilleus, hero of Troy, smiled on him. A military messenger came riding into the Forum and, seeing a squad of soldiers, reined to a halt beside them. '*Ave*, Tribune,' he saluted from horseback. 'I have news for General Antony. Do you know where I can find him?'

'We are going to him now,' answered Enobarbus. 'You may accompany us.'

The messenger slid to the ground and led his horse alongside him as he marched with stiff legs towards the Senate.

'Good news?' asked Ferrata, who was walking beside him. 'The general could do with some...'

'The first of the Macedonian legions, the *Martia*, has started disembarking in Brundisium,' gasped the messenger.

'Now that,' said Artemidorus quietly to Enobarbus, 'just has to brighten up his day.'

'And, perhaps, his mood.' Enobarbus added.

*

The tribune was right. He called Antony to the door of the Senate so the legionary could deliver his message. No sooner had Antony heard what the young soldier had to say than he peremptorily handed the chairmanship of the meeting over to Dolabella and hurried home. Apparently having forgotten all about Cicero. Paying no heed at all to the mutterings of the senators who felt insulted by his rapid exit.

In the now-vacant *atrium* of his villa – and in his changing room, office and bath – he listened to Artemidorus' report with half an ear as he changed out of his senatorial *toga*, packed away his badges of office, bathed, was shaved and put his armour on. Fulvia appeared in the midst of this process. And no sooner had she heard the news than she too was off to change.

The unsuspecting officers and men of the *Martia* legion were going to get quite a welcome, thought Artemidorus. But his wry amusement was undermined by the strong suspicion that, although his report had been delivered, it had by no means been received or understood.

'If Octavian is in Rome then you stay here too, Septem,' Antony decided. 'Keep an eye on the little rat. Stick to him like his shadow but stay unobserved yourself. Tell me where he goes and who he sees. A complete list, mind, when I get back. Tribune, you're coming to Brundisium with Fulvia and me. We're going to welcome the boys home. It'll be the start of a long party.'

Artemidorus left Antony's villa wondering how best to go about his assignment. Caesar Octavius knew him by sight. Better, perhaps than anyone except for

Enobarbus. Cyanea. And Antony himself. It seemed to him that if he was going to have a realistic chance of fulfilling his orders without alerting the subject of the surveillance that he was being watched, then he had better find someone who could stand in for him. Someone Caesar did not know – who might reasonably be expected to be hanging around the city streets.

'Ah, Septem,' said a familiar voice, breaking into his thoughts. 'Is now a good time to show you Quintus' surprise? It's an excellent one, I promise…'

He turned, and there was Ferrata. The answer to his problem. In several ways, as things turned out.

'Yes,' he said at once. 'It's a very good time.'

'Right,' said Ferrata. 'Let's go.'

Ferrata led Artemidorus across the Forum and into the maze of streets leading past the *subura* up towards the Esquiline Hill. As they walked, the legionary of the VIth Ironclads talked incessantly, bringing Artemidorus up to date with the changes set off by the dissolution of the VIIth. 'It went far beyond simply reassigning us soldiers to Antony's Praetorian Cohorts,' the old soldier explained. 'That was only the start of it. Once we were at liberty, so to speak, then a whole raft of other changes seem to have followed on. Quintus, for instance, was too old for the Praetorians. So he was forcibly retired. Which he did not take lying down, I can tell you!

'In the meantime Spurinna ran into a bit of a problem. Not the sort of problem that need trouble men like you and me, Septem, but a problem nevertheless. It appears that augurs and *haruspices* are a bit like vestals. The gods talk most clearly to those who do not indulge in the delights of the flesh. And there was poor old Spurinna, surrounded by carefully selected slaves – both male and female – who would give the Gorgons a run for their money. Suddenly giving house room to Puella, Venus and Adonis. All of whom are at the far end of the spectrum, so to speak. He went from being Perseus confronted by Medusa to being Paris choosing between the loveliest goddesses. And it seems to have confused the poor old *baro* guy.'

'I can see that it might,' said Artemidorus, remembering the warm looks Puella had given him the last time they were together. Rather than the cold, calculating comments of Venus. Though, now that he thought of Venus, there were one or two questions he might well address to her when the time was right. 'So what was the solution to all of this?'

'Wait and see,' answered Ferrata. 'You won't believe it, I swear…'

vi

155

The pair of them marched past Spurinna's villa, then Trebonius'. On up the hill into the pine grove where the would-be assassin's bolts had thumped into solid tree trunks rather than their softer, fleshy targets. Artemidorus remembered the stirring of surprise he had felt that Quintus, leading the retreat, had seemed to know where he was going. As did Ferrata now. He led Artemidorus confidently and unerringly through the pine grove that had saved their lives. Until, completely unexpectedly, the thick coppice of trees stopped. In a clearly cultivated line. That must have been laid down many years since, for all the trees along it were fully grown and tall. With no sign of any having been cut down or chopped back. There, on the far side of a considerable open space, stood a villa. That, for all its ancient design, seemed perfectly well maintained. Surrounded by carefully tended gardens full of fruit and vegetables as well as herbs and flowers. Lemon groves and orange groves. Fig trees and olive bushes. All in full flower or laden with fruit. Concealed behind walls of pine trees that stood guard on every side. Keeping the massive villa secret. Undetected. Unsuspected.

'What is this place?' asked Artemidorus, simply awestruck.

'This,' answered Ferrata ebulliently, 'this is Quintus' surprise. Though you haven't seen a tenth of it yet!'

The legionary led Artemidorus across the cultivated grounds until the pair of them reached the big front door. He hammered on the wood. Three hard knocks. Three softer ones. Two hard ones. Then he stopped and they waited. For a couple of heartbeats. Before a grille at eye level snapped open and closed. The door was opened. By an elderly man whose lean and muscular body seemed to give the lie to his white-haired, deeply lined face. Whose bright blue eyes gleamed with lively intelligence.

'This is Drusus the doorkeeper,' said Ferrata, leading Artemidorus inwards. 'Drusus, this is Septem. Second only to the tribune…'

'Welcome Centurion Iacomus Artemidorus,' said Drusus, bowing.

Ferrata led the astonished Artemidorus deeper into the house. And into the presence of the doorkeeper's female double. Whose white hair was longer. Whose body was slightly softer-looking and perhaps less muscular. Whose eyes were every bit as bright. 'And this is Drusilla, sister to the doorkeeper and *focaria* housekeeper of the villa.'

'Welcome Centurion,' she said. Her voice deeper and softer than her brother's.

'What is this place?' demanded Artemidorus, thoroughly awestruck.

'This is Colchis, land of wonders,' explained Ferrata obscurely. 'This is where the Amazons reside, where Aeetes is king, though there is no Queen Idiya. Where there are wonders belonging to the groves of the war god Ares, Greek brother to our Roman Mars. Wonders that make Jason's Golden Fleece seem like a breech-clout in comparison!'

'Don't listen to him, Septem,' said Quintus, striding into the *atrium* from the *tablinum* office area deeper in the building. 'He's just running off at the mouth.'

'What is this place, Quintus?'

'It's my home, lad. Haven't you worked that out yet? And, as the Fates would have it, my home is the very place in which we can keep our *contubernium* of secret agents housed, supplied, briefed and active.'

'Does the tribune know about this?'

'He knows about it, yes. And approves of the use I propose we make of it. But no – he hasn't been here or actually seen it.'

'Seen it?' Artemidorus was still reeling from Ferrata's description of the place as Colchis, home of the Amazons and location of the Golden Fleece, reborn. 'What is there to see?'

'More than you can imagine, Septem,' chuckled the old *triarius*. 'More than you can imagine...'

*

'For more than two hundred years my family has followed general after general in the legions. From the year 520 since the founding of the city, generation after generation of my ancestors have fought with men like Scipio Africanus; his son Scipio Aemilianus, Aemilianus Macedonicus, Marius, Sulla, Lucullus, Crassus, Pompey and Caesar all across the expanding empire of Rome's dominions and out to the edges of the world. Where others sought gold and plunder, brought home Punic artefacts from Carthage or Greek statues from Macedonia, we have sought only to make ourselves the best soldiers it was possible to be. We had no need of money...' Quintus gestured at the distant walls of the *triclinium*, the sweep of his arm encompassing not only the dining area but the villa beyond, the gardens beyond that and the groves of pine trees that capped the Esquiline Hill. Which, it seemed, he owned.

'What did we bring back from the wars, then? Knowledge and weapons. Books on warfare copied from the Libraries of Alexandria, Athens, Babylon, Carthage, Thebes... collected from repositories everywhere. Works of poetry on relevant subjects, such as *The Iliad* of Homer. Books drafted by theoreticians like Archimedes, Onasander and Asclepiodotus. By experienced observers such as Polybius; experienced soldiers such as Xenophon and Tacticus. Weapons experts like Balbus. Generals such as *Divus Julius*. Treatises in Greek, Punic, Egyptian, Latin... They are all in the library, those that need it with translations.

'And weapons. Then as now, every one of my ancestors who came across any novelty or advance in any kind of weaponry – except for siege machines and such – sent examples of it back. From all over the world. Every theatre of war the legions fought in. Year after year. For the last two centuries. Even in the matter of siegecraft we have illustrations. Archimedes' mirrors that set the ships in Syracuse harbour alight; the great crane he designed to lift entire vessels out of the water. The recipe for Greek Fire. A treatise on mines; how to dig them under city walls – and how to overcome them. Ramps – how to build them and how to destroy them. Cities – how to defend them and how to overcome them. Siege towers. Rams. *Onagers. Scorpios.* Catapults. *Ballistae.* All the rest. We even have a detailed diagram of how Hannibal's elephants were armed. But it is the actual weaponry that I know will interest you most. For anyone interested in clubs, *cestae* iron fists, knives, swords, axes, war hammers, battle scourges, armour, headgear, slings, bows, arrows, spears. You name it and this place is, as Ferrata said, Colchis. The land of unimaginable treasures.'

Quintus finished speaking and took a sip of water. His audience, varyingly entranced, consisted of Artemidorus, Hercules, Puella, Venus and Adonis, because a good deal of time had passed since Ferrata led Artemidorus to the villa – and then departed to keep watch over Caesar Octavius. They lay on couches arranged around a table laden with the remains of *cena*. The floor around them scattered, as propriety demanded, with the detritus of the meal. Olive pits, egg shells, the bones of larks, geese and a swan. Of a lamb's shoulder and a pig's trotters. The knotted ends of sausages. The peel of oranges. A slice or two of lemon. Some crumbs of *emmer* bread. All of which would be whisked away after the meal by the surprising array of servants overseen by Drusus and Drusilla.

Antistius – who would probably have been less than edified by the list of lethal weaponry – was tending Cicero. Ferrata – who would have been fascinated by the bits he didn't already know – was keeping an eye on Caesar Octavius. Enobarbus was on his way to Brundisium with Antony and Fulvia. And Spurinna was at home, seeing to his auguries; his chastity, and communication with the Deities, no longer threatened by the beautiful people currently occupying Quintus' *triclinium* dining room.

vii

Artemidorus spent the rest of the evening after *cena* following Quintus through the warlike treasure trove of his villa as darkness gathered and lamps were lit by the ever-assiduous servants. 'Servants,' emphasised Quintus. 'Not slaves. Whenever my family has bought another being, manumission is immediate. They

158

continue to serve because they want to – it is another family tradition. Like collecting examples of the art of war rather than the art of conquered nations.'

The others soon tired of watching him demonstrate one ancient or unusual weapon after another and drifted away. All except Puella. And Artemidorus came to understand several things about her. First that her interest was less on the weapons than upon himself. But secondly, although the weaponry was only her lesser interest, her wide dark eyes seemed to soak up everything Quintus was demonstrating. The neat little ears beneath the serpentine curls of her hair took in every word he spoke. And, somewhere behind that broad, ebony forehead it was all being assimilated. Every now and then, her fine nostrils would flare with excitement and the full lips would part as she asked an insightful question or requested a repetition of some particularly obscure or complicated move. Once in a while she would relieve the proud *triarius* of the weapon he was demonstrating. Her long, slim fingers would fasten purposefully around it. And her arms, body and legs would become one graceful, almost fluid movement while the dangerous end of the weapon whispered through the silent air. The tendons in her thighs and calves would tense. Her toes would spread for purchase even as her legs parted for balance. The stuff of her sheer tunic moulding itself to every curve. And, most strikingly of all, she seemed equally competent with the weapons regardless of whether she was wielding them with her right hand or her left. Artemidorus had never come across anyone before who was completely ambidextrous. In that regard – as in many others – Puella was a revelation.

But, as she moved with liquid grace, the spy was forcibly reminded of the night he freed her from Brutus' house. During the night watches before the fatal *Ides* of *Mars* dawned. The storm that they fled through then was so fierce it had burst open the menagerie behind the *Circus Maximus*. For a time they had been hunted by a black panther. Puella's elegant movements – especially with the big, two-handed Egyptian swords, put him forcefully in mind of that sleek, beautiful, utterly lethal creature.

'She's a natural,' said Quintus proudly, as she whirled an ancient Iberian *falcatta* round her head, its deadly two-cubit blade coming within a finger's width of decapitating him. 'Almost the best I've ever seen.'

Artemidorus didn't ask the obvious question. But then he didn't think he needed to.

'With a bit of practice she could be as deadly as Cyanea,' Quintus elaborated. 'Perhaps even more so. You will have noticed that she is as deadly with her left hand as she is with her right.'

159

As far as the secret agent was concerned, that was that. But Quintus mentally continued, though his mouth remained closed and silent. *Though neither of them will ever be quite as lethal as you, my boy. Dexterity, elegance and grace are one aspect. But you have speed, brutality and the best tactical brain – even one-on-one – I have ever encountered.*

After they had exhausted Quintus' main weapon collection, it was time for bed. Though there were several more rooms of even more arcane hardware to examine. And they hadn't even got as far as the library. But there was at least one more surprise in store for Artemidorus. The novel experiences of the last few hours had come so thick and fast that he hadn't really thought beyond them. It came almost as a shock, therefore, to find that he had a suite of rooms already given over not only to his bed but to all the personal clothing, equipment and armour that had been so thoughtlessly left in his tent on Tiber Island. When he went down to Pompeii – before the VIIth was officially disbanded. All of it carefully laid out on chests and stands, recently cleaned and polished, gleaming under the light of tens of lamps.

Quintus led his protégé to the first of these chambers and, as Artemidorus stood gaping with surprise, he vanished. Silently.

So that when Artemidorus turned, saying, 'But this is…' he found that only Puella remained with him. She came towards him without hesitation, coiling her arms around his neck and pressing her lips to his. Tongue-tip coyly exploring. Grinding the entire length of herself against him. The contact almost as intimate as if they were already naked. He felt himself responding at once. The scent of her. The power of her. The simple burning heat of her. With the last of his self-control, he placed his hands on the muscular fullness of her hips and gently pushed her away. Her lips reluctantly parted from his and she stepped back. Her eyes, huge in the lamplight, wide and questioning. Her breath, like his, shortened with desire as though they had run a marathon together. 'There is no need for this,' he said gently. 'Like everyone else in this strange household, you are free. You must only do what you want to do.'

'I want you,' she said simply. 'I have wanted you since I first saw you in Lord Brutus' villa disguised as a freedman, wearing that silly hat and that ridiculous red beard.'

'Even then?' he smiled.

'Even then – and ever since,' she whispered. 'And now I have you. All to myself.'

She came to him once more. And this time he did not push her away.

Later, as she lay smiling and satisfied, deeply asleep at his side, he looked down at her face gilded by the light of the last lamp. And he thought about the last spy he had taken as a lover.

And how completely she had betrayed him.

viii

Marcus Tullius Cicero rose stiffly and a little unsteadily to his feet. Pulling his recalcitrant body erect, he surveyed the white-robed ranks of the Senate. Took a deep breath and, as he had rehearsed with Tiro almost ceaselessly since the departure of the physician Antistius from his villa – not to mention the departure of Antony himself from Rome – he began. Raising his voice above the raving of a gale outside that threatened to be almost autumnal in its ferocity.

'Conscript Fathers. Before I say anything about our Republic – which I think myself bound to say at the present time – I will explain to you briefly why I recently left the city and then why I returned.' He paused for a heartbeat. Actor as much as orator, ensuring the rapt attention of his audience.

'While I believed that the Republic at last was feeling proper respect for your wisdom and authority, I thought that it was my duty to remain as a sort of sentinel. A duty which was imposed upon me by my positions as a senator and an ex-consul. I did not go anywhere, nor did I ever stop watching out for the Republic, from the day on which we were summoned to meet in the Temple of Tellus; two days after the death of Gaius Julius Caesar. In that temple, as far as I could, I laid the foundations of peace, and renewed the ancient precedent set by the Athenians. I even used the Greek word meaning *bear no malice*, which that city employed in settling political disputes. And I gave my vote to the motion that all memory of the controversy that existed then ought to be wiped out forever...'

Sitting in his usual place among the Senate secretaries, Adonis recorded every word that the great orator declaimed, secretly thankful that the old man was clearly still unwell. And speaking, therefore, more slowly than usual. For his expertise with Tiro's shorthand was enabling him to make one verbatim record for the Senate and another, secretly, for the Centurion Artemidorus and his Tribune Enobarbus. The second record to be elaborated more accurately still by his almost perfect memory of every tone and inflection in Cicero's voice as he spoke.

Getting into his stride, now, the great lawyer took hold of the folds of his *toga* nearest his left shoulder with his left hand, drew himself up even further and continued as the gale raved outside, 'The speech made by Marcus Antonius at that time was also a thoroughly admirable one.' He gestured grandly, reasonably, forgivingly, with his right hand and continued...

161

But then, over the next hour as measured by the water clocks beside the secretaries, the tone of Cicero's speech began to change. In content as well as in delivery. When Antony and his Co-consul Dolabella had behaved according to the wishes of the Senate as interpreted by Cicero himself, they had been good and upright leaders. But, little by little, they had altered. Lists of Caesar's notes and plans as accepted by the Senate had been added to – he did not say forged – and *unica* by *unica* inch by inch the two consuls had begun to leech power away from the Senate and into their own grasp. Their focus had moved away from performing their constitutional duties and towards grasping more and more naked power. Where was Antony now? Not leading the debate as was his duty but hurrying towards Brundisium to make sure of the legions landing there! And so what had started out as a constitutional friendship between the two arms of government was now marred by growing distrust. And even fear.

Adonis felt his blood run cold as he recorded what the orator was saying: 'I wish you could remember your grandfather, Antony. You have often heard me speak about him. Do you think that he would have been willing to seek even immortality at the price of being feared? What he considered life, what he considered prosperity, was being equal to the rest of we citizens in freedom. And first among equals only in worthiness. I should prefer that most bitter day of his death to the domination of Lucius Cinna which you are trying to reproduce yourself. Cinna, by whom your own grandfather was most barbarously murdered!'

The general's not going to like this! thought Adonis, his stylus busily recording the words as his ears noted the sneering tone. This amounts to a declaration of war! What is the old man up to?

But then things got even worse as Cicero continued relentlessly, his voice echoing in the hushed, horror-stricken chamber.

'But why should I try to make an impression on you by merely speaking? For, if the death of Gaius Caesar cannot scare you into choosing the love of the people rather than their fear, no speech of mine will do any good.' The right hand made that sweeping gesture once again. Encompassing Dolabella and the tiers of Antony's supporters sitting opposite. 'And those men who think you are happy wielding power through fear are miserable themselves,' he boomed. 'No one is ever happy if he lives on such terms that he may be put to death not merely with impunity, but even to the great glory of his killer!' Again that dramatic pause. The heartbeat of rhetoric as studied by every patrician boy. But rarely wielded as effectively as this.

'Therefore, Antony, who I address even in your absence, change your mind, I beg you. Look back upon your ancestors. Govern the Republic in such a way that

162

your fellow citizens may rejoice that you were born. No one can live a long life and be happy or famous otherwise.'

'By Jupiter Optimus Maximus,' said Adonis to himself, watching the point of his stylus write the words down twice. Faintly surprised that it wasn't trembling more than it was. 'The old man has just threatened Antony with the same fate as Caesar! In public. In front of the Senate!'

ix

'Has he run mad?' asked Artemidorus rhetorically, a little later in the office of Quintus' villa. 'You're sure he said this, Adonis? And in the way you acted it out?'

Adonis nodded. Venus, at his, side nodded automatically. The mimicry of expression and movement between the almost identical twins was disturbing until you got used to it, thought Artemidorus. Which in his case was not yet. But it echoed the equally disturbing manner in which Adonis had brought Cicero and his bitter words to life. He leaned forward and continued.

'Then we have a problem. Several, in fact. First, do we take this to Antony in Brundisium at once? Secondly, if we decide to do so, who should be the messenger? Because, thirdly, Cicero seems to have put the general on some kind of death list with these words. Therefore, fourthly, someone has to go through his villa checking the security. Seeing whether the other Praetorians are all they're cracked up to be…'

'You don't need to worry about the first and second problems,' said Quintus wisely. 'Adonis, you said the Senate was full?'

Venus and Adonis nodded.

'Then if Dolabella hasn't sent word yet, someone else certainly will have.'

'That's true,' said Artemidorus. 'And, now I think of it, word will have gone to Caesar Octavius as well. I'll check with Ferrata when I see him. That reminds me. Hercules. Can you relieve him? Keep an eye on Caesar and the comings and goings around him. And try to stay dry. There's quite a storm…'

The giant nodded amenably and vanished. Though just how he was going to make his enormous frame both waterproof and unremarkable in the streets round Agrippa's family home, the secret agent could hardly guess.

He caught Puella's eye. But nothing in her gaze or expression moved away from the serious consideration she was giving their problem. It was as though she was two people, he thought. Out here she was a mixture of Athena and Artemis – the wise huntress. As focused as the light from one of Archimedes' ship-burning mirrors. In the bed chamber, she was Aphrodite, astonishingly inventive and limitlessly wanton.

163

Later that afternoon, in a dry spell, Artemidorus and Quintus made their first assessment of the security at Antony's villa. Possibly because the general was away in Brundisium, possibly because of the suddenly autumnal weather, the Praetorians were relaxed. The guards lined along the *via* were more interested in each other and their conversations than in the comings and goings of strangers. The pair of spies reached the door without being challenged. Even here, the password remained *Hercules*. Which was their second guess after *Fulvia*. The guard was not unduly worried by the first incorrect attempt. 'That was yesterday's,' he explained amenably. 'It's one or the other. You just have to remember which.'

Neither the centurion nor his associate was impressed by any of this, but they made no fuss about it at the moment. Instead, having been admitted to the villa, they came back out again immediately and went down the side to the *posticum* servants' entrance. Where they employed the keys they bought from the housebreakers in Pompeii. The second one unlocked the door and they walked straight into the unguarded areas beside the *culina* kitchen.

'We'd better start making a list,' said Artemidorus. 'I wonder whether the general has taken all his secretarial staff with him.'

Antony's steward was called Promus. He and Artemidorus were well acquainted. And Promus knew precisely how the household stood at the moment. So he was able to produce one of Antony's secretaries in short order. This one was called Livius. He seemed as keen to please as Adonis, but he had not been trained in Tyro's shorthand techniques.

'Let's start with the *posticum*,' decided Artemidorus. 'Livius, note that we need more than just this old lock. Either a new lock or some secondary security. *Claustrae* bolts would be best. Top and bottom. Now, let's have a look at the windows...'

After an hour or so they had completed their initial survey. And were much less than happy with the results that Livius had painstakingly recorded for them. 'We found it easy enough to break into Minucius Basilus' place in Pompeii,' said Artemidorus. 'And, with a little preparation, I was able to get into Brutus' villa – and out again with Puella. This place is guarded while those were not, but the guards are useless. Even the passwords are obvious. We'd have to rebuild the villa or employ a crack cohort to stand a couple of men at every door or window. We don't have time to do the first. And we don't have the manpower for the second.'

'On the other hand,' said Quintus wisely, 'perhaps we just need to think like a *sicarius*. Anyone trying to break in will certainly check out the possible entry points before they make their move. If we make it clear the main ones are going to be hard to get in through, then all we need to do is leave one avenue apparently unconsidered. And be fairly certain that *that* will be the way he'll come...'

'Right,' said Artemidorus. 'Then instead of guarding the villa and its grounds as a whole we'd just have to guard that one point. Like Leonidas and his Three Hundred Spartans stopping the Persian army at the Pass of Thermopylae.'

'Yes,' agreed Quintus. 'Or like Publius Horatius Cocles holding the bridge against the army of Lars Porsena and Tarquin The Great after Brutus' forefather had thrown him out of Rome.'

X

It took them several days before they were satisfied that the villa was secure, whether or not the Praetorians were keeping a proper guard on the place. Both main door and *posticum* not only had a lock but also several bolts. The windows were mostly small – but even the smallest also had bolts and a chain to limit how wide it could be opened. Glass was reinforced with metal grilles which also secured the window as a whole. For Artemidorus had been able to come and go through Brutus' villa by using a ladder and a loosened window frame. Reaching back into his other experiences since The *Ides* of *Mars*, Artemidorus made sure that it was difficult to get over the roof into the *peristyle*. Something he had managed to do in Minucius Basilus' villa by climbing up one pine tree then swinging across into another whose branches overhung the garden.

At last there was only one method of entry left. The least likely. The almost impossible. The one they chose to watch like Leoniodas at Thermopylae. Like Horatius at the bridge.

One of the villa's greatest amenities – one of which Antony was most proud – was the bath. Ultra-modern, it consisted of *frigidarium*, *tepidarium* and *caldarium*. The *tepidarium* and the *caldarium* not only used warm – and hot – water, but they also had heated floors. These rooms were not the only ones with heated floors – and walls. The *atrium* and *triclinium* dining room were also heated, though the *tablinum*, office space, was not. The heating system was based on a series of columns almost three cubits high on which the floors sat. The *culina* kitchen was placed at the centre of this system. And here the big fire, which could roast a spitted ox, did double duty, supplying heat to the system as well as to the food. The hypocaust system, of necessity, reached from one side of the villa to the other. And, therefore, to outer walls as well as inner ones.

And that fact became relevant when Artemidorus was patrolling the streets around the villa. Looking for areas that were not covered by the Praetorian patrols. But which might give someone a chance of breaking in. Of course his main

165

attention was directed high above his head as he wondered whether this or that wall could be scaled using a ladder. A rope and grappling hook. A bolt from a *sôlênarion* or anything similar with a knotted cord attached. Looking steadfastly upward, he stubbed his toe. And stopped. Stooped, frowning. A brick had come loose and fallen into the pathway between Antony's villa and the next.

xi

'What's all this, Septem?' demanded Antony five days later. They were in the *atrium* of Antony's home. The general had returned to Rome in a dangerous mood. Which the sight of the new locks and bolts on his doors had done little to improve.

'*Securitas* Security,' answered Artemidorus.

'I don't need security! I have my Praetorians!'

'Caesar had his Spanish Guard, General. Didn't do him much good in the end.'

'But Caesar dismissed them! As you should know better than most.'

'They wouldn't have been in Pompey's *Curia* with him when the murderers struck, though, would they?' insisted Artemidorus.

'He has a point, Antony,' said Fulvia, coming onto Artemidorus' side unexpectedly. 'If anyone manages to get in here, your precious Praetorians will all be outside. Useless. Think of the children if you won't think of us.'

'Oh, very well! Septem, take Enobarbus through the villa and explain this *securitas* to him. He can assess what's worthwhile and what's a waste of time. Most of all I don't want people saying I've put all this security in place because I'm scared. Not after that old blowhard Cicero actually threatened to have me murdered like *Divus Julius*! And certainly not with that *catulus* whelp Octavian hanging around and sneering behind my back! I'm going to bathe, then eat and drink. Especially drink!'

'How did things go in Brundisium?' asked Artemidorus as he began the tribune's tour of inspection.

'Not too well. The legions are arriving slowly. Almost reluctantly. They blame the weather now it's coming towards autumn. Making the passage across rough and dangerous. But that's just an excuse. They've made it plain they don't approve of the continuing rift between Antony and Caesar Octavius. Because they want *Divus Julius* avenged.'

'I wonder who put that idea in their heads?' asked Artemidorus cynically.

'You know as well as I do that it's young Caesar,' answered Enobarbus wearily. 'He has agitators moving covertly through all the legions persuading them of his point of view. Which even now seems to be that he and Antony should combine their forces and start collecting the *Libertores*' heads at the earliest opportunity!

And it's not just the Macedonian legions he's making disaffected. He has men all over the place working on the retired, resettled VIth and even the VIIth.'

'Probably among the Praetorian Cohorts as well. Both Ferrata and Hercules have reported secret visits by the other Praetorian tribunes to Agrippa's brother's house, where Caesar has been staying most of the summer. Because he's sold everything he owns to raise the money he's bribing entire armies with. The other tribunes are making good use of your absence, I'd say. Because they know very well where your allegiance lies. They seem to be led by someone called Licinius. There's been a lot of coming and going between Caesar and Balbus as well. I'm sure that Balbus is extending him almost limitless credit. As *Divus Julius'* friend and secretary, Balbus wants to see heads in the Forum as much as any of Caesar's faction. Instead of which, Cassius and Brutus are safe and sound on their way to Athens! There's a nasty atmosphere brewing...'

'Hence all these locks and bolts, I assume.' The tribune nodded at the inside of the *posticum* door.

'Those are just the start of it,' answered Artemidorus. 'Let me tell you what I've been planning...'

*

The blade of the *gladius* slammed into his ribs on the right side hard enough to knock the breath out of his body. He jumped back, falling into a defensive stance. Feet spread, knees bent. Arms wide. Leaning forward slightly from the waist. She came after him as he knew she would, closing in for the kill. Throwing the *gladius* from hand to hand so he would never be sure which side she would hit him from. Eyes narrow, nostrils flared. Clenched teeth revealed by her killing grimace. She swung again, with the left – aiming for the damaged spot on his right side. He stepped inside the blow and drove his own *gladius* up into her belly just above her pubic bone.

Had the sword not been heavily padded and her tunic likewise, he would have opened her up from her groin to her ribs. And the point of the sword would have spitted her heart. As it was, he winded her. She toppled onto her side, choking and gasping. He collapsed onto the grass beside her. 'Never forget,' he said, his words broken by his fight for breath. 'No matter what hand holds it, the *gladius* is a stabbing sword. It has an edge, but be careful how you use it. Stab. Stab. Stab. Come up from under...'

She rolled onto her back. Her gasps became giggles. 'Like when we make love,' she said. 'And you come up from under. Stab. Stab. Stab. With that big old *gladius* of yours?'

'Do not make too much of a joke of it,' advised Quintus severely, trying – as he had during all the recent training sessions – to keep the pair of them serious and focused on their work. 'Septem is right. He uses his *gladius* better than any man I have seen. *In battle…*'

The last two words were lost as Puella went into another helpless fit of giggles.

She was still laughing and choking when Ferrata came running through into the *peristyle* of Quintus' villa. Which had now become their headquarters, equipment centre and training ground. 'Septem,' he said. 'There's something going on down at Antony's villa.'

The three men left Puella still helpless with hilarity and ran out of the villa, shoulder to shoulder. 'Any idea what's going on?' asked Artemidorus.

'No. Spurinna's slave Kyros has been working with Hercules keeping watch on the general. He delivered the message and went straight back. If we hurry we may catch up with him…'

xii

But they came across Adonis first, as the Senate secretary and secret agent came hurrying across the Forum. 'The Senate have just finished debating…' he gasped. 'Caesar Octavius has tried to get Flaminius, one of his men, elected to the post of Tribune of *Plebs*. Cicero was all for it. But Antony just said it was a trick to allow Caesar himself access to the post. And Cicero's support is just another ruse to keep him from ruling on the point of law he wants clarified. And Caesar's only nineteen years old, though it's his birthday today, they say. Even so, nineteen is far too young for such an important post. Antony insists Caesar Octavius has had no experience and isn't even qualified to go on the *Cursus Honorum*, let alone move up it so fast! Besides, he's a patrician and *Divus Filius* the son of a god. Hardly perfect qualifications for a Tribune of *Plebs…*'

'That will stir up a whole lot of trouble,' said Artemidorus. 'Antony at daggers drawn with both Cicero and Caesar at once. Go back to Quintus' villa and get a detailed report ready for the tribune. He wasn't at the Senate meeting, was he?'

'No. I heard the consul say he'd sent him to a meeting of the senior Praetorians…'

But by the time they got to Antony's villa, the tribune had returned. With a delegation consisting of all the other tribunes in the Praetorian Cohorts. Artemidorus led Quintus through into the crowded *atrium*, leaving Hercules and Ferrata guarding the door. The soldiers stood to attention, rank upon rank of them. It was just possible to see beyond them. To where Antony was seated on the great *paterfamilias'* chair in the *tablinum*. Raised on a low dais and facing them.

168

'This looks nasty,' he said to Enobarbus as they fell in beside him. He nodded silently, his expression bleak.

'General, this can't go on…' the spokesman for the tribunes was saying. Even from the back, Artemidorus recognised the tribune called Licinius. 'You must make peace with Gaius Julius Caesar Octavianus *Divus Filius*. You should not be fighting between yourselves. You should be standing side by side and avenging *Divus Julius* together. All the men think so. If you do not stand together then you will find that no one will follow either of you! No matter how great your reputation. Or how deep your purse!'

There was a growl of general agreement.

Antony sat silent for a moment. The he rose to the occasion. Literally as well as figuratively. As only Antony could do. He slowly stood up. On the dais, his Herculean frame towered intimidatingly above them. His gaze swept over them, meeting every pair of eyes. Cataloguing every face present. His thunderous frown of anger moderated to one of hurt and confusion. 'Friends,' he said. 'Licinius. I hear you. I understand your concerns. Indeed, I share them. Young Oct… Gaius Julius Caesar Octavianus and I are not enemies. The rift between us has been put there by the manipulation of Cicero and his like-minded followers. Apologists for *Divus Julius'* murderers. Who dare not see the two heirs to his name and power combine against them. Young Caesar and I are like twins in our plans and ambitions. Identical in every point. Like Castor and Pollux; Romulus and Remus…'

'That's pushing it a bit,' breathed Artemidorus. 'Though at least Castor didn't kill Pollux like Romulus murdered Remus.'

'Could be the gods speaking through him,' whispered Quintus. 'He's an augur after all.'

'Maybe Caesar and he are destined to be like Romulus and Remus in the end…' added Enobarbus, his words just one step above silence.

But Antony was continuing, in typical vein. 'Tell me what you want, friends. How can I demonstrate my willingness to live at peace with young Caesar? Would you have me do what Brutus, Cassius and I did on the day after *Divus Julius* died? Shake hands in the Forum to affirm our friendship in front of the whole of Rome?'

'Yes,' came the answer from almost every man there. 'Yes!'

But then their spokesman Licinius added, 'But not in the Forum. In the *Aedes Iovis Optimi Maximi Capitolini* Temple of Jupiter Optimus Maximus at the top of the Capitoline Hill.'

*

169

'If that *nothus* bastard with the *sôlênarion* bow is still after you, then he won't get a better chance than this,' said Ferrata as he and Artemidorus completed their swift security sweep of the Temple of Jupiter and its grounds. The weather had moderated and the afternoon was sunny, clear and hot for the season. The temple and its grounds full of dazzling surfaces. And impenetrable shadows.

'It's not me I'm worried about,' answered Artemidorus. 'It's the general.'

'Given those vicious bolts it fires, he could probably get you both with one shot if he placed himself correctly...'

'Thanks for the thought. But I'd say we're relatively safe. Yes there are hundreds of places he could hide. Most of them giving an excellent field of fire across this square. But the Temple and the precinct are full of priests and acolytes. Who tend to frown on any weapons that aren't part of the displays inside. And anyway, he hasn't got enough time to set himself up. Unless that mouthy Tribune Licinius who suggested this is hand in glove with him, the fact that Antony and Caesar Octavius will be here within the turn of a water clock will have surprised him as much as it surprised the rest of us.'

'That's good,' said Ferrata. 'You keep looking on the bright side. And if the great god Jupiter isn't watching your back, I expect your hero Achilles is!'

'If they are, then now's the time for them to focus,' said the spy. 'Here comes Antony. Surrounded by his Praetorians.'

'Just more excellent targets, if you ask me. And the general's the biggest one of all, as usual. But only because Licinius' mouth is closed for once.'

Antony came running up the one hundred steps that rose from the *Vicus Jugarius* below. His Praetorians streamed behind him, Licinius officiously in the lead. Artemidorus and Ferrata watched them approach. But as the general bounded up onto the marble flagstones of the temple precinct, Caesar Octavius led a crowd of senators and citizens out of the top of the *Vicus Capitolinus* on the other side.

'We'd better pray this all goes to plan,' said Ferrata cheerfully. 'Or there'll be more than one of us going off the edge of that.' He nodded over to the south-west corner of the precinct where the Tarpean Rock stood, overhanging the dizzying drop to the ground more than one hundred steps below.

A figure in a white *toga* over a purple-striped tunic took command of the steps leading up to the temple and began to speak. 'Senators, citizens and soldiers. We are here at the army's request to see a seal of friendship sworn between Gaius Julius Caesar Octavianus *Divus Filius* and Consul of Rome General Mark Antony...'

'Oh by the gods,' said Ferrata. 'Cicero's going to give a speech. I may just leap off the Tarpean Rock myself!'

170

'…a sign that peace and accord have returned to our city and empire. That from this time forward we may all sleep soundly in our beds, assured of tranquillity and, above all, safety!'

IX

The *sicarius* known as Myrtillus eased himself invisibly past the sleepy Praetorian who was supposed to be guarding the end of the narrow *vicus* beside Antony's villa. As he had done past a series of Praetorian guards and patrols already tonight. He was able to do this because he was dressed from head to foot in black. Everything from his hood to his boots was as dark as the River Styx. And, although the moon was bright and the stars hanging low in a cloudless autumn sky, the assassin could hardly be distinguished from the shadows through which he was creeping. He had visited the villa in secret many times since the meeting with his employer's mysterious go-between. He had even watched some of the security systems being put in place. Amused to find a challenge worthy of his talents. Knowing that when he pulled this off, his reputation would not merely be restored. It would be immeasurably enhanced.

Myrtillus knew the doors and windows were closed to him and that there was no way over the roof into the *peristyle*. He also knew precisely how many steps it took to get from the corner of the house to the section of bricks he had loosened in preparation for this moment. Whose removal would – just – allow him access to the *hypocast* heating system. And hence to the interior of the villa. Where there were no Praetorians. Or guards of any kind. Kneeling in the darkness now, he reached up and tightened the black cloth that covered his nose and mouth. Which left only a narrow band for his eyes between its upper edge and the low cowl of the hood. Then he reached down and, with hands bound, like a *cestus*, with black leather bands, he began to ease the bricks out of the wall and lay them carefully – silently – on the black cobbles of the little pathway.

His plan was simple. He would follow the air duct under the floor to the kitchen. He would ease out into the room through the *foculus*, cooking fire. Then he would go to work. Work that would end the existence in this world of everyone he could find in the villa. Starting with Antony himself. But including Fulvia and the children. Sheathed on his black belt and secured to his forearms and thighs – even tucked into his boots – were knives of various sizes and designs. From neat little Babylonian daggers to Iberian blades that were almost swords. Collected from all over the known world. All of them almost incredibly sharp. Each of them supremely suited to its single task – of ending lives swiftly and silently.

But the assassin was not relying on his armoury alone. He had managed to bribe two people. One of Antony's Praetorians and one of his slaves. He carried clearly in his memory, therefore, minutiae of the soldiers' guard dispositions and a map of the entire villa. With details of who slept in what room. There would also be a dark lantern waiting for him in the *culina* – in a prearranged spot he could find in the utter blackness. And anything that might trip him or fall and make a noise between the fireplace to the lantern had been carefully cleared away. The only risk as far as he could see was during those few dangerous moments it would take to light the lamp before he could close its shutter.

Within a few heartbeats all the bricks were safely moved – ready to be replaced when he escaped. So no one would suspect how he got in and out. To make the whole thing seem like the work of the gods. Or of the Friendly Ones. Smiling at the thought, he leaned forward, and with the slow, deliberate movements of a *stilio* chameleon, he eased himself into the hole in the wall. The darkness was absolute. The sensation of being crushed by the weight of the layers of concrete and tile above him almost overwhelming. But he had practised this. Rehearsed it in the ruins of a villa on the far side of the city. He controlled his fear and moved slowly onwards. Everything around him – above him and below – was warm. But not hot. It all reeked of smoke. But not strongly enough to make breathing difficult – even through the black mask. He closed his eyes – which were useless in any case – and concentrated on the plan of the house he carried in his memory. And imagined himself moving relentlessly across it. Towards the *culina* and liberty. And the start of his murderous task.

It took him longer than he had thought it would. But then, maybe his sense of time passing had been blunted by the situation. Still, he made it. Alerted to his approach to the kitchen by the upward slope of the tiles beneath him. Guided to the actual opening by the way the columns closed in on either side. Alerted to his arrival at the *culina* itself by the sudden cleanness of the air and the redolence of roasted meat.

Myrtillus snaked out through the flue into the *camina* kitchen fireplace. Reached up to feel the spit that normally carried sheep, boars, cows and the occasional ox. Pushed it back silently on its well-greased hinge. Came a little stiffly to his feet and paused, orientating himself. Then he moved silently along the cleared path five steps to the table where the dark lantern stood. With flint, steel and kindling wool beside it. Three strikes and the kindling caught. The dazzling light revealing the lamp. Open and ready. He touched the flame to the wick and it caught at once. A couple of heartbeats later he had extinguished the wool and was closing the shutter. Only the slimmest finger of light shone out in front of him.

Myrtillus paused, checking the weaponry strapped to his body. Making sure that every blade, no matter what its length breadth or curvature, was easily available. Then he picked up the lantern and was in action. The rooms on the ground floor were all public spaces, until they ran into the slaves' quarters at the back. Myrtillus kept clear of those – the chance of causing an alarm while slitting the throat of some nonentity it wasn't even a crime to kill was just too high. Instead he crept to the staircase and silently mounted to the second floor where the family's bedrooms were. Following the finger's width of light he crept along the *ectheta* balcony with the drop onto the *atrium* on one side and the doors into the sleeping quarters on the other. He was following the map drawn in his memory step by step. And so he knew exactly which door led to Antony's chamber.

Silently, he lifted the latch that opened the door. With his shoulder he eased it wider. In his left hand, the dark lantern gave its shard of brightness for him to follow towards the sleeping man even as his right hand felt beneath his night-black cloak for his favourite *sica* knife. The splinter of light showed the centre of the room as he swept it swiftly from side to side. The bulk of the bed with a table close by. The chests and stands containing the general's armour and the consul's robes. The hillock of the sleeping man in the high, wide expanse of the bed.

As the light fell on his face, Antony groaned and stirred. Snored and slipped back into deep sleep, sprawling on his back. His throat was a perfect target. Myrtillus slipped the razor-sharp curve of the *sica* out of its sheath. Placed the lantern on the table so that its modicum of light fell across the face and throat of the sleeping man. Took one ecstatic, victorious breath and raised his hand to strike.

When one of the nearby shadows stepped forward and clubbed him on the head. A blaze of brightness dazzled behind his eyes. Then a pit of blackness as deep as Hades opened before him and he tumbled into it.

ii

Myrtillus woke up to find himself tied tightly to a chair. He was naked. His clothing and weaponry was all piled on a table on his right. His head hurt abominably and the brightness of the lamplight surrounding him didn't help at all. 'You have to thank a woman called Puella for this particular approach,' a friendly voice assured him. 'Though I think she got a bit ahead of herself when she suggested we start by nailing your *testes* to the table. Perhaps later. What do you think?'

174

Myrtillus was gathering himself to answer when he realised the question was not addressed to him. 'I think this is an assortment of blades that I'm going to add to my own collection,' said another voice.

'In the meantime,' struck in a third. The familiar voice of Antony himself. 'It doesn't matter what we do to this *nothus* bastard as long as he answers our questions. He's going off the Tarpean Rock in any case if he lasts that long.'

'But I suppose we can make it easier for him if he tells us what we want to know,' suggested the first voice. 'If not, I think we should start with the *cestus* knuckledusters and take it from there...'

The succeeding hours became more and more uncomfortable for the *sicarius*. The men he recognised as the Centurion Artemidorus – the first of his targets – and Quintus, *triarius* of the recently disbanded VIIth, and Antony himself. Then they were joined by Fulvia – who was the most terrifying *carnifex* interrogator of them all. Then by the Tribune Enobarbus.

Myrtillus fed them the names of the Praetorian he had bribed to reveal the guard rosters. Then of the household slave who helped him with the map, the clear pathway and the dark lantern. He remained unmoved as first the soldier and then the slave were beaten to death in front of him – in vivid demonstration of what he could expect himself. But he held out against their relentless quest for the name of his employer. His only real regret – beyond the fact that he had got himself caught – being that he had failed to kill his chief interrogator. Not once but twice.

Until, at last, as he lay spreadeagled on the table, with the point of an iron nail resting icily on his scrotum and the hammer poised to drive it home, his resistance finally collapsed.

'Caesar!' he shouted brokenly. The syllables choking out of the blood-thickened phlegm in his throat; lisping through the ruin of his shredded lips and broken teeth. 'It was Caesar! He disguised himself and pretended he was speaking on someone else's behalf. But I recognised his voice. That of a boy...'

'*Caesar*!' snarled Antony. 'Just as I thought! That nasty little *nothus spurious* bastard. All that goodwill up in the Temple of Jupiter was just a *fictus* sham! Chuck this *excrementus* off the Tarpean Rock and let's get on with the war!'

The consul and general stormed out of the room, followed by his wife. 'Well,' said Artemidorus amenably, 'that seems to be that.' As he and Quintus carefully began to release and re-secure the assassin limb by limb. 'Normally, of course, a citizen would have to be arraigned before a *praetor* – perhaps even the Senate. And tried under the Twelve Tables of the Law. Before he went off the Rock. But both of the current *praetors* are on their way to Athens. And the Senate is just about to get very busy indeed. Courtesy of your testimony. The direct judgement

175

of a consul bypasses most legal quibbles in any case. And, of course, you're not actually a Roman citizen anyway, are you? I mean you're not going to start shouting, *"Civis Romanus Sum!"* halfway down off the Rock expecting Jupiter to bear you safely up after all? No. I thought not.'

Quintus turned and went through into the main body of the villa, leaving Artemidorus and Myrtillus alone.

The *carnifex* interrogator leaned forward, lowering his voice. 'And, as we're talking of thoughts at the moment, I also think you are a lying *nothus spurius*. I've been a *carnifex* for long enough to know the difference between truth and untruth. I think you know very well Caesar was not your employer. I think you know who was. And I just have to work out a way to make you tell the truth to me. Before, during or after the general's orders are followed and you get thrown off the Tarpean Rock.'

iii

But no sooner had Artemidorus uttered the words than his chance to interrogate the prisoner further came to an abrupt halt. The Praetorian Tribune Licinius arrived with a dozen burly soldiers. And orders from Antony to expedite the execution. The arrival of the officious tribune and his men somehow changed the dynamic of the situation. As they took great delight in hurting and humiliating their helpless victim, Artemidorus discovered with some surprise that he was beginning to feel some sympathy for the would-be murderer. A glimmer of respect, born during the time Myrtillus had held out against the enraged Antony and the *cestus* he wore on each fist. He might be an enemy, thought the grim centurion. But he was an enemy worthy of respect.

Which Licinius and his men did not accord him. Instead, they dragged his naked body out of the villa and into the street. Artemidorus followed, shocked to discover that it was mid morning already. Any passer-by who glanced in their direction might have been surprised to see a squad of soldiers carrying a side of beef fresh from the *macellarius* butcher's. For that's what the condemned man most resembled. Artemidorus walked beside him through the streets and across the Forum – right to the bottom of the steps up to the crest of the Capitoline. His mind was racing, conceiving and discarding questions whose answer might reveal the secrets the dying man was still keeping so close. But in the end, nothing came. And all he said, as Myrtillus was hauled upward was, 'Dive headfirst. *Don't jump, whatever you do.*' It was good advice. And well meant. From one professional to another.

Then Tribune Licinius and his death squad were gone. Their victim nothing more than a pale glimmer among them as they ran at the double up the steps

176

towards the Temple, the Precinct and the Rock. For reasons he was never able to explain, Artemidorus waited in the road. Licinius had left a secondary squad behind. Six soldiers to clear a space in the thoroughfare immediately beneath the execution place. And two more sent to summon the executioners who would complete the punishment by dragging the corpse on a big bronze hook through the streets to the Tiber. Where it would be thrown like offal into the stream.

The *Vicus Jugularis* was busy and the rumour of an impending execution made it more so. Artemidorus soon found himself at the front of a considerable crowd, pressed up against the solid shoulders of Licinius' men. Then there came a unified gasp that seemed to issue from the crowd all at once. And there, framed against a clear blue sky came Myrtillus. Upright. Legs pumping as though he still had a chance to run away from what was happening. He remained erect and running during the racing heartbeats it took for him to fall. Then he smashed onto the stones of the street, the sound of his body shattering drowned by a great, feral cheer. Artemidorus pushed through the soldiers at once. 'Keep the crowd back!' he snarled. Incandescent with frustrated rage, he ran across the open space. His mind was shouting, *Why did you not listen to me? Why did you jump?* But he said nothing.

For, shattered though he was, with fragments of bone protruding from what was left of his legs. With his pelvis clearly crushed and his back – to say the least of it – broken, Myrtillus was still alive. His chest heaved in great ragged breaths. The gap-toothed, red-lipped cavern of his mouth gaped. His eyes, wide with shock, rolled in the swollen ruin of his face. His arms made helpless movements as though they still had the power to pull him erect. There seemed to the centurion to be even more blood than there had been when *Divus Julius* died. He crashed onto his knees beside Myrtillus, pulling out his *pugio* dagger. Someone shouted. He paid no attention. 'I'm going to kill you,' he whispered urgently. 'It's the only way and I'll make it painless. You don't want to be still alive when they hook you and drag you to the river.'

Their eyes met. Something seemed to pass between them. And Myrtillus began to whisper, rapidly. His voice slurred by the state of his shattered teeth and swollen lips. His breath coming and going in great tearing gasps. 'Decimus Albinus,' he said. 'Gaius Trebonius. Minucius Basilus. And by the voice I'm sure their messenger was a woman. Kill me now.'

Artemidorus obliged. Though he was only a few heartbeats ahead of Thanatos, the god of death, he thought.

Hoof beats approached from behind him. A chain rattled. A huge, gold-coloured hook clanged onto the roadway beside him. He pulled himself to his feet, sheathed his *pugio* and turned away.

He did not watch the executioners drive the hook up under the ribcage until the point came out under the corpse's left arm. He did not see them whip the horse and drag the shattered body towards the Forum. With the excited crowd laughing and chattering close behind. But he followed the long smear of blood into the Forum, turning right, as it did, to go past the new half-built basilica. But he turned left and headed for Quintus' villa where the red smear turned right again into the *Vicus Tusculum*, heading for the *Forum Boarium* behind the *Circus Maximus* and the river docks down there.

All the way back to the secret villa, he was turning over the assassin's dying words in his mind. Testing whether he believed them because he so much wanted to or because they were the truth. *Decimus Albinus, Gaius Trebonius and Minucius Basilus. And their messenger was a woman.*

X

'What's all this about Trebonius, Decimus Albinus and Minucius Basilus?' demanded Antony. Clearly in the worst mood he had been in for some time. And with good reason, thought the Tribune Enobarbus. It had taken some time to catch up with his general right at the far end of the Appian Way. And now he wished he hadn't done so after all.

'The *sicarius* told me it was Caesar,' he snarled. 'Looked me in the eye and told me to my face. And even though the little *ricinus* tick has sworn in public – and even on the steps of my villa – that he had nothing to do with it, I for one don't believe him. Especially as I'm here in Brundisium having to sort out a bloody mess that is entirely of his making!'

'The man Myrtillus changed his story on the point of death, General,' insisted Enobarbus. 'He was all but standing on the bank of the Styx staring Charon in the eye. That has to carry some weight.'

'All right. Say I believe this deathbed confession,' Antony paused, gave a dry, humourless chuckle, 'though the stones of the *Vicus Jugarius* aren't my idea of a *bed*. Not after you've just come off the Tarpean Rock. Black enough for the River of Death, though. Still, say we give this some credit. Even the bit about the mysterious woman. What then?'

'I sent Septem to Pompeii at once with a cohort of your Praetorians to back him. They haven't been much use for anything else. My idea was at least to detain Basilus and Trebonius until you could talk to them. But the villa was closed. Basilus has disappeared. The slaves Septem talked to say they have no idea where he's gone. Though they're all terrified of him and could well just be covering his tracks. But they made no secret of the fact that Trebonius left in a hurry to take up his post as Governor of Asia. And Septem is certain the mysterious woman who gave Myrtillus his instructions is the traitress Cyanea. She went *ad orientem* eastwards with Trebonius. We think they were all scattering on the assumption that their assassin would be successful and there would be utter turmoil in the wake of your murder. So those involved had either to be invisible or securely in their appointed positions to ride out the storm.'

'Or that if the *sicarius* failed and was caught then he would hand over all of their names,' Fulvia said, breaking into the conversation. 'Which is what actually seems to have happened in the end.'

179

'Well, the bloody boy Octavius is out of reach at the moment down in Capua, surrounded by the legions he's managed to buy so far,' said Antony bitterly. All too well aware that his position with his own legions was weak. He was offering a ruinously expensive bounty of four hundred *sestertii* a man. Caesar Octavius was now offering an eye-watering two thousand. 'So I can't do much about him in any case. But Decimus is ripe for shaking. I'm going to do that myself as soon as I've settled things here. Shake him right out of Gaul once and for all. Especially if Septem's right and he's been paying *sicarii* to try and murder me. In the meantime, I think you should send my undercover *contubernium* eastwards too. Before the autumn weather closes in and makes travel really difficult from now 'til next spring. Get them to check up on Trebonius.' There was a brief silence. The air around the three speakers and the men assembled in front and behind them thrilled with tension. There were four legions awaiting exercise of his judgement against them. Hundreds of men about to die.

Antony seemed to pay it no attention. Instead, he continued, 'Meanwhile maybe it's time for Dolabella to take up his post in Syria. He can move quickly. And pick up the legion that's still in Dyrrachium into the bargain. Syria's close to Asia Province and a good place to watch Brutus and Cassius from. But maybe we should do more than just keep an eye on them. This attempt on the lives of me and my family is proof that the so-called *Libertores* are getting out of control. I've been too slow in going after them – though I've had good reason to be careful, of course.

'Perhaps it's time to start emulating the Friendly Ones,' Antony continued. 'Putting the fear of Nemesis into the entire murderous crew. I think we ought to start spiking some of their heads in the Forum. And independently of paying to have me slaughtered in my bed if Septem's right, that *nothus* Trebonius had already made it personal when he actually took me by the arm like a friend and pulled me aside to make sure I couldn't help *Divus Julius* at the vital moment. As I believe I said some time ago. So his head is certainly first on the list. It's definitely time to go and get it.'

'You are wise to keep a close eye on Cassius and Brutus,' added Fulvia. 'They're not just going to sit still in Athens. Not with Cicero praising them to the skies and calling them the saviours of the Republic. Demanding all right-minded Republicans to do everything they can to help them stand up against my Lord Antony. Begging the Senate to back them, no matter what they do. Just as the senile old *asinae* fools are supporting Decimus Albinus. And, as we all know, also suggesting that the best way forward to peace is a knife in my husband's back! And that's a situation which will only get worse once we start to kick Decimus

Albinus out of Gaul!' She turned to her husband. 'In fact, my beloved, your speech to the *Comitia* attacking Brutus, Cassius and their murderous friends has already started to make things worse!'

Antony grunted. Looked up from the little huddle they had made while having this conversation and shrugged. 'It doesn't get much worse than this,' he growled. 'Nothing I can think of is worse than a decimation.'

Enobarbus also looked up. And the scene before him stood somewhere between breathtaking and terrifying. The tension in the air was as taut as in the moments before a storm. Or a battle. And the low, seething clouds of the October sky above them simply added to the disturbing atmosphere. The countryside inland from Brundisium gathered itself into a massive, natural arena. Roofed by the low, grey overcast. A curve of hillside like the tiers of seats in a gigantic Greek theatre. A space almost as massive as the *Circus Maximus*. Large enough to hold thirty thousand men. Who were all standing there now. In full parade armour. Drawn up in ranks, cohorts and legions. Eagles and banners to the front. Looking down onto the central stage of the natural arena. Where Antony, Fulvia and their immediate staff, headed by Enobarbus himself, were standing on a low podium. And just below them, on a *centuria* of nearly one hundred acres of grass, between the legions and their general, stood three thousand soldiers – almost all centurions.

During the time since his arrival here, Antony had ordered the tribunes under his command to compile lists of all the men who had been subverted by Caesar Octavius' agitators. All those fomenting restlessness within the four Macedonian legions. Men accused of suggesting that now was the time to leave Antony and follow the young Gauis Julius Caesar Octavianus *Divus Filius* instead. The troublemakers had been split into groups of ten and each group had drawn lots composed of nine longs straws and one short one. The three hundred men who drew the short straws were just about to die.

ii

Each of the condemned troublemakers was all but naked, wearing only a *cinctus* loincloth. The nine men gathered round him were in tunics rather than in full armour. They were all armed with clubs. Most of them, as centurions, held the heavy vinestocks that were the badge of their rank. And the moment Antony gave the signal the condemned would be beaten to death. By their companions. In front of the men they had commanded.

Crassus had famously decimated his legions when they became restive during the war against Spartacus. *Divus Julius* had threatened to decimate the IXth when they mutinied during the Great Civil War demanding more pay. But Antony had never done anything like this before. And now he was decimating not one legion but four. A clear and pointed lesson about the dangers of listening to the siren voices of Caesar Octavius' *provocateurs* and their promises of two thousand *sestercii* a man.

Antony looked right and left along the front of the dais, meeting Fulvia's eyes and then Enobarbus'. Wearily, he raised his hand and the execution began.

Enobarbus watched, his face rigid. Like almost everyone present, he had heard about the ancient punishment but had never seen it done. Though somewhere at the back of his memory lay the suspicion that Quintus and perhaps Septem had done so. Even in the midst of the sheer brutality, it was possible to see popularity being rewarded and comradeship demonstrated. Well-liked men, surrounded by friends, received the first mighty blow to the side of the head or the back of the neck. Delicate temple-bones shattered. Skulls were smashed off spines. Death was instantaneous. Almost painless. And the subsequent beating, therefore, was never actually suffered by the corpses it was inflicted upon. But friendless and unpopular men endured increasing agonies – depending on the depth of animosity or revenge being taken out on them. Ribs shattered. Arms and legs splintered. Genitals were crushed. But heads remained untouched. Conscious. So that faces, at first dully Stoical soon were gasping, howling, screaming.

And then the blood came, as battered bodies began to burst. The club men were spattered, then hosed, then drenched with it. And as the ruthless procedure continued seemingly endlessly, so the clubs themselves, coated with the stuff, began to spray droplets far and wide as they rose and fell. The restless air itself seemed to become one red cloud, smelling and tasting of iron. Enobarbus suddenly felt drops of liquid fall across his hand and stepped back.

His mind withdrew from the immediate horror all around him, effectively shutting his eyes and ears as he worked his way through the implications of Antony's orders. Trebonius was on the way to Asia Province. Many senior officials were on their way to their posts now. Although they might not actually take up their responsibilities until the government's new year dawned at the *calends* of *Januarius*, there was usually a period of handing over. Furthermore, although the weather in Rome was still warm, the travelling season was rapidly drawing to a close as late-autumn storms threatened the seas all around Italy, with winter approaching fast.

Trebonius could travel swiftly because all he needed to take with him were his orders, his badges of office and his immediate household. Including Cyanea, apparently. The current governor, Marcus Apuleus, had tax money and soldiers in place. The province was peaceful as were all the cities within it. It would be a simple handover from one governor to another. The problem was that they were both deeply committed to Brutus' and Cassius' faction. Which was why Antony was sending his Co-consul Dolabella eastwards as well. He would not be able to travel so swiftly if he was going to pick up an entire legion and take it with him to Syria. He would at least have to plan how to provision several thousand soldiers and several hundred more hangers-on. The route east along the seven hundred and fifty military *miles* of the *Via Egnatia* was bleak. Passing through the wilds of Macedonia and the high mountain passes north of Epirus, through Moesia where the Getae threatened to come south of the *Fluvius Danubius* to Thrace.

And Dolabella could not by any means be sure of the welcome he would receive when he reached the end of the *via* and had to cross Asia Province to get himself and his men to Syria. Living off the land would be a challenge – especially at this time of year. And foraging slowed the legion's progress into the bargain. But there was no doubt that, once in place, stationed in Tripolis, it would be easy enough for Dolabella to observe events in both Smyrna and Athens just across the strait beyond it. Watching Brutus and Cassius. And Trebonius – for as long as he kept his head.

But even though he was Antony's co-consul, Dolabella was by no means a reliable ally. He was completely self-serving. Always putting his own ambitions first. Was greedy. A terrible disciplinarian, notoriously bad at keeping control of his men. And, of course, he was Cicero's ex-son-in-law. Widowed husband to the old lawyer's beloved – dead – daughter Tullia.

Which brought the tribune back to Septem and Antony's plans for him. How the secret agent fitted into this rapidly expanding puzzle. Like the coping stone holding a huge arch unshakably in place. But as Enobarbus' reasoning reached this stage, he was recalled to the present. There was a sharp hissing intake of breath. He looked across to see Fulvia standing there on Antony's left, wide-eyed, lips parted. Her face liberally sprinkled with bright red dots. Spots that spread like a rash down the front of her formal *stola* – to decorate her rapidly heaving breast. It was hard to be certain whether the expression on her face was one of revulsion or exhilaration.

'That's enough!' bellowed Antony. 'Stop now. Dismiss. And clear this carrion away!'

iii

Venus frowned thoughtfully. Her exquisite countenance seeming even more beautiful as it reflected her ready intelligence. 'I have seen it happen,' she said, her voice, as usual, a throaty purr. 'When someone fears she may become the victim of some brutal diversion for the pleasure of her masters. Instead of lying quiet and hoping for the best, she begins to join the game. Becomes an active

183

participant, little by little. Takes a measure of control. Becomes complicit by finding victims other than herself. And then – rarely but occasionally – she might manage to make herself a vital part of the sport. So that the men cannot play it properly without her. And so she takes control of everything.' Adonis nodded in ready agreement. But so, to be fair, did most of the others.

'So she goes from being the sufferer to being the accessory,' said Artemidorus. 'Yes. I have seen that working with bullies and their victims in the legions. But I had never thought of it happening in the manner you describe. However, now you mention it, I can see Cyanea playing a game like that. But I still don't see why she went back to him.'

'Where else was there for her to go?' asked Venus, rhetorically.

'She couldn't come back to you or any of the team, could she, Septem?' answered Ferrata, who did not understand rhetoric and was finding this conversation fascinating. Quite apart from anything else, it was the first time Venus had decided she trusted them all enough to open up. The legionary clearly hoped that now she was beginning to open her mind to them, she might open other aspects of herself to him. 'I mean, she could see as clearly as the rest of us that the information she gave Basilus was directly responsible for the failure of your mission and the death of *Divus Julius*. A point you had rather forcefully driven home by leaving her tied naked to a whipping post and presented to the less than charming companions I happened to pick up in the middle of a riot.'

'That was a terrible thing to do,' said Puella.

'I know. I regretted it at once. And have done so ever since.' The words came easily as he tried to reassure her. But he was by no means certain they were true.

What he was regretting now was leaving the bitch alive.

'You don't regret it as much as the first two morons who tried to take her,' said Ferrata. 'By the time they got up beside her she'd worked one hand free. Rapist number one had a *pugio* in his belt and she cut his throat with it while he was still trying to loosen his *braccae* trousers. Number two was no cleverer and didn't last any longer. Everyone stood back for a moment. She cut herself free and came towards us like one of the Friendly Ones dressed in nothing but hot blood. It was a cold night and she was actually smoking! Well, *steaming* I suppose. No wonder everyone retreated! Then someone tried to stop her and got his face slit open for his trouble. Then she sliced the face off another one – an innocent bystander with a torch. She took the torch and threw it into Basilus' *tablinum* where all his books and scrolls were scattered. By the time she vanished into the night the whole lot was ablaze and we only just made it out of there ourselves.'

184

'I see why she couldn't come back to us – or anyone we'd worked with,' said Artemidorus. 'But why go back to Basilus?'

'Perhaps because she knew he wanted her,' suggested Venus. 'Better to be wanted than discarded…'

'But he wanted her whipped for his pleasure. Humiliated. Screaming. That's how he *wanted* her…'

'Well, boy,' concluded Quintus. 'She must have had some kind of a plan. Because it worked. You and I have seen the truth of that. It worked so well that by all accounts she's now the mistress of the Governor of Asia Province. And on her way to Smyrna with him.'

*

'Antony wants you to follow Trebonius,' said Enobarbus on his return from Brundisium. 'Dolabella will be ahead of you – with the last of the Macedonian legions when he gets through Dyrrachium. But you're to focus on Trebonius.' He was talking to Artemidorus but the whole *contubernium* was there, except for Spurinna and Antistius, who were both about their professional callings. The secret agents were in the *tablinum* of Quintus' villa, which had been adapted to their purposes with a table large enough to carry maps or plans and seats for a dozen people around it. Even Adonis was present because, although the Senate had been called, it wasn't due to meet yet. Not with Antony still away and Dolabella out of town preparing for his journey. With the consuls absent, it was the *praetors'* responsibility to arrange Senate sittings. But both of the *praetors*, Brutus and Cassius, were in Athens. So in many ways the Senate was hamstrung for the moment.

'The general wants you to see what Trebonius gets up to,' continued the tribune. 'He's relieving Marcus Apulius out there. They're both dyed in the wool *Libertores* and there's a fortune in tax revenues unaccounted for. And he wants you to bring back Trebonius' head. Especially if you find he's up to mischief.'

'His head?' said Artemidorus. 'That's a big step down a dangerous road.'

'Trebonius, Basilus and Decimus Albinus took the first step down that road when they sent Myrtillus after the general,' said Enobarbus. 'And after *you*, of course,' he added, after a pause.

'It's nice to be an afterthought,' said Artemidorus with wry amusement.

'But I'd have thought *that* was probably Cyanea's doing,' added Ferrata. 'A little extra paragraph added to the original contract perhaps.'

'But if that's true, why didn't she do more when she discovered us in Basilus' villa?' Artemidorus returned to a subject that had been at the heart of a good few conferences lately.

185

'You can ask her when you get to Smyrna,' said Enobarbus impatiently. 'But if we don't start planning this mission soon she'll be dead of old age before you arrive.'

'Right,' said Quintus, taking control. 'One decision leads to another. First decision – how many do we think should go? Did the general dictate a number, Tribune? Is it to be just Septem here – or can he take more of us to watch his back while he's taking Trebonius' head? Once we've decided that, we'll need to consider speed, route, provisions, supplies. Staging posts, ships… Travel at this time of year is always a problem unless the gods are with you, each and all. Greek and Roman both.'

iv

Artemidorus decided that they should travel as a six-man military unit, using military transport and equipment. Following military roads. That way they could use the *mansio* military staging posts that *Divus Julius* had been putting in place to facilitate communications and support during the Parthian campaign he had never undertaken. Following hard on Dolabella's heels, close enough to call on his legion for help if they ever required it. But still with the capacity to overtake him if they felt the need. Although the secret agent much preferred to work alone – or, *in extremis* as one of a pair – six seemed the smallest unit likely to travel safely from here to Smyrna, the capital of Asia Province. Even in the footsteps of a legion.

In Italy they would probably be safe enough as they sped down the Appian Way to Brundisium and paused there to take ship across the Adriatic to Dyrrachium. 'Brundisium should be quiet now,' Enobarbus told them. 'Antony has sent the four Macedonian legions that landed there north to wait for him at Ariminium just south of the Rubicon. Which is the border with Cisalpine Gaul. Ready to move north with him when he decides to shake Decimus Albinus loose. He plans to be back here soon to organise the Senate.'

'After we land in Dyrrachium, we follow the *Via Egnatia* eastwards through Macedonia,' said Ferrata, taking up the plan. 'Then it's another voyage. From the most convenient port we can find across to Smyrna.'

'Good,' said Quintus at a nod from Artemidorus, summoning up all his courage in the face of not one sea voyage but two. The second one a long one – and in stormy weather too. 'We should have no trouble travelling along the first leg to Brundisium and boarding a ship to sail us across the *Mare Hadriaticum* Adriatic and into Dyrrachium. The only possible problem will be the weather, of course.'

Ferrata leaned forward once more, to add a little streetwise information. 'But the *Via Egnatia* which joins Dyrrachium with Byzantium goes through some wild

186

and dangerous country. If Dolabella isn't careful with his legion and what it gets up to – or if the Getae are really considering an invasion of Macedonia – we could find ourselves walking into a war zone. I'd like to suggest we plan to stop at Philippi and take ship from Neapolis Orientalis, the port that serves it. The most convenient jumping-off point in my opinion. A slightly longer voyage should lessen the danger all round. If, as I say, we can actually get to Philippi. And find a ship willing to make the voyage when we arrive there.'

Quintus closed his eyes as he nodded his curt agreement to the suggestion. The voyage from Brundisium to Dyrrachium was bad enough at a hundred *miles*. Neapolis Orientalis to Smyrna was well over twice that distance. And the weather was likely to become increasingly stormy as late autumn became early winter.

Once the initial decisions were taken, Enobarbus went off about his increasingly important duties with the Praetorian Cohorts and the four decimated legions, leaving Artemidorus, Quintus and Ferrata to iron out the details of their mission. Whose three places were taken as a matter of course. Hercules was technically still tutor to young Gaius Lepidus, but the elder Lepidus was happy for him to remain with the *contubernium*. And as he taught boxing, wrestling, sword fighting, a range of other weaponry and horse riding as well as logic and rhetoric, the gigantic tutor was a welcome addition. So that only left two places to be filled. Adonis was too valuable to be removed from his place as Senate Secretary. And taking either of the women did not seem to be a realistic option. Though, as Quintus gruffly pointed out, Puella was as ready as Cyanea had ever been to undertake such a dangerous mission. Especially given her almost supernatural ambidexterity.

The next obvious contender was Spurinna's slave Kyros, the quick-thinking young Greek who had been of valuable service to the *contubernium* before. So, leaving Puella working off her frustration on the progressively more breathless Ferrata, sword on sword, two hands against one, Septem and Quintus went to see Spurinna.

The Augur's villa was much nearer the Forum than Quintus' villa was. And, as the two men approached it, they became sidetracked by the bustle of an increasingly agitated crowd, all heading down past the Macellum market and the stalls of the *Basilica Aemilia*. Frowning with gathering concern, Artemidorus led Quintus into the crowded Forum. The soldiers shouldered their way to the front of the throng, who were standing looking up at a long line of papyrus sheets that had been secured to the door of the Senate House.

187

Artemidorus pushed closer still to the first sheet, recognising as he did so, the distinctive penmanship of Cicero's *amanuensis* secretary Tyro. 'What does it say?' demanded Quintus from further back.

Artemidorus started to read at once: '*Conscript Fathers, I ask by what bad luck it is, that for the last twenty years everyone who has been an enemy to the Republic has at the same time declared war against me? I don't need to name any particular person; you yourselves will remember examples that prove what I say. All these enemies have suffered more terrible fates than even I could have wished for them. But I marvel that* Antonius *does not fear the possibility of sharing the dreadful deaths of these men whose conduct he is imitating* now.'

'By Mars,' breathed Quintus. 'It's the speech he would have given had the Senate been in session... What else is there?'

'More than twenty pages by the look of things,' answered Artemidorus. 'I'll scan it for the highlights.' And so he pushed his way through the front line of the crowd, calling over his shoulder. 'It says here that Antony is so ruthlessly ambitious that he is worse than Catiline – and you remember that Cicero slaughtered Catiline's supporters himself. Including Antony's stepfather. Without the inconvenience of a trial. Strangled with bowstrings in the *tullianum* prison. Then it goes on to say Antony's worse even than Clodius Pulcher – who was Antony's friend – and Fulvia's first husband until Cicero's associate Milo murdered him on the Appian Way. It adds that Antony is a helpless drunkard. That he has been from his youth a pervert. That he dressed as a woman. Had a longstanding affair with the young aristocrat Gaius Scribonius Curio. Sold himself as a prostitute when money ran low. Charged the highest prices, too. And even played the woman's part with many men. Which is much the same as was said about *Divus Julius* and Nichomedes of Bythnia.

'But this next section looks more focused and relevant. I'll read it word for word. "*However, notice how stupid this man Antony is, I should rather say, of this brute beast is. For he said: 'Marcus Brutus – who I honour – holding up a bloody dagger, called upon Cicero. From which it must be obvious that Cicero was an accomplice in Caesar's evil murder.'*"'

'Wait!' said Quintus. 'I thought you took Brutus' dagger from *Divus Julius'* corpse. I thought that was the dagger you gave to young Octavius.'

'That's true,' nodded Artemidorus, surprised. 'But it's probably poetic licence. You know Cicero. Never let the facts get in the way of a well-turned phrase. Now what does he say next? "*Am I then called wicked because Antony suspects that I suspected something? And is Brutus, who openly displayed this dagger dripping with Caesar's blood, called an honourable man by Antony? This is the sort of stupidity we find in everything Antony says. But how much greater is it in whatever he thinks and does? Decide matters this way if you want,* Consul Antonius. *Call the cause of Brutus, Cassius, Decimus Albinus, Trebonius and the rest whatever you like. Sleep off that drunkenness of yours! Sleep it off and take a deep breath. Must we put a blazing torch under you to waken you while you are sleeping over such an important affair? As you have already threatened to do to me? Will you never understand that you have to decide whether those men who killed Gaius Julius Caesar are foul homicides or glorious heroes?*

"*Just think a little; and for a moment consider the situation like a sober man. I, who, as I confess, am an intimate friend of those men and a would-be accomplice of theirs, deny that there is any room for argument between these alternatives. I confess that if these men are not saviours of the Roman people and of the Republic, then they must be worse than assassins! Worse than homicides! Worse even than patricides! For it is a far more terrible thing to murder the father of one's country, than to kill one's own father. What do you say to this, you wise and thoughtful man? If they are patricides, why do you always call them, both in the Senate and before the Roman people,* honourable men? *Why has Marcus Brutus been, on your authority and at your insistence, excused from obedience to our laws and allowed to travel abroad? Why were provinces given to Brutus and Cassius? Why were extra magistrates assigned to them? Why was the number of their lieutenants augmented? And all these measures were suggested by you. They are not homicides then. Nor patricides either! It follows that in your opinion they are heroic deliverers of their country and saviours of the Republic, since there can be no other alternative explanation for the actions you have taken!*'"

Artemidorus turned to Quintus, his face pale. 'That's it then!' he said. 'Cicero has ruled on *Divus Julius'* dying words at last. What Antony has been forced into doing for political expediency has completely undermined the case he was trying to build against Brutus as a patricide. This has to mean total war with Cicero and with the Senate. There is no other way forward. And it looks to me as though the faster we start collecting *Libertores'* heads, the happier the general will be!'

189

XI

i

Kyros looked at his five companions with nothing short of awe. And at their surroundings with stunned disbelief. Born in Greece, he had been sold into slavery as a child and, apart from a brief, unpleasant visit to the slave market in Ephesus, he had lived his life in Rome. Rome was just about all he could remember, and the strict but kindly ownership of the augur and *haruspex* Spurinna. And here he was now, recently manumitted, a freedman, added to the tribune's *contubernium* of spies under Septem's command, all heading *ad orientam* eastwards. Far beyond his native Greece. Right to the far edge of the world as he understood it. Looking down at this moment on the dockside of Brundisium. Expecting to take ship on the next tide in a massive military *quinquireme*, with five banks of oars, bound across the narrow Adriatic to Dyrrachium in Macedonia. His mind simply reeled at the prospect. His chest threatened to burst with excitement.

The six secret agents were attended by four slaves, military men, experienced and reliable. In a fight as well as on the road. Borrowed from Antony's Praetorian Cohorts, many of which were being disbanded now or reassigned. But the spies who had been slaves were all, like Kyros, free. And technically one of the last independent Praetorian units still functioning. Even the striking woman they called Puella seemed to be free. Though how they had arranged her manumission was still a mystery to the young Greek. For her papers of ownership must be either in Rome or Athens – wherever the household documents of Marcus Junius Brutus, her original owner, were stored. But Puella was mysterious in more ways than one.

For a start, Puella was dressed and treated like a man. And she seemed to expect nothing else. Perhaps it was part of the price she paid for her participation in this adventure, Kyros speculated. And dressed not just as a man – but as a Praetorian legionary. She wore *braccae* leather trousers and hobnailed *caligae* boots. A padded tunic. A backplate and breastplate of armour over it. Adjusted, it must be admitted to allow for the added volume of her breasts. She even had a helmet with a legionary's crest stowed somewhere in the baggage train. And she rode fully armed. *Gladius* on her right hip, *pugio* on her left. Weapons with which she was impressively competent. Able to use each one in either hand – something the young Greek had never seen before. Skills she honed relentlessly at every opportunity. Usually against the square, capable, cheerfully ribald Ferrata.

Occasionally against the gigantic Hercules. And once – but only once – against the terrifying *triarius* Quintus. Because he wished to polish her technique and show her a new move.

Only Septem remained aloof. As befitted the little group's leader. Kyros suspected that the dazzling woman and the handsome unit commander were lovers. Just the manner in which they seemed to avoid each other gave the game away. But he had no evidence beyond the vague suspicion. True, her eyes seemed to sparkle with excitement whenever she looked at him. But then, her eyes seemed to sparkle with excitement almost all the time. As did his own, he suspected. Like Kyros himself, Puella was in the middle of the most exciting adventure she could ever have imagined and was loving every heartbeat of it.

*

Artemidorus led the little group down onto the dockside. There was stabling here for the horses they had ridden from the last *mansio* way station. Where they had swapped the mounts they picked up in Capua. They were planning to ride from *mansio* to *mansio* or township to township along the *Via Egnatia*, swapping horses at each one. Once they had requisitioned or purchased the best that they could find across the *Mare Hadriaticum* Adriatic Sea in the military port-city of Dyrrachium.

In order to facilitate this, Artemidorus was once again carrying letters of authority from Antony. Letters which included one manumitting the slave Puella. As the Consul of Rome had the legal power to do. And assigning her to the command of Iacomus Artemidorus, centurion seconded to the consul's personal Praetorian Cohorts. And, amongst his other effects, the secret agent also carried a strongbox full of gold.

The military *quinquireme* was called *Salacia* in honour of Neptune's queen. Her commander was a tribune called Vitus. He raised an eyebrow when a tall centurion ran uninvited up his gangplank but proved to be amenable enough. The moment Artemidorus showed him Antony's order, he called the rest of the *contubernium* aboard and sent crewmen to help with their baggage. 'We sail with the tide after our sacrifices are done,' he said. 'It's a straight run over to Dyrrachium. We're just carrying supplies to restock the warehouses over there now that Consul Dolabella has taken the last Macedonian legion eastwards to support him as Governor of Syria. The weather looks calm enough, given that it's so late in the season – and the sacrifices will clarify that one way or another. I'm lucky to have an excellent *haruspex* aboard. And I'm an augur myself.'

And so they set off. Kyros watched the *haruspex* sacrifice a white lamb and read *calm seas and prosperous voyage* from its entrails before approving the fortunate sacrifice for roasting and consumption by the officers and their guests. The young spy was unimpressed by the man's technique, however. It didn't begin to compare to Spurinna's.

He was just turning away from the bloody sacrifice, overwhelmed by the procedure of setting sail, when Artemidorus called him over. The rest of the *contubernium* were assembled on the raised afterdeck, near where Tribune Vitus was overseeing the vessel's departure. The drum beat of the timekeeper ensuring the five banks of oars on each side rose and fell in unison. The deck crew scurrying around both here and high above as the great square sail bellied with the wind. The way the deck moved was a sensation unlike anything he had ever felt. The closest he could come was a vague memory of an earthquake he experienced as a child.

No sooner had Kyros staggered over to the group than Quintus and Ferrata ran for the siderails and looked steadfastly downwards. Seemingly fascinated by the way the long, sleek hull was sliding through the water. 'We'll be aboard overnight at least,' Artemidorus said. 'This is one of the few voyages where the ship goes out of sight of land and keeps going – though slowly – in the dark. And the crew have already started looking sideways at Puella. Women aboard ships are either out of reach, bad luck or fair game. I want to ensure Puella stays out of reach, understand?'

'Yes Septem,' said Kyros. Although he didn't really understand at all.

'So I want you and Puella to go through a series of training exercises. As though she is teaching you how to use both hands to wield your weapons in the same way as she does. Work hard. Put on a show with both *gladius* and *pugio*. I want every sailor aboard this vessel to have a clear idea of what Puella is capable of doing to them if they put one finger out of place. Understand?'

'Yes, Septem,' said Kyros. And this time he was telling the truth.

ii

Dyrrachium seemed eerily empty as they disembarked next day. There was an air of desolation about the place. Only a month or two ago, there had been five legions and all their ancillaries stationed here. Legions that had been in place for more than a year. Now they were all gone – four via Brundisium to the south bank of the Rubicon at Antony's order. Ready to try and shake Decimus out of Gaul. The fifth with Dolabella heading *ad orientem*. That was thousands upon thousands of soldiers. Plus their support units. Often as not, their families. Certainly their camp-followers. Their needs, wishes, desires. But, most of all, their pay. Millions of *sestertii* gone from the local economy. The *tabernae* were deserted. The *lupanaria* brothels abandoned, she-wolves underused, bored and bellicose. The stalls and shops empty, their shelves bare; their holders and keepers fearing a long, lean winter. The augurs, *divias* fortune-tellers and *strigae* witches all unemployed – the future crystal clear to all of them.

Salacia's crew, therefore, received the warmest possible welcome when they docked next day in the deserted port. For they brought not only goods in her cargo hold, but men, money and employment. Temporary though it might be. Kyros and the others in Artemidorus' *contubernium* also could have made themselves free of the city. But the spy refused to be distracted. As their equipment was being unloaded, he came ashore personally to find the *hospitium* that best suited their needs. Quintus came with him, instantly rejuvenated when his feet touched solid ground. The *hospitium* they found was also able to supply a dozen good horses for hire and several pack animals as well. The reason Artemidorus selected it was simple. It was the start of the communication system that would allow his team to swap their horses at *mansios* and townships all along the *Via Egnatia*. As far as Philippi, at least. They planned, following Ferrata's observations, to make the city of Philippi their next destination. It lay nearly five hundred military *miles* distant and at least three weeks' hard travelling away, just inland from the port of Neapolis that served it. Where they would take ship one last time. Heading for the port-city of Smyrna, their final destination.

And so they proceeded as planned, over mountain and valley, from *mansio* to *mansio*, village to village, town to town – in the wake of Dolabella's legion. Their welcome always curt – at the least – for Dolabella's men had been almost rapacious. And notoriously ill-controlled. Their general infinitely greedy. Demanding extra taxes whenever he thought he saw prosperity. With gathering concern, they passed through the towns of Claudiana, Heraclea, Edessa and Pella, Thessaloniki and the local provincial capital, Amphipolis. In the end it took them more than a month to reach the soggy plain below the township of Philippi where they turned towards the coast and the port of Neapolis Orientalis. Where they found a ship willing to take them through the wintery seas to Smyrna. A neat little *trireme* called *Triteia*.

*

Like Dyrrachium, Smyrna seemed eerily deserted when they arrived there with the early days of the new administrative year 711 since the founding of the city. In the consulship of Aulus Hirtius and Gaius Vibius Pansa. This might have been explained by the pounding downpour that greeted *Triteia* as she docked. But as soon as Artemidorus stepped off the gangplank onto the quay, he sensed an unsettling atmosphere. Which was something more subtle than a mere atmospheric disturbance. More dangerous. The port, which should have been busy even on an overpoweringly wet mid-winter's day, seemed deserted. Once their baggage had been unloaded into a dockside warehouse, leaving the well-armed slaves to guard it, Artemidorus led his *contubernium* up from the waterfront slowly. As though he was taking them into enemy territory.

There had been good reason for Dyrrachium to seem like this, Artemidorus thought. With five legions recently departed and the town yet to readjust to their absence. But Smyrna was a garrison town. There were cohorts stationed here permanently. Occasionally legions. And, as far as he knew, none of them had been reposted. It was just possible, Artemidorus reflected, that Dolabella, passing through Asia Province on his way to Syria with the last of the Macedonian legions, had borrowed some extra cohorts from Governor Trebonius. But even that should not have left behind this unsettling air of emptiness. Tension. Such as they had experienced along the *Via Egnatia* in the footsteps of Dolabella and his legion, as they came across looted villages and burned-out farmsteads. Towns with their gates closed and their walls manned as though besieged. Perhaps Dolabella was after more than a cohort or two from the Governor of Asia Province. Whatever the reason, as soon as they were all ashore, he called to the others, 'Form up!'

The long journey aboard *Triteia* from Philippi and Neapolis had been further lengthened by contrary winds and two storms from which they had sheltered in the lee of islands and the welcoming sanctuary of deep bays in mountainous shores. The extra time had allowed the little unit to hone and extend their skills. Not only with sword and dagger, right hand and left. But also with bow and arrow, slingshot and *pilum*. Though spears and arrows were tied to lengths of cord so they would not be lost overboard. When slings ran out of bullets, they raided the ballast for pebbles. The extra time allowed Quintus and Ferrata to find their sea legs. And finally it allowed some changes to the way the *contubernium* was constructed – especially when it was heading for trouble.

As his curt order still echoed on the deserted dockside, therefore, Artemidorus took the lead at the point of an arrowhead. Behind him at his right shoulder came Quintus, in the middle towered Hercules, and at his left shoulder Puella. This arrangement allowed Quintus to use his right hand to wield his *gladius*. And Puella to use her left. Hercules was tall enough to see even over his centurion's crest. This also allowed each of them to use Artemidorus as a shield even as they guarded his back. For none of them carried a *scutum*. Behind them came Ferrata on the right and Kyros on the left. Guarding their backs in turn – but alert for the slightest sound or movement at their rear – at which they would whirl and form a circle of sharp steel. Almost comparable to the *testudo* tortoise the legions were trained to form with their shields. Kyros, who was beginning to share some of Puella's ability to wield his weapons with either hand.

iii

But as Artemidorus led his tight-knit command up the hill from the docks towards the town itself – birthplace of Homer, whose poetry recorded the deeds of his personal protective deity Achilleus at the twenty-year siege of Illium, also known as Troy – the streaming *vias* remained empty. The threat he felt was in the air – not on the streets. For the moment, at least. Artemidorus' eyes were narrow. And not because of the rain. He didn't know Smyrna – except by reputation. But he knew cities. This was a commercial neighbourhood. The one closest to the docks always was. Merchants' villas liberally interspersed with their warehouses and shops. *Hospitae. Tabernae. Lupanaria.* Serving the city and the travellers who came and went through the port. Not to mention the *nautae* sailors who transported them. But all he saw on either side were closed doors and fastened shutters. It was as though Smyrna was under siege like Troy. But that could not be – the seaways were clear and the docks were open. There was something else going on here that he didn't yet understand.

Until he reached the city's main forum. And found the Governor of Asia Province crucified against the door of the town hall.

Artemidorus could not identify Trebonius at first, for the body hanging against a wooden cross propped against the wooden doorway was so battered and bruised it was scarcely recognisable as human. Only the scantiest loincloth preserved some element of modesty. Above it, the belly and breast were a mass of welts and bruises. Open wounds and black burn marks. Below it, the legs, clearly disjointed and broken, reached down to crushed and blackened feet. Ropes had been secured round ankles and knees; wrists, elbows and shoulders. Though the outstretched arms and hands in no better shape than the legs and feet. At first glance, the rope holding the outspread arms seemed to be a kindness. But Artemidorus knew better. For, at the end of the Third Servile War against Spartacus he had seen six thousand men crucified by Marcus Licinius Crassus all along the *Via Appia*. And he knew that crucified men often died because they could not breathe properly. So the ropes were just a way of saving the tortured victim from asphyxiation – and so extending his agony. The head hung down, hair pulled forward by the weight of sweat and blood. For the door of the *curia* was protected from the rain by a formal colonnade that stretched across the width of the building at the top of an impressive set of marble steps. And, even as Artemidorus stood, stunned by simple shock, the head moved. Lifted. Revealing the smashed and battered face that, after a moment of utter disbelief, he realised he knew.

195

On either side of the cross, lines of legionaries stood guard beneath the colonnades. Armoured and fully armed. As though on parade. Artemidorus recognised their insignia at once. They were from the legion he had followed all the way down the *Via Egnatia*. The last Macedonian legion which Dolabella had brought with him from Dyrrachium.

Dolabella had done this!

Artemidorus' mind reeled. That one governor should torture and crucify another governor. Both Roman citizens. Patricians. Generals into the bargain. It was scarcely comprehensible. Under Roman law, slaves could be tortured – could only give evidence in court if there was proof that they had been tortured. But to torture a Roman citizen was to declare war against the city and the state. And if anyone other than Cicero himself should be fully aware of this, it must surely be his ex-son-in-law. As these thoughts span through Artemidorus' head, he was mildly surprised to find his *gladius* in his fist. And, beneath the relentless roaring of the rain he heard the hiss of five more swords sliding out of their soaking scabbards.

'Forward!' he ordered, and the tight little arrowhead moved across the forum behind him.

As his mind grappled with the horrific fate of Governor Trebonius, so he began to see the implications – and understand why the citizens of Smyrna were all in hiding. To begin with, they might well be terrified by the possibility that Dolabella planned that they should share the fate of their governor. Or simply that he proposed to unleash the legionaries on them. Or alternatively there was the very real prospect that the Senate would want to take revenge for the treatment of their duly appointed governor as soon as the news reached Rome. Vengeance not only on the people who did this to him – but upon the people who did not stop them doing this to him.

The moment Artemidorus' foot went onto the bottom step, the centurion in charge of the guards stepped forward. Stood solidly in front of the dying man, just inside the warm, dry colonnade. Looking down through the relentless curtains of rain. 'No closer,' he said. 'On pain of death.' His face was set like marble. 'And, as you can see, I do mean *pain*…'

'I am here on the commission of Consul and General Mark Antony,' said Artemidorus, so used to using the phrase that he forgot Antony had not been Consul since the *calends* beginning of the month. 'I carry his seal and authority. I speak with his voice.'

'You'd better speak to General Dolabella then,' answered the centurion. 'He's in the governor's palace.' He gestured with his chin towards an imposing building on the right-hand side of the square.

But something in Artemidorus' ringing declaration of his authority seemed to get through to Trebonius. The head beyond the centurion's shoulder stirred again. The battered face came up. The swollen, blood-crusted lips moved. Trebonius shouted a message to the spy and courier. The words came out as a garbled whisper and were only uttered once. The head fell forward once again, overcome by the effort of communication. Artemidorus had turned and begun to lead his command towards the palace before he fully understood what the words had been.

'My woman. Dolabella has her…'

iv

Publius Cornelius Dolabella was exactly as Artemidorus remembered him. A spare man with a long face and thinning mud-coloured hair. Cold, narrow eyes. A downturned, pouting mouth above a weak, receding chin. It was difficult to imagine what Cicero's daughter Tullia had seen in him. Other than a political marriage to further her father's ambitions. But it was easy to see why his ex-father in law found it so easy to dislike him now that she was dead and his ambitions lay in other quarters. But Artemidorus was still staggered that the man was capable of such unbelievable cruelty.

'So…' Dolabella raised those cold, calculating eyes from his perusal of Artemidorus' letters of authority which lay spread across the table in front of him. 'What exactly is it that Antony wants you to do, Centurion? You and the five companions waiting for you outside?'

'To establish precisely what is going on in Smyrna – was going on before your arrival at any rate. To prepare a report for him. And to bring him Trebonius' head if he has been involved in any actions against the general and his interests.'

'That's quite an assignment. For a centurion and five helpers.'

'Catiline sent Centurion Gaius Manlius north to raise an army.'

'And look what happened to them. Courtesy of my revered ex-father-in-law. But I take your point. Centurion Manlius raised a considerable army. On his own. We should never underestimate what a centurion is capable of.' The Governor of Syria stood up. The whiteness of his *toga* cast a bright reflection over Antony's orders. 'Well, I am prepared to help Antony, even though the *calends* of *Januarius* has passed and we are replaced as co-consuls by Hirtius and Pansa. It so happens that the foolish ex-governor of Syria Province not only refused to give assistance and support me and my legion as we passed through his territory. He also put his trust in a woman.'

'Really?' grated Artemidorus. 'What woman is that?'

'Some *canicula* bitch of no account. Who, when I put the case to her forcefully enough, was happy to recount all the pillow talk the *stultus* fool shared with her.'

197

'Forcefully enough…' Artemidorus' voice was husky. His throat dry. How he wished he had been allowed to wear his sword or dagger in here. Or even to bring his five companions into the room with him.

'Making her watch the beginning of Trebonius' questioning was enough to break her down. In every regard except one. Which is why she is awaiting my pleasure. When I have finished with her ex-lover.'

'And that is?'

'Where he has hidden the gold he brought out from Rome with him.'

'He brought gold, Governor? I thought – the general thought – he was relying on the taxes collected by Governor Marcus Apuleius, the man he was relieving.'

'That's what Antony thought, was it? Unusually naive of him, I'd say…'

Artemidorus frowned, trying to work out what Dolabella was driving at. But before he could even get his thoughts in order, the governor slapped his palm onto the tabletop beside Antony's letters of commission. 'I think you need to see the lady in question. Talk things over with her. Then you'll understand.'

'Understand, Governor?'

'What I have done and why I did it. And you can report it all to Antony when you hand over Trebonius' head. Which, in due course I will give to you. When I finally allow him to die.'

*

The guard Dolabella assigned to guide Artemidorus had no orders concerning his five companions. As they, like their leader, had been disarmed at the door, he allowed them to accompany him as he led them through the governor's palace. In common with many other great official buildings, it was not furnished with dungeons. Which were reserved for the local *carcer* prison. Instead, there were storerooms with heavy doors secured by Greek locks that could be locked against people breaking out as well as against people breaking in.

The six of them followed the legionary down steps into the lower floors of the palace, where the air was fragrant with the smell of cooking. Dolabella, Artemidorus recalled, always preferred a well-furnished table. Which seemed to have no effect on his lean, spare figure. Perhaps he was a regular visitor to the *vomitorium*, emptying his belly after each course – as some Epicureans were said to do. The guard led them past the *culina* kitchen itself and into the corridors beyond. Here, heavy doors secured all sorts of supplies – mostly vegetable, mineral, oleaginous and alcoholic – against theft. At the end of the corridor, a door stood ajar, opening out onto a rainwashed street and a small paddock full of fatted animals.

The animals being outside, thought Artemidorus, made it clear what lay behind the last door – through which it was possible to hear movement and ragged breathing.

With a flourish, the legionary thrust a massive key into the simple lock, turned it and threw the door wide.

The occupant of the room came out like a wildcat, springing for the soldier's face. It was more by luck than judgement that he stepped back – thus saving his eyes if not his cheeks. But the shock of the attack wore off almost instantly and he caught his assailant's wrists and threw her back. Stepped forward as she staggered, still on her feet and ready for a fight. Punched her with all his strength immediately between her breasts. She crashed backwards into the darkness of the room. 'You wait, bitch,' he said. 'I'll see you pay for that in ways you can't even imagine...'

Artemidorus stepped past him. 'That will do, soldier. You are dismissed!' he said, pushing the door wide to allow some light into the place. Whose occupant was already rolling over onto her side, ready to pull herself onto her feet. As the enraged legionary pushed roughly past Puella and vanished.

But when she saw Artemidorus she froze.

'*Salve*, Cyanea,' he said, his voice unexpectedly gentle.

v

Cyanea shook with simple, scarcely controllable rage. 'Why,' she demanded. 'Why am I always surrounded by men whose dreams and plans are so much bigger than their brains? So much greater than their reach?'

Artemidorus was here to ask questions – not to answer them. And in any case, he realised that this question was rhetorical. Born from the frustration of defeat. The prospect of a truly terrifying death. The present state of her hair, which was a tangled mess. Of her clothing which was filthy and spattered with what looked like blood. Probably Trebonius'. Of her face – which was no cleaner than her clothing. And of her nails which were packed with skin from the legionary's cheeks. She was not a vain woman. Especially considering how beautiful she was. But, cat-like, preferred to stay neat and tidy. Filthiness had always appalled her.

However, he was having trouble putting the questions he wanted answered into any kind of order. So, logical to his Greek fingertips, he started with the most immediate. 'What was Trebonius up to, Cyanea? What made Dolabella do these terrible things to him?'

Cyanea's eyes narrowed. Even so, they seemed to catch the light of the lamp Ferrata was holding. And gleam like blue-green chalcedony. '*Up to*? He was helping Brutus and Cassius of course. Trying to make up for the mistake they made in leaving Antony alive on The *Ides* of *Mars* last year. Specifically, he arrived with the huge cache of arms and armour Caesar left in Dyrrachuim to supply his Parthian Campaign. Then the moment he made contact with Governor Marcus Apuleius, who he was relieving here, he sent Apuleius south with the arms and the entire year's tax revenue from Asia Province. When Brutus gets the money, and Apuleius as a new lieutenant, he will be better off by two hundred million *sestertii*!

'And Brutus is on the move with Cassius, by the way. He has plans to recruit the men from Pompey's army who escaped after the battle of Pharsalus and settled in Greece, Macedonia and Syria. While Brutus is working up in the north, Cassius may go as far south as Egypt on his recruiting drive. Though I don't know how Cleopatra's going to feel about that! The fact is, you can build a good many legions with two hundred million *sestertii*. Especially if the men you're recruiting came from Pompey's command. An army Caesar defeated. Who loved the man whose head he took. Some of whom, into the bargain, have had farms and townships raided by Dolabella's legion as they made their way out here.

'And Cassius, of course, is still amazingly popular with the men he led to safety after Crassus' defeat at Carrhae just over ten years ago. There are thousands of them settled locally as well. When they hear the news about the money and the armaments he'll have to fight them off, they'll be so eager to join him. Almost at one stroke, Trebonius has turned the situation in the East on its head. He was enormously proud of that. Until Dolabella arrived, at any rate. Probably still is. All he's actually said, even under torture, is "*Civis Romanum sum*! I am a Roman citizen!"'

'But Dolabella's concerns are even more immediate than arms and tax revenue, Brutus and Cassius, aren't they?' probed the spy.

'Trebonius' gold, you mean?' shrugged Cyanea. 'Yes. That's the one thing I haven't told him yet.'

'But you know where it is...'

By way of answer, Cyanea changed the subject. 'These are the spies you've replaced Telos and me with are they? I know Spurinna's slave boy Kyros here. And Ferrata. Quintus, of course. I seem to remember the giant. And the girl you stole from Brutus. Is she your new mistress? She looks the part, I must say. You being Greek and her being dressed as a boy...'

'I look more the part than you do,' snapped Puella. 'Even in armour!' Artemidorus swung round. Puella was looking down her long nose at the bedraggled Cyanea. Her expression one of pure, aristocratic disdain. A few weeks ago she had been a slave. A possession; a thing. Hardly even human. Now she

200

was using icy looks he had only ever seen displayed by Cleopatra at her haughtiest.

*

Dolabella agreed to accommodate them in the governor's palace. There was plenty of room. And they were, after all, Antony's emissaries. As his guests, they were welcome to use the baths, and while they did so, a messenger went down to the docks to summon their slaves and their baggage. Then, clean and appropriately dressed, they were invited to *cena* dinner. Only Artemidorus, however, was invited to the *triclinium* formal dining room. Here he found Dolabella, his tribunes, and several leading citizens of Smyrna. Nine guests in all, arranged in traditional threes on the couches around the central table. The others – even Puella – ate with the centurions in the officers' dining room.

Artemidorus was preoccupied, as he mentally wrote and rewrote the report he would send to Antony. Which he would take to Antony in person if matters moved on as quickly as he hoped. Along with Trebonius' head. He was sufficiently part of the conversation, however, to note that the local dignitaries were nervous on several counts. Who, they wondered, would take over from Governor Trebonius? Who would run their city when Dolabella and his troops moved on? How would the Senate in Rome react to what had happened here? And, perhaps most worryingly, how were the citizens of Smyrna going to react when the shock of their governor's death began to wear off? There had been talk of riots…

'If they riot, then we know how to settle things,' answered Dolabella roundly, nodding at Artemidorus, and beaming with self-satisfaction. 'We had enough practice in controlling riots last *Mars* in Rome.'

After *cena*, Artemidorus excused himself and retired to the bedroom he had been assigned, leaving the other guests to philosophical and political debate. And *amphora* after *amphora* of Trebonius' best wine. He had been assigned a sizeable chamber that contained not only a bed but also a desk. The bed, as with all Roman beds, was tall and ornate. The headboard and footboard were carved with intricate designs. The whole thing stood so high that there was a footstool at its side to allow the sleeper to climb aboard. The room was bright with a range of lamps and candles, smelling of scented oil. One of the palace body-slaves was waiting to help him get ready for bed, but he sent the man in search of an *amanuensis* secretary instead. After a while, the slave returned with a young Greek carrying a writing box, a stylus and tablets, ink and papyrus.

Artemidorus dismissed the body-slave and began to dictate the report he planned to send – or take – to Antony. He was just putting the finishing touches to it when the chamber door opened and Puella entered, carrying a lamp. 'I thought

201

I'd never find you,' she whispered. 'This place is like the maze of Daedalus. And you will be my Minotaur; part man, part bull...' Her eyes widened when she saw that they were not alone, but Artemidorus dismissed the scribe. Then, in spite of the temptation of the pleasant distractions she presented, he settled Puella in a comfortable chair and read the report to her.

One read-through was sufficient to establish that he was thoroughly satisfied with what had been written. He put the papyrus scroll aside. She came to him at once and, with the practised movements of a well-trained handmaid, she helped him to disrobe. She herself was wearing a light tunic, and when he had been stripped down to his, he held her hand. Literally. As she was just about to lift the tunic over his head. She looked up at him, the faintest of frowns marring the perfection of her forehead. Wide eyes gleaming in the lamplight. But questioning. Then filled with sudden understanding.

'You cannot leave her down there,' she said. 'You would rather let her escape than let her share Governor Trebonius' fate. Despite the fact that she betrayed you. Caused Caesar's death with her treachery. Even though, as Ferrata says, she wants to see you dead and burning. And is more relentless than the Friendly Ones and Nemesis combined...'

vi

Now that they were guests, their weapons had been returned to them. Together with all their personal items from their baggage. Which, in the spy's case, included two pouches. One containing the Balearic sling he habitually carried nowadays. The other full of the keys with which he had broken into Minucius Basilus' villa in Pompeii. Keys designed to open locks like those on the storeroom doors – in case the legionary with the scratched face had taken the key to Cyanea's cell away when he stalked angrily down the corridor. Artemidorus strapped his sword-belt on, therefore, and fastened the pouch of keys to it. Beside the winged phallus good-luck charms Ferrata had given him. Beside the tiny pouch that held the sling. He took the largest of the lamps. 'Come on,' he whispered.

Puella and he crept into the corridor side by side. Puella's search for her lover's chamber had the unexpected benefit of familiarising her with the maze of corridors they were passing through. Dolabella seemed dangerously overconfident, thought Artemidorus. Had the spy been in the governor's place – with Trebonius crucified and slowly dying, scant *pedes* feet away – he would have posted guards inside the palace as well as outside. But there were none. And, in spite of the reputation of the legion and its lax commander, it seemed that everyone was in bed. Perhaps exhausted by all the pillaging, carousing and ravishing they had performed on the way here, he thought wryly. The only sounds the pair of them heard as they slid silently through the shadows was that of distant snoring.

Even if Puella had not been so confident a guide, thought Artemidorus, he would probably have found the storerooms. Simply by following his nose. For the heady scents of *cena* still hung heavy on the air. Getting stronger and stronger as they approached the *culina* kitchen. After leaving Cyanea, he had subconsciously counted the number of storeroom doors separating her makeshift prison from the kitchen itself. And he counted them back now, knowing that there should be six. For some reason far beyond his understanding, he pushed his hand against each of them as he and Puella passed. They all remained solidly shut. Until he reached the sixth.

The pressure of his palm against the cool wood made the door swing open at once. He froze. Puella, sensitive at his shoulder, froze as well. The door swung inwards through several *pedes* feet then stopped as it came up against something solid enough to halt its movement. Artemidorus slid his *pugio* out of its sheath – regretting as he often did the fact that he had given the dagger with the almost magical blade to Caesar Octavius. But this one was almost its equal, he consoled himself, as he stepped forward, following the brightness thrown by the lamp. Feeling Puella stirring into movement behind him, even as her left hand brushed his hip intimately. As she lifted his *gladius* out of its sheath. Then she was at his side. Armed and ready to face whatever was going on.

The brightness of two lamps lit the whole storeroom. But neither the spy nor his companion paid any attention to the bales of herbs or sacks of grain that lined the walls. Their attention was taken by the head and shoulders of the body that had stopped the door from opening. It was dressed in a tunic. Lying on its back, facing upwards. The face was that of the legionary Cyanea had scratched. The red trenches still marred the skin of his cheeks. His left eye seemed to stare balefully at the intruders. But where his right eye should have been there was only a gaping red wound.

'He must have come back to take his revenge,' breathed Puella.

'Underestimating his victim,' nodded Artemidorus. 'And still wearing his dagger, the stupid bastard.'

'Well, she's got it now. And she's out there somewhere...' For the first time since the *Ides* of *Mars*, Puella sounded nervous.

No sooner had she finished speaking than there came a pandemonium of shouting and screaming from somewhere up above them. 'FIRE! FIRE!' someone shouted. 'Quick! The palace is on fire!'

Side by side they turned and began to retrace their steps. As they did so, the sound of snoring was replaced by the noises of people stirring. Waking, beginning to react to the warnings. Even so, they made it back to Artemidorus' room before they met anyone. The spy looked over the bedchamber and what was in it, making a rapid mental calculation of what he needed to save. But then Puella took his shoulder and he realised she had been speaking. 'I hear the warnings,' she was saying. 'But I don't smell the smoke...'

Puella was right. Artemidorus decided to risk leaving the contents of the room just as they were. Together they ran out into the corridor again. And this time it was full of confused people milling about. Most of them looking for a fire. There was panic and puzzlement. Until, just as Artemidorus was about to take command and restore some sort of order, Dolabella himself appeared, accompanied by two boys and two girls. Slaves who had clearly been his bed companions, though they were scarcely more than children. 'Down to the *atrium*!' he ordered, his voice cracking with the strain of shouting over the disorder. Everyone obediently trooped off while the governor, proving what an effective leader he could be – commanded a series of slaves and soldiers to check for a fire and report back.

While everyone went down to the *atrium*, Artemidorus collected his *contubernium* around him. 'Cyanea has escaped,' he said. 'Keep careful watch. There is no telling what she has planned. Though, knowing her as I do, I suspect she will be after Trebonius' treasure. Or as much of it as she can carry safely away with her...'

'She won't be coming after you?' wondered Puella.

'She will eventually,' he agreed. 'But I doubt she will tonight. She has other priorities. And as long as I'm alive, she can afford to wait. Knowing her and her appetite for vengeance, she'll probably wait until I'm at my happiest, my most fulfilled – with most to look forward to. And then she'll strike. Probably starting with my wife and children. Working her way towards me...'

'That's horrible!' whispered Puella.

'That's Cyanea,' answered Ferrata.

vii

None of Dolabella's teams found anything to report. The whole thing had clearly been a false alarm. So after a while everyone was told to return to their rooms. Artemidorus and Puella returned to his. But they had hardly settled – had yet to start undressing – before a slave was knocking discreetly but insistently on the door. 'Wait here,' ordered Artemidorus as he followed the slave.

Who led him to Dolabella's bedchamber. And to the enraged governor. 'Look at this!' Dolabella shouted. 'Just look at this!' He was so angry that he hardly seemed to have registered that his catamites and little girls were huddled in his huge bed. Their eyes wide with terror. The footboard of the massive bed stood open. A secret panel gaped, revealing a hidden compartment. Out of which stuck a metal-bound strongbox. Its lid thrown back, to reveal that it was less than half full. Two bulging leather sacks were squashed into the bottom of the box. And clearly there had been at least two others on top of them. But the topmost ones were gone now.

Disregarding the outraged Dolabella, Artemidorus crossed to the box and eased the last two bags out of it. They were tied together at the neck, which made them easy to carry – slung across a shoulder, saddle-bow or the withers of a horse, he calculated. And they needed to be easy to carry for they were very heavy. He swung them down onto the floor and squatted, pulling the neck of the nearest wide. To reveal a hoard of gold coins. Freshly minted and still so new that they glittered in the lamplight. 'It's Trebonius' treasure,' he said. 'Some of it at least. Whatever this part of it the *bitch of no account*, as you called her, has left you. Because she's escaped with the rest and I doubt you'll see her again. Unless you're on her kill list, in which case you might get a fleeting glimpse of her as she slits your throat one night.'

'Don't be ridiculous! She's little better than a she-wolf in a *lupinaria*. Though I find it hard to believe she just sat there and watched as we questioned Trebonius. All he said was "*Civis Romanus sum!*" Even when the red hot pincers went to work. And she could have stopped it. With one word she could have stopped it!'

'She did that once before,' Artemidorus said, wearily, straightening. 'Stopped someone being tortured with a word or two. Or thought she had. But actually she hadn't – he was still beaten to death. And in the end, those were the words that got Caesar killed.'

Dolabella swung round and looked at Artemidorus, frowning. 'So that was *her*!' he said. 'I thought you threw her to the mob.'

'I did. She came back. Left a good few of them dead into the bargain. That reminds me, there's a dead legionary in the storeroom you had her locked in down by the *culinea*.'

'By the gods below, I've had enough of this!' snarled Dolabella. He slammed out of the room, calling for soldiers and lamps. Artemidorus followed him as he stormed through the palace, the dark heart of a gathering river of brightness as the attendants he summoned joined him. Out through the door they went and into the forum. Which was still dripping but no longer rainswept. There wasn't even enough breeze to stir the lamp flames as they all ran up the steps of the *curia's* colonnade.

Without hesitation, Dolabella strode up to the crucified man. Trebonius seemed to be deep in an uneasy sleep. Dolabella woke him with two explosive slaps – forehand and backhand – across his ruined face.

'*Civis Romanum sum*,' he mumbled.

'Your bitch, who is definitely not a Roman citizen, just ran away with a good deal of your treasure,' snarled Dolabella. 'I just wanted you to know I'll be back in the morning. And I'll be asking about the rest of it.' He snatched at the front of Trebonius' loincloth and tore it off. Grabbed the testicles his action revealed. 'And this is where we'll start the questioning,' he spat.

*

Artemidorus and Puella were woken next morning by Quintus. 'There's trouble brewing,' he said. 'Apparently the loincloth was a step too far. A Rubicon Dolabella shouldn't have crossed, you might say.'

There was no modesty within the *contubernium*. He didn't even turn his back as they climbed out of bed and into their clothing. The other three were waiting for them outside the bedroom door. All six went down together, stepping three abreast out of the big double doors of the governor's palace into a clear, blustery dawn. And into a forum that seemed packed with people. All, at the moment, standing quietly. Looking at the naked wreck of their legally appointed governor. And at the man who had tortured him to the very edge of death.

Dolabella stood in front of Trebonius, in parade armour and helmet; every inch the general. Flanked by his tribunes, backed by his centurions who were in turn standing in front of long lines of legionaries.

As riots went, it was a quiet, short-lived, almost sedate affair. The shops, stalls, courts and public buildings round the forum were all closed. There was nothing to break or to burn. A few of the assembled citizens had armed themselves with stones, but as soon as these were thrown half-heartedly towards Dolabella and his troops, he ordered the legionaries to clear the square. Which they proceeded to do, employing a great deal more violence than anything that had been used against them. Dolabella himself took the lead in both elements of this, striding forward, safe in his full armour, laying about him with his *gladius*. Thankfully mostly with the flat of the blade rather than the edge or the point.

Artemidorus watched as the lines of soldiers followed their leader, leaving Trebonius guarded by the two lines of legionaries. Who moved to the forward edge of the colonnade, the toes of their *caligae* boots overhanging the top step of the marble stairway, watching their colleagues at work. He looked at the tortured man hanging naked and shamed from the cross half a dozen feet behind them. The marble beneath him soiled with all sorts of solids and liquids. Having nothing left to look forward to but more agony and eventual emasculation. On a sudden impulse, the secret agent stooped. Picked a round stone off the cobbles of the forum and walked purposefully towards the western end of the colonnade, nearest the governor's palace. 'You are all dismissed,' he said to his companions. 'I don't want you to see this.'

As they moved obediently away, Artemidorus glanced around. It seemed that Trebonius and he were alone in the forum except for the guards who stood with their backs to both of them. So they were unobserved. For the moment at least. He pulled his sling out of its tiny pouch on his belt, unrolled it, put the loop over his index finger and slid the stone into its soft leather pocket. Level with the dying man, perhaps forty paces distant from him, and out of sight of everyone, even the guards, the secret agent turned, whirling the sling with deadly expertise. Releasing the string at the moment of maximum power. Sending the stone faster than the eye could see down the length of the colonnade.

There was a crisp SLAP! As the stone connected with Trebonius' temple. But none of the guards moved. The hanging head jerked sideways. Artemidorus remembered Quintus' melons. The way they burst and leaked red flesh from gaping wounds. He could see no new wound on Trebonius' already battered head. But the way the body slumped in the ropes securing it to the cross was a giveaway. As though every bone in his body had suddenly melted like wax. Especially the bones of the neck, which seemed oddly to stretch under the sudden weight of the ruined head. There was no doubt in his mind that the fragile bones of Trebonius' skull must be shattered.

And he was dead.

viii

'*Dead!*' spat Dolabella. 'This just keeps getting worse and worse. I have only found a tiny fraction of the treasure he was supposed to have brought. And I only have that because that bitch of his left what she couldn't carry when she took the rest out of the box hidden in their bed. Now she's vanished and he's beyond my reach! It must have been one of the stones the rioters threw that did it! The guards saw nothing but there was a stone in the *excrementum* shit on the ground beside the cross. And the side of his head was caved in!'

The governor was pacing up and down across the *tablinum* office area of the palace, waving his arms as he shouted. His tribunes were there, and one or two senior centurions. Together with the leading citizens he had entertained to dinner yesterday evening. And Artemidorus.

'What I think I'll do is to search out the ringleaders of that mob. Maybe replace Trebonius with one or two of them...'

The leading citizens paled at the thought. Clearly calculating the likelihood of ending up there themselves.

But Artemidorus stepped forward. 'General, Governor,' he said. 'I'm sure you have thought through the implications of the situation you have discovered here. Which I will report to my General Antony at the earliest opportunity. But it seems to me that if Brutus and Cassius have the money and arms sent south by Trebonius, they will have built an army several legions strong in a very short time.'

'I understand that,' said Dolabella. 'But I don't see how it affects me...'

'If Brutus is recruiting in Greece and Macedonia and Cassius is busy in Egypt and Arabia, then what are the provinces most at risk?'

'Asia,' breathed Dolabella, in the grip of a sudden revelation. 'Asia and *Syria*! *My* province...'

'And the Syrian capital of Laodicia must be almost a thousand *miles* from here, General. You have another long march in prospect, unless you want to ship your legion south...'

'Legions!' snapped Dolabella. 'I'll be taking Trebonius' men under my *imperium* leadership. But I see what you mean. Yes. I must get matters settled here and move on as swiftly as I can. It could take me until *Aprilis* to get to Syria if we go by land. Even if the roads are clear and the weather clement. And it would be a disaster to arrive, only to find Cassius waiting there for me. Gentlemen,' he swung round to face the city's leading citizens. 'I will need a precise accounting of all the vessels in the immediate vicinity large enough to transport my men! Under the circumstances I will not be able to hire them. So I will have to commandeer them. A final gift to you from your late governor!' he added with a sneer. And as they hurried out, dismissed by his abrupt announcement, he turned back and met Artemidorus' level stare. 'But there are matters that must be attended to before I leave,' he concluded.

*

Dolabella ruled that Trebonius' body be left secured to the cross. A table large enough to bear it was carried out of the governor's palace and placed in the colonnade. The cross was lifted onto it. And laid so that the dead man's body was uppermost. His battered face staring up at the ceiling under which he had died. The table was then positioned so that the top of Trebonius' head pointed out into the forum. Where Dolabella's legion was paraded. Or as many of them as would fit into the cramped space. The balding pate of the middle-aged corpse seeming suddenly frail and almost pathetic in the thin winter sunlight. Soldiers and citizens crowded the streets leading off the square. Artemidorus and his command were given positions of importance beside the tribunes on the steps. Witnesses to carry the report of proceedings back to Antony.

Two of the legionaries standing guard at the time of the late governor's death stood on either side of his head and adjusted it so that the chin was raised and the throat exposed. Then Dolabella himself came forward. He was armed, not with a *gladius* but with a longer, curved sword that looked like an Iberian *falcata* or a Greek *kopis*. Examples of which Artemidorus had seen and wielded in Quintus' secret villa. A long blade, slightly curving, almost leaf-shaped with a strong spine up its back. And a well-honed edge that gleamed wickedly even on a dull day like this one.

There was no ceremony. Nobody spoke. The governor raised the big sword above his shoulder and brought it down with all his might onto the exposed throat. The edge of the blade cut through the dead man's flesh and buried itself in the wood of the cross. Blood sprayed sluggishly. The head jerked up and down, the back of the skull landing with a *CRACK!* that echoed across the silent square. Frowning, Dolabella worked the sword free, raised it once more and brought it down again, unerringly, into the wound he had just created. The head rolled grotesquely. But still did not fall free. Dolabella jerked the blade out of the wood impatiently, raised the sword for a third time, taking the hilt in both hands now.

'Should have done that first time,' breathed Quintus knowledgeably. 'This'll do it though. Watch out...'

Dolabella brought the sword down with all his force. The head seemed to leap off the wood. It flew through the air and went bouncing down the steps like a ball. So much like a ball, indeed, that the soldier at whose feet it landed kicked it without a second thought. Within a heartbeat the head had vanished beneath the legion's feet and was being booted from side to side across the forum by several hundred hobnailed *caligae*. Dolabella waited, watching, as Trebonius' blood slowly pooled on the marble at his feet. Then, 'That's enough!' he bellowed. 'Bring the traitor's head to me!'

The shoving and jostling stopped. Someone stooped and retrieved the thing. Picked it up by the thinning hair on its scalp. Raised it above his head. Passed it to the man in front. Who passed it on in turn. Like a piece of flotsam on the crest of a wave, the head swept forward until a soldier from the foremost rank came and placed it at Dolabella's feet. Had it been battered before, now it was utterly unrecognisable. The nose was flat, smeared across black-bruised cheekbones. One of which was split open to the bone. One ear was missing. The eyes were swollen almost shut. The eyeball visible through the slit on the side the fatal sling-stone hit was bright red. The jaw was broken and most of the teeth were gone. The

209

tongue seemed unnaturally swollen and lolled out of the side of the lipless mouth like that of a *stupidus* idiot.

'There you are, Centurion,' said the governor to Artemidorus, gesturing towards the horror at his feet. 'I will arrange to have the body sent back to Rome. And you may take the head to Antony.'

XII

At much the same moment as Trebonius' head was bouncing down the steps of the *curia* in Smyrna, Antony's tribune and spymaster Enobarbus was standing on the steps of the Temple of Jupiter Optimus Maximus Capitolinus in Rome. Watching Marcus Tullius Cicero through narrowed eyes. Cicero was standing down in the precinct, surrounded by his cronies. A headcount of Antony's greatest enemies, thought the spy. Cicero was glaring with simple outrage at Antony's wife Fulvia, his mother Julia and his son Marcus Antonius Antyllus. Who were up in the colonnade that fronted the oldest and most sacred space in the city. They were all dressed in mourning black. And were here to attend the Senate meeting which had been dragging on in one location or another for several days. Which was convened in the Temple of Jupiter today.

Enobarbus was here with Antony's spokesman, *Divus Julius'* father-in-law Lucius Calpurnius Piso. Under orders from his general to watch and report events. Because the turning of the year changed everything in a heartbeat. Just as Trebonius' treachery in Smyrna had – although they didn't know that yet.

At the *calends* of *Januarius*, the first day of the administrative new year, the new Consuls Aulus Hirtius and Gaius Vibius Pansa had taken up their responsibilities, relieving the absent Consuls Dolabella and Antony. Just as Brutus and Cassius had been relieved in their turn as *praetors*. So that the Senate could finally be formally summoned. For the last four days, Piso reported faithfully, and the records of Senate Secretary Adonis confirmed, Cicero had argued that the Senate, on behalf of the People of Rome, should remove Antony's *imperium* generalship and the governorship of Cisalpine Gaul. The governorship and *imperium* awarded him by the *Comitia of the People* in exchange for his surrendering the governorship of Macedonia which *Divus Julius* had planned for him this year. Cicero was demanding that the Senate should in fact pronounce Antony *hostis* enemy of the state. And then declare war against him if he persisted in trying to replace Decimus Albinus as governor of that vital province. From which, famously, *Divus Julius* had launched his bid for absolute power by crossing the River Rubicon heading south with his legions. A fact that lay very near the heart of Cicero's worries about Antony and his true motives.

Because Antony was currently encamped with three full legions – the IInd Sabine, the Vth *Alaude* Larks and the XXXVth – as well as a range of auxiliaries including a thousand Gaulish cavalry, just north of the Rubicon, within striking

211

distance of Mutina. The walled city which Decimus Albinus had chosen as his bulwark to defend his claim to the governorship of Cisalpine Gaul. A city into which he had moved his own legions. Antony being the legitimate ruler of the province by the will of the People. Decimus Albinus holding it on the orders of the Senate.

Gaius Julius Caesar Octavianus *Divus Filius* being also encamped nearby with several more legions he had managed to assemble. The wondrous boy, in Cicero's words, on whom the Senate and People could rely for protection against the monster Antony. Particularly if he could be persuaded to share some of his power and a large number of his soldiers with the Consuls Hirtius and Pansa – who were tasked with leading Rome's senatorial armies when she went to war.

*

In fact, Adonis and his sister Venus had proved to be invaluable in reporting and interpreting all this. For when Cicero spoke, there was as much communication in his tone and gesture as there was in his words. So, when Adonis recounted the lawyer's orations as recorded in the secret minutes he kept in parallel to the official ones, he mimicked Cicero's delivery with disturbing accuracy. And Venus, with almost uncanny insight, interpreted and extrapolated every gesture. Every shift in timbre. Every calculating nod and knowing wink.

But the increasingly desperate tribune had gone well past merely being an observer of the events unfolding so rapidly here. Fulvia and Julia were at the Senate's door with young Antyllus because Cicero's plan of declaring Antony an enemy of the state not only allowed any citizen anywhere in the empire the right – the duty – to kill him on sight. It also took everything he owned into the state's possession. Throwing his family, dependants, servants and slaves all out onto the street. Something Antony's family were just about to plead should not be done to them.

Antony's tribune and Caesar's father-in-law had discussed this move at length with Fulvia, all increasingly well aware that Cicero's bitter condemnation of Antony in speech after speech was turning the Senate against him in a way that his dwindling list of friends could no longer stop. Cicero had even started boasting that he should call the speeches his *Philippics*, after a series of speeches the great Greek orator Demosthenes had given in his attempt to destroy Philip II of Macedon exactly three hundred years earlier. There was no doubt in the Senate – or in the city itself – that Cicero saw himself as the one man who could stop Antony fulfilling for himself the ambition that got Caesar killed.

A hand clapped Enobarbus on the shoulder. 'Time to go,' said Piso as he strode past. And he walked up the steps, gathering the black-clad family together and ushering them into the temple. Cicero threw the tribune a cold glance and followed them into the Senate meeting. Enobarbus turned away and ran down the steps. All too well aware that even if Fulvia's pleading saved Antony today, it would not stop Cicero's venomous attacks. Only death would do that.

Antony's death. Or Cicero's.

ii

Enobarbus sat and listened as Adonis performed Cicero's latest speech attacking Antony. Things had changed for the worse in the last month, even though the ploy of presenting the black-clad family to the Senate had had some effect. Enobarbus and Piso had managed to convince Fulvia that she should make plans for the inevitable day that Cicero would convince the Senate to call Antony an enemy of the state. Something which must happen, if not in the next month, *Mars*, must certainly happen in *Aprilis*, the month after. For, if the Senate wavered indecisively, Antony remained adamant and unvarying in his purpose.

In the meantime, the Senate had sent a delegation through the icy winter weather to negotiate with Antony. Their proposals had fallen on deaf ears. Worse, one of the senators in the group, Cicero's old friend Servius Sulpicious Rufus, had died on the way back. A sad coincidence that had somehow – in Cicero's mind and speeches – become Antony's fault. Along with everything else. Now, the great man's every word, intonation and gesture rang out across the *atrium* of Quintus' villa, continuing a debate as to whether Antony's actions in Cisalpine Gaul actually constituted a state of war. Or merely a serious civil disorder. The one punishable by *hostis*. The other merely calling for continued negotiation.

'As there is no middle ground between war and peace,' declaimed Adonis in Cicero's voice, 'it is quite plain that civil disorder, if it is not a sort of war, must be a sort of peace. And what can be said or imagined which is more absurd than that? However, we have said too much about one single word. As we have all too often done in the past. Let us rather look to the facts. We are unwilling to admit that the *civil disorder* generated by Antony appears to be a state of war. If it is *not* war, then why are we giving authority to the local towns to close their gates against Antony and his men? Why are we authorizing their citizens to be enlisted at once into our legions? Permitting them to raise money for the assistance of the Republic in raising our own armies?

'For if the name of war is taken away from the situation by our continued hesitancy, the zeal of those municipalities will be taken away too. And the unanimous enthusiasm of the Roman people which at present pours itself into our cause against Antony, if we appear to be hesitant, must inevitably run dry. But why do I need to say any more? Decimus Albinus is being attacked. Is that not

213

war? The city of Mutina is being besieged. Is that not war? Cisalpine Gaul is being laid waste. What *peace* can be more obvious than that? Who on earth could even think of calling all these things a *war*?

'But that thoroughly admirable young man Gaius Caesar, has not waited for our decrees. He has undertaken to wage war against Antony on our behalf even without our authority; for there was no time to pass a formal decree after all our hesitation and debate. And he sees all too clearly that, if he misses the opportunity of waging war on our behalf, then, when Antony inevitably crushes the Republic, it will be too late to pass any decrees at all.

'Therefore, I demand the following: That anyone currently serving with Mark Antony, who deserts from his army and comes over either to Caius Pansa or Aulus Hirtius; or to Decimus Albinus or to Gaius Caesar, before the *calends* first day of *Mars*, shall not be liable to prosecution for having been with Antony in the first place. And that, after this resolution of the Senate, anyone who stays with Antony or goes to join his army shall be considered, with Antony himself, *hostis* – an enemy of the state.'

'Did they pass that motion?' asked Enobarbus, frowning with worry. The inevitable ruling of *hostis* was getting closer and closer day by day.

'Not entirely,' answered Adonis, becoming himself again. 'They agreed to make any soldiers who stay with Lord Antony enemies of the state. But they haven't decided about Lord Antony himself yet. In spite of Cicero's demands. There's gossip among the secretarial staff, many of whom are friends of Tiro's, that Cicero is in correspondence with both Brutus and Cassius, who are raising armies in Macedonia and Arabia. As well as with Decimus Albinus.

'Decimus Albinus sends messages out of Mutina by pigeon as well as by secret messenger, apparently. Most of them asking for help. From the Senate, of course. And from Caesar Octavius, who may not be as fully committed as Cicero says. And who is unwell in any case. Cicero is also writing to General Lepidus in Gallia Narbonenesis, trying to get him to back Decimus Albinus. And even to General Lucius Plancus Proconsul of Gallia Comata trying to get him involved. But I think he places most of his hopes on Caesar Octavius.'

'That's a relationship we must find a way of breaking down,' said Enobarbus.

'There might be a way of doing just that,' said Venus quietly. 'It may be nothing. It might just have been a slip of the tongue, but... Go on Adonis. Tell him what you were telling me last night.'

'It could be nothing at all,' emphasised Adonis. 'And, as often happens with Cicero, it turns on the meaning of a single word. A pun. A joke.'

'All right,' said Enobarbus. 'Tell me...'

'Close your eyes and just listen, Tribune,' suggested Venus. 'Then say what you think.'

Enobarbus was used to Venus' ways by now and had grown to respect her insights and her ideas. So he did as she requested. And listened.

'Cicero was discussing young Gaius Julius Caesar Octavianus,' Adonis began. 'The conversation went into debate of what the Senate should do about him after Antony is defeated. There's a real worry that he'll continue building his army and get too powerful for the Senate to control. He is a Caesar after all. So, in this particular exchange, Cicero said he understood their worries, although he does not share them. He thinks the boy – as he calls him – can easily be manipulated. Is, in fact, being manipulated very successfully by Cicero himself at the moment. But in the meantime Caesar is "*Adolescens laudandus, ornandus, tollendus*": a young man we should celebrate, decorate and tolerate.'

Adonis fell silent. Enobarbus opened his eyes in some confusion. 'What's wrong with that?' he asked.

'*Tollendus*,' said Venus. 'Think about it. About all of the meanings that word has. Then listen again. With your eyes open.'

Tollendus thought Enobarbus. It was an ancient word that originally described a specific act; in time, drawing wider meanings and implications from that. The act of a father holding his newborn son for the first time. In a ceremony almost as old as time itself, the father would raise the child and either acknowledge him as son or throw him aside as unacceptable in some way. So the word could mean, at the same time, accept or reject. Raise or raze.

Adonis brought these thoughts to a halt by becoming Cicero once more. Puffing himself up, assuming the sly and knowing expression the orator put on when making one of his clever jokes. This time the words were accompanied by a smirk and a knowing wink. Which changed the impact of the words '*Adolescens laudandus, ornandus, tollendus*' entirely.

From: 'celebrate, decorate and tolerate'.

To: 'celebrate, decorate and *exterminate*'.

Enobarbus was just beginning to see the implications of the phrase when there came a thunderous banging at the front door. Still deep in thought, the tribune went behind the *ostiarius* doorkeeper to see what the commotion was all about. The door opened to reveal a group of six weary-looking travellers. The leader stepped into the hall and raised a sack he was carrying. It contained something the size of a large cabbage. Heavy enough to make the material bulge and swing.

'Here's Trebonius' head,' he said. 'Where's the general?'

iii

215

'This is no good to me,' snapped Antony. They had ridden in with the last of the night. But as usual when he was on campaign the general was up and about early. And sober. If not sunny and smiling. 'It's no bloody good at all! It's got no face! How is anyone ever going to recognise it? Even if I put a notice under it that evil bastard Cicero will only say it's the head of some slave put up there for effect. Not Trebonius' head at all!'

Artemidorus and Enobarbus exchanged a look. The siege of Mutina was not going well. It would soon be *Mars* – hardly three weeks to the anniversary of Caesar's murder – and it seemed that it was Antony rather than Decimus Albinus who was feeling trapped and frustrated here.

'The rest of the body will arrive in Rome soon,' said Artemidorus. 'If it hasn't done so already.'

'Even so,' snapped Antony. 'This might just as well be a melon for all the use it is to me. When I put a head up in the Forum I want everyone to see precisely whose head it is. To know exactly whose body it once sat on top of – until I had them separated!'

'Very well, General. What do you want us to do with it?'

'If the body's back in Rome then send this down to join it. It's no bloody use to me!'

'*Omne mandatum quod praeceperat Dominus faciemus et erimus parati!*' said Artemidorus formally, angered that so much work and time seemed to have been simply wasted. 'We will do what is ordered and at every command we will be ready.'

'Yes, yes,' said Antony, waving his hand in dismissal of the formal reply. 'I'm sure you are and will be.' He looked up suddenly and his gaunt, exhausted face splitting in a broad, conspiratorial grin. 'Give the monstrosity to one of the useless buggers from the Vth to take back to Rome and Trebonius' grieving family. Don't think I don't appreciate what it's taken in time and effort to get it! I do. And I have more important work for you and your spies here at Mutina, friend Septem. Starting with a detailed briefing on everything you found out while you were in Smyrna. And while you tell me all the gory details, let's have some breakfast, shall we?'

*

'Looks like someone's been studying Aeneas Tacticus on Siege Warfare,' said Enobarbus grimly an hour or so later.

'Looks like they both have,' said Quintus and Artemidorus nodded his agreement, 'Maybe Polybius too.'

216

They were sitting astride three of the Gaulish cavalry unit's best horses, looking up at the walled city of Mutina from a low ridge some five hundred paces away. Just out of range of bows, slings, *ballistae* and catapults. Assessing the position from an intelligence perspective as Antony had ordered. He himself had assessed things as a military man – and ordered his legates and tribunes to do the same. But all any of them could see was a stalemate in the short term, unless something radical changed. 'I'm like Agamemnon at the siege of Troy, Septem,' Antony said at the end of the breakfast briefing. 'And I need you to be my Ulysses and come up with a wooden horse…'

The besieged town sat like a stone crown on the top of a hill. The hill itself was not particularly high or steep. But there was enough of a slope to discourage siege towers. Unless Antony decided to build special ramps for them. In their place, Antony was currently relying on *ballista* catapults and huge siege bows to hurl rocks and massive iron bolts, kegs of explosive Greek Fire and rotting, infested carcasses at and over the walls. Decimus Albinus in the besieged city was answering with much the same sort of artillery, but neither one seemed to be making much of an impression in the other. Though Antony had started hurling rotten carcases into the besieged garrison in the belief it was running low on food. But apparently not yet low enough to be forced into making a break for it. Or – as Antony no doubt hoped – to open the gates secretly and let the besiegers in. Laden with fresh food and drink.

'I'd suggest he tries some mining,' said Quintus. 'If he hasn't already done so. Unless that hill's made of rock too solid to dig through.'

'Or earth too soft to support a shaft,' added Artemidorus. 'And the lower slopes – outside artillery range – look as though whatever gets dug in them will flood almost immediately.'

Mutina had been built in an excellent defensive position. To the west of the fortified hill, a river wound down into an area of swampland that looked to be proof against soldiers and siege machinery alike. Then the river wound on out of the swamps to curl round the north side of the hill. At its narrowest point, a viaduct stepped over it, carrying the *Via Aemilia* on its arrow-straight way from Ariminium on the coast to Placentia at the foot of the Alps. Beyond the bridge the river all but met another stream that flowed down the east side. Thus three sides of the city were protected by water as well as hillsides and walls.

All of the waterways were swollen with spring rain, making them in themselves formidable barriers against attack by men or machines. Antony had drawn up the bulk of his army perforce to the south of the city – the only part unprotected by water. Here the Vth, the *Alaude* Larks, and the rest of his force were camped, using the southern section of the *Via Aemilia* as a solid base. 'No way out and no way in,' said Quintus approvingly. 'Antony's planning to starve Decimus Albinus out. At first glance, that looks like his only option. Unless you can come up with the wooden horse he wants, Septem.'

'He's running out of time, though,' said Enobarbus. 'And so are we. Caesar Octavius has his base down in Ariminium at the other end of the *via*. Three days' march away. With at least four legions – including the Macedonian legions Antony decimated – who followed the IVth and the Martia in deserting him and going over to Caesar almost immediately afterwards. Cicero and the Senate want him to move against Antony's rear.'

'Bugger him in more ways than one.' Quintus growled.

'Caesar Octavius will probably wait until the consuls actually take to the field with whatever legions the Senate can scare up,' said Artemidorus, who felt he knew the young man better than any of the others. 'I think he still sees Antony as a more natural ally than Cicero. Especially as Cicero is starting to seriously underestimate his abilities. And take him for granted. I told you about the *laudandus, ornandus, tollendus* crack. Perhaps we should have sent Trebonius' head to *him*. I just wish we had a clearer idea of his plans…'

Their conversation was interrupted by Puella who rode up towards them with Hercules at her side. She had a bow slung across her shoulders and was carrying a dead bird. 'We saw this come out of the city,' she said as she came closer. 'I got in a lucky shot and brought it down. There's a message strapped to its leg.'

'Did the people in the city see it fall?' asked Quintus at once.

'Yes, they did. So we made a great show of riding away then we hid and waited. They sent another one when they were sure we had gone. Ferrata's doing his best to follow it. Until he gets a clear idea of where it's heading, at any rate.'

'Good man!' said Quintus. 'Good work, all of you! So in a short while we'll know where the message was headed.'

'And therefore who it was for,' added Artemidorus. 'So all we need to do now is find out what it says.'

iv

The *contubernium* of spies and their spymaster sat round a table in the tent Antony had assigned to them. The dead pigeon lay discarded on the floor. The message it had carried was spread on the table in front of them. A series of Roman letters on a long, thin strip of papyrus. 'It's in code of course,' said Kyros, who had been instrumental in breaking other codes Artemidorus and his spies had come up against. 'I can try Caesar's transposition code and see how we get on with that. It's not a long message, but it may take some time. So you don't need to hang around if you have anything better to do.'

The little group were just going back out of the tent when Ferrata rode up on a sweat-lathered horse. 'It went down the *via*, straight as an arrow, he gasped. 'Heading for Ariminium. I'd bet my life on it.'

'Ariminium,' said Artemidorus. 'That means Caesar Octavius. I wonder if he'll reply...'

'Let's assume he will,' suggested Enobarbus. 'Quintus, what's the most likely method he'll use?'

'Well,' said the legionary slowly. 'Let's start with the possibility Caesar like Decimus Albinus has a supply of trained pigeons ready to fly into Mutina. How likely is that?'

'Not very,' answered Artemidorus at once. 'Decimus Albinus had a good deal of warning about this siege. Time to lay in supplies and so forth, even if he's running low now. Time to sort out some birds trained to home in on some of the nearest towns. Those like Ariminium and Bononia that might make good bases for anyone coming to his aid. Not so Caesar Octavius. He may have taken his time arriving at Ariminium. But not enough time to get a flock of birds trained to fly into Mutina. So if he wants to reply to Decimus Albinus' message, he'll have to send a messenger.'

'Who will probably be coming up the *via* – or across country parallel to it on one side or the other.'

'Where we can be waiting,' said Ferrata, with some relish.

'To do what?' asked Puella.

'We'll know that when we get the messenger,' said Artemidorus. 'And get some idea of what the original message says.'

*

'It uses a transposition code,' said Kyros. 'But it's different from Caesar's. Caesar moved the letters three spaces to the right and allowed an overlap. So A,B,C,D,E became X,Y,Z,A,B and so forth. But this one just moves the letters one place to the left. So A,B,C,D,E becomes B,C,D,E,F and so on. There are no Zs in the message so I don't know whether Z is A or AA – or something else altogether. But I've deciphered it all right.'

'Fascinating,' said Artemidorus with just a trace of irony. 'What does it say?'

'*Must have food or support. Must break out soon. But need your plans. Message. Pass Res Publica.*'

'Hmm,' said Quintus. 'Let's hope the second pigeon carried the same message.'

'Let's assume it did,' said Enobarbus. 'Where does that get us?'

'Quite a long way,' said Artemidorus. 'We can report to the general that Decimus Albinus is genuinely desperate for food and appears to be on the point of breaking out. But he needs to co-ordinate with Caesar Octavius – or Consuls Hirtius or Pansa if they have arrived yet – before he dares do so. And he wants a messenger to come in and confirm the plan. The password is *Res Publica* Republic.'

'We should take this to Antony at once,' said Enobarbus. 'He needs to know the potential it has.'

'Yes,' Artemidorus agreed. 'If we can catch Caesar's messenger and at least get an idea of what they plan to do, then the general can be prepared for whatever they have in mind. Perhaps lay a trap of his own. In fact,' he added, 'now that we have the password we might even be able to take things further still.'

V

'This is excellent,' said Antony. 'I've been sitting here with the Vth and all the rest, banging my head against a brick wall, waiting to get *pedicare* shafted by the Senate at Cicero's request or by that little shit Octavius, and within a couple of days you have given me the chance of breaking the stalemate. This is very good work. What do you propose to do next?'

'Lay a trap for Caesar's messenger and take it from there,' said Artemidorus. 'Do you need us to report to you stage by stage?'

'No,' answered Antony decisively. 'Coming to me before every decision will only slow you down.' He looked at them with a grin, then gave a chuckle and continued, 'You've done more in that couple of days than I've managed to do so far this year. *I* should be coming to *you*…'

'So,' said Artemidorus as they came out of Antony's tent. 'We simply set up a line of spies – us – hidden on either side of the *via* tonight. And every night until we catch Caesar's messenger. Or until it becomes clear that he hasn't sent one.'

'Or,' said Quintus, 'until it becomes clear that they've got another way in that we don't know about.'

But when Artemidorus led them to the *via* itself and stood on the crest of the nine *passus* pace thirty-foot width of it, looking south-east towards Ariminium away down on the coast, several things soon became obvious to him. First, that the ditches on either side of the sloping road, awash with run-off though they were, would make good pathways for anyone wishing to approach Mutina in secret. Especially as they led directly to within a few paces of the main gate. Secondly that the land on the right of the road would almost certainly be closed to Caesar Octavius' man because that was where Antony's legions were encamped, their lines extended by the constantly manned and guarded siege weapons. Thirdly, therefore, that the best way to approach the beleaguered town in secret was to come up the ditch then strike north across the river on his left. Towards a small postern gate that was all too easily overlooked. The ground there was marshy – except for the ridge running up towards the village of Forum Gallorum. Too soft and wet for camps or heavy artillery. Perfect, therefore, for one man sneaking inwards.

'Assuming that the pigeon got to Caesar Octavius within the turn or two of a water clock,' he said thoughtfully, 'Caesar could write a reply and give it to a messenger who could come up the *via* on horseback. It's almost exactly one hundred *miles*. A legion would take two or three days to get here. A messenger on horseback could do it in an afternoon if the horse was strong enough. Tether his mount a *mile* or so away and come the rest of the way on foot in secret.'

'So,' said Enobarbus, 'we'd better keep watch from sunset…'

*

The early spring weather was cold and wet. The line of spies huddled under cloaks within call of each other, trying to stay hidden, warm, dry and alert. Even staying awake was a challenge, thought Artemidorus. But he rather suspected that sleep would be dangerously close to death in these conditions. Which, oddly, were worsened as the drizzling overcast was swept away by a keen northerly that seemed to blow directly off the crest of the ice-clad Alps. But at least a low moon gave some welcome light.

Artemidorus was on point duty, furthest forward, and closest to the little gate he suspected would be the messenger's target. Then Quintus ten paces on his right. Then, Hercules, Kyros, Ferrata and lastly Puella closest to the road. Ferrata was only five paces from Puella because they reckoned that if the messenger wasn't coming across the open ground towards Artemidorus and the gate, then he would be coming up the ditch beside the road. Their plan was simple. Flexible. They would catch him with the minimum noise, stun him – not kill him. And take it from there.

As it chanced, Caesar's secret messenger crawled straight into Hercules. So stunning him was not a problem. Nor was carrying his unconscious body to their tent. The gigantic tutor didn't even need the help the others offered as they trooped together through the frosty night. The courier was wearing a dark cloak and had blackened his face, arms and legs with mud. But even so, the first thing Quintus said when they lit their lamps and got a good close look at him was, 'I know this man. He's from the old VIIth.'

'Yes,' agreed Artemidorus. 'He's not from my cohort, but I recognise him too.'

'Does that mean we go easy on him when it comes to questioning and other *carnifex* work?' mused Ferrata as he finished tying their prisoner to a solid chair. He was from the VIth and there was no love lost between the legions.

'I don't know what it means,' said Artemidorus. 'Kyros, get some water. We'll wash him off and wake him up.'

Caesar's go-between woke the moment the icy water splashed over his face. 'He looked around, dazed and frowning. Confused. 'Hey,' he said. 'I know you...'

'We're all from the old VIIth,' said Artemidorus. 'Except Ferrata here who's from the Ironclads. But we're a Praetorian unit on General Antony's staff now. What are you doing with Caesar?'

'Earning two thousand *sestertii*. Plus a bonus if we beat Antony and the Larks.' All of them growled companionably. 'There was no love lost between the VIIth, the VIth and the Vth *Alaude* either. 'Antony settled me in that mud-pit north of Capua,' continued the old soldier. 'But I found out pretty quickly I wasn't cut out to be a farmer. Or a husband. Or a *paterfamilias*. So I'm back doing the one thing I'm really good at.'

'And in the meantime taking messages between Caesar and Decimus Albinus...'

'I served with General Albinus in Gaul against Vercingetorex. Caesar thought that might make me a good contact. This is my first time, though. I have to be particularly careful with the password.' The suspiciously detailed nature of his answer was explained by his next question. 'What are you going to do with me?'

'We're going to take your message and copy it,' said Artemidorus, entering into the spirit of openness between ex-colleagues. 'Then I'm going to take your place and go into the city. I can risk that if this is, as you say, your first time. Then, when I come back we'll talk further. If I don't come back, of course, you will meet an incredibly unpleasant end. So if there's anything else at this point...'

The go-between shook his head. 'Nothing.'

'Well, I think I will risk it then.'

'You'll have several options to consider in the meantime,' said Quintus as Artemidorus went off to change his clothing and blacken his face. He ticked them off on his fingers as he spoke. 'Join Antony's army and take your chances with us when Caesar finally gets off his *culus* arse and the war starts. Agree to return to Caesar but work for us as a double agent. Keep coming back and forth between Caesar and Albinus – but always via this tent. Both of those will involve you telling us anything else we want to know. The second option will also involve us offering you a certain amount of bribery.'

Ferrata took over. 'The third option is that you refuse to tell us anything and so we kill you. And the fourth option is that you refuse to tell us anything and we turn our *carnifex* loose on you and you die screaming. Sometime far in a truly unpleasant future.'

'Your choice,' said Quintus accommodatingly.

vi

Artemidorus eased himself into the icy water of the swollen river east of Mutina and swam across as swiftly as he could. Carefully keeping his mud-blackened face clear of the water which was washing his arms and legs clean as he swam. Pushing a carefully wrapped waterproof bundle ahead of him. A bundle containing a dry – hopefully warm – cloak. Around his neck hung a tube made of thinly beaten lead. In which was wrapped a piece of parchment. On which young Caesar Octavius' message was written in code. The ends were sealed with wax to make it waterproof. The code was the same one as the pigeon's message had been written in and Kyros had translated it almost as quickly as the messenger had decided to play double agent. His name was Felix but they had code-named him *Mercurius* Mercury the messenger. Quintus and Ferrata were still arguing through the precise nature of the bribe needed to keep him loyal to them as the secret agent went to take his place.

Artemidorus paused on the bank and slipped his dry cloak over his wet shoulders. Then he jogged up the slope to the little gate that stood half-hidden behind a buttress in the wall. He tapped on the wood lightly. '*Res Publica*,' he said.

A small door in the corner of the larger one opened. 'You're late,' said a low voice.

'They have guards out. I was nearly captured.'

The door opened wider. There was light inside. A flambeau was burning. 'But they didn't suspect?' demanded a hoarse voice.

'No. I went out of my way but I got past without them noticing.'

'Good enough.' The guard officer gave him a cursory glance. Not that there was much to see in the shadows immediately outside the postern. 'I'll take you straight to General Albinus and you can deliver the message to him yourself. Come on in.'

Immediately inside the door was a squad of heavily armed legionaries. And, although it was night, the streets through which they escorted Artemidorus were well lit and bustling. Most of the activity was by soldiers making repairs to buildings smashed or burned by Antony's barrage. But there were squads replenishing the ammunition beside the massive slings, catapults – *ballistas* and *onagers* – as well as scorpions looking like gigantic crossbows on wheels. Many

223

of which – but by no means all – were up on the walls. Especially on the extra buttressing and in the towers guarding the main gate. The one area where besiegers had easy access to the city walls. Here there were also cauldrons and fires. Though, thought the spy, there would be no need to heat water, oil or sand for the moment. Not until Antony decided to deploy siege ladders or battering rams by bringing them straight up the *via* itself.

The air of the town stank. The men all around him stank. The odour was more than one of fear – though these were frightened men in a dangerous trap, he reckoned. It was the stench of corpses going unburied. Of disease threatening. Of bodies going unwashed as the garrison fought to preserve water. And – in the face of the rain of rotting carcases Antony was sending them – food.

But there was no doubt in Artemidorus' mind that Decimus Albinus was going to hold this place unless Antony came up with something truly unexpected. And if the general was really relying on Artemidorus to mimic Ulysses at Troy and develop a plan equal to the wooden horse, then he was going to be disappointed.

The governor's palace was as closely guarded as everywhere else. Artemidorus had to repeat the password several more times before he was shown into the general's quarters. Brought face to face with the commander of the besieged garrison. If Antony was pale, exhausted, his features gaunt and his eyes dark-ringed, this was as nothing to the way Decimus Albinus looked. But he was still sharp. 'Do I know you?' he demanded at once. His tone of voice made everyone else in the *tablinum* office area look at the newcomer. Most of them just glanced up and then down. The only one whose gaze lingered was Pontius Aquila. The deep-set eyes beneath that one straight eyebrow stayed on his face for a few heart-stopping moments. Then turned away. Clearly Aquila had been too preoccupied on the day Artemidorus saw him at Brutus' villa in Antium to register the identity of the Senate's messenger. Artemidorus relaxed infinitesimally. He felt he had passed the test at least.

Apart from Pontius Aquila, there were a couple of legates, judging by their badges. A couple of tribunes. Two secretaries with piles of papyrus and wax tablets in front of them. Some blank and some already covered with writing. Servants holding *amphorae* of wine and water. Trays of bread, oil and honey. Very small *amphorae*. Very tiny trays.

'Yes General.' Artemidorus came to attention. Went into Mercury's story – in case Caesar Octavius had found any opportunity to inform Decimus Albinus why he had selected this particular messenger. 'That's why Caesar chose me as his messenger. I served with you in the campaign against Vercingetorex in Gaul and aboard your flagship in the battle for Massalia.' Like Pontius Aquila, Albinus glanced away almost immediately. Before the spy finished speaking. Apparently satisfied. 'That must be it,' he nodded. 'You have Caesar's message?'

'Here, General.' Artemidorus handed the lead cylinder over and Albinus passed it directly to a secretary. 'And when does Caesar propose to come to my rescue?' he demanded as the secretary began to unroll the secret message.

'I'm sure his message will tell you that, General. There are no obvious preparations in his camp, though. We are simply doing our usual daily training. Performing our ordinary duties. Breaking in the new men as they come streaming to Caesar after their two thousand *sestertii* bounty.'

'Well. Go and get something to eat and drink. Then come back when I call. I'll have messages for Caesar and for other people as well to be passed on by him.'

As Artemidorus followed one of the general's soldiers out, the man muttered, 'I hope you're not hungry, though. Or thirsty.' And indeed, Artemidorus spent the succeeding, uncalculated time in a mess hall that was barren of anything to eat and drink. Empty apart from some tough-looking legionaries from the squad that had escorted him here. Who met his questions with tight-lipped silence, so that he too soon fell silent. And when he stood, stretched and strolled towards a window overlooking the town's forum, they too rose. And put themselves between him and anything worth looking at. But at least there was a fire. And they didn't put themselves between Artemidorus and that.

vii

Artemidorus delivered all of Decimus Albinus' secret message to his *contubernium* of spies. Those in code were written in the same code as before. Kyros started translating and transcribing them at once. Enobarbus and Hercules scanned those in plain text, and set about copying the most important paragraphs. Quintus went to rouse some of Antony's secretarial staff – or the task would take all night. Antony himself returned and looked with simple awe at the treasure trove of correspondence the spies had brought him. 'You're going to need more help,' he decided. 'You'll certainly need a larger team. And I think you'd better get a bigger tent.'

In the meantime, Artemidorus snatched a moment with Ferrata and Puella. And Mercury. 'What's the agreement?' he asked.

The double agent remained silent, apparently embarrassed.

'He wants us to match Caesar's two thousand *sestertii*,' said Ferrata. 'So that would be four thousand. In gold. Held safely for him here.'

'An excellent motivation to keep him coming back,' nodded Artemidorus. 'I think we can agree to that.' He glanced across at Enobarbus, who nodded his acceptance of Mercury's terms.

225

'And,' added Puella, 'he wants me.'

'*What?*'

'Every time he comes to us and you take the messages on into the city, he spends the waiting time with me,' she explained. 'If he can have me, then he'll do everything we want.'

Artemidorus' expression folded into such a frown that Mercury stepped back, pale as a spirit on the shore of the Styx.

'Don't be angry.' She placed herself between the men and looked Artemidorus straight in the eye. 'I've already agreed.'

'You have!'

'And it is my decision. Mine alone, Septem! Because it's my body. Less than a year ago I was a chattel. A thing. My body belonged to Lord Brutus and he could do whatever he liked with it. Even something as horrible as what you tell me Lord Basilus likes to do. But then you freed me. Manumitted me into a freedwoman. And my body became my own. You and Quintus taught it how to do things and visit places I have never heard of other slave women even dreaming about! And I choose to share my body with you because I love you. But I serve Lord Antony now, as you do. Because you do. And if I can serve him better by lending my body to Mercury once in a while, then that is what I choose to do!'

Artemidorus opened his mouth to argue. To answer at least. But then he discovered that there was nothing he could say. The woman was free. Free, therefore, to do what she wished.

And so the bargain was struck.

*

Every ten days or so Mercury would appear. The vastly enhanced secret secretarial team would decode Caesar's letters that Artemidorus took into the beleaguered city once he had memorised each new password. And transcribe the ever-more desperate pleas to Caesar, Cicero and the Senate that Artemidorus brought out. Antony was forced to send the scavengers from the Vth further and further up the *Via Aemilia* towards the Alps in search of provender for his troops, and Enobarbus led these alongside the general's brother Lucius, leaving Artemidorus to concentrate on the intelligence work. But apart from that, nothing seemed to change on the ground. Not in Italy at any rate.

But incoming information told a different story in the East where Brutus had made himself Master of Macedonia and Cassius of everywhere from the borders of Egypt to northernmost Syria. And, at Cicero's prompting, they were awarded the governorships which they now held *de facto*. Antony had three legions under his immediate command. The IInd Sabine, the Vth Larks and the XXXVth. And his Gaulish cavalry. His enemies – not even counting the masterly inactive Caesar Octavius, commander of the legions that deserted Antony after the decimation – now had almost ten times that number.

And so the *calends* of *Mars* crawled into the *ides* fifteen days later. The anniversary of *Divus Julius'* death passed without note or ceremony. The *calends* of *Aprilis* came and went.

Then, thirteen days later, on the *ides* of *Aprilis*, everything blew up like one of the barrels of Greek Fire Antony's men were lobbing into the starving city.

XIII

Mercury started it. He came riding full tilt into the camp in the last night watch of the twelfth of *Aprilis*. Lucky not to have been stopped or killed by Antony's admittedly lackadaisical outer perimeter. Nothing had happened for so long that not even Antony could stop his legionaries getting lax and lazy. Apart from the men working the siege engines. And Artemidorus' expanded *contubernium* of spies, codebreakers and secretaries.

The double agent was not motivated by his concern for Antony.

Or Antony's legions, the IInd Sabine and the Vth *Alaudae* or the XXXVth. The other cohorts he still commanded together with more than a thousand Gaulish Cavalrymen. Or the bits and pieces of the VIth and VIIth the general seemed to have accrued.

Or his handler Artemidorus and his *contubernium*.

Or for the four thousand *sestertii* in gold the spies were holding for him.

His concern was all for the woman he loved.

He reined in his horse outside the much enlarged tent that now housed the *contubernium* of spies, together with their secretarial support, and leaped to the ground. Naturally he went to Puella first, but as soon as he started giving his garbled message, she took him to Artemidorus. Who in turn took him to Antony after the first few broken sentences.

The reputation of the undercover operatives was such that Artemidorus had instant access to the general no matter when he demanded it. Even in the middle of the night. And Antony came straight out of a late strategy meeting with his legates and tribunes to hear what his spies and their double agent had to tell him.

'Caesar is on the move,' gasped Mercury. 'No. That's not quite right Caesar is unwell and keeping to his bed. But his legions are on the move. Led by the Consul Gaius Vibius Pansa, who has just arrived from Rome. With the authority of the Senate – at last – to take direct action against you, Lord Antony.'

'On the move?' probed Antony, eyes narrow.

'Straight up the *Via Aemilia*. The shortest, fastest, most direct route.'

'But no one's alerted Decimus Albinus. How will the two armies co-ordinate?' demanded Antony. 'I assume they will want to try a pincer movement – one in my face; the other at my back. Much as they handled things with *Divus Julius* on the *Ides* of *Mars* thirteen months ago.'

228

'They will have warned him,' answered Mercury breathlessly. 'As soon as my message is delivered...'

'I see,' said Antony. 'Well, forewarned is forearmed. When is Consul Pansa due to be in a position to offer battle?'

'The day after tomorrow. On the fourteenth.'

'We have time to make counterplans, then. Septem, look further into this and report to me.'

Artemidorus took Mercury back to the tent occupied by the intelligence unit. Who were all now up and very much awake. 'Is the message for Decimus Albinus in writing or are you to deliver it in person?' he asked.

'In writing. As usual.'

'Right. I'll take it to him. As usual. But this time I think we'll change the routine. Kyros. Can you copy the message in the same hand it was written in? So that Albinus won't be able to tell it's not the original?'

'Yes, Septem.'

'Good. Because there are one or two elements I want you to change...'

And so the *contubernium* went from recording and dispensing information to generating disinformation.

*

'*Triumphus*.' Artemidorus gave the password for the day and was ushered through the tiny door into Mutina's flame-lit streets. During the weeks of his visits here disguised as Caesar's messenger, he had seen even the brawniest of the legionaries seem to wilt. As starved flesh vanished from their increasingly scrawny bones. Whenever he caught a glimpse of the city's residents – those few not directly involved in the defence of the place – their faces were gaunt and their eyes sunken and huge. The children's bellies were blown up to enormous proportions. Their little faces skeletal.

Under other circumstances he would have felt pity for them. Perhaps even guilt at what he was doing. But he was Antony's man. While these were Antony's implacable enemies. And if Artemidorus or Antony failed here, then it would be Antony's head spiked in the Forum. Rather than Decimus Albinus', as was still the current plan. Or, indeed, that of his right-hand man Pontius Aquila, who was also one of the men who plunged a dagger into *Divus Julius'* back on the *Ides*.

The main head in question was thrust out of the *tablinum* door. 'The message?' snapped Decimus Albinus.

'Here, General,' answered Artemidorus, handing it over. His heart was racing. His scrotum clenched. As though he was in the coldest *frigidarium* bath of a northern bathhouse in winter. While he might have become inured to passing

229

messages back and forth, this was the first forgery he had tried to pass on. While the original message had given Pansa's simple battle plan and asked Albinus to bring his men out of the main gate at dawn on the fourteenth, this new message asked him to mount an unexpected sally at noon.

By which time Antony planned to have engaged and defeated Pansa's legions and be waiting to mop up Albinus' men as well.

This time the spy was not asked to wait in the empty, unsupplied dining hall. Decimus sent an acknowledgement and agreement to the plan in one short, coded reply. Artemidorus was back in his tent by dawn and Mercury was off down the *Via Aemilia* with his lusts satisfied and his message secure. For the last time. It had to be the last time whatever the outcome. For Caesar Octavius was no fool, even if he was sick in bed. When Decimus Albinus came out at noon instead of at dawn, he would have given the game away. Caesar would know immediately that his messages were being tampered with. And the traitor Mercury would either be hiding with relative safety in the midst of Antony's troops or hanging on a cross somewhere.

ii

The *haruspex* straightened, his arms red to the elbow from examining the sacrifice's intestines and liver. It was a white bull and it had been offered, as was traditional, to Mars and Venus *Victrix*, deities of battle and victory. *Divus Julius'* favourite deities in fact. Who were his companions in Olympus now.

'The gods foresee a fortunate victory in today's battle,' he intoned. A wave of relief went through the assembled legions in front of whom the sacrifice had been made. The *haruspex* dropped his voice so that only Antony and his immediate circle could hear. 'But they advise great caution.'

'I'm going into battle against an army more than twice the size of my own. Of course I'll exercise great caution!' hissed Antony. Also keeping his voice low. Artemidorus kept a straight face. He had seen Antony in battle and 'caution' was among the last words he would have chosen to describe him. 'So the odds are still stacked pretty high against us,' continued Antony. 'And I have to say that, as an augur, I do not like the look of those *corvi* crows either.' He nodded at a black cloud of the birds hanging in the left quadrant of the sky. Above the little village of Forum Gallorum which sat on a low eminence above the marshy plain Antony proposed to use as his battlefield.

'You know what they say, General,' said Artemidorus. '"*Trust in what the gods tell you – but always check for yourself.*"'

Antony gave a grunt of amusement. 'Well, let's get busy,' he said. 'We all know what we're expected to do today, so it's time to get on with it.' He clasped hands with his senior officers, legates and tribunes. The infantry commanders in charge of the legions of foot soldiers. The cavalry commanders. Antony always preferred to deploy and lead cavalry himself. And had brought several *alae* wings home with him from his campaigns in Gaul.

Other men brought gold and slaves, mused Artemidorus. Antony brought warriors and their mounts – two mouths to feed for every cavalryman in his *velites* units; *alae* wings. Perhaps that was why he was always in debt. His massive cavalry contingent was split into two cohorts today. Each of several hundred soldiers. One would be led by Antony himself. The other by Gretorex, his Gaulish legate. And that was important because Artemidorus and his *contubernium* had been assigned to ride with Gretorex. The Gauls were all huge, blond warriors. They wore their hair and moustaches long as a sign of manliness. Used a range of weapons strange to most legionaries. Favoured brightly patterned trousers and tunics made of skin, lined with fur. Over which they wore chain mail. Sometimes – but by no means always. There was something cowardly about wearing armour, they suspected. Real men fought naked and berserk. Like the Ghost Warriors of Germania.

'This is a woman!' Gretorex had shouted in astonishment when he first realised Puella's gender. 'No woman has ever ridden with my horsemen.'

'This one will,' said Artemidorus. 'And she will help you to a great victory. Put her to the test.'

Gretorex turned away in apparent disgust, pulling his horse's head to the right with his left hand. While his right hand reached across his belly in one smooth movement to pull his long *spada* double-edged cavalry sword out of its sheath. And throw it at Puella.

Who caught it in mid flight with her left hand while drawing her *gladius* with her right. At the same time urging her mount forward using knees and heels alone. The horse obediently charged into Gretorex' mount's shoulder to shoulder. The grip of her iron-muscled thighs kept her safe. Thighs that only a few hours ago had been clasped almost as fiercely round Artemidorus' hips. Gretorex was taken by surprise, even though he had started the test himself. An instant later, the Gaulish commander was on his back in the mud. A heartbeat after that, Puella was kneeling astride his chest with the *spada* buried in the earth a finger-width from his right ear and the *gladius* a finger-width from his left.

'By Camulos, god of war,' he boomed. 'I thought for a moment this woman was going to cut my hair!' He gave a great bellow of laughter – echoed by his men. He thrust his hand out and Puella grasped it as she stood, helping him to his feet. 'Very well,' he said. 'She rides with us. But I will not call her Puella – girl.

This is not a name of due respect! When she rides with us she is *Spiritum Bellatrix* Ghost Warrior Woman!'

Artemidorus shivered at the name. For he had fought Ghost Warriors in the dark forests of the north. In Gaul and Germania. Warriors who painted their faces and bodies black and crept from shadow to shadow, silently and invisibly, spreading death and terror. But mostly death.

*

The mission Antony had given Gretorex, Artemidorus and their command was simple. But crucial. It sprang directly from what his secret agent had discovered and what he had done. As the general's legions formed up on his chosen battlefield during the last of the darkness before the dawn of the fourteenth day of *Aprilis*, waiting to face Consul and General Pansa's much larger army at sunrise, the cavalry unit rode silently and secretly into a hiding place behind the village of Forum Gallorum.

The men and women who lived in the tiny hamlet had no cause to love Decimus Albinus and his men in Mutina. Who had stolen all the food the village possessed in order to feed their starving garrison. The villagers were only still alive because Antony had given orders that his well-supplied legions should share their food. It was easy enough, therefore, for several hundred horsemen – and one black-faced Ghost Warrior woman – to hide themselves there. Those that could not be accommodated in stables and barns thronged the streets and hid behind the village houses. Gretorex and Artemidorus climbed to the top of the highest building, a modest temple to Apollo. From this vantage point, the pair of them had an excellent view of the battlefield, the road beyond it and the south-east quadrant of Mutina's walls. Including both the little postern gate Artemidorus came and went through in his disguise – and the huge main gate leading out onto the *via* which had withstood even the largest of Antony's siege rams for week after week.

The sun rose through a low mist, glinting off the armour and weaponry of Antony's army. And off those of the seemingly endless snake of Pansa's men as they came up the *via* from Arminium and Bolonia marching ten abreast to the beat of military drums and the howling of signal trumpets. Consul and General Pansa himself rode in the lead, with his senior commanders grouped around him.

'No sign of Caesar,' said Artemidorus, scanning the generals' standards as well as the legions' eagles.

'Could he be bringing up more troops?' wondered Gretorex.

'My spy says he's still too ill to fight,' answered Artemidorus.

The solid target offered by Pansa and his immediate lieutenants suddenly split and scattered. As Antony's slingers went to work. Followed almost immediately by his archers. It was impossible to see where the slingers were stationed. But the archers were in a solid group three rows back, with the *triarii* men looking after them. Men like Quintus. Antony's army was experienced, battle-hardened and ready. By the look of things, most of Pansa's troops were little short of being raw recruits. Quantity rather than quality. With the exception, a couple of legions back, of a thousand or so who marched with a confident swagger and looked disturbingly familiar as they approached. The legion called Martia.

Although Pansa himself had served with *Divus Julius* in Gaul, he was by no means an experienced general. And he did not control his men with anything like Antony's steady grip. Pansa's troops leaped over the roadside ditch and formed up opposite Antony's army. Sinking to their ankles in the marshy soil. They left dead and wounded on the road and in the ditch as testimony to the effectiveness of Antony's slingers and archers. But not in anything like sufficient numbers to make a difference. The *aquilifers* put their eagles at the front of their legions. The *signifers* put their banners in front of their cohorts. The officers took their places. Everything moved into place as though this were a parade ground. And stopped, like troops awaiting the general's inspection. The pause became a hesitation. Even though Antony's arrows clouded the sky and his invisible slingshots took their toll.

'They're wondering where Decimus Albinus is,' said Artemidorus. 'It's dawn and he's not where they expected him to be.'

But the hesitation lasted only a few moments. The *cornicens* sounded. Their trumpeting lost in a huge bellow. The Martia broke ranks, hurling forward and driving the raw recruits before them. The armies clashed together like a storm swell hitting a cliff. And the battle began.

iii

As the sun rose inexorably up the bright, frost-clear sky behind them, heading for noon, Artemidorus and Gretorex watched the slaughter. Wave after wave of Pansa's inexperienced troops dashed themselves hopelessly against the iron wall of Antony's Vth *Alaude* Larks and IInd Sabine legions. Pushed forward by the impatience of the uncontrolled Martia legion immediately behind them.

Antony held his own cavalry back until the crucial moment. As he was doing with Gretorex' wing. The moment when, inexperienced though they were, Pansa's troops finally chopped and stabbed their way to the third rank. Sheer weight of numbers threatening to overcome everything standing against them. And the Martia finally broke through to confront soldiers who were, at last, their equals. At that moment, just as the raw recruits found themselves trapped between the iron jaws of two great legions, finding out the hard way what real soldiers could do to them, Antony led several hundred heavily armed horsemen into the right flank of Pansa's army. Many of the raw recruits had never experienced a cavalry charge before. And the impact of the horses, the sheer weight of them with their armoured breastplates, not to mention the sharp-edged, slicing *spadas* that the cavalrymen wielded, came as a massive shock to the beleaguered lines of inexperienced soldiers.

Which wavered. Almost broke there and then. But managed to hang on, steadied by the Martia men. Hoping increasingly desperately, Artemidorus' intuition told him, for support from Decimus Albinus and his troops in Mutina.

But that support did not arrive until noon, when it was more or less too late.

The great gate of the city opened on cue and Decimus Albinus' troops stormed out. There was no cavalry. They had eaten all the horses long ago. But they came bravely, like Pansa's men, ten abreast and following the *via*. His cavalry running as fast as they could – charging on foot instead of in the saddle. A great bellow of relief came up from Pansa's legions. Who saw in that flood of soldiers streaming towards the rear of Antony's army, the prospect of immediate relief. And eventual victory.

But this was the moment Artemidorus and Gretorex had been waiting for. Even as the main gate creaked open, they were mounting their horses. And as Decimus Albinus' men charged out of the city, they leaped into their saddles and began their countercharge.

Nearly five hundred heavily armed Gaulish cavalrymen followed that ridge of firmer ground on the south bank of the river which led round the northern edge of the battlefield towards Mutina's main gate. And so they were able to hit Albinus' legions side-on just at the moment they were about to attack Antony's rearmost cohorts. From the IInd Sabine legion. Who, prewarned, turned and offered cold steel instead of confusion and surprise. The surprise and confusion swept through the betrayed legions under Decimus Albinus' and Pontius Aquila's command, therefore. Gretorex led the charge, as was his right. He insisted Ghost Warrior ride close behind him. Not so that he could protect her, but so that she could watch his back, he said. Artemidorus and Ferrata rode either side of her. Both coming close to being awed by the ease and dexterity with which she visited death and destruction upon their enemies. With a *spada* in one hand and a *gladius* in the other.

What had started out as a concerted charge by Decimus Albinus' men, to surprise Antony's army and support their comrades in arms, turned into a rout that not only failed to help but also shattered their morale. Pansa's army began to retreat in confusion. Not even the Martia men could steady them now. And they, too, began to fall back. While Antony's legions moved forward relentlessly like the Friendly Ones. As Gretorex' cavalry rode straight through the column of shocked and all but helpless legionaries from the city. Artemidorus swept through and through the melee looking for Albinus or Aquila, keen to take a head for Antony. But he found no one of note. He began to wonder whether Decimus Albinus and Pontius Aquila had actually led the charge in person. Or whether, like Caesar Octavius, they had preferred to stay in bed and direct the battle from there.

Puella and Ferrata rode straight on, however. Exhaustively trained with weapons but less so with horses. Unable, once their steeds were galloping in the full charge, to stop them. Or even to turn them from their course. And so the pair of them careered almost helplessly southwards as Gretorex, Artemidorus and the rest of the cavalry unit began to pursue the broken legionaries back towards Mutina. All too well aware that, behind them, Antony's legions were creating mayhem among Pansa's shattered command.

But then everything turned again. As though on a cast of the dice or the flip of a coin.

Ghost Warrior and Ferrata suddenly came back, riding north into the carnage Gretorex' men were creating, hardly able to control their horses. Or their tongues. Puella found Artemidorus. Her mount crashed against his almost as forcefully as it had against Gretorex'.

'There's another army,' she gasped as he rocked in the saddle.

'*What?*' he was almost as stunned as he had been to hear that she was willing to sleep with Mercury to keep him faithful to their *contubernium*. 'Another *army*?'

'It's huge. I don't know how many legions. And it's marching north. I've no idea where it's come from. Rome maybe. But it's coming straight at us.'

'When will it be here? Could you tell?'

'I don't know exactly. But soon!'

'Right. You and Ferrata come with me. Guard my back. I need to get to Antony!' He dragged his horse's head viciously to the left and galloped off towards the main battlefield. Feeling as he did so, Puella and Ferrata falling behind each of his shoulders.

So far today, until the wild charge at noon, he had seen the battle only at a distance. But now they were galloping right into the heart of it. Artemidorus, holding himself as tall in the saddle as he could, looking for the *draconarius* standard that would give him an idea of where Antony was. In the middle of the mayhem if he was any judge.

It was only the sure-footedness of his well-trained war horse that allowed him to proceed as swiftly as he did. Right into the heart of the battle, where Antony's battle flag waved cheek by jowl with Pansa's own. He was not concerned with attacking or killing the men he rode by – or rode over. He trusted his greaves to keep his legs safe from those few enemy soldiers who remained erect after the armoured breast of his charger smashed through them. And remained quick thinking enough to consider retaliation. In the heartbeats before Puella or Ferrata, hard on his heels, slaughtered them.

He found Antony in the middle of the battlefield. Still on his horse. Covered head to foot in other people's blood and almost drunk with bloodlust. Surrounded by senior officers including Enobarbus. Hacking to left and right with a cavalry *spada*. 'Have you seen Pansa?' Antony bellowed over the deafening din of battle. 'I'm pretty sure I wounded him. But he's gone now...'

'General,' shouted Artemidorus. 'General, there's another army. Coming north. It will hit us very soon. It must be Consul Hirtius bringing Pansa's reinforcements.'

'Hirtius!' spat Antony. 'He's a much more experienced leader! He was *Divus Julius'* legate. Dined with him on the night he crossed the Rubicon.'

'If he has fresh troops then this could be serious, General!' shouted Enobarbus.

'Puella and Ferrata say he has several legions,' yelled Artemidorus.

'And they'll be fresh and battle-ready. Not like our poor men who have been hard at it all day. *Excrementum*! We'd better pull back to our lines.' Antony sat tall in his saddle looking around the massive field of battle. 'It breaks my heart but we'll have to tell the men to just drop their eagles and leave their standards. And just get the *hades* out of here. I'd rather lose all our eagles than any of our men. Because there'll be an even tougher battle once they get organised in a day or two!' He turned to the command group who surrounded him at all times. Not so much to protect him as to allow him to communicate with the army he was leading. '*Buicinator*,' he bellowed to the nearest bugler. 'Sound the retreat!'

iv

Consul and General Aulus Hirtius arrived with his legions as the last of Antony's men were leaving the field. These were mostly diehards who had gone back for their standards and their eagles. All of which fell into Hirtius' possession while he announced a great victory; *bucilators* and *cornicens* blasting the air with their triumphant trumpet calls.

'Just like Pompey,' said Antony wearily as he surveyed the scene from the relative safety of his own fortified lines. 'Arriving when all the hard work is done and claiming victory for himself!'

'I remember Pompey doing that when Crassus had all but defeated Spartacus and his gladiators,' nodded Artemidorus. 'Crassus never really forgave him.'

236

Antony nodded. Turned. 'Check on your *contubernium* and report to Gretorex as he was technically your commanding officer in the battle, Septem. He'll report to me. They all will. I need to know how many men we've lost and how many I can count on when Hirtius, Pansa and that bloody boy come after us again. After you've done that I want you to take a flag of truce into their camp and see if you can negotiate the recovery of our wounded. Make it fast before too many of them start dying. And I hardly need to tell you to keep your eyes open and your wits about you. Enobarbus, you stay here. I want a good intelligence officer to do the negotiation but I can't afford to risk you both. Report back as soon as you can, Septem. After I get the briefing from my legates and tribunes I'll be with the wounded in the field *hospitium*. Report to Enobarbus if you can't find me.'

'Yes General. I'll take two of my *contubernium* with me if I may. But what will my proof of authority be?'

Antony paused for an instant, then pulled a badge off the front of his breastplate. 'I got it when I was first hailed *Imperator*,' he said. 'I won't be needing it for a day or two. But bring it back. Or it's your head...' And his tone said very clearly that he wasn't joking. 'Unless you're already dead of course.'

*

Hirtius had set up his camp fewer than two military *miles* from Mutina astride the *Via Aemilia*. It was plain that he was an effective leader simply from the speed and efficiency with which his legions had constructed and manned their fortified encampments. And that he was not afraid of Antony – for the complex of encampments was within sight both of Mutina and Antony's lines. Which also suggested Hirtius was an able strategist. Simply by setting up camp where he had, he promised almost immediate relief to Decimus Albinus and his beleaguered garrison. And threatened Antony's men with almost inevitable annihilation. Artemidorus, Quintus and Ferrata were met at the gate of a palisade every bit as solid as the one surrounding Antony's much smaller camp and taken to the command tent under armed guard.

Hirtius was a tall, lean, eagle-faced man. As Artemidorus waited in the *vestibulum* of the command tent, surrounded by the guards who had conducted him and his associates here, he was able to glimpse the general through in the *atrium*. And, equally tall and gaunt, beside him stood Caesar Octavius' relative, Quintus Pedius, whose daughter had been murdered by Balbus' messenger Flaccus. But there was no sign of either Caesar Octavius or Pansa. Maybe both Mercury and Antony were right – Caesar was sick and Pansa was wounded. He strained his ears to hear what they were saying. Snatches of conversation came and went.

237

'...held the Fourth back...' Hirtius was saying, '...but the Martia ran out of control...'

'...lucky Caesar held the Fourth at least,' Quintus Pedius answered. 'They might have been slaughtered like the inexperienced men Pansa sent up first...'

'...but the Fourth might have made all the difference. Made victory more assured. And remember, he is now officially *hostis*, enemy of the state by the ruling of the Senate. That has to be a potent motivator...'

'...What does it matter?' Added a new voice. 'We won. We'll catch him soon enough...'

'Won? Barely! In spite of all the eagles and standards we took. Antony must have had warning of our arrival. Retreated in good order. But yes. As you say. We won. Though I think you'll find him harder to catch than you suppose...'

'... at what cost?' Demanded Quintus Pedius. 'Won at what cost?'

'High. We'll need to regroup...' said Hirtius.

But then the leader of the guards broke into their conference. And the subject turned to Artemidorus himself. 'A messenger?' asked Hirtius.

'Came in with two companions under a flag of truce. Says he's from Mark Antony, General. Showed me this...'

'That's Antony's all right,' said Hirtius. 'I was there when he was acclaimed *Imperator*. What does this messenger want?'

'Show him in and let him tell us himself,' suggested Quintus Pedius.

'With any luck Antony wants to surrender...' added the third – vaguely familiar – voice.

'I'll believe that when I see Antony on his knees in front of me. Which I never will!' answered Quintus Pedius. He turned as he spoke and a look of recognition swept over his face. 'I know you,' he said.

'Yes sir,' said Artemidorus. 'We met on the Appian Way and we went together with Caesar Octavius to Rome. I hope Caesar is not too unwell?' He saw the immediate reaction in Quintus Pedius' eyes. But they must already be certain that Antony had spies in their camp. Because of Decimus Albinus' unscheduled arrival – and the way he charged straight into the jaws of a trap. No harm in rubbing it in, though. Especially as he recognised the third man now – Balbus' right-hand man Nobilitor. Companion to the murderous Flaccus. Whose account had been so unexpectedly settled by the assassin Myrtillus. No wonder Caesar Octavius could afford to buy – and bribe – so many legions. If he was using Balbus' famously bottomless purse.

'I suspect Antony does not share your sentiments on the subject of Caesar's health, Centurion,' said Quintus Pedius. 'What does your commander want?'

'Permission to retrieve his dead and wounded.'

Consul Hirtius and Quintus Pedius looked at each other. Nobilitor looked into the distance. Dressed as a legate but clearly out of his depth here. No more of a soldier than Pansa. Artemidorus could almost read the minds of the two professional commanders, however. They would be disappointed Antony was not admitting defeat as Nobilitor had hoped. But not really surprised. Then they would be going through a rapid series of calculations as to the immediate future and their own plans in it. Which – in broad terms – would be to throw the full might of their combined legions straight at Antony at the earliest opportunity. But the conversation so far suggested they would not be able to do this in the immediate future. And they needed to do something about their own wounded. Before the already battered morale of Pansa's legions began to suffer further, infecting the other men. As the strength of their command already had – as evidenced by the Martia's uncontrolled behaviour.

If they refused his request, then collecting their own – much greater – tally of dead and wounded might be problematic. Especially for Decimus Albinus who would have to let his men come in and out of the besieged city – something Antony could well want to take advantage of. But Antony was an honourable man. If he gave his word on a truce then he would keep it. Furthermore, he suspected that Hirtius and Pedius would be speculating that a large number of wounded would slow Antony down if he did decide to retreat. Make him easier to catch up with when they sorted out the near disaster of Pansa's engagement.

v

The three of them galloped back towards the battlefield in the gathering darkness with the news that Antony could have his truce. As they did so, they came across walking wounded in greater and greater numbers. Soldiers at first staggering towards Hirtius and Pansa's camp, but then increasing crowds of Antony's men heading in the opposite direction. And, there amongst them, Mercury. Artemidorus did not recognise him at first, but the double agent recognised him and called his name. Artemidorus reined to a stop and looked around. A few moments later Mercury was precariously perched behind him as they raced towards Antony's camp. Ferrata took Mercury to the nearest medical tent as Artemidorus went to report to the general.

As ever, Antony put the welfare of his men first, so it was Ferrata who found him, among the wounded who had made it this far – and who were already being tended by the *medicii, clinicii* and *capsariors* doctors attached to the legions. It was Ferrata therefore who gave the news of the truce which sent most of the *medicii* hurrying out onto the battlefield – together with cohort after cohort of able-bodied helpers. Bearing torches as the night closed in. Though the brightness of Hirtius and Caesar's campfires outshone the moon and almost made flambeaus and lamps unnecessary.

Artemidorus found Enobarbus and as they walked side by side from the intelligence tent to the medical facility, they discussed the information that Artemidorus was taking to Antony. 'So the general has finally officially been declared *hostis*. I'm not sure how he'll take that. In the meantime Caesar Octavius is sick, but in full control. Quintus Pedius is liaising for him with Hirtius – and Pansa I assume. But it looks as though Antony could well be right and the consul is badly wounded. Also Nobilitor is there – which means Balbus is financing everything that the Senate isn't paying for. Agrippa and Rufus weren't there which means they were with Caesar. Who might still be in Ariminium. But I doubt it. If I was him I'd have moved up much closer by now – into Cisalpine Gaul now the Senate has ruled. He could be as close as Bononia. That's only a day's march or an hour's hard ride away from Hirtius' new position just down the road.

'Pansa tried to deploy the Fourth today when the Martia went out of control. But Caesar Octavius held them back. Which has to mean he was close enough to take command decisions. Bononia's most likely, as I say. And he was probably wise – the Fourth used to be Antony's men and might well be a little hesitant to attack him full on. Even after the decimations in Brundisium. Especially as they'd find themselves facing the Thirty-fifth, the Second Sabine and Fifth Larks. All experienced and battle-hardened. The Fifth especially, with the general's brother Lucius leading them. But Hirtius and Quintus Pedius seem to be blaming Pansa for what they view as a near disaster rather than a great victory. And you can see their point. Antony is still here. And Decimus Albinus is still trapped in Mutina. And they have about four times as many dead and wounded as we do. Though that's just a rough estimate.'

At this point in their conversation, they entered the tent and found Antony deep in conversation with Mercury, whose wound turned out to be a deep cut to his cheek which was open from ear to chin. That was being cauterised and stitched shut as the pair talked. Mercury had never been pretty but not even a mother could love him now. 'Ah, Septem,' said the general as the spy approached. 'Your man here saw Pansa after I did. He was badly wounded. His guards had to carry him off the battlefield. Sounds as though he'll be lucky to last the night.'

*

'It's simple mathematics,' said Antony as the next day threatened to dawn. 'I don't need spies to add to the figures. Or Pythagoras and Euclid to explain them. And the fact that they've declared me *hostis* doesn't make any immediate difference. Certainly not on the ground here. I command four legions, though after yesterday's battle, I'm really only left with two full legions and some auxiliaries. The Second Sabine and the Fifth Larks, though I could just about reconstitute the Thirty-fifth. Decimus Albinus has more than that in Mutina – though to be fair they are disheartened, weakened and starving. Pansa had four. So did Hirtius. And Octavius has the Fourth, the Martia – which Pansa couldn't control – and a couple of others that he's still training up. Even so, that's the better part of sixteen legions all in all. Plus cavalry and Praetorian Cohorts. We're outnumbered by a factor somewhere between four to one and eight to one. Any suggestions?'

'Attack,' said Artemidorus at once. 'Use the truce for as long as you can to strengthen your men and their numbers – then attack the moment it's over.'

Antony gave a shout of laughter. 'My thoughts exactly! But explain your reasoning Septem. Let's see how close your ideas are to my own.'

'You need to keep the initiative and that's the way to do it,' the spy said forcefully. 'If you sit and wait they'll catch you on the back foot and annihilate you. You have very little chance of winning an outright victory but the best chance is surprise. Which an attack certainly would be. In the meantime, you need to secure a clear route for an orderly retreat. I'm pretty certain you've been thinking along those lines already because you've been using my tribune here and your brother General Lucius to organise a series of *speculatores* and *exploratores* from his Fifth Legion to scout the north-western extension of the *Via Aemilia* up past Placentia to *Castra Taurinmorum* military camp and beyond. Which I suppose is your escape route. Perhaps the least likely one you could choose. Certainly Pansa and Hirtius must reckon they have you trapped against the Alps. But it's an escape route that also takes you towards Gaius Lepidus in Narbonnese Gaul with at least five legions which he may be willing to share with you, even if you are a proscribed outlaw. And to General Pollio in Further Spain with at least two more. And General Plancus beside them in Transalpine Gaul with five more who might be persuaded to join whichever side looks the stronger. If Mars and Venus *Victrix* stay with you, you could go into the mountains with two legions and come back out again with fifteen.'

'Very good!' said Antony, clearly impressed. 'My thoughts almost exactly. Except for one element. An important one to you, as it happens.'

'Yes, General? What is that?'

'Not what – *who*. My old friend General Publius Ventidius Bassus is in the ancient Etruscan capital of Arretium. He's no friend to Cicero or the *Libertores* faction in the Senate. He gave me his word that if ever I was declared *hostis* outlaw and enemy of the state, he would help me rather than hunt me. It's time to see

241

whether he will keep his promise. If he does, then Cicero may well have saved my life by demanding my death! As soon as we finish this battle you suggest we start, I want you to go and get him and bring him to me if he will agree to come. Over in Gaul, as you suggest. Him and the three legions he commands. Which, if we can pull it off, will give us an army that will outnumber everything that the Senate, Pansa, Hirtius, Decimus Albinus and that bloody boy can bring into the field against us.'

vi

'Right,' said Antony three days later as the truce at last came towards its end. 'It's a bit underhanded, but this is what I want you and your *contubernium* to do, Septem. While I, my brothers, legates and tribunes conduct the battle on the wider scale, I want you to go in as a separate unit. Disguised in the armour we stripped from Pansa's dead legionaries for precisely this purpose. Wearing their legionary badges. Pretending to be on their side. In the confusion of battle that shouldn't be too hard to do. Then your mission is simple. Find the leaders of the enemy troops and kill them by whatever means you can. Pansa, if he's recovered from that wound I gave him. Hirtius. Decimus Albinus and don't forget his head. That slimy *nothus* bastard Pontius Aquila who you say is his right-hand man. Young Caesar, if he's well enough to have got himself out of bed. His two bumboys Agrippa and Rufus. I don't care how you get them. Stab them in the back if you have to – it's what most of them did to *Divus Julius* after all. Consider yourselves *cryptia* Spartan undercover elite. The heart and soul of The Three Hundred at Thermopylae. Because if I'm not Agamemnon at the gates of Troy, then I'm Leonidas at the Pass!'

The only other person present at the briefing was Enobarbus. Even the general's trusted brother Lucius was elsewhere. Both he and Artemidorus stared at Antony stony-faced. There was no doubt they would obey his orders. And both men understood the reference to the Spartan army's secret super elite, who only became eligible to join the *cryptaia* after they had murdered in cold blood to prove their willingness to kill or die whatever the odds.

But neither man liked what the *contubernium* was being ordered to do. Though, to be fair, this was not the first time they had been commanded to put on their opponents' armour and legionary identification badges. Each night since the battle, the spies had dressed in disguise and tried to infiltrate Hirtius and Pansa's camp. Further visits to Mutina being out of the question now that Caesar Octavius and Albinus knew their correspondence had been tampered with. Albinus possibly knew the face of the man responsible for delivering the forged letters that almost got him and his entire command wiped out. Even though the face in question had

242

been blacked each time they met. And if he did not, then Pontius Aquila almost certainly did.

The best they had been able to achieve was reports of guards' gossip overheard. Which informed them that Pansa was still clinging to life. That Caesar Octavius was recovering – and had demanded that the truce be extended with no further attacks on Antony until he was well enough to lead his men in person. Hirtius had acquiesced. For the Senate was beginning to hand out honours and the promise of a triumph. And neither man wished to miss his chance at any of this. Each of them wishing their actions to be clearly seen and accurately recorded. So that the Senate's gratitude could be precisely targeted and richly fulfilled. In the golden days that would follow Antony's defeat, disgrace and death.

And as Antony had at last been declared *hostis*, his goods and possessions, villas and all that could be found of his personal fortune had been confiscated. Fulvia, Julia, Antyllus and the other children thrown out onto the street. And the word had gone out. The man who killed or captured Antony would be rewarded with every brick of building, every stick of furniture, every *sestertius* of the fortune that had been taken away from him.

In reaction, however, many people felt Antony was being shabbily treated by a Senate biased by Cicero's Philippics into unreasoning support of *Divus Julius'* murderers. Were beginning to wonder whether things had gone too far. Whether it was Cicero rather than Antony who was really the enemy of Rome. And whether the time had come to go to Antony's aid. Men like Marcus Aemilius Lepidus Governor of Narbonese Gaul. Lucius Munacius Plancus Governor of Transalpine Gaul. Gaius Antonius Pollo, Governor of Further Spain.

Men like General Publius Ventidius Bassus with his three legions stationed in Arrteium.

XIV

Artemidorus, Quintus, Ferrata, Puella, Hercules, Kyros and Mercury eased themselves silently through the scrubby bush separating them from Hirtius' camp. The night was dark but not black. There was no moon and a light overcast but the stars and the campfires of the opposing legions cast a little light. The *contubernium* spread out as they crept silently forward. But they did not separate so widely that they could not communicate with each other and keep control of the ground between them. Behind them, moving almost as silently, came a line of legionaries from *Legio V* who had been carefully prepared for this duty. The spies were the first line of defence against infiltration from Hirtius' spies. The legionaries were the second. Any man coming from the Senate's legions would die silently and be left where he lay. For, although it was still just after sunset, Antony's attack was under way. The first *ballista* shot would announce the end of the truce at dawn tomorrow.

The briefing he had given Artemidorus and Enobarbus was one among many that the spy and his chief had attended – and participated in. Their role as disguised *cryptaeia* assassins was only one element of a much larger plan which was going into action now. As silently as possible, slowly and carefully, Antony's siege weapons were being moved. Repositioned. Turned to face away from Mutina. Creating a field of fire centred on Hirtius' camp instead. Antony and his artillery officers calculated that, although the *ballistae*, *onagers*, *scorpios* and slings had been of limited effect against the battlements of Mutina, they would be devastatingly effective against Hirtius' stockade. Further, while the months of the siege had forced the men working the siege weapons to target them with increasing accuracy, the huge camp containing twelve legions' tents was an objective they could hardly miss. Pinpoint precision coming a long way second behind the impact of an unexpected bombardment. In *any* case, the fires, as numerous as stars – which Hirtius calculated would sap the morale of Antony's troop – provided a perfect mark to aim at.

But the plan depended on surprise. And Artemidorus was in charge of ensuring that surprise was total. Using the *contubernium* as a Spartan *cryptaia* ruthless killing machine to ensure no one from the enemy camp saw anything suspicious and survived. Employing a technique he had first seen used by Cilician pirates in his youth, Artemidorus clenched his dagger between his teeth. For once glad that he had given Brutus' uncannily sharp dagger to Caesar Octavius. Closing his lips against the cold steel in case his teeth glinted. Hooding his eyes for the same reason. This freed both hands to crawl or fight, and kept the dagger ready for immediate use – far more accessible than it would be in its sheath. The only problem with the technique was the fact that, although not quite the equal of Brutus', the dagger was razor sharp on each edge. As the pirates had taught him to do, he clenched his teeth on the ridge that ran down the middle of the blade. Which kept his mouth safe from being widened into a smile that might stretch from ear to ear. His face was black, as were his arms, legs and clothing. As were the others'. And, indeed, as were those of the line of legionaries crawling out into no-man's-land behind them.

A low whistle made Artemidorus freeze. His *contubernium* and the legionaries supporting them had been warned against making any sound. And were relying on Antony's artillerymen to go about their business equally quietly. The whistle had come from one of Hirtius' men, therefore. He raised his head, scanning the stunted bushes. A black figure detached itself from the shadows in front of him, visible only as a darker shape in the darkness. Discernible only because it moved, slowly and stealthily, in a half crouch. Artemidorus waited without moving a muscle. A signal meant at least two *speculatores*, maybe more. And he wanted them all stopped. No one running back to camp and managing to raise the alarm. His patience was soon rewarded. Another figure rose into visibility. A third. A fourth. Hirtius' men were doing exactly what Artemidorus *contubernium* were doing. Just not quite as well. When he was certain that his spies would have seen their opponents, he moved. Like a lizard on a warm stone, he raised his right hand and took his dagger from between his teeth. Tensed his whole body, but especially his legs. As the enemy soldier came closer, still unaware that he was approaching danger, he rose up on his knees. The dagger went straight into the other man's belly, just beneath his breastbone, driving upwards to his heart. There was a flood of hot liquid over his hand. The dead man deflated like a bursting bladder. Collapsing silently. Artemidorus looked around. There was no longer any sign of the opposing spies; and, in a flash of movement, the line of his own agents vanished into the black undergrowth once again.

*

Just before dawn, safe in the knowledge that no enemy *speculatores* had penetrated their defences, Artemidorus led his *contubernium* back through the row of backup legionaries and into the silent bustle that was the artillery line. Only the larger torsion catapults had been moved – the *onagers* and *ballistae*, both capable of firing bolts – huge metal arrows – or rocks and stones. Or, as soon a surprise was no longer a vital element, burning barrels full of Greek Fire. If they had time they might employ the smaller, anti-personnel *scorpios* later, either swung round and pointed at Hirtius' men – or in their current position against Decimus Albinus when he sallied out to support his rescuers. But the plan was to start with the heavy artillery at dawn.

Artemidorus and his command reported to Enobarbus and then changed into the arms and armour recovered from Pansa's dead soldiers. 'You will not take part in the initial attack,' the tribune confirmed, fresh from Antony's final briefing. 'You are to think of yourselves exclusively as a Spartan *cryptaia* unit. Licensed to kill outside the normal rules of warfare. The general wants you to wait in the camp here and join in when Hirtius' and Caesar Octavius' troops overrun it. Going in behind the enemy as they come past, driving our men back. The Thirty-fifth Legion will take the brunt of the first retaliatory attack. Which is likely to be fierce, as the general is also bending the rules of war with this unexpected and undeclared artillery assault. They will fall back until the Second Sabines can support them. But it is vital that they retreat in good order while seeming to break and run. They will abandon this camp with a maximum of apparent confusion but a minimum of actual resistance. Just enough to make it look good and give you a chance to seek and destroy anyone in an obvious leadership role as discussed.

'The Fifth *Alaude*, Antony's Larks, will be commanded as usual by the general's brother Lucius. They will oversee the retreat up the *Via Aemilia*, which he and I have already scouted. Past Placentia and into the mountains if we make it. The plan is that Antony's army will simply vanish, leaving Hirtius, Caesar and Decimus Albinus – if they are still alive – in possession of an empty camp, the dead and any wounded who are too weak to move.

'If you do your work well, there will be further confusion among Hirtius and Caesar's men because many of their leaders and senior officers will be dead. You will then use the cover of this confusion to run south. Gretorex will leave you an *alae* wing of his best horses in the woods a *mile* south of here. And will be there to escort and guide you if he can. You should be able to reach Ventidius Bassus within three days. And get him to rendezvous with us by early *Maius* if he is still willing to keep his word. We'll be easy for you to follow and find. Antony has already agreed most of the route with Gretorex and the Gaulish cavalry who know the mountains – distantly if not intimately. All clear?'

'They'll be easy enough to follow if anything goes wrong,' said Ferrata after Enobarbus left. 'Because the *Via Aemilia* will just be one long line of dead Larks.'

ii

246

Artemidorus stood at the top of an east-facing watchtower, looking towards Hirtius' and Caesar's lines. The tower was part of the wooden wall of the palisade that marked the perimeter of Antony's camp. He was dressed in full armour with the identification badges of a centurion in the Martia legion. In Antony's camp behind him, the general's *haruspex* was sacrificing another white bull. Antony had already made it clear to the man that, no matter what he saw when he studied the beast's prophetic liver, he would pronounce the signs as positive. Today was going to be a good day no matter what the gods predicted. Artemidorus was put in mind of the *Ides* of *Mars* last year when *Divus Julius* also had paid no attention to what the gods were telling him. Or to what Artemidorus and his secret agents had discovered about the conspiracy against him, come to that. Which was why he was in Olympus now and they were all here. It was strange, thought the centurion, how the entire weight of history sometimes seemed to turn on one action or failure of action. Like a great gate turning on a hinge.

The centurion's dark reflective mood had several causes. The main one of which was Antony's order that he should kill his enemies while disguised as one of them. He knew well enough about Leonides' Spartan *cryptaia* special troops. Had he been living several hundred years in the past, he would probably have been one of them, running forward in secret to try and murder Xerxes in his tent the night before the Persians threw their army at Thermopylae. But he was uneasy about emulating them here and now. He could see Antony's reasoning, and the necessity for working outside the rules of war. A necessity dictated by the general's desperate situation and the increasingly effective machinations of Cicero in the Senate. There had been thirteen so-called Philippics so far – and no sign that they would stop, even though Antony was now officially an outlaw. But what he had been ordered to do – like the unannounced artillery bombardment which would be under way in almost no time now – seemed to the brooding spy to signal a change in Antony's character. The bluff, charming, inspirational leader – and occasional bellicose drunkard – was being replaced by someone much more cold and calculating. Someone more like Cassius.

Someone more like young Caesar Octavius.

'Well, Septem?' Quintus arrived at his side as he spoke. Recalling Artemidorus to himself and refocusing him on the scene he was looking down upon. 'When the enemy comes over – or through – this wall,' Quintus continued, 'I will be removing all the badges that identify me as a soldier in the Martia legion. I will fight as an anonymous legionary rather than go to war as a lie.'

'I was thinking of doing that as well,' said Artemidorus. 'We'll brief the others. But our targets remain the same. I will not betray the general's trust.'

247

'Neither will I. But I will not follow his orders either. Not in this.'

The two men stood side by side looking down and waiting. During the last few heartbeats of peace.

The whole battlefield between their lines and the enemy's was a milky lake of mist, just becoming visible in the gathering light of a spring dawn. The low fog heaved gently, like the surface of a calm sea, trapped between the stout wooden walls of Antony's lines and those of Hirtius. There, as here, a watchtower stood every hundred paces. Rearing above the milky surface like the *pharos* lighthouse of Alexandria. Manned, as this one was, with guards. Guards who must surely understand precisely what the mist concealed at any moment now. For the light was growing inexorably stronger as the sun approached the eastern horizon. But the horizon – and the sun – was behind the enemy, casting a darkening shadow that served to further conceal what was going on between the two camps.

From their vantage point it was just possible for Artemidorus and Quintus to see dark figures and angular constructions sunk deep within the undulating haze. But they could only tell what was actually there because they knew. In the distance, the artillery. Behind it, the ranks of *Legio XXXV*. Behind them, *Legio II Sabine*. Standing as silently as they had arrived. Ready. Waiting. To their right, down a slight incline, even deeper in the mist, Gretorex and his *alae* wing of five hundred cavalry. And Antony would be up on the *via* – on their left – with the rest of the cavalry as soon as the pre-battle rituals were completed. In the ditches along the roadway, Antony's slingers and archers waited for the enemy to show themselves.

The sun pushed its red disc up above the eastern horizon and the watchkeeper Antony had placed in the tower above the Temple of Apollo in Forum Gallorum gave the signal. And the battle commenced.

A cacophony of trumpet calls shattered the silence. Flames flared, making the vapour glow like a sea of molten gold. The artillery opened fire. Suddenly the mist's calm surface was torn by flight after flight of metal bolts, rocks and stones. The vague grey-brown wall of Hirtius' wooden palisade shivered and began to give way under an assault designed to shatter massive city walls. Distant concussions echoing back strangely out of time with the twangs and crashes of the launching. And with the sights of destruction as the missiles hit their targets. The watchtower opposite Artemidorus' was shattered with a rending *crash!* The men within it smashed to a red haze by a rock the size of an elephant flying faster than a pigeon. The next wave of iron bolts was followed by blazing barrels of Greek Fire. The smell of burning swept back towards them as the dawn wind began to stir.

During his boyhood in Greece, before he fell into the hands of Cilician pirates, Artemidorus had been brought up in the old-fashioned Spartan way. But in between the bouts of training he had managed to fit in many youthful adventures. One of which involved throwing a rock at a huge nest of enormous hornets he found hanging in a wild olive bush. The result of that experiment came into his memory now. As Hirtius' legions reacted to Antony's unannounced attack.

But, unlike the angry hornets, these legions did not boil out of their shattered camp and counter-attack as a cloud of individuals. Even as they ran out of their tents tightening their armour and settling their helmets, buckling their sword-belts and easing their *gladii* in their scabbards. They grabbed their *pilum* spears and *scutum* shields as they fell into their *contubernium* groups. Which coalesced into their cohorts as the *decanii* sergeants got them organised. Then the cohorts joined their centuries as the centurions arrived with the *signifer* standard bearers. These were with their legions in an astonishingly short time – even under the weight of Antony's unrelenting artillery fire. By the time his Thirty-fifth Legion had marched through the line of war machines and began to approach the enemy encampment, Hirtius' legions were almost ready to meet them, tribunes in place, *aquilifers* holding the legionary eagles high. The generals arrived then, attended by their legates and surrounded by the Praetorian Cohorts of their bodyguards. And all of them threw themselves into the battle.

Artemidorus and Quintus were joined by the rest of the *contubernium* then and they silently watched Antony's plan begin to unfold. Even Puella was dressed in armour covered with the identification marks of a Martia legionary, her face set, eyes narrow. With Mercury close behind her, his face hideously swollen, the line of his wound a red trench held closed with a network of black stitches. The pain must have been immense, thought Artemidorus. But the depth of his infatuation with the beautiful spy outweighed it. She had not trained for this as the men around her had and it was difficult to assess how she felt about being ordered to break almost all of the normal rules governing military combat. 'When the enemy breaks through and we go to work,' he shouted, raising his voice above the increasing din of battle, 'Quintus and I are going to remove all the badges that identify us as being members of their legions. We will fight as ordered. But not disguised as enemy soldiers.'

The others all nodded their agreement. Even Puella. And so the matter was settled.

iii

The Martia legion swept over Antony's artillery line soon after the mist cleared. And Hirtius' own men immediately set to swinging the machines into position so

249

that they could return the damage to Antony's lines. Not even the pincer-shaped intervention of the two cavalry wings could stop this. Although Antony and Gretorex appeared to be using all of their skill and power, they could not drive their enemies off the siege engines – or even do much to incapacitate them. They withdrew in apparent confusion. And the bolts, rocks and barrels of Greek Fire began to rain down on Antony's camp instead. Under cover of this fire, the Martia legion moved forward, sweeping the XXXVth before them. The IVth joined them, and it became immediately clear that Caesar Octavius had joined Hirtius on the battlefield. At the same time, the great gate of Mutina swung open and Decimus Albinus led his men out onto the *Via Aemilia* in a full charge. Twelve full legions were now engaged on the Senate's side. And those under Antony's command were showing every sign of crumbling. Sensing victory already, the three columns of the Senate's legions swung towards Antony's encampment where the last of his forces seemed to be trapped with their camp-followers, slaves and wounded. The three generals, Albinus, Hirtius and Caesar Octavius, their legates and Praetorian bodyguards were to the fore. Where the danger was greatest. But also where the chances of glory were the highest. Of fabulous rewards from a grateful Senate. And of political advancement to ultimate power.

*

'Here they come,' called Artemidorus. He threw the dead Martia centurion's identification badges on the ground, drew his sword, gripped his shield and prepared for battle. This was cut-and-thrust warfare. The disciplined lines of legionaries had broken up. In this section of the battlefield at least. Some soldiers still carried their shields but they had all thrown their *pila* spears and were using their *gladii* swords now. They came boiling through the ruined palisade as the last of the XXXVth and Second Sabine Legions fell back, still fighting fiercely, hand to hand.

In this sort of situation, the *contubernium* of spies had a distinct edge. More than one, in fact. Their opponents did not see them immediately as enemies, for they wore no legionary identification badges. They were in a tight group, offering protection and support to each other – while the units of Caesar Octavius' army had split up long ago – or been whittled down by death. They were using the arrowhead formation they had used in Smyrna. But this time most of them carried shields as well as swords. The spies were fresh and focused. Their opponents exhausted and caught in the confusion of battle. That being said, Septem's little command was still thrusting itself into the middle of a battlefield. And there was no guarantee of protection – even from the gods who were appealed to by the

250

good-luck charms. Which were the only additions to the dead men's armour they did not throw away.

Artemidorus had chosen their battleground carefully, however. They were fighting inside Antony's camp which gave them several more elements that might be to their advantage. They knew the lie of the land. Every alley between every tent. Those still standing at least. Between all the supply wagons that were still left. Where the wounded were. Where the general's command tent was. A list of advantages that meant they were likely to be safe from slings and arrows which would be difficult to deploy in the cramped space. They could be sure their feet would not be snagged by unexpected guy ropes or slip on unseen areas of mud. That, if the worst came to the worst, they knew where the best hiding places could be found nearby. That it would be difficult for anyone to bring much in the way of cavalry in here. Especially Praetorian cavalry – those bodyguard units that the leaders of the armies needed to surround themselves with. And yet the three generals might well need to come in here themselves. Even if they weren't looking for Antony himself, they would want to know what he had left in his command tent, which, as with most other commanders, he shared with his *quaestor* paymaster general. In the way of expensive personal items. Gold. Coin. Battle tactics. Escape plans.

The *contubernium* of spies started out in their tight arrowhead wedge therefore. Artemidorus in the lead with his left side protected by his *scutum*, Quintus with his shield on his left – and Puella left-handed on his right shoulder – *gladius* in her right hand, a sharp-edged cavalry spada instead of a shield in her left, Ferrata and Kyros on theirs, Kyros also with a *spada* instead of a *scutum*; Hercules and Mercury at the rear. Though Artemidorus was as unsure of controlling the lovesick messenger as Pansa had been of controlling the Martia legion.

The first soldiers they met were the retreating Thirty-fifth Legion, and it was immediately obvious that removing the enemy legion badges had been a good idea. For the moment at least. Antony's men were happy to retreat past them without getting involved in more sword-play. And when the next wave of his army came past there were even men from the old disbanded VIIth who recognised Artemidorus and Quintus. And from the VIth who recognised Ferrata. But the spurious peace could not last long. As Antony's men worked their way back through the camp towards the northern arm of the *Via Aemilia* and the Vth *Alae* who were controlling it under Lucius' command, so the first of their opponents arrived. The spies' orders were clear – focus on the generals and their senior officers. And yet, at first at least, they had to deal with ordinary soldiers from the Martia and the IVth who were drunk with bloodlust and keen to slaughter anyone

251

they came across. Especially after the way they had been attacked without warning. Subjected to an artillery barrage while in their beds believing themselves still protected by a truce. But bloodlust, like drunkenness, adds to self-confidence while undermining ability. The first soldier who threw himself at Artemidorus raised his *gladius* as though it was a sharp-edged cavalry *spada*. And raised his chin as he did so. The spy's *gladius* stabbed straight through the exposed throat and the entire *contubernium* were blooded by the result.

iv

Artemidorus' focus closed down after that. There was no more strategy; no more overall view. As he had observed to Quintus long ago – the first thing that died in a battle was the plan. This battle became one duel to the death after another. And he slowly became less and less aware of the men and woman fighting at his back as Caesar Octavius' legions swept into Antony's camp, already scenting victory. Single opponents became groups that challenged the tight squad of the *contubernium*. But there was always that fatal hesitation as the Senate's men took a second look at the anonymous oncoming soldiers.

Then, behind the increasing numbers of legionaries, the senior officers began to appear. And the work of cutting their way through became harder. Artemidorus felt the tight structure of the *contubernium* begin to unravel as he found himself face to face with a grim centurion who might have been his own reflection. Quintus and Puella, then each of the others in turn also became involved in a personal conflict. Artemidorus defeated the centurion in the end by using a gladiator's trick – letting go of his *scutum*, going down on one knee and driving the point of his sword past the edge of his opponent's shield under the studded leather apron of his armour and into the top of his inner thigh. Destroying the tendons that kept the man upright and opening the femoral artery – which bled out in half a dozen heartbeats while he floundered helplessly in the rust-coloured mud.

As Artemidorus leaned on his shield and pulled himself to his feet, he saw the first horse. Which was a telltale sign that there were senior officers close by. Only Praetorian guards amongst the enemy would be riding horses into this restricted killing ground. And even then only to protect the men whose bodyguards they were. He glanced back and beckoned to the others to re-form on him. Half a dozen heartbeats later they were back in that tight wedge, and Artemidorus was back in the hunt for the enemy leaders as ordered.

Where the generals were in relation to their standards and their eagles would vary from man to man. Some, like *Divus Julius* and Antony, liked to be in the thick of things – on horse or on foot – close to their standard and the eagle of their favourite legion so they set the sort of an example men would fight and die to

252

follow. Others preferred to hold back. Take a more considered view. This was Brutus' style of leadership. Also, sometimes, Cassius'. And, apparently, Caesar Octavius'. There were even generals who used common soldiers who resembled them as doubles on the battlefield, sending the stand-in to the front line while hanging back themselves. Men who fought like this rarely progressed far – either as commanders or as politicians. But the whole point was that, even in the noise and confusion of battle, with soldiers and horses from either side charging this way and that, the eagles and the standards stood tall, offering rallying points to the men on one side. Offering targets to the men on the other.

The first standard Artemidorus saw was Decimus Albinus'. Which seemed as logical as any argument in Aristotle's *Analytics*. After so many months of siege and humiliation, Decimus must want Antony's head as much as Antony wanted his. Artemidorus began to hack and stab his way towards it, hurling himself at rank after rank of enemy soldiers as though he and his companions were a bolt from a *ballista*. Their opponents became more and more challenging the closer they came to Albinus' standard. Thin and half starved they might be. But they were also desperate. Agonisingly aware of the alternatives before them – victory, starvation or death. Well led, they had used the time of their imprisonment behind Mutina's walls, to train and train for this very moment. And, like any sensible leader, Albinus surrounded himself with his best soldiers – not even counting his special Praetorian Cohorts.

Then, in the blink of an eye, the stakes of the game escalated. Artemidorus found himself confronted by a tight-knit group similar to his own. And it was led by Decimus Albinus' right-hand man legate, Senator and murderer of *Divus Julius*, Pontius Aquila. Aquila did not hesitate as many of his soldiers had done, for he was not looking at the spy's armour. He was looking him in the face. And he recognised the man who had delivered the deceitful message that almost got his legions wiped out a week ago. The eyes beneath that one long eyebrow narrowed. The lips thinned back from yellow teeth in a snarl that would have done credit to a wolf. Aquila threw himself forward and his men all came with him. Like Antony's soldiers, they were covered in the blood of the men they had slaughtered already. Unlike Artemidorus' little command, they were backed up by a complete army. And, by the look of things, by a wing of cavalry from Hirtius' or Caesar Ocatavius' command.

As their leaders' shields slammed together, so each arrowhead spread out until there was another line of hand-to-hand duels being fought in the middle of the mayhem. Both the centurion and the legate were too well trained and expert to leave themselves open to the classic upthrust their *gladius* swords were designed for. They were equally matched in size and strength, though the spy had some advantage in being the less exhausted of the two. Aquila, however, was incandescent with rage and burning to exact revenge. So every thrust was parried, every cut countered. Even as they were jostled by the duels being fought on either side of them.

Artemidorus fought almost mechanically, his mind detached, assessing his opponent's strengths, which were many, and his weaknesses which were few. Then he began to go through the catalogue of feints and tricks that had kept him alive in the arena, and eventually earned him *Rudiarius*, and the wooden sword of honourable retirement.

Little by little he began to give ground. Moving back as though weakening under Pontius Aquila's onslaught. Keeping his focus flickering between Aquila's eyes and his *gladius*. The sword strokes started coming more swiftly as the enemy scented victory. The expression in the narrow eyes showed no suspicion. Showed nothing but gathering triumph. Aquila really thought he was winning. That he was within heartbeats of killing this enemy spy who had fooled him and his general and nearly destroyed them both. But he was mistaken.

As soon as he was free of the jostling line of one-on-one duels and had a momentary space on his left, Artemidorus let go of his shield and threw it aside. In the same movement, he snatched the *pugio* out of its sheath with his empty left hand as he stepped forward, smashing his breastplate against Aquila's shield. Disregarding the shock and pain. The legate was too surprised to think of pushing back.

Instead, perfectly trained in legionary sword-play as he was, he drove his *gladius* upward. But even as he did so, Artemidorus stepped inside the blow so the blade slid past his ribs and missed him altogether. Their faces were so close that Artemidorus could smell the rank breath of the starving man as it came through clenched teeth over the top of his *scutum*. Could look deep into his narrowed eyes beneath the ridge of his helmet and the one long line of his brow, savouring the confusion dawning in them.

'*Vale, interfector!* Goodbye assassin!' He spat.

Then he drove the dagger in his left fist unerringly into Aquila's right ear. Burying it to the hilt in his skull. Jerking it out and stepping back. As the dead man stood there for an instant longer, unaware that his battle was lost and his life was over.

'*Septem!*' bellowed a huge voice, and a leg clad in checked material astride a horse appeared as if by magic. A *spada* flashed down. And the murderer's head, already assaulted by the spy's *pugio*, was chopped in half. Gretorex' blade sliced through the crown of Aquila's helmet past the eye-ridge and split the face beneath it. For the first and last time in his existence Pontius Aquila had two eyebrows. Separated by the cavalry commander's sword-blade as it sat bizarrely on the bridge of the dead man's nose.

As Gretorex jerked the *spada* free, Aquila's body toppled backwards beneath the stamping hooves of the Gaulish cavalry horse. And the already bifurcated face was crushed out of existence in an instant as it was trampled into the thick red mud.

All Artemidorus could think of as he sheathed his *pugio*, retrieved his shield and returned to the battle, was how angry Antony was going to be. Pontius Aquila was the second of *Divus Julius'* assassins to die. And the general still didn't have a clearly identifiable head that he could spike in the Forum.

V

Gretorex wasn't here by accident. 'Septem!' he bellowed again. 'We've been looking for you! Follow!'

Artemidorus glanced along the line of his *contubernium*. Those who hadn't settled matters personally had been helped by the unexpected arrival of the cavalry. Aquila and his bodyguard were all dead. 'Form on me!' he bellowed, his voice almost as loud as Gretorex'. Then, 'Where?' he called to the *decurio* cavalry commander as they fell into the familiar arrowhead formation behind him. Speeded and protected by parallel lines of Gaulish horsemen, they ran through the battlefield. Across the wreck of Antony's camp.

Gretorex answered, but the only word Artemidorus understood was, 'Hirtius!'

Gretorex and his men took them unerringly to where the fighting was most intense. A section of the battlefield which seemed unnaturally well endowed with standards and eagles. Most of which were those of Antony's enemies. And Artemidorus could see at once why Gretorex had called for him. The most intense fighting was on the entire width of the *via* itself. Where the three attacking armies were thrust up hard against the steely hearts of the IInd Sabines and the Vth *Alaude* whose duty was to guard the road as an escape route for the rest of Antony's army. Under the immediate command of another ex-gladiator, Antony's brother Lucius. Thousands of men had died here – their corpses filling the roadside ditches and flooding out onto the fields beyond. The stones of the roadway were icily slick with blood and a range of other fluids. It was hard enough for men to stand. A slimy deathtrap for horses.

And yet, there in the centre of it all were the eagles of the IVth and the Martia, as well as Hirtius' personal standard. It was clear that the Larks and the Sabines were fighting a solid defensive rearguard action. They were holding the line as

255

they slowly retreated. And the line stretched from one corpse-filled ditch to the other. There was no sign of the dashing Antony's maxim that the best form of defence is attack. The axiom Artemidorus had in mind himself when advising Antony several days since. But, he thought now, he and his *contubernium* had been specifically designed and detailed by Antony to make up for his legions' orders. In the face of two legions falling back and twelve legions pushing forward, the six soldiers of his *contubernium* were under orders to attack. At all times. Under every circumstance. Like Leonides' *cryptaia*.

Which was precisely what they were going to do now.

As Gretorex and his *alae* peeled away, Artemidorus led his command across the ditch, treading lightly but uneasily on the solidly packed bodies of the dead and dying. The roadway itself was crammed solid with soldiers. Two straight lines of legionaries stood shield to shield across it, fighting in the old style. As the Senate's army pressed relentlessly forward – and Antony's men slowly gave ground. Because of that measured retreat, the roadway was jammed. No one was going anywhere at any speed. The Senate's legions were packed tight but effectively held almost still. And in the midst of them, hemmed in and with apparently nowhere to go, were the Praetorian horsemen whose primary duty was to protect Hirtius and Caesar Octavius. Whose standards waved beside the eagles of their legions.

The spies attacked from the side just behind the foremost line of Martia legionaries but ahead of the hard men of the *triarii* line. Here was where the generals and their senior officers could most often be found. Just behind the first lines, confident that their men would dull the edge of the opposing legions. Surrounded by their own Praetorian bodyguards. Backed up by the solid *triarii*. And yet up with the standards, cheek by jowl with the eagles. Where the glory was.

Artemidorus put his professional conscience away. He had to. It seemed to him that the surprised legionaries he slaughtered before they even had a chance to turn and face him were dying outside the rules of civilised combat he was being ordered to disregard. If the idea of civilised combat was something that had ever really existed – beyond the stories of his Spartan childhood. Which, oddly, had failed to say much about the *cryptaia* and their licence to kill. And yet, as ever, there was the larger picture. He understood all too well that if he failed here – if the *contubernium* failed here – then Antony's plan might also fail. And the fate of the empire as he understood it would turn once again. Like a great gate on a hinge.

He felt some empathy for the men he was slaughtering in this almost underhand manner. And, in a strange way that he was never able to understand, he also felt a kind of sympathy for the horses. As though they too were enemy soldiers he was attacking unfairly. The Praetorians sat on them almost uselessly. They were grouped around their generals, but were otherwise trapped and held helpless by the press of legionaries around them on the *via*. They could not deploy themselves as Gretorex and his *alae* could – or Antony and his cavalry wing. There was no space for them to charge. Nor opportunity to do so. Nor surface safe enough to allow it.

Instead, as Artemidorus slashed the last legionary away and came up against the first Praetorian mount, he took immediate and fatal action. Shield raised in case the rider was quick thinking enough to slash down with his *spada* as Gretorex had just done to Aquila. Aware that it would be unlikely – he was coming in from the rider's left – the shield side, not the sword side. Without pausing, just as he had done with the nameless centurion, he went low and stabbed inwards with his *gladius*. He had no idea of the names of the muscles or tendons he was severing in the horse's foreleg – nor of the veins and arteries lying beneath them. But he knew that if he was fast enough and had a long enough reach he could extend his arm beneath the horse's chest and sever the tendons and muscles of its far foreleg. The horse would collapse at once. Falling away from Artemidorus. Pitching its rider to the ground in the middle of a cavalry melee. And, as likely as not, knocking the rider off the horse beside it. Two men down at once – and with any luck, killed or crippled beneath the falling bodies and plunging hooves of their mounts. While, focused on their leader and quick thinking as ever, the rest of the *contubernium* were soon doing the same.

The first horse's chest and belly swelled like a brown barrel above him as he drove inwards. The stench of blood was momentarily replaced by the warm scent of the stable. Then his *gladius* reached its target. Point first, but also relying on the sharpness of the edge, he drove the blade through the brown column of the horse's far foreleg. Watching in something like horror as the gash exploded in a welter of blood and the thin line of the wound yawned the moment the muscles and tendons separated. The leg simply collapsed. And the horse toppled sideways away from him. Exactly as planned. And the five horses behind it did exactly the same as the rest of the *contubernium* struck.

As they realised what was going on, the Praetorians reacted. Not by turning their horses' heads towards their attackers. Something they could not do in any case because of the wall of crippled, dying horseflesh between them. Instead, they turned their horses' heads away and retreated as best they could across the road packed with legionaries and the corpse-filled ditch beyond it. Into the field where the battle beneath Forum Gallorum had been fought six days ago. But as they did this, the horsemen spread panic and confusion among the foot soldiers surrounding them. Regardless of rank or importance.

Running through the line of screaming, thrashing horses, dispatching as many of the animals and their fallen riders as they could on the way, Artemidorus' *contubernium* fell upon the mayhem left in the wake of the fleeing cavalry like the Friendly Ones themselves. But almost immediately, Artemidorus raised his right hand, sword dripping and steaming in his fist. The five men and one woman behind him ceased their slaughter. Looked around at the chaos on the blood-slick roadway and wondered what was going on now.

vi

Artemidorus found himself confronted by a sight he had never even dreamed that he would see. The uncontrolled retreat of the mounted Praetorians had caused total chaos. There were legionaries of all sorts and ranks lying hurt and dying on the roadway. Who had been knocked aside by the armoured breasts of the fleeing horses. Who had slipped and been trampled as they tried to run out of the way. Who were endeavouring to pull themselves up on the red-running icy slickness even now.

A standard bearer lay on his side amid the corpses filling the farther ditch. Still alive and fighting to find his feet and raise his standard. Beside him, face-up on the roadway, staring at the sky with lifeless eyes, the owner of the standard. Consul and General Aulus Hirtius. Whether he had been thrown from a horse or trampled as he fought on foot, the spy would never know. Beside him, face-down with the back of his helmet crushed, the *Aquila* eagle bearer of the Martia legion.

As the stunned centurion began to register the utter havoc he and his command had caused, he saw a slight figure begin to pull itself out from among the dead men packed in the ditch between the Martia legion's eagle and General Hirtius' standard. Even as a kind of horrified recognition began to dawn, his attention was claimed by something else. A flash of movement. There, on the far side of the ditch full of dead men, stood Decimus Albinus himself. Frozen. Staring with a terrible intensity at the slender figure dragging itself erect. As though in the grip of utter drunkenness – like Antony on the night of Caesar's murder when Cleopatra left for Alexandria – the slim, blood-covered figure reeled onto the roadway. When Artemidorus looked again, Decimus Albinus was gone. Leaving the lone legionary to his fate.

By the grace of the gods, the young soldier's unsteady footsteps did not slip. He staggered to the fallen eagle and tried to pick it up. But the dead *aquilifer* had lashed the pole to his body. The slim figure pulled out his *pugio* and cut it free with a couple of deft slashes. Then, clutching both the pole and the dagger in his

258

left hand, using the eagle's pole as a crutch to steady himself, he limped over to Hirtius' dead body. Stooped, reached down and took a grip on the top of the dead man's breastplate. Clearly planning to pull the general out of the battle to some place where his corpse could be treated with the respect it deserved.

Seeing what was happening – and who was watching events narrow-eyed, smoking sword in hand, with five equally fearsome companions at his back – the nearest of Hirtius' soldiers fell back, wide-eyed and silent. The soldier holding the eagle, unaware of the scrutiny, pulled at the dead general's armour but slipped on the ice-slick road and fell to his knees once more.

Driven by motivation he did not understand. That he would never understand. In the grip, perhaps, of the will of the gods themselves, Artemidorus moved forward at last, sheathing his *gladius*. He reached down and took Hirtius' breastplate at the throat. Heaved the corpse into a half-sitting position so he could be moved more easily. Leaned it against the belly of a dead horse as he reached down once again. Took the free hand of the young man fighting to pull himself upright on the Martia's eagle standard. Dragged him to his feet as he spoke.

'Take care Caesar,' he said, his voice carrying in a sudden, breathless silence. 'With Hirtius dead and Pansa so badly wounded, you have the command of these eight legions in your grasp. You're doing well for someone only nineteen summers old. But I'd advise you not to slip again.'

The battered, boyish face split into a weary grin. 'Cicero says it. You do it, Septem. What did he declare? *Laudandus, ornandus, tollendus.* You've elevated me, congratulated me. What comes next? Exterminate me?'

Even had he wished to answer Caesar's question, Artemidorus got no opportunity to do so. Agrippa and Rufus appeared with the re-formed Praetorians then, crowding into a threatening line of cavalry just beyond the ditch full of corpses.

'It's all right,' called Caesar. 'My friend Septem and I were just discussing jokes and gifts.' He swung the eagle so that the dagger was clearly displayed, held in his grip against the standard's pole. 'Antony never sent me this pugio, did he? You did.'

'That's right, Caesar.' The spy was too weary to lie. 'I thought a conciliatory gesture would help you both come to an understanding.'

'But it *is* the dagger Brutus used to kill my father *Divus Julius*?'

'It is, Caesar. I swear it on my life.'

'Even though Cicero says Brutus brought it dripping from the murder?'

'Even so…'

'Then we will all have a settling of debts. Brutus and I. Antony and I. You and I. But not today. Today I have other work to do. Other accounts to settle. Which, I must admit, you have managed to bring to my mind with your typically clear analysis of my position. There are some horses over there that you left uninjured. Take them and go.'

*

The six of them took three uninjured horses from the pandemonium they had created on the *Via Aemilia* and rode two-to-a-horse back the way they had come. Off the roadway, over the corpse-filled ditch and onto that part of the battlefield Gretorex and his men had guided them through.

It was quieter now. For the XXXVth, the Sabines and the Larks had vanished from the burning wreck of Antony's camp. Leaving only dead and dying in their wake. Pansa's legions and now Hirtius' were leaderless, rudderless. Unopposed. With nowhere to go. Caesar's legions hardly more focused or motivated, for the moment. Decimus Albinus' starved soldiers had reached the end of their strength. Some of them, no doubt, looking at the dead horses. Their mouths watering. No one tried to stop three mounts carrying six assorted legionaries as they galloped south out of the battlefield, past the walking wounded and the deserters. Down to a grove of trees where six strong cavalry horses were waiting to carry them south to Arretium.

And, when they arrived there, they discovered not only the promised mounts but also Gretorex and his *alae* cavalry wing. 'Ah, Septem, you have survived! And your *cryptaia* suicide squad into the bargain. All still alive. I am surprised but very pleased. Well done all of you!' boomed the Gaulish decurion and legate to the general. 'Antony asked us to look after you if you managed to make it this far. He's worried you might have become tired out by your exertions today. So he wants us to take you south and make sure you get safely to General Publius Ventidius Bassus. And the three legions he has promised to take to Antony.'

XV

'This is it,' said Antony. 'The end of the road.'

'You can say that again,' grated his brother Lucius.

And Enobarbus nodded his silent agreement.

Their horses whinnied softly, tossing their heads and shifting their hooves, as though overcome by their situation. And the enormity of what confronted them.

Behind them the *Alaude* legion, the Sabines, the XXXVth, what was left of the Gaulish cavalry with Gretorex away, Antony's Praetorian Cohorts together with bits and pieces of the VIth and VIIth, all stretched in a line almost as far back as Castra Torinorum. The last camp on the *Via Aemilia*. Where they had overnighted. And finalised the plans that had brought them here to this desolate place. The end of the road indeed. Almost, it seemed, the edge of the empire. The end of the world.

Ahead of them reared the Alps. Green-grey and white capped. Like the fangs of some unimaginable wolf trying to tear the throat out of the stormy sky. A bitter wind whirled down off the peaks, cutting into them like cold steel. They sat astride their nervous horses at the mouth of a valley which wound into the mountains, vanishing out of sight all too swiftly between the sheer slopes of interlocking spurs. Which filled their vision almost as far as they could see on either hand. And even when looking up towards the low, scudding overcast. There was a river flowing out of the sheer-sided valley, steel grey, swollen by spring rains and early run-off from the lower ice fields. But there was no road. No path. Not even any track. Only the desolate slopes gathering into rocky scree and absolute precipice before them.

'Are you sure about this, Antony?' asked Lucius.

Antony gave his great, booming laugh. 'Look, Lucius,' he said, his voice echoing back from the mountains and carrying down the roadway to the men behind, borne on that bitter wind. Full of cheerful virility and utter self-confidence. 'Haven't you read your Polybius? This is where Hannibal crossed! If some Punic general could get over these mountains a couple of hundred years ago with a bunch of Carthaginians and thirty bloody great elephants, then I can do it with an army which is mostly composed of Larks!'

*

And, thought Enobarbus with a secret smile as they began to move forward into the jaws of the trackless valley, most of an *alae* cavalry wing composed almost entirely of Gauls – who know their way around these mountains pretty well. Who are also related to half the Alleborge *barbari* who still guarded the passes.

Last night's meeting had made Antony's plans and the reasoning behind them very clear. The death of Hirtius gave them a considerable breathing space. Even if Pansa was still alive. Which Antony maintained was unlikely. As he was certain he'd inflicted the fatal wound himself. The one remaining consul was in no condition to lead an army in pursuit. If he was dead, then the Senate would almost certainly order Caesar Octavius to hand over the consular legions to the command of Decimus Albinus. Who was, according to Cicero, an experienced and capable commander. On the assumption that Albinus would come after Antony like Nemesis.

'I can't see Caesar doing that,' Enobarbus said. 'I don't know him as well as Septem does, but we've talked over his likely actions and reactions to a range of scenarios at briefings of our *contubernium*. The Senate has been made very nervous by the general's actions as we know. As I have seen – and as Lucius Piso keeps reporting. Consequently Cicero has been pleading that they grant *Imperium* to Caesar Octavius as well as to Hirtius and Pansa. Because the old man is still certain he can control the young man like a puppet and get rid of him if he gets too big for them to manage easily. Maybe grant him a gold statue or something of the sort to keep him quiet in the meantime. Then when his usefulness is at an end, the Catiline approach – a bowstring round the throat one night. You heard the joke he made. Everyone has. "*Adolescens laudandus, ornandus, tollendus* – He's a young man we can congratulate, elevate, exterminate."

'The Senate has done what Cicero advises on this assurance. But Cicero is wrong. They all are. Look at it from Caesar's point of view. He's been given powers no ordinary nineteen-year-old could ever dream of. He has four legions of his own – which will become eight now that Hirtius is dead. And probably twelve if Pansa goes too. Which will follow him to Hades if he asks. Not only for the pay he offers them but also because of his name – *Caesar*! The only thing he lacks to take absolute power is a consulship. He's not going to hand all that back.

'No. Pansa will die if he's not dead already. The Senate will tell Caesar Octavius to give his armies to Albinus so that Albinus can pursue us. He will refuse. He may come up with some excuse – he can't control the legions any better than Pansa; they won't work with one of *Divus Julius'* assassins – some such. But he will refuse. Albinus will hesitate. The general will escape, and we will escape with him. Caesar Octavius will demand a consulship as the price of stopping us.

Something he can afford to do. Because he will be the only *imperator* with a serious army left in Italy. Only when he gets that assurance will he think of joining Decimus Albinus and coming after us.'

'There!' said Antony. 'That is the whole point of maintaining a *contubernium* of spies and secret agents – so that they can come up with an analysis that agrees precisely with what I want to hear! Well done, Tribune! Keep up the good work!'

Enobarbus smiled and allowed the gust of laughter to pass.

'And, don't forget, General, although they seem to have missed Caesar Octavius himself, Septem and his spies were, it is reported, intimately involved in the deaths of Hirtius and Pontius Aquila. And if anyone can get Ventidius Bassus with his three legions to you, it is Septem. Who, may I remind you brought you Trebonius' head as ordered, and has sworn to bring you Decimus Albinus' head as well.'

ii

Publius Ventidius Bassus was a hard man. A balding, square-faced, square-bodied soldier. With short, thick legs and the arms of a blacksmith. A down-to-earth no-nonsense leader. He had been one of Caesar's closest associates, in spite of his unusual birth and background. A commoner who had been taken prisoner as a child and paraded in chains at a triumph; a slave who had sold mules to make a living before joining the army as a common legionary and working his way up by sheer merit. Who in time had become one of Caesar's most able and reliable commanders. Campaigning with him in Gaul and Britain as well as against Pompey.

And becoming a close friend of Antony's into the bargain. Antony who, typically – and almost uniquely in the snobbish, patrician Senate – saw the soldier not the slave; the man and not the mule-seller. Artemidorus, also the result of a chequered career, also saw the man. Bassus, in return, saw how vital the secret agent's work could be – and how much more useful a properly organised military intelligence unit might become in the future. Not to mention a full-blown secret service. Consequently, the pair of them had always got along very well.

Bassus welcomed them to his camp in Arretium, one hundred and fifty *miles* south of Mutina through the trackless Apennine mountains, therefore, when they arrived three hard-riding days after the battle. Just as Antony was entering the mouth of that valley three hundred and fifty *miles* north. And taking the first steps of his epic journey across the Alps.

The Greek centurion and secret agent knew the route that Antony proposed to adopt. The Gaulish cavalry commander knew the best way to follow their general across the mountains to Governor Lepidus' province of Gallia Narbonensis. The

263

widely experienced general of three legions knew how vital it would be to bring more than just his men with him. And to that end he had begun to assemble supplies of everything an army on the move though harsh and hostile country might require. But carts and cattle, sheep and supply wagons, goats and grain transports all travel slowly. And Antony, as ever, was in a hurry. So there was a delicate balance to be struck. Which the *contubernium*, the Gaulish legate, General Bassus and his senior officers debated far into the night. Before setting out at dawn next day.

*

One of the many benefits of taking the coast roads from Arretium rather than going back north through the Apennines, Artemidorus thought on the afternoon of the second day, was the fact that it was the quickest route from the north-west section of Cisalpine Gaul to Rome. It was, therefore, the route by which the governor of that province, finally marching his legions in pursuit of Antony, chose to communicate with the Senate.

Decimus Albinus' messenger sat, his face flushed with outrage, on the ground beside his horse. Tied hand and foot. With Gretorex' *spada* sword uncomfortably close to his throat. Artemidorus broke the seal of the message tube, unrolled the papyrus scroll it contained and glanced at the contents. Which weren't even in code.

'Decimus Albinus sends greetings to his friend Marcus Tullius Cicero and the Senate,' he paraphrased. Glancing up at his audience – which consisted of his *contubernium* as well as General Bassus and his senior officers. 'The governor expresses great concern at the situation in which he finds himself and lists a series of complaints as the cause. First, that Marcus Aemilius Lepidus, Governor of Gallia Narbonensis, is apparently hesitant about stopping Antony should Antony succeed in crossing the Alps. A disappointment paralleled, secondly and thirdly, by Albinus' mistrust of both Governors Plancus in Transalpine Gaul and Pollio in Further Spain. Compounded, fourthly and perhaps most importantly, by Caesar Octavius' continued refusal to lend him any of the legions he now commands as a result of the deaths of both Consuls Hirtius and latterly Pansa.'

Artemidorus paused, glanced round, added – speaking slowly. Giving what he was saying added weight. 'A note here adds the observation that Pansa's *quaestor* second in command suspects that Pansa may not have died as a result of his wound but because he has been poisoned. The physician Glycon is suspected. And, it is observed, Caesar Octavian visited the ailing Pansa on the night he was found dead.

'As a result, Governor Albinus, with the legions from Mutina, still weak and half starved though they are, will pursue Antony alone and unsupported…

'Ah! Now this is very interesting too. Apparently Albinus has also received word that Antony's friend General Publius Ventidius Bassus is on the move. He has asked Caesar Octavius whether, as he refuses to pursue Antony, he would consider cutting off General Bassus' legions if they come north. He assesses that Caesar is unlikely to do this either. Therefore he will take his own legions through Castra Torinorum and perhaps as far south as Genua in the hope of coming across Bassus himself. Even so, he concludes hopefully, his legions should easily outmatch the ones Antony currently commands. If and when he catches up with him...'

Bassus gave a great bellow of laughter, reminding the spy irresistibly of Antony himself. 'Well, now we know where Albinus will be, we'll make sure we're somewhere else. That way when it comes right down to it we're still going to come as an unpleasant surprise to the snivelling little back-stabber!'

iii

'Here?' said Ventidius Bassus incredulously three days later. 'He went in *here*?'

'That was the plan, General,' Artemidorus assured him. 'If anyone's to blame its Polybius the Historian. Antony's taken his description of Hannibal crossing the Alps as a personal challenge.'

'But it's a *desertum* wilderness. No tracks to follow. Nothing to scavenge! And you said he had no supplies with him. Hardly anything at all to eat or drink. And, what, three thousand men? Maybe more?' General Bassus shook his head in wonder and disbelief. 'How long did he calculate it would take to get across?'

'Apparently Hannibal took sixteen days to come the opposite way,' said the spy. 'And he had thirty elephants. The general believes he can do it in two of *Divus Julius'* new weeks. Maybe less.'

'Well, we'd better get after him then. Gretorex. Is there a way round? Or do we just have to follow in his footsteps and hope we can catch up?' Bassus had already discussed the danger of coming up against the rear of Antony's army on a path too narrow to allow overtaking.

'General Antony is following the most direct route,' answered the Gaulish legate. 'But if we strike south, there, I can take you to a lower pass. The route is longer but we may be able to move more swiftly. And your men are fresher, fitter and better supplied. Then, after the lower pass we can swing north again and meet Antony as he descends into Gallia Narbonensis. Just in case Governor Lepidus decides he wants to side with Cicero after all.'

'Very well. The legions are all briefed and prepared. We will follow your longer but swifter route. Lead on.'

265

Artemidorus and the *contubernium*, now more or less part of Gretorex' *alae*, went with the Gaulish leader as he rode into the valley. The spy had no difficulty in seeing the tracks left by Antony's legions as they followed the right-hand bank. But as the mountain slopes closed around them and the light dimmed in the valley foot, Gretorex led them across a section of the river where it ran wide and shallow to the left bank. After a *mile* or so, a smaller, tributary valley led off southward, and soon the route taken by Antony and his legions was left far behind.

They camped the first night in a pine forest. The trees broke the power of the wind while the pines scented the restless air. The wild scent of the great black forests of northern Gaul and Germania. Not the civilised aroma of Roman pines. But the ground was made soft by layers of pine needles and the pinecones made good kindling for the legionaries' cooking-fires. Bassus was a strong disciplinarian and he liked to do things according to military tradition, but, accepting Gretorex' assurances of absolute safety from local tribes, he did not insist that the legions build a palisaded perimeter. Though he set extra guards. Protection against wolves, bears, lynx and other predators.

The next day took them slowly higher and the third higher still. Until the forests at last gave way to great grey-green meadows. The route was not hard to follow, though as they climbed higher, some of the men began to find it more difficult to breathe. Two further days took them out of the meadows and into the snow fields. Where the challenge of breathing went hand in hand with that of keeping warm – particularly at night. For the nights were crystal clear and icily cold, the chill of the altitude outweighing the gathering warmth of spring. The stars so huge and low that it was only the difference in colour that distinguished them from the legions' campfires.

iv

Enobarbus crouched at the top of the cliff, gasping for breath. He was so high that he really felt that if he stood erect and stretched his hands up he would be able to touch the sky. Or the clouds at least. Behind him was the slope he had just scaled, coming at it crabwise from a good way back along the path that Antony and the rest of his command were following. The tribune had read his Polybius and knew that this was one of the points at which the local tribes nearly brought the Carthaginian invasion to an abrupt end by raining rocks down upon Hannibal's army. If this was indeed the path that Hannibal took – something that was still open to debate. Everywhere but in Antony's mind apparently. And there were rocks piled nearby. Large, rounded boulders which could never have arrived here naturally. Indeed, the whole slope was dotted with great grey rocks of various sizes. Apparently left ready to resupply anyone rolling those nearest over the edge.

Enobarbus glanced over his shoulder. He had a disturbing feeling that he was being watched and wished for a moment that he had brought a bodyguard of Gaulish warriors with him. But the locals were apparently friendly. To Antony at least. Because Antony was at war with Decimus Albinus whose legions had run riot in the high country before Antony trapped them all in Mutina. With whom, therefore, the local chieftains had several scores to settle. Still, it was an uncomfortable feeling.

Enobarbus dragged his mind back and looked in front of himself. The view was at once spectacular and disturbing. The clear, thin air stretched away to another peak in the distance. A peak that seemed to be burning as the wind lifted clouds of snow like smoke off its flanks. Between them was a valley of immense depth whose sides were so steep that it seemed miraculous that they could ever meet at the bottom. The tribune was used to measuring distances – had done some work with *ballistae* catapults in the past. But he couldn't even begin to guess how deep this valley was. Perhaps the sheer sides never met at all, he thought fancifully. Perhaps the valley simply opened through the roof of Hades' dark kingdom itself. Went on down until it met the surface of the River Styx. Or even the fires of Tartarus far below even the river of the dead.

And part way down this sheer side, perhaps two hundred *pedes* feet directly beneath him, was a ledge. And on the ledge, a track perhaps a third as wide as the *Via Aemilia*. And on that track was Antony, leading his horse, at the head of his army. Like a line of ants walking along the thinnest twig at the top of the tallest pine tree in Rome.

Enobarbus would never know what made him glance back over his shoulder then. As a lone wolf the size of a British war dog came charging up the slope towards him. It came silently and incredibly swiftly. The tribune had no time to reach for his *gladius* or his *pugio*. He threw himself downslope away from the precipice, turning as he did so to try and meet the monster head-on. As he straightened, the thing took one long last bound and leaped for his throat.

Enobarbus had served with Caesar in Britannia. Had faced the native war dogs which were often as big as their ponies. So he was by no means frightened. Even though he knew his situation was desperate. If his attacker was alone he might stand a chance. If it was the leader of a pack, then he was dead. He had a flashing image of a lean grey muzzle, burning golden eyes and long yellow teeth. A blood-red tongue, dripping drool. The stench of its breath in his face. Grabbing it by the throat he fell backwards, praying that he had come in from the edge just far enough to stop himself going over. But not far enough to stop the wolf going over. As he fell, he heaved with all his might, kicking up with his right leg even as the back

267

of his helmet and the shoulders of his backplate hit the icy ground. And the wolf was gone. Cartwheeled away by the momentum of its own attack. Thrown over his head entirely. Pitched over the edge of the cliff immediately beyond. Its howl of rage seeming to echo endlessly towards silence as it fell.

*

'Typical!' bellowed Antony later, as Enobarbus and he waited for his army to edge gingerly off the precipitous path. 'The one thing with a bit of meat on it that we've come across in this forsaken place and you chuck it off a cliff!'

'I wasn't thinking of it as food at the time,' answered Enobarbus.

'That's just about all I do think about at the moment.' Antony admitted. 'I've even stopped thinking about women!' He stooped and cupped a scoop of puddle water in his hands, drank and spat. 'Horse piss,' he said. And Enobarbus knew he meant it. Literally. 'Well, almost,' he continued. 'Cleopatra somehow sneaks into my thoughts every now and then. But largely because she serves such amazing feasts! What I wouldn't give for a wild boar or two at the moment. Stuffed with Nile perch and flamingo. Roasted over sandalwood...' he wiped the back of his hand over his mouth and down the front of his thickening beard which was now wet with saliva as well as horse piss.

'The best you're likely to get in the immediate future is the nuts out of the pine cones when we get back down to the tree line,' said Lucius, joining the tribune and his elder brother. 'Or, if we're lucky there might be some grass. But, if we get really desperate, there's always the horses...'

'That's what Decimus Albinus did, Lucius. Stupid little pederast! Not for me, brother. I'll need my cavalry able to *ride* at the enemy. Not *run!*' His lip curled with disdain. 'To tell you the truth, I'd rather the men ate each other than the horses.'

'Don't let anyone hear you suggesting that, General,' said Enobarbus. 'Because I'd say you're still the plumpest of all of us.'

'He's right, Antony!' laughed Lucius as he climbed into the saddle. 'There'd be a lot of good eating on that great big carcase of yours!'

v

Artemidorus and Gretorex came across them first, for they were scouting ahead of Bassus' column as they came down from the lower pass and out onto the flat plains near the river Rodonos. Turning north as planned, in search of Antony's legions as they too came out of the mountains. Artemidorus could hardly believe the change in them. Even Antony, famously as robust as Hercules, was lean. The face beneath the wild hair and lengthening beard all sunken eyes, lines and angles. Cheekbone and hollow cheek. Enobarbus and the other legates and tribunes of his senior staff were gaunt to put it mildly. And the legions following on behind were almost ghostly. Two weeks without real food or potable water had taken a terrible toll.

And yet their spirits seemed high.

'SEPTEM!' bellowed Antony as he recognised the riders galloping towards him. 'Well met! Have you anything to eat? I've eaten nothing but bits of trees for a week and if I see another pine cone on the menu it's the *vomitorium* for me!'

'General Bassus will bring up supplies as soon as he knows we've made contact, General. But we should be able to scavenge something more immediate. At the very least there will be early grapes down here in the valley. It's *Maius* after all.'

'An excellent notion, Septem. But I would rather we started making use of the big fat birds that feed on the grapes. And the equally plump animals that feed on the birds. Did I mention that my tribune here threw a perfectly edible wolf off a precipice? I mean it went right over my head and away before I could catch it. Let alone kill it and cook it. That was more than a week ago and there's been nothing to eat since! I think I'm going to have to get a smaller breastplate.'

Artemidorus, his *contubernium* and a squad of Gretorex' men oversaw the supply column as General Bassus sent it forward past his own hungry legions. And necessarily so. The route through the lower valley had been no easier than Antony's route over the high col. The only difference was the fact of that supply column. And that Bassus' men had been less hungry at the outset. Even so, they needed to exercise all their self-discipline as they watched the food they craved go forward. Though they knew it was going to feed legionaries in far worse straits than they were in themselves.

But the *contubernium* of secret agents proved to be a greater asset than either Antony or Bassus calculated. For as the six legions, cavalry *alae* and ancillaries settled into encampments along the bank of the river whose valley they were occupying, so Artemidorus and the others led the legionary scavengers to pools and reaches aswim with fine fat fish. To stands of reeds packed with ducks, geese, herons, coots and grebes. And that was before the *quaestors* and quartermasters made contact with local farmers and bought up all the grain, olives, oil, bread, goats, sheep, cows and oxen that could be spared.

This was only the beginning, however. For, as Antony's and Bassus' legions settled in on the eastern bank of the river, so the legions commanded by Marcus Aemilius Lepidus marched onto the west bank opposite. Settled and set up their camps. Antony, Bassus and their legions were, after all, in the province of Gallia Narbonensis now. And the governor was under direct orders from the Senate to

269

arrest the *hostis* outlaw Antony and bring either his body in chains or his head to impale on a spike to the Forum in Rome.

*

At this point the river was wide but shallow. Artemidorus reckoned that if he was careful he would be able to wade across most of it and only be forced to swim in one or two of the deeper sections. But the stream was swollen by snowmelt which added to the power of the current as well as to the simple volume of water rushing between the widespread banks. And, of course, to the lowering of the temperature. Even on an early summer's night like this, the water seemed to give off a sinister chill that could be felt far away from the banksides.

'Are you sure this is a good idea?' demanded Ferrata on behalf of all the others.

'We need to know what they're thinking and planning over there,' said Artemidorus. 'We should have gone over earlier. I'm surprised Lepidus hasn't sent spies across to sound out our men.'

'No you're not,' observed Quintus. 'Lepidus is just playing a waiting game and you know it. He doesn't want to precipitate anything. Certainly he doesn't want to do anything that might irritate Antony and bring things to a head here. And spies running around in each other's camps are the sort of thing that will do that.'

'Are *we* going to precipitate anything then?' asked Puella. Not that she cared, thought Artemidorus. She was bored and itching for action. And she was by no means alone in that.

'Not if we can avoid it,' said Artemidorus decisively. 'We're just going over to poke around. Listen outside a few tents. Get the lie of the land as they say. Test the breeze. Check the atmosphere.'

'Right,' said Puella. 'Just so long as I don't have to sleep with anybody. Keeping on top of you two is more than enough for me as things stand.'

Somehow, although she was still besotted by Artemidorus, Mercury's calf-love seemed to weaken her resistance every now and then. That and a good deal of pity for the state of his face. Certainly, they all concurred, no other woman would ever have him. Unless he agreed to wear a sack over his head at all times.

Artemidorus stepped down into the icy rush of the water and waded out towards midstream. The brightness of the fires behind him coming from Antony's encampments and that ahead coming from Lepidus' was augmented by a low moon hanging in a clear spring sky. Wishing he had thought to bring a pole with him to test the water depth immediately ahead, he proceeded slowly and carefully. Miraculously remaining upright, leading the others in a steady line. At last he felt the riverbed begin to slope away and he leaned forward, careful to make a

270

minimum of noise. As, like Horatius having kept the Bridge, he swam in full armour towards the far bank.

But he need hardly have bothered. There were no sentries. No sign of any security at all, in fact. Away to his right, upstream as he pulled himself ashore, he could just make out the black square of a palisade that no doubt surrounded the camp of Lepidus' Praetorian bodyguard, his senior officers and the governor himself. But down here there were only leather-roofed tents, campfires, and the relaxed banter of several thousand soldiers with nothing much to worry about. In fact, as he stood shivering amid the bankside reeds, he was able to make out a surprising number of figures coming and going across the river from one camp to the other. Not spies, he reckoned. Certainly not counterspies. For these would have to come from his own *contubernium*.

Just friends fraternising.

As the other six came ashore behind him, they split into pairs. Puella as Ghost Warrior, would watch his back. Mercury would watch hers. Then Kyros and Hercules would go one way and Quintus and Ferrata another. All to meet back here by moonset. To swim back to camp and prepare a report to give to Antony at his morning briefing tomorrow at dawn.

vi

'Here?' said Antony next morning. 'We cross here?'

'Yes, General,' answered Artemidorus. 'It's where we crossed last night.'

Antony scratched his chin through his thick black beard. 'What do you think, brother Lucius?'

'Looks all right to me, Antony.'

'And Septem here has never let you down yet,' added Bassus. 'Has he, Tribune?'

'No, General,' answered Enobarbus at once.

'Right then,' decided Antony. 'Over we go.' He waded into the water. 'Better clench your scrotums, boys. This water's cold enough to freeze your *testes* bollocks off.'

'It was colder than this last night,' said Artemidorus quietly. 'And I've still got mine.'

'As Puella can attest,' observed Enobarbus drily.

'But there are no guards!' said Bassus, his sense of professionalism outraged. 'And you say there were none last night, Septem?'

'None, General. We wandered around the camp without even being challenged.'

'Outrageous!' huffed Bassus. '*Divus Julius* would have had them decimated!'

271

'Don't complain too loudly, Bassus,' called Antony. 'It's all working out to our advantage after all! As long as we're still able to fornicate when we get out of this freezing water.'

*

No one tried to stop the little group as they heaved themselves out of the river and onto the far bank. There were no real lines here – just a city of tents. Outside which men were sitting cooking or eating *jentaculum* breakfast.

'I'd have been fighting for a share of that a week or so ago,' observed Antony as he led them up the riverbank towards the palisade that formed the only proper defensive position in the entire camp. 'I'd probably have been happy to eat the leather of the tents. But have I told you how Cleopatra has whole boars roasted, crispy skin and all? *Divus Julius* used to say he sometimes found it hard to choose between her dining room and her bedroom...'

It was surprising how quickly the general had filled out now that he was able to eat properly again, thought Artemidorus. His Herculean stature was almost fully re-established. But for some reason he had resisted the urge to see the legion's *tonsors*, so his beard was beginning to bush out. His black hair was falling in waves towards his shoulders, its ends beginning to form virile curls. And, judging from his conversation, women of all sorts were beginning to replace food in his thoughts and dreams.

But even Cleopatra and her *culina* kitchen could not entirely fill his dreams, thought the spy. For Antony was also dreaming of revenge. And the men on whom he planned to visit his Nemesis formed a long and lengthening list. In a strange, subtle way, this Antony was different from the Antony who had led the Larks, the Sabines, the XXXVth and all the others into the mountains. He was certainly very different from the man who had crossed the Rubicon heading north to shake Decimus Albinus out of Cisalpine Gaul. It was as though, somewhere in the long journey he had made since leaving Rome soon after *Divus Julius'* murder, one of the Friendly Ones had crept into his soul and taken up residence there. And the comparison suddenly shocked him. Antony was fast becoming the masculine equivalent of the vengeful Cyanea.

Antony led the group behind him through Lepidus' camp, turning the heads of the soldiers he strode past, almost as though he were the ghost of *Divus Julius* himself. By the time he reached the gate of the governor's palisade, he had acquired quite a following. Needless to say, the gate into the simple fortification was standing wide open. But at least there was a guard.

'*Qui est ibi*? Who goes there?' he challenged nervously as the cohort led by the gigantic figure swept towards him.

272

'The *hostis* outlaw General Marcus Antonius and his senior officers,' Antony answered. 'Here to see Governor Marcus Aemilius Lepidus.'

The guard looked around in a panic, but there was no one nearby to help. And Antony had no intention of stopping. So he strode on into the makeshift fort and followed the familiar layout of the paths to Lepidus' command tent. Even when he got there, he did not hesitate. With Bassus at one shoulder, Artemidorus and Enobarbus at the other, Antony swept the leather door wide and strode on in.

Lepidus and his senior officers were grouped around a table, surrounding a map that appeared to Artemidorus to show most of the land between Hispania Posterior and the Rubicon. The area from which a competent leader could control the whole of Italy. Pieces of fruit and bits of bread were placed on top of it. Breakfast serving as battle plan.

Lepidus glanced up, frowning at the unexpected interruption. His face went blank for an instant. Then a strange combination of dawning recognition and sheer horror swept across it. 'Antony!' he said. 'What on earth are you doing here?'

'I've come to discuss the terms of surrender,' answered Antony cheerfully.

'Surrender? *Surrender*!' Lepidus' expression was almost comical in its utter confusion. He glanced down at the food-covered map then up at his equally horrified companions. 'You're surrendering?' he demanded, as though utterly unable to believe what was happening here. 'You're surrendering? To *me*?'

Antony gave a huge bellow of laughter, then he spoke as though addressing a backward infant. 'No, Marcus Aemilius! No! *You*. Are. Surrendering. To *me*!'

Epilogue

Decimus Junius Brutus Albinus, Pro-praetor and Governor of *Gallia Cisalpinus*, favourite of Cicero and the Senate, late defender of the besieged city of Mutina, murderer of *Divus Julius Caesar* and enemy to the death of Marcus Antonius, leaned forward in the saddle to ease his aching buttocks. One day, he thought, someone will do something to a saddle that will allow the rider to take some of his weight on his feet. He tensed his weary thighs and rocked towards his horse's neck until the saddle-horn dug into his lower belly. Reminding him he had not relieved himself in several hours. Not since they left yet another makeshift camp, in fact. Easing back a little, he kicked his heels into the sides of his ambling mount. Without noticeable effect. Decimus and his horse were exhausted, like his ten centurion bodyguards and their animals. After so many days in the mountains, the only ones there who seemed active and sprightly were the Gallic guide and his sturdy mountain pony.

Had Decimus been less fatigued, he might have appreciated the grandeur of the country he was riding through. The high Alps in summer were a feast for the senses of almost Lucullan proportions. The mountain peaks towered like the fangs of gigantic bears, angular and sharp-pointed. Their tips dazzling white with snow. Their lower slopes carpeted with wild flowers all in full bloom. And, between, tall green stands of trees. Whose heady scent came and went on the breezes blowing up and down the valleys. Intermixed with the aroma of those countless blossoms. None of which made any impression on the increasingly desperate man.

He looked back over his shoulder. As he had done ever more nervously during the last week, surrendering to the eerie certainty that someone, somewhere, was watching his every move. Following every footstep he had taken since Caesar Octavius refused to help or support him and his legions had leached away. Ultimately forcing the governor to leave his command and run eastwards through the mountains in hope of reaching the other *Libertores*. Far distant though they were and in spite of the fact that he was still in command of the entire province as far as Cicero and the Senate were concerned. Therefore he remained oblivious to the multi-coloured slopes and blazing peaks outlined against a cloudless cerulean sky stretching away behind him. But when he looked forward, up ahead, the heavens were grey and darkening far too rapidly for his taste. There was a bad storm coming. 'Hey,' he called to no one in particular, 'ask the guide if there's any shelter nearby.'

The guide was the only Gaul amongst the Roman soldiers and Decimus Albinus did not trust him. There was good reason for that. Even beyond the fact that the promised three- or four-day journey had almost doubled in length. During his term as Pro-praetorial Governor of Cisalpine Gaul, which included the area he had been riding through for so long, he had trained and motivated his legions by letting them have free rein to loot the local countryside. To fight the local men and rape the local women. Steal the local livestock and enslave the local children.

It was a strategy he had been forced into, he told himself, because the Senate, who appointed and supported him, swayed by Cicero's eloquence, were fatally slow to pay him. They sent messengers when they should have sent money. Good wishes instead of gold. And he had needed that gold desperately. For, Decimus was bitterly forced to admit, he was not the sort of leader men would follow for love. He was no Mark Antony. He was no *Divus Julius*. Though he had defeated the former in battle last April. And murdered the latter in Pompey's *Curia* thirteen months before that. He looked around. And saw the proof of his failing leadership. Of all the legions he had commanded, all the thousands upon thousands of soldiers, he only had ten men left.

But letting his legions loose up here was a strategy he bitterly regretted now. And regretted more keenly with every burned-out farm and deserted village they passed. For it had ultimately made matters so much worse. The legions he commanded simply made unforgiving enemies of the local tribes. To little or no purpose. Instead of winning pitched battles, booty and glory, they ended up besieged and mutinous in Mutina. Confined. Afraid. Starving, towards the end.

And even when the siege was lifted, they had been slow and unwilling to pursue the man who besieged them. In spite of the prompting of Cicero and his puppet senators. Mark Antony. Who retreated into the icy mountains and apparently to certain death, followed faithfully by men who trusted – almost worshipped – him. As he had led his legions, seemingly defeated in the Battle of Mutina, in good order up the *Via Aemilia* and its less imposing extension north past Placentia, Castra Taurinum and into the Alps. At the bitter end of a lingering winter when many of the passes were still blocked with snow and provisions non-existent. And, miraculously, they had survived. Burgeoned, in fact. Had been joined by three more legions en route and then merged with the legions of Gallia Narbonensis, Transalpine Gaul and Hispania.

His own legions, however, knew the reputation they now had in the mountains. And were very wisely unwilling to put themselves between Antony's well-ordered retreating Vth, *Divus Julius'* deadly *Alaudae* Larks, the IInd Sabines and the

XXXVth and the vengeful Gaulish warriors who called these oft-ravaged mountains home.

Decimus had hoped for help and backing from young Octavius, who called himself Caesar now. But Caesar did not see him as an ally. The arrogant boy made it all too plain that he saw Decimus Albinus only as the man who led his adoptive father to the slaughter. Literally. By the hand. Overcoming the advice of his friends who warned him exactly what was going to happen. Friends like Tribune Enobarbus, centurion Artemidorus, code-named Septem, the augur Spurinna and the rest. So, in the absence of the money and support he had been promised to keep his men loyal, Decimus found his disgruntled troops sneaking away to join the boy Caesar's legions. As the young commander waited in the warmth around relieved and grateful Mutina. Promising fortunes to everyone just for serving with him. Some other of Albinus' ex-legionaries even following the charismatic Antony's legions further into Gaul, hoping for fame before fortune; glory rather than gold. Leaving the increasingly pathetic governor his meagre bodyguard and his guide.

Only desperation forced Decimus to trust the Gaulish guide Gretorex without holding his wife or children hostage. For, although he had served here on more than one occasion and even spoke Gaulish, he did not know the mountain passes. Nor did the centurions who formed his bodyguard. And he was relying on sneaking slowly but anonymously through the mountains and down to the coast. Because his only hope of salvation now was to take the first available passage to the East. So he could join the *Libertore* army in Illyria. Help Brutus move down from Macedonia in the north as Cassius moved up from Syria in the south to crush the treacherous Dolabella in the central province of Asia. Caught in the middle between them as he was, like a nut in a nutcracker. To take vengeance for what he had done to Gaius Trebonius nearly six months ago.

A brutal wind came blustering down the valley. It felt like knives against Decimus' cheeks. Set his squinting eyes to streaming. Blew his hood back onto his shoulders. Brought his thoughts back to the present. It did not smell of Alpine forests or flowers. It smelt of the snow and ice in the high peaks. The roaring it made lingered, echoed, became part of a low snarl of thunder. 'Shelter,' bellowed Decimus. 'What does he say?'

'Up ahead,' came the answer. 'There's some kind of building. Cattle byre or stable…'

The black thundercloud came spilling over the valley head at that moment, streaming forward on the storm wind like the smoke of a burning city. A wall of hail hung beneath it like chain mail made of ice. The exhausted horses pushed onward without prompting. Lowering their heads and speeding almost to a trot. As though they knew where shelter lay as clearly as the guide did. Decimus pulled his hood up once again, to cover his thinning hair, and leaned further forward. Taking the lashing hail on bowed shoulders. As though it was some kind of scourge. Following the guide, the Romans fell into single file as they veered to the right and mounted a narrow path up the valley side.

ii

The mountain slope up which the path led became a cliff wall reaching skywards on their left. At least it cut the wind, thought Decimus. Though the hail continued relentlessly. And the thunder became deafening. But after a few moments, the path widened into a considerable rock shelf. At whose back, someone had erected a big strong-looking building. Using the cliff face itself as its rear wall. The other walls were roughly fashioned of boulders wedged in place with smaller stones. And those made sound with slate and gravel. The roof was slate. The stable doors were made of unfinished pine planks. As, no doubt, were the roof beams.

The guide reined in before the double doors and gestured. Chilled to the marrow, Decimus dismounted, staggering a little on legs that felt like wood. Handed his reins to one of the guards and entered the building. Swinging the heavy wooden door wide then letting it slam behind him. It was disorientatingly calm inside the stable. That was the first thing that struck him. No wind. No hail. The stillness of the air made it seem warm. He blinked his streaming eyes and realised there was more to the warmth than still air. There was a fire in a makeshift grate at the very back of the place. Giving a little light as well as warmth. With no further thought, he crossed towards it.

There was a rough table in front of it surrounded by crude stools. On one of which sat a man, very much at his ease. As Decimus' vision cleared, he saw that the stranger was dressed in simple Gaulish clothes. His hair was wild, but not long. His cheeks and chin were stubbled, not bearded. He wore it all like a disguise; not like a native.

'Storm coming,' observed Decimus in his best Gaulish.

'More than a storm,' answered the stranger in liquid Latin. 'Much more than a storm. Please take a seat, Governor.'

Decimus turned at that, every nerve alert as he realised that this was a trap. Simple but effective.

'Please sit down,' repeated the stranger gently. 'It's far too late to think of running anymore. Besides. You are quite alone.'

'My guards...'

277

'Gone, I'm afraid. Without even an obol beneath their tongues to pay the ferryman. Off the cliff, likely as not. It's a good deal higher than the Tarpeian Rock.'

Decimus turned back to face the stranger. And realised in some vague way that the man by the fire was not a stranger after all. 'I know you,' said the governor.

'I think "know" might be too strong a word. You have seen me on occasion, I'm sure. But you didn't really notice me…'

Intrigued in spite of himself, Decimus moved forward. Towards the fire, the table and the seat the half-familiar stranger indicated.

'The last time you saw me was at the Battle of Mutina,' said the gently flowing, softly modulated voice. 'Just at the moment young Caesar reached Consul Hirtius' body and tried to retrieve it. The eagle bearer beside him was dead. You stepped back, no doubt calculating that the boy would not survive such a dangerous moment. One less leader likely to challenge your position and your plans. One less Caesar in the world. And I must admit that I too had orders concerning him. But Caesar freed the eagle. And I found that, unlike you, I could not leave him to his fate.'

The stranger rocked back slightly on his stool, watching Decimus with strange smoke-coloured eyes. The light gleaming on his stubbled chin as though it had been dusted with copper. 'Before that, I delivered messages to you in rolls of lead. I swam the river outside Mutina carrying them and was allowed through your lines and into your city. Into your quarters, in fact. For I had the passwords. You were too interested in the messages' contents to look closely at the messenger. Though, I'm sorry to say that the communications I brought you were by no means always accurate. And the replies bound for Caesar and the Senate often went to Antony instead.

'But enough of this,' he said, rocking forward again, as though tiring of a childish, painful game. 'What you really need to know is the one truly important time you saw me and did not notice me. That was when I was standing on the steps of Pompey's *Curia* as you led *Divus Julius Caesar* by the hand in to meet his murderers. I was trying to make Antony intervene, but you and Trebonius outmanoeuvred me.'

The mellifluous voice stopped for a heartbeat or two. Then continued, changing the subject suddenly. 'You may not be aware of this, but you have been the focus of some intense negotiations as we watched you wander through the mountains guided by my friend and associate Antony's cavalry legate Gretorex. We, being Gretorex, me, my spies, Antony and the local chieftain. Whose son your legions killed and whose wife and daughter they dishonoured. Who wishes the fullest

278

possible recompense, as you will easily understand. Messengers have been riding up and down the *Via Aemelia* at full gallop day and night. Antony and young Caesar want you dead. As does the chieftain. Cicero and the Senate want you alive. And, as always, in the end it's come down to the matter of payment. Who will pay the most and soonest.'

He hesitated for a heartbeat. 'And you know the outcome of all that communication. Negotiation. Your life depending entirely on Cicero and the Senate acting swiftly and decisively. And generously. With bags of gold instead of volumes of words.

'So. How would you like to die, Governor? Not like Pontius Aquila, with your head cut open to the bridge of your nose. Certainly not like Gaius Trebonius after two days at the mercy of Dolabella. His *carnifexes* with their racks, whips and red-hot irons. And we're too late for you to go the way *Divus Julius* said he'd like to go at the *cena* dinner you gave him the night before you slaughtered him – "unexpectedly". No. The best I can offer you is swiftly and relatively painlessly...'

'Swiftly,' said Decimus Albinus, raising his chin in an attempt at Patrician pride. Meeting the inevitable with a last show of soldierly disdain.

The stranger moved with astonishing speed. Decimus Albinus felt a searing pain on the left side of his throat. A disturbing, penetrating sensation from one side of his neck to the other. An abrupt tug, which jerked his chin forward. His torso rocked to and fro. Apparently of their own volition, understanding far more than his stunned mind, his hands reached for his throat. Only to be covered in a burning, pumping liquid. Where they should have felt a column of flesh there was only a strange, gaping vacancy. They gripped his neck with a strangler's power. But could not close the massive wound. Could not stanch the pulsing blood.

He rocked back, unbalanced by the fierceness of the grip. Found himself on his back on the cold stone floor. He gasped with the shock of the fall, but found he could not breathe. His laggard brain began to understand that his throat had just been cut. There was a rhythmic, hissing scream. He wondered whether he was making the sound. Then realised he could not be doing so. Because he could neither breathe nor speak. It was the sound his lifeblood made as it came streaming out of his body like steam from a boiling kettle.

As though the liquid fountaining out of him was falling directly onto its flames, the light of the fire dwindled. Above the failing rhythm of the throbbing squeal, he heard the stranger say, gently, 'Swift, then. If not quite painless. Swifter than Caesar's at least.'

The last thing Decimus Junius Brutus Albinus, Governor of Cisalpine Gaul and assassin of *Divus Julius Caesar*, saw was the blade of a heavy Gallic woodsman's axe as the stranger hefted it with grim expertise. Swung it up into the shadows reaching from the last faint pinpoint of earthly fire to the top of the celestial *aether* at the feet of the gods themselves.

iii

Mark Antony was sitting at the map table in what had once been Lepidus' command tent. A tent which was now Antony's command tent. Even if he had been awarded *Imperium* by his lieutenants rather than by the Senate. He was sluiced, scrubbed, tonsured, strigilled, shaved, shining and sober. And, as usual, in his full battle armour. His Herculean lion skin on his shoulders. His helmet on the ground by his feet. Almost as much of a myth as a man.

And in an exceedingly sunny mood, thought Tribune Enobarbus. In spite of the fact that he was still *hostis* an outlaw in the eyes of the Senate. For Antony was now the leader of a gang of outlaws. An army of outlaws. Several armies of outlaws, in fact. Their individual leaders, also all in full battle dress, sat round the table beside him. Lepidus, of course, at his right hand. Outlawed by the Senate at the insistence of his own brother. Inevitably with the vocal support of Marcus Tullius Cicero. In spite of the fact that Lepidus was still *Pontifex Maximus* Chief Priest of the empire. Beside him sat Ventidius Bassus, whose perfidy had yet to register with Cicero and his minions. Beside Bassus, still holding a warrant from the Senate – for the time being at least – sat Lucius Munatius Plancus, Governor of Transalpine Gaul, who had been commissioned to ensure Lepidus stayed faithful to the Senate. But had joined Antony himself instead. And, finally, Gaius Asilius Pollo, Governor of Further Spain who was also here to throw his hand – and his legions – in with the general.

If this meeting continued to go as well as it had so far, thought the tribune, his general would, almost at a stroke, jump from being a fugitive in command of a couple of recently defeated legions and some hangers-on to the commander of the most powerful force in the empire. With the better part of twenty legions at his command. Fair enough, most of them were still encamped in Narbonese and Transalpine Gaul and Farther Spain. Though there were eight or so camped on either side of the river outside, resting, relaxing and gorging themselves on fish.

It very much looked, thought Enobarbus, as if the general was certain to end up with an army of a hundred thousand men before the end of the day. Most of them battle hardened and ready for war. Especially against the men who killed their beloved *Divus Julius Caesar* and the politicians still supporting them, led by Cicero. Between here and Rome stood only whatever forces Decimus Junius

Brutus Albinus still controlled and the eleven legions under the *imperium* (also unofficial) of the young, self-appointed General Caesar Octavius. Fifty-five thousand men at most, though word was that more were flocking in. And, as Caesar Octavius' treatment of Decimus had shown already, if Antony was willing to make war on the men who murdered *Divus Julius Caesar*, his great-nephew and adopted son would be more likely to join him than fight him. No wonder there were rumours the Senate was trying to get a couple of legions over from Africa.

'Well,' boomed Antony. 'Let's get down to business, shall we? The day is wasting and it'll soon be time for a goblet of Falernian. But we have some final details to agree before then...'

Before anyone could answer, however, a tall man dressed in Gaulish clothing was admitted by a rigid guard. His hair was wild and his chin lightly bearded. He looked threatening enough to make Plancis and Pollo at least reach for their swords. Not so Antony, who swung round, his bright gaze resting on the interloper as though he was now the most important man there.

'Ah, Septem,' said the general. 'Is it done?'

'Yes, General,' answered the stranger. He lifted into view a roughly woven sack which he had been carrying.

'Well, let's have a look, man. Don't be shy!'

Septem put the sack on the table and opened it so that its contents were visible. He stepped back so everyone could see. Decimus Junius Brutus Albinus regarded the assembled commanders with wide, glassy eyes. His expression one of mild shock. As though the removal of his head had been a minor insult rather than a brutally efficient execution. 'Have it packed in ice,' ordered Antony. 'The gods know, there's enough ice and snow about, even now! I want everyone to recognise it when it's spiked in the Forum. I want to send a message...'

'That this is the fate awaiting anyone who had a hand in Caesar's murder?' asked Lepidus.

'That this is what happens to anyone who dares to stand against *me*!' snapped Antony.

There was a tense moment as Antony's notoriously volatile mood wavered. But Septem broke the tension by stepping forward again. Closing the sack over its horrific contents. 'Packed in ice, General. Yes. Immediately.'

He stepped back. And Antony, in his sunny mood once more, slapped his hands together and rubbed them briskly. 'That's the first one I can actually put on display,' he said. 'Given the state of Trebonius' and Pontius Aquila's. First spiked in the Forum but third one down. Twenty more to go, eh Septem? Tribune? Three down. Nineteen to go.

'But now that I have so many legions to support my actions, I think I might just go home to Rome and take you all with me. Yes. That would be the best move. We'll all go back together. Pay a visit to Cicero and his friends in the Senate. Then I'll happily let them watch me stick this first head up there in the *Forum Romanum* myself…'